Catch the Dragon's Tail

Book Three
Of
The Jolie Chronicles

Also by E.F. Winters:

MEMELOOSE: The Island of the Dead
First in category winner
Somerset Awards
Chanticleer Writing Competition

SHARKS AND MINNOWS
Book One of the
Jolie Chronicles

GHOSTS in the GRAVEYARD
Book Two of the
Jolie Chronicles

THE PEOPLE'S GIFT

SIGNEY'S BEAR

Watch for:

EBULON
Book One of
The Keepers of the Truths

Catch the Dragon's Tail

Book Three of

The Jolie Chronicles

E.F. Winters

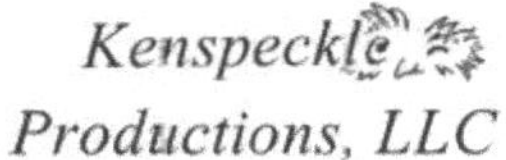

Kenspeckle
Productions, LLC

Dedicated to the memory of The Reverend Dashi Steven Baugh who said," Yes, as long as you don't make me fly or some crazy sh**". The Sifu in Jolie's story is not him, but he was in my thoughts every day while I wrote this book. He will forever have my deepest gratitude for his teachings and his friendship.

My thanks go out as well to my life partner in all things who helps stories become books, and to my Beta Reader, Laura, who has stuck with Jolie the whole way. We all need Beta Readers, but it's extra special when they are also a cheerleader and a friend.

2024 Kenspeckle Production LLC

Copyright © 1-14078585971 2024
by E.F.Winters All rights reserved.

Published in the United States by Kenspeckle Productions LLC
Distributed by IngramSpark and
Lightning Source as Print on Demand

Library of Congress Cataloging-in-Publications Data
E.F.Winters & Kenspeckle Productions
ISBN 978-1-940531-06-9

Printed in the United States of America

Book design by E.F.Winters & J.L.Winters

Chapter One

The umbrella over Jolie's head felt like a hovering, malevolent black bird above her. Marble-sized raindrops thundered against its dark dome, falling from the umbrella's edge in a silver curtain, closing the teen into a world of private mourning.

Iris brought an umbrella. Of course, she did. Who in Las Vegas still owns an umbrella?
An umbrella--like the castoff sweaters that filled Las Vegas's thrift shop bins—revealed people as transplants. In a town where former CEOs worked as casino bakers, it was taboo to hold onto your past. Las Vegas, Nevada was a city of reinvention, whether your preferred method was self-discovery or pretension. No one gave a crap about who you were before you got here.

Even with the umbrella, Jolie felt wet through—porous, like a sponge. Maybe, all this rain would fill the holes inside her.

Then I can go through life all squishy and leaking on people's floors, she thought, wrapping sarcasm around her like a comfortable blanket, hoping it would help her feel better, hoping it would help her feel something.

Vegas was marketed as a place of eternal sunshine, except of course, during monsoon season when it let go of the stress it pretended not to have and blubbered rain like a toddler throwing a tantrum. In the Mojave Desert, rain came in two types: non-existent, or biblical deluge.

Just go ahead and wash the whole damned place away, Jolie taunted. *This place could use a good Noah's Ark-style cleansing.* Of course, not everyone would drown. The Mormons probably had an ark hidden in one of the mammoth airplane hangers scattered around the city, leftovers from when it had been Howard Hughes' sandbox.

When a rainstorm started, water-starved dry-creek beds suddenly remembered their true identities, engorging into raging rivers that washed out roadways and turned city streets back into the streams they had been before being paved over. Cars then floated down the paved creek beds--flooding rich folk's delusions of invulnerability--leaving them rotting in the glaring sun.

Post-monsoon Vegas was always one giant steam bath. It ran the makeup down the cheeks of showgirls and stuck casino executives' crisp shirts to their armpits like decoupage. Right now, the water puddling in the turf at Jolie's feet was soaking into her high-top tennis shoes, making her feet cold and clammy. She knew high-tops were not exactly funeral wear, but they were the only shoes she had this morning when she got dressed at Child Haven, the facility run by the county to house juvenile delinquents, youth rescued from questionable homes, and the recently orphaned—which was now her. Funeral or not, no one at Child Haven had shown any willingness to help Jolie fetch personal items, clothes, or anything else from the cabin she and her mom had been living in just over the Nevada border in Tecopa, California.

The rhythm of the rain pounding against the umbrella's taut material nudged her from her current circumstances toward happier childhood memories seeded in the neglected soil of her past--memories saturated by the sights and scents of lush Southern gardens, the distinct decay of bayous, flavored by statues of saints, voodoo folk art, music, and all the spices that made up the unique cultural mix of New Orleans.

The Boulet family tree had deep roots in NOLA. It had grown broad and strong over the centuries going back to before the native Chitimacha tribe had begun to mix with Spanish, French, or English invaders, and the immigrants of all races who came with them. The living testimony to this cultural mix now lured tourists to view its brightly, polished, dark secrets.

Jessie Lynn Figg, Jolie's mother, had been a rootless kid who had grown up to be a rootless adult, without family or connections, except for her only child: Jolie. She had jealously refused to share this singular child, even with her father's family, the Boulet's, stealing her away, and cutting off all contact.

But now Jessie Lynn was dead, the victim of a relapsed overdose, and Jolie was alone. Jolie didn't know how she would have gotten her mother buried if it weren't for Iris.

Iris Fadgeon had burst like an indomitable weed from the cracked sidewalks of the male-dominated New York fashion world in the late sixties and refused to leave until she decided she wanted a different kind of adventure than what Manhattan now offered.

The older woman's silk-gloved hand clutched the black umbrella's glossy burlwood handle with the same strength it once used to clutch protest signs, her redlipsticked mouth a finish-line of determination. A citrus and floral scent misted off the older woman, pushing back the exhaust rolling across the cemetery lawn from the traffic on Eastern Avenue.

Liquid money, Jolie mused. One bottle of Iris' perfume cost more than what Jolie and her mom lived on for a month. Jolie stopped herself mid-thought. *No, not me and Mom, just me, now.* There was no her and Jessie anymore.

"Good perfume is like walking around in your own little cloud of joy," Iris had told Jolie. "It helps shield you from the harshness of the world."

When had Iris said that? Weeks ago? Months? Clocks and calendars didn't mean much anymore. After Iris' and Jolie's friend Faith had died, there had been Bodhi and Jessie Lynn, without a breath between. Jolie's losses loomed large, shrinking everything else.

But that had not been the whole story.

You were a shitty mother, Jolie thought. *But you were my shitty mother and the two of us made a kind of family. And now that's gone.*

Jolie's view of her mother's casket being lowered into the slick, gray rectangle of the open grave was blurred by the curtain of rain falling from the umbrella's edge. The funeral people had put up a canopy over the open grave. *Probably so the casket won't float back up like a Beetlejuice-themed paddleboard,* Jolie joked darkly. Someone had thought of everything.

Except me.

In the final moments before her death, when Jessie Lynn Figg must have faced a choice: letting go, or fighting to stay alive, deciding not to be a mom anymore, choosing instead to become part of something else-- anything else. Not that she had been good at being a mom. There was no point in romanticizing it or pretending. Jolie felt her mom's abandonment as yet another betrayal.

"Steady, Jo." Iris' aged whisky contralto melded with the rain's rumble. "It's almost done. You can do this."

Of course, she *could*, Jolie thought to herself. But she shouldn't have to. Single mothers were not supposed to die, leaving their daughters alone. If a person was determined to parent solo, they owed it to their kid to stay alive until they were old enough to make their own way. But then Jessie Lynn Figg had never been a planner. Her selfish pursuit of some unidentified "magic bean" that would make their lives better, defined Jolie's short childhood. Jessie Lynn called it "living spontaneously". Other people called it "flaky", but whatever label was attached to it, Jolie now faced the outcome: no house, no savings, no family support. Aside from Jolie, the only thing Jessie Lynn left behind was a bunch of creepy art that looked like storyboards for a horror film, testimonials to her frame of mind in the weeks leading up to her death.

Iris' arm around Jolie's shoulders felt like an emotional shackle and she shrugged it off.

"Sorry. I don't mean to intrude," Iris said, not offended. "I just want you to know you're not alone, Jo."

But I am alone, Jolie wanted to shout. "Iris, if you start singing 'It's a Small World' I'm gonna barf," she said instead. Prickly wit was Jolie's armor of choice, a survival tool that kept people at a distance. She had let it slip since the last Solstice. She'd gotten soft. It was a mistake she did not intend to repeat.

Iris' perfectly painted lips pursed and the muscles supporting her powdered cheeks worked beneath her paper-thin skin.

"That song is culturally horrifying in so many ways, but the underlying message is not untrue. We are all connected, Jo. You of all people know this."

Iris was one of the women Jolie had helped save last winter when a local Solstice celebration had gone horrifically wrong, hijacked by dark magic. Faith and Iris and a few of their mother-hen Wiccan friends had taken Jolie under their wings, working their heart magic to soften the teenager's raw edges and try to give her a few more years of childhood. Of course, they were years too late. Jessie Lynn had held the title of "mother", but she had never been the adult in their family of two.

After the Winter Solstice adventure, Jolie had tried to avoid getting involved in any more psychic mumbo-jumbo, stumbling into a small group of outsiders at school. That was how she wound up being on Mount Charleston the night the "Ridge Walkers", an annual ceremony performed by local spiritual leaders, called the lost dead and helped them cross over to the spirit world. The calling had included the deranged spirit of a man who had bonded a demon and who blamed Jolie for his death. It was also where Jolie was when her mother's spirit showed up, having just died of an overdose.

Jolie wiggled her toes in the puddle of her canvas shoes. The umbrella's thunder-drumming was giving her a headache. She wondered where the little blob of a demon that had stalked her before switching over to possessing her mother was now. It had tried to play nice, offering itself to Jolie, like a genie with innumerable wishes, but there were some things you just could not forgive a recalcitrant demon, and aiding and abetting in the death of your mother scored high on that list.

The hum of the motor lowering Jessie Lynn's casket ended in a jarring clunk, returning Jolie's mind to current events. She sniffed the snot back before it dripped out of her nose and wiped her heartbreak away like steam on a bathroom mirror.

Suddenly, everything was quiet. The rain slowed to a misting drizzle, the orchestral drip off the cemetery's trees and the umbrella's edge, slowing like a pendulum that was winding down. Jolie could hear her breath and her heartbeat, but mostly she heard the anger buzzing in her head; wasps committing hari-kari against her skull.

Mickey, another of the women from Solstice, stepped up behind Jolie.

"Do you want to say something, honey, or put anything in with her?" she asked. Mickey's mini-me daughters in their pink and yellow rain slickers looked up at Jolie, tears swimming in their innocent eyes.

"Why are you crying?" Jolie demanded of the girls, too sharply. "You didn't even know my mom."

"They know *you*," Mickey said gently. "They're crying for you."

"Because you can't," the young mother added silently. Mickey shared Jolie's dubious "gift" of hearing other people's thoughts and had passed that talent on to

her daughters, just as Jolie's Paternal grandmother, Mem, had passed her abilities down to Jolie.

"I'm sorry," Jolie apologized. "I'm just—"

"Grieving," Mickey finished for her. "We know, Jo. It's all right. The girls understand."

Jolie could have punched her. How could Mickey's girls understand when Jolie didn't? She hated it when people were nice to her. It made her want to cry, which made her feel weak, which made her feel angry.

Maybe it was better that none of her school friends came to the funeral. They wouldn't have known what to say or do. They would have just hung around looking sad and droopy, expecting Jolie to pay attention to them. Then she would have felt bad for not helping them deal with their confused feelings. People didn't come to funerals for the dead. They came for themselves.

"Jo," Mickey tried to get Jolie's attention. "Do you want to put any kind of remembrance in with your mom, a picture, a flower?"

"I don't have anything," Jolie mumbled. "Everything's still in Tecopa. They wouldn't let me go back." It was all sitting there in the cabin just the way she and Jessie Lynn had left it; a time capsule to the life Jolie was leaving behind. She looked down at her ratty high-tops, fighting tears.

Iris' red lips pursed in disapproval. "I'll talk to your Probation Officer. Wrangler is his name, isn't it?"

Jolie nodded.

And so, it's done. The finality kicked her hard in the gut. How did you walk away from your mother's grave?

Her life plan had been to survive her mandatory sentence tied to Jessie Lynn's messes, then, as soon as she turned eighteen, move out. But she had never planned to cut the ties between her and her mom.

Jolie had no plan for dealing with this new chapter that had been inserted into her life. However much she pretended otherwise, the truth was, she was terrified.

No one could know.

"We're done here." She walked out from under Iris's umbrella and headed for the car.

Back inside Iris's classic Cadillac the old woman announced, "Jo, we need to talk about your future." The mix of leather upholstery and perfume made Jolie think of the Sherlock Holmes movie with Robert Downey Junior where his sketchy ex-girlfriend-turned-nemesis shows up at his flat to invade his gentleman's retreat, and he knows she's been there because he smells her lingering scent. "I promised I would have you back at Child Haven by five, so we have just enough time to get you something decent to eat. I can't imagine that whatever they feed you at that place has any nutritional value." Jolie offered no opinion. She hadn't been interested in eating. "I've asked my lawyer to look into filing the paperwork for me to become a foster parent," Iris, the organizer of all things, went on. After the low-budget horror film that last winter's Solstice Ceremony had become, Iris had taken on managing their friend, Faith's, finances when her home situation required a change. "Once I'm in the system," Iris went on, "if your Probation Officer recommends you live with me, there shouldn't be a problem having you assigned to me, but the system is slow. It's going to take time, maybe as long as a few months. Are you going to be okay?"

Jolie snorted. "I've lived in rougher places than Child Haven. I'm not your kid, Iris. I'm not your responsibility." She felt bad as soon as she'd said it. After all that Iris, Faith, and Jolie had shared, saying something like she just had was a slap in the face. Iris's gloved hands clenched the steering wheel, but she was East Coast Yankee stock, resilient, and as hard-shelled as hell. Her thin shoulders pulled back against the leather seat, her perfectly powdered face maintaining polite neutrality.

"I'm not blood, but I care, Jo. It's a terrible situation and it's probably unfair to ask you to make these kinds of decisions right now, but we need to figure out what happens next. I don't want to push you or presume anything, but I am asking you if coming to live with me is what you want, or if there's somewhere else you would rather go. You have people in New Orleans, and I would understand If you'd rather try to work that out. I'll help in any way I can. But you have to let me know what you want to do."

What did she want? Jolie hadn't thought beyond getting through her mother's funeral. She was five the last time she had been in New Orleans, and back then her grandmother, Mem, had been alive. Mem had been everything to Jolie; Mem, and Topi, whom Jolie had been sure was going to be her new dad. But Jessie Lynn had messed that up too, and then in the middle of the night she had taken Jolie away.

A lot had happened in New Orleans since then: hurricanes, deaths, marriages, births. When Jolie found her mom's old phone book last winter and called the number, she thought was Mem's house, she learned her grandmother had been dead for years. The conversation with Topi had been short and awkward, but the takeaway for Jolie had been that Topi and Tessa of the beautiful hair were together now and had kids of their own and no self-respecting mama bear was going to welcome the half-grown cub of a former rival into her cave, no matter how softhearted papa bear was.

Jolie's great aunt and uncle, Mem's sister and brother-in-law, might take her in out of a sense of familial duty but the Blancflors were old--the same generation as Mem and probably not up for taking on a teenager they didn't know anymore.

Iris fidgeted, nervously. "Jo?"

Jolie pushed past the fog in her brain. "I don't know about New Orleans."

"But is that what you really want?" Iris repeated. "To go live with your family there? It's okay if it is. I understand how you might feel more comfortable with them."

Feel more comfortable? The subtext cut like a shank to Jolie's neck.

Iris doesn't want me. Not really. She'll take me in because that's what Faith would have done, but if I say I want to go to New Orleans, she'll be relieved.

Iris had been there when Faith's daughter-in-law accused Jolie of almost killing Faith. She knew all about Solstice and Rory's death. Nobody else still alive knew how closely Jolie had been involved in that situation, except Iris. Maybe Iris worried that Jolie was dangerous.

Maybe, under all her desire to do good, Iris was secretly afraid that Jolie would hurt her. Harboring a teenager who could read your thoughts and had a history of attracting seriously dangerous situations would certainly complicate Iris's well-ordered plans for retirement. What adult in their right mind would choose to be part of any of the crap Jolie seemed to attract?

Jolie hunched down in the car's front seat, crossing her arms over her chest.

"Whatever. It doesn't matter. It's just a few more years. What I really want is to get emancipated. I've been almost on my own since I was five anyway. I don't see why it would be different now."

In a small corner of her mind and a larger corner of her heart, Jolie thought that if Iris wanted her, she'd fight for her. But Iris did not fight. She did not say anything.

So, she doesn't want me.

No one did. There was no place that Jolie belonged.

Chapter Two

The dreamscape was familiar, the glistening webbing of possibility imposing patterns on the obliterating darkness, connecting planets and stars that sat like dew drops balanced among the tangled threads.

Jolie had been here before.

The act of recognizing the patterns woven into the universe had captivated and encouraged the gifted psychic, but they looked so much less vibrant now, faded, like sun-bleached curtains waving from the windows of abandoned cabins in the desert. Once upon a time, she skipped gazelle-like across the glittering web but her body, or whatever part of her substituted for it here, now felt like an anchor, too heavy to move, like it was stuck in the crab shell she had worn and discarded when she had been here before.

Jolie looked down and saw the old crab shell lying beside her. It was still upside down. Its weight held her back, but she knew she no longer carried it. So, what was the source of her heaviness?

The empty crab shell's tiny crustacean eyes looked up at her, crying, the weight of its tears pulling the web down while the wet rose in a pool below.

"The door is still there," a voice said.

Jolie looked up and recognized the spiral staircase the demon had chased her up. It was no longer whole, a crumbling skeleton, without purpose. She no longer needed the illusion it had provided.

"The door still exists," the voice prompted again. But the door and the stairway were part of an older story where the demon pursued her and she ran from it in fear; a story she had let go. The Jolie of today was no longer that person and the demon was no longer her bogeyman.

The door grew brighter, more solid, the staircase rebuilding, triggering the fear and desperation her phantom body remembered.

"No," Jolie denied the structure and whatever wished to rebuild this renewal. Instantly, the stairway crumbed, falling into the dark nothing: the dust of a nightmare denied.

The fading door at the top became smaller and smaller, zooming away until it flared in a starburst of light and disappeared.

"I will not be afraid," she declared before waking up.

Jolie was lying on the plastic-covered mattress on the floor at Child Haven. Facing away from the cell-like room, she watched the slats of light coming through the high horizontal windows across the institutional white wall, shredded by the blinds.

Well, there was nothing else to do.

She sensed when the squat, gray demon appeared, wriggling out from the linoleum floor as if from a hidden trap door to another dimension.

"Come to gloat?" she asked, not looking at it. The demon did not rise to the bait. "Go away. There's nothing for you here," she mumbled, keeping her face to the wall so the camera in the corner of the room wouldn't catch her talking to herself. Having the staff decide she was having a mental breakdown would not be helpful.

"*You* are here," the demon declared, sounding more like a petulant four-year-old than a scary monster. Four was about the level of its social skills.

"I *have* to be here, *you* don't," she said. Without the influence of a master the demon's energy felt different. No longer the slavering devil who had pursued her in and out of her dreams, this self-conscious gray blob looked more like the base of an ash-stained snowman than the frightening creature she remembered. Maybe people just got used to things—even demons.

"You said with my last master gone, I am no longer required to obey someone else's commands, that I am free." How could a demon sound whiney and petulant?

"I say a lot of things," Jolie rebuffed the vague attempt to make peace, settling into sullen.

"You said that I should figure out what *I* wanted. Well, that has been difficult. I have never had to do that before and well, I don't know. I have thought about it, however, and I have decided that I wish to stay with you."

Jolie whipped around. "No!" It was an instinctive reaction, not thought out, and would be sure to grab attention if anyone happened to be monitoring the camera in her room. She quickly turned back to the wall. "You've been making trouble for me since before I knew you existed. You've been behind all the bad crap that has happened to me over the past six months. Go away!"

"*I* didn't kill your mother," the demon almost whispered. "That was her—and the drugs."

"Don't you talk about my mother," Jolie growled, her voice deepening with the effort it took to push the

15

anger past her larynx. Axel had used the demon to possess Jessie Lynn, splintering Jolie's mother's mind and toppling her off the no drugs or alcohol wagon.

"That was not me. It was Axel—" The creature's anxiety was so great that its gray, jelly-like body trembled.

"And you!" Jolie sat up, eyes glaring. "You were there, pushing her into places you knew weren't safe for her. I warned you to leave her alone. Without you, Axel would have just been dead that first night. End of story."

"That was not *my* doing," the demon pointed out.

No, that was on Jolie. She had not meant to kill the old man. It had been an accident. She had not known she was capable of doing what she did, but Axel-- drunk out of his mind--had been choking her, and when she pushed him away using her energy, he had been thrown against a chair so forcefully his spine had broken.

"I must do what my master requires," the demon sued for its innocence. "It is how I was created."

"I don't care what story you tell yourself to try and feel better, demon. What you *tried* to do, and what you did were unforgivable. You and I are done. Do you understand? We have no connection. I am not interested in anything you have to offer." She sank back down onto the mattress trying to cover her anger with the grief that would be easier to explain to the facility's staff than arguing with a demon. "Just please leave me alone. My life is complicated enough without having a demon on a leash." She rolled back over to face the wall, her eyes welling.

"Yanna Maria is still out there looking for me," the demon said plaintively.

"So, stay away from her."

"That is not so easy. She is a Santeria."

Jolie let out an exasperated sigh. "She is only human, and you are a demon. I'm sure there are places you can go where she won't find you."

Jolie felt bad. She did not believe the demon had meant to hurt Jessie Lynn. Axel wouldn't have cared, except that he wanted a body to inhabit, but the demon had no reason to bear Jessie Lynn's ill will. It had been acting on its master's instructions. Axel had been the one in charge, and even if he had wanted to, the demon could not have refused his master's requests. How much responsibility did a creature under such a guise have for actions taken at someone else's command?

I should be thinking about biology and algebra and boys, not this shit, Jolie groused. Her head hurt and her eyes burned, and it felt like her heart had all the hope wrung out of it.

"I can't think about this anymore," she muttered into her fist. "I just can't. Please, just go away."

"Go where?" the demon's plea was a child's, tremulous and small.

"Wherever you want, just away from me." Jolie pushed away the compassion that might have dissolved her bitterness. No, the demon was not the same as it had been when Axel commanded it. It had picked up some new tricks. That was what they were though, right? Just tricks? It was pretty good at them.

A long silence followed before compassion; a subtle but persistent emotion snuck back.

"You had nothing to do with Mom's death?" Jolie asked softly. "Don't lie, because I'll know if you do."

"I *found* her by the road and came to tell you so you could save her. That is the truth."

Tears dripped across Jolie's nose and onto her pillow, strands of her pink-tinted hair sticking to the sadness on her face, doodled curlicues of it looping over her caramel cheeks.

"Okay. But I can't talk to you right now. Really. I mean it, please, please, go."

Jolie felt it when the creature finally disappeared, leaving her alone. And that was what she wanted, wasn't it?

"Just don't go back to Yanna Maria, demon," she whispered. "She'll hurt you."

When Jolie opened her eyes, rubbing heavy sleep and salty tear-crust from her eyelids, she could feel the cold floor through the thin, plastic-wrapped mattress, a cold that seeped from the cement block walls and floor. The whole building smelled like an overchlorinated swimming pool. The hospital surplus blanket she had been given was spongy with no strength to it, chosen no doubt because it would not hold the weight of a body and therefore would be unusable for a distraught kid to use to try and hang themself. Places like this were always thinking about that stuff, even before kids did, which Jolie figured was the point. She guessed, too, that her mother's recent death and the funeral were why she had been given a private room instead of being put in the girl's dormitory with all the other girls. But that would change.

Child Haven was a lonely place, except when you were out in the common areas with the other girls. Then it was dangerous.

It was the law of juvy jungle; what you had lived with, you would repeat, inflicting the sins you had endured on others. That was the way the world worked in the only model many of them knew. Kids who had been treated badly thought everyone treated everyone badly, and Child Haven was full of tough girls desperate to establish dominance over anyone to feel better. The only ones available were either other tough girls trying to do the same or girls whose role in life had been victim to some abuser. Predator or prey; sharks and minnows, a microcosm of high school: everyone was one or the other.

Jolie had no interest in playing this game but that would not stop her from becoming a pawn. The only option was to become a knight, a king, a queen, maybe a bishop.

When the automatic door lock on her room was finally released, a voice came over the speaker announcing; "Lunch is being served in the cafeteria until 12:30. There won't be another meal until dinner at 5:00. So, eat now."

Finally hungry, Jolie got herself up and cautiously pushed down the metal handle on the door.

A lone girl was leaning against the wall in the hallway outside. Her white skull was nicked in several spots from a bad hair shave. Her clothes were threadbare enough to have lost all shape and she smelled like poverty: unwashed, ill-fed, with a dash of ode de propane: a typical trailer park bully who lived on the rough side until she landed here. Jolie had seen a dozen like her in a dozen different towns. It was a type: the girl who decides their only way to move forward is to clear their path by denying other girls any place along it.

Jolie and the new girl eyed each other uneasily, determining where the other stood on the tough teenager poverty ladder. It was a weighted system, with no goody two shoes around to affect the bell curve.

"What are you in for?" the shaved head girl asked, sucking her teeth to look tough.

"It doesn't matter," Jolie replied. "I won't be here long, and we're not going to be friends." The shaved head girl cracked her knuckles. Jolie wanted to just walk on as if the wordless threat was meaningless, but her back was tingling. The shaved head girl would attack as soon as Jolie provided a target.

Coward, she thought. She did not say it out loud because that would have started the fight the girl wanted.

"You know, it can get worse," Jolie warned her self-appointed rival instead. "Whatever you think they've taken from you, they can take more. And if they decide you're a fighter, they'll make it their quarterly goal."

"What do you know about it?" The girl looked at Jolie from beneath heavily hooded eyes.

"I know they won't tolerate any of that violent crap. They can't. Their system is too vulnerable. They have to beat out any tendency we have to fight back. They don't care if you have good reasons, just like they don't care if they helped put it there in the first place."

"Woa, big words." The girl sneered.

"The staff here aren't the screwed-up adults we learned how to work before we learned to walk. They hold all the power, they know it, and they won't hesitate to use it against us. Our best play is to learn the rules *they* play by and figure out how to turn those rules to our advantage."

The girl turned her face away, looking down the hall. "If we play by their rules, they win."

"If we fight them, they'll grind us into the dust," Jolie countered. "Using our heads to survive the system isn't giving in. It's being smart."

"If you're so damned smart, how come you're locked up here with the rest of us?"

"My mother died," Jolie said. "Overdose."

The girl glared at Jolie, but she walked off without throwing a punch.

Mission accomplished. Today Jolie got lunch.

The menu was some kind of ground entrails in a burger and fries. There was no vegetarian option. Jolie skipped the burger. Moving through the line, she took some fries, some runny coleslaw, and a chocolate chip cookie, then found a table where no one else was sitting.

Aside from the physical danger and emotional stress of being in a room with dozens of girl grenades a thread away from having their pins pulled, Jolie was being assaulted by the very loud "private" thoughts of every inmate and staff member within an undefined area of awkward nearness.

She tried a fry, then took a bite of the cookie before lifting her plate and tipping it from side to side to watch the puddle of mayo water seeping from the coleslaw move back and forth across her plate. "Wonderful."

"What's your crime?" the girl who had been behind her in line interrupted the mesmerizing motion.

Jolie looked up, groaning inwardly. This was what passed for conversation here?

"I killed my mom," she answered not looking up from the puddling plate. It was sort of true.

"Huh. That's dark." The girl was not scared off. "Mind if I sit?"

"It's not my table." Jolie got up. She was not looking forward to listening to her own thoughts, but anything would be better than finishing this conversation.

"Everyone needs a friend," the girl called after her.

"Nope," Jolie refused the offer.

"You need to eat," the staff person watching the lunchroom stopped her before she exited.

"I need to eat *food*," Jolie quipped. "Not whatever that is." She waved her hand to indicate the cafeteria offerings.

The lunchroom monitor's eyes narrowed. "A smart-ass, eh?"

"Or just honest, depends on your point of view." Jolie shrugged.

"My point of view is you're working yourself up to cause trouble, New Girl, and that's the wrong way to go in here."

"Always is. Hey, did they ask you for suggestions when they named this place?" The monitor looked confused. "I didn't think so. Because the sign outside says "Child Haven" not dumbass adult's hell for kids. You're here to protect us, Staff Person Goble," Jolie read the name on the woman's badge. "Not bully us."

Staff Person Goble smiled cruelly. "What can I say? It's a skill. 'Can't seem to do one without the other."

Jolie wanted to tell her that if that was true, she lacked creativity, but it was probably one goad too many. She had already said too much.

"You're not going to cry, are you, New Girl? Because if you do, I'll have to put you on suicide watch."

Jolie pulled her cheeks down away from her eyes. "Dry as a bone. Have a nice day." She didn't care if the monitor thought she was still being a smart-ass. If the woman wanted to get her in trouble, she had a hundred ways at her disposal.

"I need to get out of here," Jolie grumbled silently.

"I can get you out." Jolie wasn't sure if it was the demon speaking in her head or her imagination reminding her that the possibility of bonding him provided her with an option.

"Not that way," she declared firmly. "I'm not bonding you."

"Stubborn human," the demon growled back.

By the time her counseling appointment rolled around, Jolie had been sitting in her room for most of the day and she was a coil ready to be sprung. The office of the counselor she had been assigned to was more a closet than an office, with a desk so out of scale to the size of the room that it must have arrived in a box, then been assembled in the tiny space. It was landscaped by stacks of paperwork, notebooks, reference books, and the counselor herself, Ms. Lee. A thin woman with a frail build, her long, dark hair was pulled back in a legitimate horse's tail, not just a pony's. Ms. Lee shimmied sideways to get behind her desk, squeezing into the chair behind it. Fortunately, she was still small enough to do that. Jolie wondered how many new graduates in the Social Services field would still have chosen their field if recruiters were honest and told them, "And throughout your career, you will gain twenty pounds every two years due to stress."

"Relax, Jolie, this is a safe space," Counselor Lee's voice was carefully modulated to express professional concern with just the right amount of friendliness. The corners of her eyes had traces of smile wrinkles, but it was a practiced smile, not one of honest humor. Dark brown eyes revealed a quick intelligence, but though Lee was trying to give the impression she was an open book, all Jolie saw were blank pages.

The teen groaned inside at the counselor's pat statement about safety. How could this person have any idea what made Jolie or any of the kids here feel safe? There wasn't a girl at Child Haven that didn't have a story, and from what Jolie was picking up, most had landed here for doing the smart thing and running away from abuse, or fighting someone who was trying to assault them, or leaving home so there would be more food for younger brothers and sisters. But to the county apparently, it did not matter how right or righteous your reasons were for leaving home. Here you were treated like the statistic you were expected to become if you didn't figure out a way to turn your life around. Society had prejudices toward the poor, the houseless, single moms who assuaged their adult passions with socially undesirable men thereby putting their children at risk-- self-perpetuating prejudices. But those pinhole tears in the fabric of society were nothing compared to the way they viewed minority girls, inside, or outside the system.

There were benefits to a girl like Jolie who could not easily be pigeonholed by race or culture because of her skin color.

Jolie knew letting an adult know what she was thinking was not usually in her best interests. Revealing frustration because she was being forced to undergo counseling due to her mom having died and leaving her on her own would only make her case seem like a savory challenge--an enticement she did not want to dangle before a bleeding-heart counselor's trauma-pocked heart. In Jolie's experience, counselors who went into the field to "give back" relished reliving the way their baggage had been worked out and too many tried to replicate their breakthroughs from the other side of the desk. On the other side, those who did not come with baggage had no clue about the realities a girl like Jolie faced.

Jolie's best and shortest route out of Child Haven and mandatory counseling was to appear to buy in, giving the counselor just enough of what they expected to feel satisfied over having done their job that day while not being obvious about it.

"Really, Jolie, relax. It's okay." Counselor Lee's professional smile was the period at the end of her sentence.

"If I relax it could look like I'm slouching and you might think I have self-esteem issues," Jolie retorted. "I don't."

"Okay." The delicate crinkles at the edges of the slightly raised outer edges of her eyes looked like bird tracks in wet sand. "So, what do you want to talk about?"

"I don't," Jolie replied bluntly.

"Too soon? That's understandable. We don't have to talk. We can just hang out for an hour. Do you want some paper and pencils so you can draw or doodle?"

"No," Jolie's mind jumped to the dark, blotchy sketches her mom had plastered like horror movie wallpaper on the cabin in Tecopa. The images of malevolent eyes and gaping mouths indicated by emotionally charged black, charcoal, pencil strokes were not easily dismissed. Jessie Lynn's art had been a reflection of her haunted mind, an attempt to communicate her desperation at Axel's attempts to steal her life.

My god, Mom. What was happening in your head? Tears sprang to Jolie's eyes.

She wiped them away, pretending to scratch her face.

"How about a mindful coloring page?" Counselor Lee spread a selection of intricate design coloring books on the desk and opened a box of markers and pens. "Some of my clients find it helps to have something to do if we're not going to talk."

"If we're not going to talk, how about if I just leave? Then not talking makes even more sense."

The counselor shook her head. "Whether you talk or not, you're scheduled for an hour. We need to get the process started. It's policy."

"I get it, it's your job." Jolie picked up the book and began to leaf through it. Not talking was not a problem. She didn't need to talk to find out what she needed to know about people. All she had to do was listen. People hated silence, especially in social situations. They felt compelled to fill in the spaces, even if they only did it in their heads, which for Jolie was the same as if they spoke out loud. Most of the time she hated her gift, but it had advantages.

"I spoke with Officer Wrangler," Ms. Lee said casually as she chose a deep Persian blue crayon and began methodically coloring the edges of a butterfly wing on the page before her. "He told me what happened to you. I am so sorry, Jolie. This must be hard for you. Wrangler was the one who requested I be assigned to your case, by the way. I think he felt like I would understand your experiences better since I'm bi-racial as well. I'm Chinese and Latina. Sometimes having multiple perspectives can make a person more accepting of other people's differences."

"And sometimes it means no one wants to claim you so you don't belong anywhere," Jolie retorted. It wasn't hard to see what Lee was trying to do; saying that she could be trusted not to dismiss Jolie's experiences because she could relate, but Jolie was pretty sure this nice Asian-Latina had no experiences that would help her relate to Jolie's circumstances. Ms. Lee struck Jolie as the kind of person who made statements like "I'll believe you", without knowing what she was promising. It was a common thing to say, but meaningless because it was not true. Jolie couldn't explain most of what had happened to her, even if she wanted to--which she didn't. None of it sounded real and her reward for the excruciating reliving of her misadventures would probably be years of counselling and a roller coaster of trial-and-error medications to cure her of her "extra sight".

"My friend Rose says her people believe you shouldn't talk about your personal spiritual experiences," Jolie countered. "They believe that trying to fit something spiritual into words changes it."

"Are you Native?" Lena flipped open Jolie's file, scanning the pages.

"I'm a mutt; Chitimacha, Creole, Latina on my father's side, and who knows what on my mother's. I'm so mixed that I'm nothing," Jolie said.

"I wouldn't say that." The counselor picked up on the phrase as a classic marker of low self-esteem and depression.

"I don't mean that *I'm* nothing," Jolie corrected the misperception. "I mean that my cultural background and spirituality aren't going to match any of the checkboxes on the forms in that file. And my spirituality is personal."

"Fair enough." Lena closed the file and set it aside. "I'm not trying to hurt you or trip you up, Jolie. I'm just trying to let you know that you don't need to worry about being judged by me."

You've been judging me since I walked in, Jolie thought. *Sizing me up based on my hair, my clothes, my tone, my words, my posture.* "And yet, that's what human beings do, isn't it?" she replied. "We're wired to judge strangers who come into our village. We don't have long to decide if they're friend or foe, so we size them up and judge them quickly so we can either shout and raise the alarm, or smile and bring out the welcoming committee. Being open-minded doesn't mean you've lost that self-preservation instinct, Ms. Lee. It means you're smart enough to let those judgments evolve as you get new information."

Lee chuckled, smiling as if Jolie had just passed some sort of test. "Cliff said you were smart. That's why he said you need to be placed in a home where there are strong boundaries." Jolie's hackles came up.

"I don't need someone else to give me boundaries. I've been doing that for myself since I was five. My mom was the dysfunctional one in our family. *I'm* fine."

"Are you?" Lena examined Jolie through her psychologist's lens.

"I'm sad, okay, but then I should be. My mom just died. Even though she had problems, and wasn't grown up enough to be much of a parent by most people's standards, she was all that I had, and we were a family.

"And I'm worried; same reason," Jolie ticked off a list. "Because even though I've had to take care of myself for most of my life because mom was struggling to stay sober and pay the bills, her death means I've been thrown into a system that assumes I don't know how or when to wipe my butt, so they're going to tell me. So, besides losing my mother, I've lost my freedom, my ability to make decisions for myself--everything that makes me a unique human being, and that sucks."

"It's not personal," Lee insisted.

"It feels personal."

"It's not, and it's not meant to be a reflection on you or your maturity. But there can't be different rules for different kids. There are a lot of angry, messed up kids struggling to cope here who need structure."

No, you need the structure, Jolie thought. The kids at the center far outnumbered the staff. If the staff failed to keep them in line, the whole system would come unseamed.

"So, give *those* kids structure, but leave me out of it."

"The system doesn't work that way."

"There are things I need to do, Ms. Lee, and I can't do them stuck in here waiting for whatever happens next—which no one is sharing with me by the way."

"Legally you're a minor, Jolie."

"Unless I'm emancipated. I don't belong here, Ms. Lee. Emancipate me."

"Every kid who walks through that door says that same thing. Very few manage it. There are a lot of pieces that need to be in place to prove that you can stand on your own two feet and function like an adult when technically you're not one."

"I can handle them." Jolie stood up. "Ask Wrangler."

"Okay, we can look at that, but the process takes time, and still includes counseling. You need to make your peace with that. It doesn't have to be me. If you prefer one of my colleagues I won't be offended, but you have to see someone, Jo. You'll also have to be in school during the school year, you'll need to have good attendance, maintain good grades, and hold down an approved job that allows you to help pay for your expenses. There won't be time for partying or being a kid anymore. It's a tall order. Meanwhile, you'll need a place to stay until all that can be put in place."

They looked at each other across the desk. Neither blinked.

Jolie heard Lee think, *"She's strong. She might just be able to do this."* It was the first internal dialogue she'd picked up from the woman. Maybe Lena Lee wasn't just another bleeding-heart liberal.

Jolie sat back down. "What do you want to know?"

"Let's start with what made you so emotional when I asked about art?"

"*Shit,*" Jolie thought silently.

CHAPTER THREE

Text #1 Tru: Got a cruise ship band gig! Lead singer for other band sick. Headed for Bahamas. Back in a few weeks."

Text #2 Remy: "Bodhi's funeral 3:00. C U there?"

Text #3 Hugo: "Need a ride to the funeral?"

Text #4 Remy: "Missed you at funeral. Will I C U B 4 I leave?"

Text #5 Hugo: "R U OK?"

Text # 6 Remy: "R you ok? Call me."

Text #7 Remy: "Is something wrong?"

Text #8 Remy: "Did I do something wrong?"

Text #9 Hugo: "Had a weird talk with my mom. Feels like everything's coming down all at once. Can we talk?"

Text #10 Remy: "Seriously, what's going on? TALK TO ME".

Text #11 Remy: "OMG just heard what happened with your mom. I'm here for you. Call me."

Text #12 Tru: "Having an amazing time. Can't wait to share!"

Text # 13 Hugo: "OMG. Just heard about your mom. So sorry, Jo. Meet at coffee shop?"

Text #14 Iris: "Family emergency. Leaving town for a few weeks. Let me know if I can do anything to help with the New Orleans plan."

Text #15 Remy: "Back in Reno. Text me when U R ready to talk."

32

Text #16 Hugo: "Text so I know U R OK."

Text #17 Remy: "Call as soon as you get this. I'm worried."

Text #18 Remy: "Why aren't you answering?"

"I'm without my cell phone for a few weeks and the whole world goes nuts," Jolie grumbled.

"A lot of messages?" The case worker driving Jolie to the foster home was trying to be cool and make a connection, but Jolie wasn't interested in a five-minute friend. The young staffer looked to be fresh out of college, too new to be jaded or have emotional calluses yet.

"A lot's been happening with my friends lately," Jolie muttered vaguely continuing to read her messages.

Text #19 Hugo: "I'm worried about U. Text me."

Text #20 Remy: "I'm worrying. Text me."

Text # 21 Hugo: "Send me a sign U R OK."

Text # 22 Hugo: "That was dumb. Of course, U R not OK but I'm UR friend. Don't shut me out."

Message #23 Tru: "Rose texted about your mom. Hate that we're not there." (Sad emoji.)

Message #24 Tru: "Cell range sucks. Texting's better. I'll text back when can. Marty sends (heart emoji). Says 'hang in there". B back next week."

Message#25 Madison: "I DK what happened between U and Remy but he's going nuts. PLZ text him."

Message #26 Hugo: "R U OK? Remy's freaking out. Just text the dude already."

Message #27 Tru: "Contract's extended. Yay? Sorry. Have to stay. Need $. Stay strong."

Message #28 Remy: "Rose says U R in Child Haven. Did you and Iris have a fight?"

The staffers at juvy handed Jolie's cell phone back to her as she checked out of Child Haven. Its battery was almost dead, and her charger was still in Tecopa with the rest of her belongings, so she needed to make her replies short and to the point.

Maybe someone at the foster home would have a compatible charger she could borrow, but that did not fix the larger problem. The bill for the family plan she and Jessie Lynn had would come due in a few days and Jolie had no way of paying it. Would the new foster family pay for her cell service? They were getting paid to take care of her, including money that was supposed to be spent for her upkeep, so it seemed logical, but Jolie had low confidence in adult logic when it came to a kid's tech needs. Maybe they would front Jolie the money until she could get a job and then she could pay them back. She should get a job first thing. A job meant having her own money and that meant independence.

"Don't you just hate drama?" the young driver dove in with all the cheery confidence of a newbie. They probably had a class in "jumping to conclusions" for new social workers, teaching it like it was an important career skill--a shortcut to establishing common ground with a juvenile. "I guess you've had more than your share, huh?" the young woman added a lame 'personal note' but four years of college did not make this young woman an expert on Jolie's life, and it was presumptuous and entitled for her to assume it did. Jolie wondered what the county intern had read in Jolie's file. Apparently, everybody had access to it except Jolie.

The staff at Child Haven had been vague and cagey, refusing to answer Jolie's questions about what she could expect next. Then suddenly, this case manager intern had breezed into Jolie's room, bundled Jolie and her backpack into this crap of a county car that reeked of unwashed boy, and driven off like there was a fire sale on teenage girls. Jolie felt like she was a piece of embarrassing dirty laundry being swept out of sight a half second before guests walked in. She was hoping Tru and Marty, or Iris, or somebody would come back to town, and she'd get fast-tracked to being housed with one of them, but that hadn't happened. The whole foster care placement thing was feeling arbitrary and random. Classic administrative bull at best. Purposely belittling and dehumanizing at worst. And the barrage of frantic messages from her friends did not make Jolie feel any better. Sending a text was so easy. Caring enough to make the effort to act said more, and the unspoken expectation that now they had texted, her it was up to her to do something, just added to her stress.

Jolie texted a quick "I'm OK. Headed for foster home," in a mass text, adding, "Cell battery dying. No service for a while. Later," in a second message. She pushed 'send', feeling as flat as Wiley Coyote after the asphalt roller drives over him.

She and Jessie had experienced a lot of close calls with skanky boyfriends, psycho-landlords, and the random misadventures poverty threw at females. Still, there had always been two of them working it out—one of them at least chronologically an adult. Jessie Lynn had been able to present an adult face to the world and legally was old enough to make financial decisions, even if her status as an adult was only a half-truth. As Swiss-cheese holey as Jolie's upbringing had been, her future without

35

her mom looked even more grim. Jolie's school friends were just kids and had no power to do anything to help her. Tru and Marty were out of the country. Faced with Jolie being dumped on her, Iris sprinted out of town. Remy was in Reno at college, and his Aunt Rose…well, how long could you expect relatives of your ex-boyfriend to keep doing you favors?

She watched the city passing outside the car window. The other girls at juvy viewed placement at a new foster home as being forced to play Russian Roulette. You landed where you felt safe, or you didn't. You landed with a family you could tolerate, or not, either way, you were stuck with whatever you got. Jolie figured whatever was next had to be an improvement over Child Haven. Tossing all the damaged kids together was just stupid. What a kid didn't know about being rebellious they were going to learn. In a hundred years, social researchers discuss the well-intentioned but misguided social experiments run on kids in institutional housing. A lot of the situations justified as "policy", reeked of the institutional belittling and character assassination that was standard fare at religious and government-sponsored schools for Native American children. Strong-willed kids who knew who they were, were the first to be targeted. It was harder to manipulate a person with a strong sense of self, but once they were beaten down, they were more compliant.

Jolie understood there were committed, responsible counselors and staff in Social Services, but they did not understand Jolie's world, and their assumptions that they did, created barriers against them helping her sort things out.

The county car turned off the main artery onto a side street.

It took real effort to look depressing in sunny Las Vegas, but the eternal sun did more than cast a golden glow over everything. The flip side of eternal sunshine was how the blazing hot sun sucked the life out of everything it touched.

Small one-story houses in need of paint had been planted along the street, their bib yards sprouting sun-bleached tchotchkes. A bleached-out yard gnome, his colors so faded he appeared nearly transparent, giving the impression the little guy was slowly fading away. Each yard had a wild-eyed, wide-jawed dog with a curling lip, each pockmarked driveway a carport. Rusty car parts poked out of the dry Nevada clay like emerging fossils. There were no garages. A garage was four walls too expensive.

This neighborhood Southeast of the marketing mecca of The Strip had never been much even when it was new, but it had not fared well under Las Vegas's new standard of worth. Left behind by age and poverty, opportunity was not knocking on these doors. These folk were shut out of the booming service economy that recruited attractive upscale presenting doormen, valets, and casino dealers, able to pull down upper-middle-class incomes in tips from high rollers and weekend pretenders: no college required.

Vegas had been born the undesirable relative to Los Angeles--one that lived close, but not too close to be ignored. Marketing itself as a playground where the rich and wishful could pretend they were something more than they were had made the desert mecca fashionable, but its popularity was founded on providing shiny newness for public consumption. If it was an illusion, no one cared. The tourists did not stay around long enough to see the men behind the curtains, the showgirls and cocktail waitresses living under threat of age and weight notices, the historic buildings being imploded to make way for a new attraction designed to separate people from their money.

Fountains of flowing water, green golf courses, glittering showgirls with tan partners; illusions abounded. Surviving to become one of the fastest growing cities in the United States, Vegas had become a young, beautiful city. The kind of city that eats its young; not a place to grow old or be poor. To belong in Las Vegas, you needed to be fantastic.

In the mid to late 1990s and through the transition into the new millennium, it had become infamous for mass-producing cookie-cutter mini "McMansions" that announced their owner's importance. The houses were so alike, down to the landscaping, people got lost in their neighborhoods. Many of these developments were painted in shades of pink. No one knew why.

The young case manager driving Jolie turned another corner and Jolie's skin began to prickle like sharp pins were being jabbed into her. Driving deeper into the old development, the underbelly of poverty revealed a toothless grin with prejudice as ripe as an overflowing septic tank bubbling up in the packed dirt yards.

The first house on the corner had a yard sign declaring: "Protected by Smith and Wesson." Three doors down another sign read: "Forget about the dog; beware of owner." The picture placed the sign's viewer as looking down the barrel of a gun. Yet another stated; "My kid can beat up your Honor Roll student."

"Great," Jolie mumbled as the county staffer turned into the driveway of a house two doors down.

"Here we are." The case manager's teeth were clenched, her expression grim, but she flashed Jolie a forced smile. "Don't forget anything."

"Small chance. All my stuff is still out in Tecopa where my mom and I were living. Do you think you could arrange for me to go there and get my things? I need some clothes and I really should go through my mom's stuff, the important papers, family pictures…."

The case manager frowned. "Tecopa? That's in California, isn't it? You're a ward of the court now, Jolie. You can't cross state lines without permission. It's a federal offense."

"That's why I'm asking, so you can give me permission," Jolie pointed out. "We can make an appointment now and you can drive me."

The case manager hesitated. "You'll have to ask your new foster parents about it. If they think it's okay, they can let the state know."

"You're going to have to learn to just say no when that's what you mean," Jolie advised the intern. "Passing decisions off to others just makes you look weak." She got out of the car, shucked her backpack onto her shoulder, and stomped up onto the porch.

Empty boxes and a collection of broken toys created a wall within a wall. The floorboards hidden by rotting, fake grass floor covering, gave an inch when Jolie stepped on it.

"They're getting another one?!" Jolie "heard" the exclamation of the neighbor across the street. *"Maybe this one will burn the dump down and that jerk with it."*

So, the family is popular in the neighborhood, Jolie surmised, sarcasm intact.

The case manager--avoided looking at Jolie--stepping onto the porch as if she were avoiding land mines. She pushed the corroded, paint-splattered doorbell beside an oddly neatly lettered block of wood screwed in beside it spelling out the family name: "The Bozovics."

Jolie could feel the neighbors watching through their windows as she and the county intern baked on the porch, her Spidey senses tingling. Maybe the Bozovics wouldn't answer, and the case manager would have to take her back to Child Haven. Who would have thought that would suddenly feel like an improvement?

The intern, nervous and eager to be away, opened the tattered screen door. It squeaked like a Halloween soundtrack.

"Hello?" she rapped on the door. "Mr. and Mrs. Bozovic? It's Heather from Child Protective Services. I've brought—"

The door stuttered open. A sad-eyed woman gave Heather, and Jolie furtive glances before returning her gaze to her pudgy feet smashed into worn-out Crocs.

"Mrs. Bozovic?" Heather's tone inferred she hoped she was in the wrong place.

"Yes," the bedraggled whispered. One pop tart away from a straight jacket and a long rest, the woman ventured a fearful check of whatever was behind her. "I'm Tulip." Though she could not have been over forty, her hair was thin, dull, and as gray as her skin. If she had gone out of the house in the past decade, the sun would have already been down. Her oversized clothes hung off her like her shoulders were a hanger, the material skimming the bulges of middle age. She smelled like rancid oil and cheap dryer sheets.

"Is that the nosy bitch from across the street?" an unseen man inside the house demanded. "You tell her to get off my porch and mind her own damn business, Tulip."

"It's Child Protective Services with the new girl, Reuben," frightened Tulip answered, blinking like she was sending an SOS to Heather to save her.

"Well, if they're coming in, tell them to hurry up. The swamp cooler's running and we aren't made of money." The Pillsbury Dough Boy appeared, waddling toward the front door. He wore a filthy, too-small T-shirt that rode up over his belly, leaving an inappropriate gap between its tattered hem and the jogging pants below. The hand he held out looked like pizza dough that needed to be punched down.

Or a dog that should be put down, Jolie thought with a shudder.

"Reuben Bozovic." The dough boy's smile lacked sincerity and several teeth.

Tulip Bozovic stepped back to let Heather and Jolie inside while her husband's hand wrapped itself around Heather the intern's like a large clump of dough around a skinny hotdog. He turned a piebald eye to Jolie. "And this must be Julie."

Jolie almost gagged as any hope of her new situation working out drained away, leaving only dread in its place.

"Jolie," Heather corrected the man of the house and gave Jolie time to recover. Doughboy Bozovic's face wrinkled into an alluvial plain. This was a man who was always right and did not tolerate being told otherwise.

"Whatever."

On the outside, Reuben Bozovic smelled like bitter sweat and the cheap beer being pressed through his pigskin pores. On the inside, he smelled like deceit, abuse, and a very special misogynistic red-neck narcissism.

This was not going to go well.

"I can't stay here," Jolie blurted out. Reuben's eyes compressed to knife slits. Heather bumped her with her elbow. "What I mean is thank you for offering to take me in, but it's only temporary," she tried to correct her mistake, working to catch the intern's eye. Heather, however, was deep in her lizard brain and had already chosen flight over fighting.

"Well, I have to run," she announced with forced cheer. "I'll leave you to get Jolie settled. Someone will be by to check up on things in a few days."

You can't leave me here!" Jolie shouted silently to the staffer.

"Yeah, we know the drill," Bozovic assured the intern.

"Right." Heather tossed Jolie an apologetic smile and ran to her car like a scared rabbit.

"Coward," Jolie muttered.

Bozovic snorted. "Face it, kid, your mommy and daddy don't want you. They aren't coming back for you, and they're not going to win the lottery tomorrow. You should be grateful we're willing to try you out."

Scratching his bloated belly, Reuben Bozovic waddled back into the invisible room. Jolie was just glad he had not scratched his butt.

"Ha!" a small boy with a head of licorice curls jumped out like a playful puppy from behind the kitchen wall. His mop-top hair made his head so much larger than his skinny body that he looked like he would topple over. "You're here!" he shouted exuberantly as if he had been awaiting her arrival. Bolting forward, he wrapped his little arms around Jolie's waist. "Gerith was waiting and waiting for you." Two bright eyes sparking with life blinked up at Jolie, a pair of chipmunk cheeks plumping up below the warm, chocolate chip eyes as his brown face bloomed into a spring morning smile.

"Gerith is… special," Tulip said apologetically.

She dropped down to one knee to be at his level. "I'm Jolie Figg."

Gerith frowned. "No. Not your name."

"Now Gerith, don't be rude," Tulip scolded the boy. "I think Jolie knows her name."

"Not Figg." Gerith crossed his pudgy brown arms over his tiny chest.

"Stop being stubborn—" Tulip began.

"I am Jolie Figg-Boulet," Jolie corrected herself. "Boulet is my father's family name."

Gerith's round face beamed. "Boo-lay," the charming little urchin rolled the syllables around inside his mouth as if tasting them. "Yes, that's your name."

"None of your nonsense, Geri, you little monkey!" Reuben Bozovic shouted from the other room. Jolie stiffened at the racial slur. The sound of a pop tab being pulled from a beer can interrupt the white noise of the game show on the TV.

Tulip scowled. "You shouldn't encourage him."

"It's no big deal." Jolie shrugged. "He's just a little kid."

"There are no holidays from righteousness, Jolie. In this house, we don't hold with fanciful lies. We raise god-fearing Christian children here." Tulip glanced furtively toward Reuben sitting in front of the television. "We have standards, and we expect the children living under our roof to hold to them," she continued her little memorized speech.

Jolie's insides churned. A century ago, people like this woman would have burned someone like Jolie at the stake or tossed them into a pond with a stone tied to her leg to see if she would float. If she didn't, she would be declared innocent of being a witch. She would also be dead. For someone with Jolie's gifts, this house, with its rules, was a minefield.

"Just follow the rules and leave Mister to watch his programs," Tulip's frightened eyes glanced toward the room where the television blared. "Things go much better that way. It's best if you understand that straight off." She led Jolie to a narrow stairway and stopped. "Gerith, why don't you take Jolie upstairs and show her the girls' room? Stairs are hard on my knees these days," she explained apologetically.

At the top of the steep stairs, Gerith jumped through the undersized doorway like a kangaroo. It was not a real door--more like a homemade makeshift sort of door for an attic space and that's what the girl's room was really: attic space. Crammed into the low-ceilinged room were two cots with just enough space between them for a young person to slip in sideways. Gerith sat on the cot on the outside wall.

"Jolie's bed," he announced bouncing. The cot did not bounce back. Gerith pointed to the other bed. "Luce's bed."

Jolie let her backpack slip from her hand, sitting on the bed that was not Luce's. Was this Jolie's home now? It did not feel like it.

"Where is Luce?" she asked.

Gerith thought about it. "School?" He leaned over to peek under the cot, then popped back up, giggling. "Look, hooties!"

Jolie leaned over to peek under the bed. When she touched it, she got a flash image of the girl who slept there. She was ill and had been for a long time. She had been neglected, abused, and lonely most of her life, but here with Tulip and Gerith, she had found a home. Luce's feeling that this was a good place was humbling. What must the girl's life have been like before to have this place seem like a good one?

"You like Luce?" Jolie asked Gerith.

"Love Looos," the little boy stretched out the name.

"Gerith," Tulip called from downstairs. "Come down and leave Jolie to get settled."

The little boy smiled, waved, then skipped out of the attic room, tripping like a gnome down the stairs.

It took all of two minutes for Jolie to stash her meager belongings, toothbrush, hairbrush, travel-sized toothpaste from Child Haven, two sets of spare underpants, an extra bra, and a t-shirt that wasn't the one she was wearing. It took another minute to toss all of it back into her backpack. She didn't know how long she'd be here, but it wouldn't be long.

She looked around the tiny room. Above Luce's bed were a cross and a picture of Mary, the mother of Jesus. Over a plain, dingy white bedspread a piece of material with large, bright flowers splashed across it had been added. A soft mat set on the floor. Someone tried to make the place homey. Jolie thought about how she had tried to make a home for her and Jessie Lynn in Tecopa. It was the same instinct, but for Jolie, this would never be home.

How long would it be until Tru and Marty came back? The young musicians were eternally broke, drove a vintage pickup, and lived in a converted garage/shack behind a friend's house. They were part of an Indie band and lived gig to gig, eternally trying to keep their financial lives together in a town that mistrusted originality, only hiring slick cover bands who could play music made popular by someone else a decade or more ago—music to please the Fruit Loop tourists who flocked to the city to forget their real lives. Jolie knew Tru and Marty would not want to leave her in a place like this, but they weren't there. Once they got back from their cruise gig, they'd probably kidnap her just to make sure she was safe. Jolie grinned. But her hippie-artist friends were probably not the kind of candidate the state looked for in foster parents, though if the Bozovics were the state's idea of a good family, the system was a hot mess.

Maybe, if Jolie promised to be really, really, good, and not cause any trouble Iris would reconsider taking her in. Faith would do it. Faith would have moved heaven and earth no matter what kind of barriers the state threw up.

Just keep your head down, Jolie, she told herself. *Something will come up.*

Something skittered across the floor underneath Luce's bed.

Oh God! Was that a rat? Jolie leaned over, squinting into the darkness. Several pairs of large eyes and an unexplainable number of blue sticklike arms and legs blinked back at her from under the bed.

"I'll be damned, hooties."

CHAPTER FOUR

Jolie vaulted across the bed and grabbed her cell phone before the first buzz ended.

"Oh my God, you picked up!" It was Remy. "Are you okay? Where are you?"

"I'm at the foster home. I just got here." Jolie's eyes teared up just hearing Remy's voice. She knew it was dumb, but he was the first friend she had talked to since her mom died.

"You sound *off*," Remy said. "Are they weird or something?"

"Probably." Jolie sighed. "I'm still trying to figure things out, you know?" Of course, he didn't know. Remy would never have to go to foster care. His Grandpa Hoke, or Rose, or someone else would have taken him in, no question. She flopped down on the cot. "It doesn't matter. I'm just glad to hear your voice, Rem. How are you holding up?" She didn't want to say, "after Bodhi's funeral." They both knew that it was implied.

"It's not easy, but I'm doing okay. I've missed you, but I've got my family to lean on." Jolie envied her friend the support he had, people who understood that Bodhi had been more to him than just a friend and could help him deal with his grief over his boyfriend's suicide. "The good news is I've been chosen for a summer internship at Pine Ridge Reservation helping get hot water solar systems and electricity installed on houses there. Lots of them don't have either one. It's important work and it will help me get in touch with my people and keep me out of my head, which seems like a good thing right now. Helping other people with their problems kind of puts mine in perspective. So, that's cool. I'll be gone for a while though."

"Okay." Jolie felt an anvil suspended over her head.

"I'm leaving next week." And boom, it dropped.

Jolie and Remy were just good friends, something they had figured out when Remy realized he was in love with Bodhi. She hoped they were still close friends but with Jessie Lynn and Bodhi both dying the same night and Jolie being locked up and offline it was hard to say where they were.

"How long will you be gone?" she asked.

"All summer. You're not alone though, Jo," Remy hurried to add. "Hoke will be back and forth between Vegas and the res, Rose will still be in Red Rock, and you've got the Kung Fu boys. If you need something, call them. All you need to do is ask."

"Sure. I know," Jolie lied. People said that stuff, but she never felt like she could burden her friends with her troubles. No one wanted to hear about all the crap she was going through, and she didn't want to relive it by explaining it either. There was a line between unburdening yourself and "getting it all out" and reliving trauma. She didn't know where that line was, but there was one. Holding on to your stories could become an addiction--a way to define yourself as a victim. She was not a victim. Jolie's way of dealing with things was not to talk about them. She was on her own, she had always been on her own. Nothing had changed.

"I guess I should thank you," Remy said, so much uncertainty and pain in his voice that it was hard for Jolie to hear it.

"For what, Rem?"

"The accident happened, but I didn't die."

"You almost did." Jolie remembered Remy trying to follow Bodhi through the vortex to the spirit world. Only Bodhi0's insistence that his boyfriend go back kept Remy from crossing over. "I didn't stop you." They both knew who did.

"But it was you who told Madison to make Dad hold on until Hoke got there. If you hadn't, things would have been different."

Jolie wondered how different. If she had not tried to interfere and stop her vision of Remy's death from happening, would Jessie Lynn have died? Had there been some cosmic tradeoff for her interference; a life for a life? Remy was probably asking that question, too, and worrying about the answer.

"I owe you something, Jo. Everything, really."

Jolie's eyes teared up. "You don't Rem. We're friends. That's what we do for each other; everything we can."

"Yeah," Remy agreed. "They say that cell service on the res sucks," Remy warned. "So, text me. I'll text back when I can. I just don't want you to think I'm ignoring you."

"I wouldn't. Don't worry about me, Rem. Go do this. It's a great opportunity for you." They were the right words to say but Jolie couldn't stop the tiny, pinching voice that saw Remy's summer job as one more abandonment. She was not going to say that though. She was going to pretend Remy's leaving didn't hurt and that she didn't need anyone to lean on. She would keep pretending that until she believed it.

Luce reminded Jolie of old linens, like the ones Mem had kept folded in the dark cedar sideboard in her dining room in the big house in New Orleans. Bright white like they had an inner light, crisply starched by determination, there had been an old-fashioned gentility to those linens and Jolie saw it in her new roommate. Luce had delicate Latina features, and bone-thin limbs that looked like windswept driftwood, curved, and turned in surprising ways.

"Can't the doctors do anything?" Jolie asked when her roommate explained the slow advance of her Multiple Sclerosis.

Luce's thin braid snaked across her skeletal back, her bones pushing up her thin undershirt in ridges.

"No. This is the challenge God has given me. I carry it like my own cross."

She sounded like Tulip. Jolie glanced at the picture of Mary.

"You're Catholic, aren't you, Luce?"

"I was baptized in the Catholic Church right after I was born," the girl clarified. "But the true church doesn't need gold-plated crosses or red carpeting to dress it up. We are all true Christians in this house. I have been here for over two years now--Gerith has been here one," Luce declared proudly, not recognizing any issues with the statement. Despite Gerith's affection for his foster sister, Jolie did not think Luce's statement included Gerith, the great bedeviler and player of tricks, who had hooties under the bed. Jolie wondered why adults always wanted to pass on their prejudices to kids like those prejudices were candy apples.

"We've seen a lot of kids like you come and go, Jolie," Luce told Jolie. "It is unfair for you to judge Reuben and Tulip when you don't really know them. Tulip has a good heart, and she does the best she can for us."

"And Reuben?" Jolie asked.

Luce's face hardened. "As long as he stays in front of his TV and no one disturbs him, Reuben is usually harmless. Don't provoke him and he'll ignore you, unless you cross Tulip, but give him an excuse, and he feels he needs to establish dominance and flex his muscles."

And his anger, Jolie deduced. "Thanks for the advice." It had been a telling conversation. Other foster kids were disposable. They came and went, and Luce would never ally with them. Her loyalties were aligned with the people who controlled her life.

Jolie went downstairs.

"I need to charge my cell phone, Mrs. Bozovic." She held the phone up. "Do you have a charger that might work?" she asked.

The woman looked at her like she'd asked for a snack of chocolate-covered cockroaches.

"No."

"Maybe an old one that one of the other kids left?"

"No. You can call me Tulip, Jolie. All the kids do."

"Could you check, Tulip?" The woman opened a junk drawer in the kitchen and did a cursory rummaging through it. "Oh, and I wanted to ask you, the bill for my cell service is coming due and--"

"Do you have money?" Tulip glanced at the next room. The TV was roaring for a touchdown. Reuben was not paying attention to them.

"Not right now but I could get a job or work around here." Jolie looked around the kitchen. "I could clean, or do yard work, help take care of--"

"You think my house is dirty?" Tulip retorted sharply. "That I can't take care of my own house?"

"No. I only said I could help," Jolie protested.

"For money," Tulip sneered. "We take you in, and right away you start asking for money for helping out when you should be showing how grateful you are by helping out for free?" Her words were angry, but she kept her voice below the TV's volume, conscious of avoiding Reuben becoming aware of the conversation. "Mister Bozovic didn't want you," she hissed between gapped teeth. "I fought to bring you here. He said that spawn like you can't be saved, and you would only cause trouble. So, don't start causing trouble!"

"I said I could get a job," Jolie repeated, trying to avoid the guilt chunks Tulip was spewing at her. "I'm not asking for a handout, Tulip. The state gives you money to take care of my needs. I need a phone, and a ride to Tecopa to get my clothes and my mom's important papers. It won't take me long, there's not much there that's worth keeping, but I need to go, and no one has taken me since…you know since…." She couldn't finish, the reality of her mother's death suddenly rushing her.

"And no one's gonna," Reuben joined the conversation. "We're not driving you all over the countryside, using our gas--"

"But I need--"

"You don't *need* anything," Dough Boy snarled. "We provide everything you need: food, a roof over your head, and a bed to sleep in. The rest: a cell phone, being driven all over--that's stuff you *want*, not stuff you *need*. There's a perfectly good phone right there on that wall." He pointed to an old olive-green phone hanging on the kitchen wall. It was older than Original Sin. "If you ask nice, you might earn permission to use it, but don't be tying up the line talking to your friends for hours. I can't be missing any important calls."

Jolie stopped herself from laughing. She couldn't imagine anyone would have anything important to say to Reuben Bozovic. She took a deep breath.

"I'm not here because I did anything wrong," she tried a strategy of reason. "I'm here because my last living parent died." She turned to address Tulip. "And okay, I get it, you feel like you do enough, and you can't do anymore. I don't want to add to your burden. I've pretty much been on my own since I was five and I can take care of myself. I'm just asking for this little bit of help and afterwards, you can ignore me and leave me on my own. I won't mind and I won't say a word to CPS."

"That's not the way it works," Tulip huffed. "As your foster parents, it is our duty to mold your character to the Lord's purpose. We're here to help you find your way to a righteous life, Jolie Figg--to straighten you out."

"We're *kids*, Tulip. Not tablecloths," Jolie shot back. "We don't need to be 'ironed out'." Tulip's eyes looked like they were going to pop out of her head. Jolie could practically see the steam coming out of her ears like in the old cartoons. It even made her feel kind of bad for the poor, downtrodden woman. Kind of.

"Go to your room," Tulip commanded.

"Yes, Ma'am." Jolie felt steam building in her head too. "Dammit Mom, why did you have to go and die on me?" she muttered under her breath as she tried not to stomp up the stairs.

Maybe she should keep the damned demon.

CHAPTER FIVE

Jessie Lynn was screaming her daughter's entry into life. Cold hands pulled Jolie's tiny body from the birth canal, her cries dead-ending her mother's.

"Give her to me. She's mine." Jessie Lynn's eyes were fierce, fiery orbs in her color-drained face. A quick look took in the spirits surrounding the birthbed. "Back off, all of you. She's mine!" Jessie Lynn spat. Flinching from the heat of the new mother's anger, Jolie's family stepped back into the shadows though they continued to linger. Only Jolie's father, Lucian, held his ground beside mother and daughter.

"She needs you, Jolie," he whispered to the infant as if it were an old spirit who would understand and not newly born. "Your mother is not whole." The red of Jessie Lynn's lifeblood spread like spilled ink flushing the sheets with the threat of death.

"Quick! We must save her!" Jolie's spirit leaped from the baby, a grown teen, and ran out through the hospital room's door.

A mountain of red plastic bio-hazard bags barred her way, the walls around it drawn in the dark charcoal strokes of Jessie Lynn's nightmare art. Jolie threw herself onto the pile, crawling through the bags, checking each and tossing them aside as she searched for The One.

The demon poked up from out of the bags, pressing one bag forward. The bag rolled down to the foot of the pile and lay there, glowing with Jessie Lynn's life-

essence. But it looked different than it had in Jolie's dreams before this--deflated like a popped balloon.

"What have you done?" she demanded, grabbing the bag, and tearing it open. Jolie's father, Lucian, appeared.

"What you are looking for is not there. Your mother's essence is no longer here, Jolie. She is gone, remember? But she left you this." Lucien gestured toward the demon. Lucian held out a necklace of twisted white cords, ruby red threads, and thick, gelatinous ribbons with a pearlescent surface. Shining tear droplets were caught and woven in among the twisted threads. Jolie took the braided intestines, veins, and corded muscles and placed them around her neck. Jessie Lynn's tears glistened among the red and pink viscera like scattered diamonds.

"This is your mother's life essence--her legacy to you, Jolie. The moment she decided to love you and carry you in her womb, her life was forfeited in favor of your own. Jessie Lynn Figg was not selfless. She tried to get it back, but she couldn't. Your life power was too strong."

Jolie looked up at the demon.

"I told you it was not me, Jolie. It was not me," he repeated as liquid blue pearls etched streams down the lumpy grid of his gray face.

Jolie wanted to blame someone for her mother's death. If not the demon, then who else was there?

Yourself.

No. It was not my fault, Jolie reminded herself. I am just a kid. I can't make choices for other people. Mom made her own choices; right or wrong.

Mostly wrong.

Jolie waited until Reuben got out of his chair and Tulip left the kitchen before going for the wall phone. One or the other of the Bozovics seemed to always be near the front door as if on guard duty protecting against a kid making a jailbreak, and Jolie had waited days for her chance to have the kitchen and the phone to herself, working at the kitchen table to complete her online classes in hopes that Tulip would leave.

Giving up, she decided on a new strategy. Changing her study place to the top step by the girl's bedroom, she could lean down and see the kitchen without being noticed.

I need my stuff. Handwashing the same three T-shirts and a pair of jeans was time-consuming and inconvenient. Tulip had offered to wash them with the rest of the laundry, but Jolie had seen the woman's disgust at her Princess Leia "A woman's place is in the resistance" T-shirt, and she wasn't willing to take the chance that her shirts would mysteriously be eaten by the washing machine's spin cycle.

Jolie tiptoed down the stairs, turning her cell phone on just long enough to bring up her mother's old boyfriend's number and scribbling it down on a post-it note. Quickly shutting her phone back down, she dialed, letting out a sigh of relief when Brett picked up.

"Brett, it's Jolie," she said straight off, knowing he would be questioning the unfamiliar number.

"Jolie? Hey, kid, what's going on? Where are you? I'm sorry I couldn't make it to your mom's funeral. I had this out-of-state conference, and I was giving the talk so I couldn't bail. Did you see the flowers? I sent flowers. I know it's not the same as being there but were they okay?"

"They were perfect," Jolie lied. She had been way too out of it at the time to notice the cards on the wreaths and bouquets at Jessie Lynn's gravesite. "I'm at a foster home for now."

"Really?" he sounded genuinely surprised. "How's that? I would have thought one of those old lady friends of yours would have--"

"It's a long story," Jolie stopped him. "Look, I don't have much time, but I wanted to apologize for leaving Chase's truck on the highway the night Mom died. I know it's not an excuse, but I wasn't thinking very clearly."

"It's fine, Jo. "No big deal. Really." Brett assured her.

"So, did you find the tow place that took it?"

"Yeah. JJ's on Highway One Sixty near the Fifteen. They're storing it for me until I can make it back down to Nevada." Brett had a ranch in Montana among other business concerns. He was far above the level of most of Jessie Lynn's boyfriends, but of course, Jessie had mucked that relationship up. But Brett was too nice a person not to help Jessie and Jolie when they were in a jam and had arranged the no-rent cabin in Tecopa, put in a working fridge, repaired a window, and the door, and filled the cupboards with groceries.

"Let me help out," Jolie suggested. "I can pick up the truck and drive it back to the cabin. It was my fault it got towed. I'd feel a lot better if you'd let me do the responsible thing." She heard his hesitation in the hairs' breadth of a pause. "I need to go back up to the cabin to pick up some things anyway," she added, hoping that wouldn't raise any red flags or additional questions. But Brett seemed distracted. Jolie could hear the bee buzz of voices in the background. Some woman was calling his name.

"I'm sorry, Jo, I'm going to have to go, but we can-_"

"Just text or call the tow place and let them know that it's okay for me to pick the truck up, okay? I'll do the rest. Please, Brett, you did so much for Mom and me. Let me do something for you." The woman on Brett's end hailed him again and his judgment fractured.

"Okay. Leave the keys under the visor like before so Chase will know where to find them."

"Absolutely. Thanks, Brett, and good luck with your speech."

"Thanks, Jo. Okay, okay, I'm coming, his voice became fainter as he moved the phone away from his face and ended the call, his focus already somewhere else.

Jolie put the receiver back on the wall phone and headed toward the fridge as Tulip reappeared.

"No snacks. It's too close to dinner," the woman snapped.

"But I'm starving." Jolie sucked in her cheeks. Tulip almost smiled.

"You're too dramatic for your own good," she scolded instead. "A little self-discipline won't hurt you, Jolie. Oh, there was a call for you today," she changed the subject. "The number's there on the pad. I couldn't understand the name of the place, something foreign. Chinese maybe?"

Jolie found the pad. The number was written in middle school perfect script with elegant swooshes and old-world flourishes. Jolie raised an eyebrow and pointed to the pad asking a silent *yours*? "Very nice." Tulip blushed. "Do you do calligraphy?" Tulip shook her head, embarrassed.

"No."

"Well, you should. People pay good money for handwritten invitations for events these days, weddings and showers, and stuff like that. With penmanship like yours and a decent calligraphy pen or two, you could make some money, Tulip." It wasn't a lie. The woman might do something with her perfect penmanship if the beer-pissing flesh ball in the other room didn't keep her chained to the stove. Also, a little flattery might help Jolie navigate her way around some of Tulip's many rules. Jolie made a sudden decision and took a chance. "You're worth something, you know, Tulip?" She glanced toward Reuben, an overgrown toad shuffling back to his lily pad in front of the television. "Life doesn't have to be like this. It could be better for you." She knew the instant she had said it she had made a mistake. People did not appreciate having their poor choices pointed out to them, particularly those who were complicit in their imprisonment because they refused to use the door. Tulip's eyes went mean.

"Go to your room and don't come down."

"But I'm--"

"Not for anything," Tulip interrupted.

"Can I just call--?" Jolie lifted the pad with the number up.

"Upstairs now!" Tulip pointed, ripping the pad from Jolie's hand.

"What's going on in there, Tu?" Reuben asked, raising his voice over the television.

"Nothing. Everything's fine, Reuben." Tulip lied. She was angry at Jolie for seeing too much but that did not mean she was going to risk her husband's wrath. She pulled the top sheet off the pad and threw it at Jolie. "And not another word or you'll be grounded," she hissed.

Jolie resisted rolling her eyes until she'd turned away so Tulip wouldn't see the small act of insolence.

Being a kid sucked.

In a ribald festival of color and ferocious paper mâché' Chinese Lion heads grinned from the loft balcony above the Kung Fu school's main practice room. Slender Chen-style straight swords and curvy broadswords with bright red tassels hanging from their pommels took focus while hand-buffed wooden staves made meticulous military lines on the walls. Sifu's long-handled Kwan Do, a heavy pole with a broadsword blade on the end, had a special place on the wall. Though heavy and cumbersome, the master teacher spun it around like a toothpick.

Copies of Taoist and Buddhist paintings of gods, goddesses, demons, and spirits also hung on the walls, though Jolie couldn't tell which was which. Among Taoists, ugly did not mean evil and the images depicted immortals, philosophers, and sages followed by lumbering creatures plucked from the pages of "Where the Wild Things Are".

A four-foot statue of General Tsao dominated the altar at the North end of the main room with pictures of the school's lineage masters, and other sacred objects-- Jolie did not understand--placed below it. Three incense sticks burned in a large black ceramic burner whenever someone was in the building. Even when it was not burning incense the scent of Nag Champa permeated the air, nearly covering the sweat and smells of stale fast food.

Jolie let her backpack slip from her shoulder to the floor by the wall then slid down beside it to watch her friends and the other students move from pose to pose in the form they were learning. No one noticed her, their focus entirely on perfecting the stances that Sifu's right-hand man, Rance, was teaching them.

Even filled with so much aggressive male energy, the school felt safe, like a sanctuary, an underlying sense of peace held within the four walls.

Jolie looked up at the small office that let out onto the loft/balcony above. A light glowed through a curtained window. When the curtains were open the person inside could look out over the practice room and observe what was going on below.

That's where Sifu is.

An old Chinese man came out of Sifu's office, looking out over the practice room before starting down the stairs.

"Thank you, Master Yinchen," Sifu's voice rolled over the balcony edge.

Jolie felt the tension slough from her, the emotions she had kept stuffed deep inside trickling out. Sadness, like condensation pressed at the bones of her face, settling behind her eyes, stuffing up her nose. The rawness of the emotions made her feel weak and exposed. She drew her knees up to her chest, lowering her face down onto her folded arms, trying to gather the strings of emotion and tuck them back where they would not be seen as Master Yinchen walked by.

"When you do this move, the goal is to push Qi along your arms and out through the palms of your hands." Rance demonstrated. Jolie's shy school friend, Hugo, had changed so much since starting at the school that he was nearly unrecognizable. Hugo, Remy, their friend, Brutus, plus Bodhi's younger brother, Jiu, worked alongside each other, focused and precise.

In her former status as Remy's girlfriend, Jolie had been on the fringes of the group until Remy and Bodhi became an item, but by then both boys had become entangled in the drama of Jolie's mom being shot by her ex-boyfriend and Jolie running amuck because of the demon trying to possess her. Now, without her connection to Remy, she wasn't sure how she fit in here, or even why she had come to the school. She wasn't a student. She couldn't afford to be one, but something whispered at her, drawing her, compelling her.

When Jolie was found, after being lost wandering in the Spring Range Mountains after watching her mother cross over, it was Sifu who tended the fire for the ceremony to bring her spirit back to her body. Afterward, he asked her if she wanted to study at the school.

Maybe she was here to decide.

As she sat by the wall, the mirrors opposite her caught Jolie's attention. A stripey, green wash clouded their gleaming silver as if someone had painted them with a dry paintbrush, leaving streaks of darker and lighter shades of green partially covering the shining surface. She frowned, wondering why the mirrors were painted. How did the students see themselves, or their teacher, with all the green paint hiding their reflections?

Class ended and her friends moved into their intimate circle.

"It's true!" Jolie caught a bit of their conversation. "Sifu talked about it in Spiritual Warrior class last week," Brutus insisted. "The Eight Immortals are like superheroes who understand how the world works."

"You're making that up," Hugo insisted. "Sifu didn't call them superheroes."

"Pretty close."

Hugo saw Jolie and his face lit up.

"Jo!" He ran toward her, stopping himself just before he grabbed her in a hug that would have embarrassed them both. "I'm so glad to see you. How are you?"

"Eh. You know, I'm okay. I'm 'job hunting', so the fosters let me out for a few hours."

Brutus sauntered up. "Sounds like prison."

"Feels like it," Jolie agreed.

"We were sorry to hear about your mom," Hugo said.

"Yeah. So, what are you going to do now, Jo?" Brutus asked. Hugo jabbed him in the side with his elbow. "What? I'm just letting her know we care," the teen defended himself.

Jolie shrugged. "It's okay. No one knows what to say in this situation and what they do say mostly sucks." She noticed a fleeting expression of agreement cross Jiu's face. The night she lost her mother, Jiu's brother, Bodhi, had died as well. She caught his eye. *I'm so sorry, Jiu,* she said silently, knowing he would not hear her but that he might see her sincere compassion.

"Is there anything we can do to help?" Hugo asked Jolie.

"Find me a ride to Tecopa to get my stuff? Except it's across the state line which makes it a felony." She rolled her eyes.

"Shouldn't your new foster parents take care of that kind of stuff?" Brutus asked, wiping his face with a towel from his sports bag.

"They're not that kind of foster parent. You know, the kind who do stuff for the kids who live with them? They're the other kind."

Brutus scowled. "That sucks."

"So, what about that old lady friend of yours, Iris?" Hugo asked. "I thought she'd want you to live with her."

Jolie's jaw tightened. "Maybe, but she had to go back East on some family emergency, and getting approved through the system takes time."

"So, when she gets back then," Hugo suggested Iris would iron things out.

"When she gets back." Jolie nodded. This was not the time or place to go into her fears about Iris's reluctance.

As they talked, they had meandered out of the school building and were now lingering in the front courtyard, a two-story entry area defined by concrete brick half-walls outside the porch's tall columns.

They sat on the low wall in the twilight as cars drove into the parking lot to pick kids up from class. Older students with cars were hanging out by their vehicles. Those who were old enough to not be chauffeured began heading across the street to the Chinese restaurant in the strip mall.

"I'm starving," Brutus announced. "Who wants to eat? Hugo? Jo?"

Hugo looked at Jolie to see what she wanted. She shook her head.

"Okay. See you later." Brutus put an arm around Jiu's shoulders and lumbered off to catch up with the others.

"It's okay, Hugo, you can go with them," Jolie told her friend. "I need to get back anyway."

"No, I'm good." Hugo found her hand and took it in his.

"The school's been good for you," Jolie said, awkwardly. The boy she remembered from just a few weeks ago had slimmed down, muscled up, and grown a few inches. His round, side-kick face showed signs of maturing into something resembling a young Latin American heartthrob. Jolie wasn't the only one noticing.

"Hi, Hugo," a middle school-aged girl called out, swaying her skinny girl hips in her skinny jeans and crop top as she passed.

There weren't many girl students at the school but there was always a parade of faces at car windows, wide-eyed and breathless, eager for a glimpse into the inner sanctum of this boy's club with its budding knights-in-training. A few local girls might dream of becoming Mulan, but most of the sisters were still looking for Prince Charming.

Hugo raised a hand in a half-hearted greeting to the girl who flashed him a smile that made promises she was too young to understand or keep. Jolie wondered how many hours she had practiced that flirty smile alone in her bedroom mirror.

She nudged her friend. "Wow. When did that happen?"

"Coby's sister." Hugo shrugged, embarrassed. "I guess I should be flattered, but girls just seem like such a distraction."

"You don't like girls now?" Jolie teased.

"I like girls fine," Hugo corrected her. "Just not *these* girls." Suddenly Jolie felt awkward. "Seriously, Jo, we've--*I've* been worried about you. Nobody should have to go through what you have alone, and you didn't have to. We would have been there--"

"To do what? Hold my hand?" Jolie's eyes and temper snapped. "They don't allow that sort of thing at Child Haven. They didn't allow us to have our cell phones". Jolie could feel him studying her, his dark eyes serious, thoughtful, and sad. Hugo Matias was a steady, loyal friend. The kind of person people underestimated and who got hurt because of it. People took the Hugo's of the world for granted, never realizing how rare and special they were, or how much they relied on them until their own Hugo decided he'd had enough and moved on. Then, they were missed.

Boys like Hugo got their hearts broken because they gave their affections completely whether the object of their affection was deserving or not. They cared too much and committed too strongly, and though their affections might change in time, they were too good and compassionate to ever stop caring. Jolie wondered what all that meant for her and Hugo's future friendship.

"I'm sorry, I didn't reach out and ask for help, Hugo," she said. "I know you meant well, but really, I've just been trying to survive."

Jolie could feel his pulse in the hand clasped around hers. He cared. How much? She was afraid to look into his eyes and find out, risking a friendship for something that would not last and that she could not return with the same commitment.

"I'm not very good company these days." She slowly pulled her hand out of his so it would not seem like a dismissal of his feelings. Loss and isolation flooded over her. "I just don't have anything to say to people. I have nothing in common with any of this." She swept her hand to indicate the kids being picked up by mothers, fathers, or nannies.

Hugo sighed. "It's been a weird year."

"It has," Jolie agreed.

"My mom's been seeing this psychic--some friends recommended her, and this woman seems to know stuff I can't explain. So, I'm thinking maybe she's the real thing, like you? I don't know. But she's got my mom all worried, telling her that I have some special destiny to fulfill and that it puts me in danger. So now my mom thinks she needs to bring me to this woman so she can do some protective thing on me."

Suddenly Hugo had Jolie's full attention. "You mean like a spell?" Hugo shrugged. "Have you told Sifu?"

"No! I'm not going to Sifu with some dumb superstitious stuff that my mom's into. And I didn't agree to do it. It's just hard because Mom keeps pestering me about it and, you know, she's my mom."

Jolie frowned. "I thought your family was Catholic."

"Yeah, but South American Mountain Native Catholic. We didn't let go of our old beliefs, we just added the Catholic stuff in, mixed it all up together, and it's been simmering on the back of the stove ever since."

"You don't think Sifu should know that this person is trying to get her hands on your energy?" Jolie stayed on topic.

"Whatever line this woman is feeding my mom to keep her coming back and paying for another session, I know that I'm not important. Repeating their claims to Sifu would just sound like a lame plea for attention. I want Sifu to notice me for the work I put in, not some drama cooked up by a strange woman who sucked my mom into her stuff to make a buck."

Ever since Hugo began talking about the situation, Jolie was fighting a sick feeling in her gut.

"What's her name, this psychic?" She tried to make her interest sound casual.

"I don't know. I wasn't paying attention."

"Find out and tell me, okay?"

Hugo looked confused but agreed. "Okay. Did you get your phone working?"

"No, but there's a landline at the house" Jolie got out a pen and scribbled the Bozovic's number on Hugo's hand. "The mom, Tulip, will probably screen my calls, but if you need to get hold of me, this is the best way, for now." Jolie stood. "I've got to go, or I'll miss my bus."

She stopped and turned back. "Hey, you haven't seen any weird-looking creatures hanging around have you--shadows moving out of the corner of your eye or anything weird like that?"

Hugo looked disgusted. "God no! I'm not doing that Iron Body stuff." Jolie looked at him without understanding. "Last week in Spiritual Warrior class Sifu taught Iron Body. It makes you really strong, but you also start seeing spirits and stuff and if you don't keep doing it for all one hundred eight days, you can get sick."

"Seriously?"

"Yeah. This Taoist stuff isn't fluff, Jo. It's the real deal. You've got to be careful and committed if you want to go all the way. Brutus is excited but I just don't know." Hugo shook his head.

"Who in their right mind would want that?"

"He thinks it's going to be so cool," Hugo mimicked his friend. "Like it's going to make him into a superhero or something."

"It's not that cool. Trust me," Jolie disagreed. "So, no creepy little gray brain-like beings in your dreams or weird things happening to you? No one offering you free wishes?"

"No. No bottles and no Geni's, Jo. Cross my heart," Hugo teased.

"I'm serious, Hugo. I want you to promise me that you won't go wishing on pennies in fountains or birthday candles, or any of that right now, however innocent or tempting it seems. Promise me."

Hugo's eyes scrunched down to slits. "You are the weirdest girl." He studied her again. This time there was nothing vaguely romantic about it.

"It's a weird world," Jolie insisted.

"When you're around."

"It's the same weird whether I'm there or not, you just don't notice it," Jolie informed him. "Find out the name of that psychic and don't make any wishes." She tossed her backpack over her shoulder. "Now I've really got to run." And she did, barely making the first bus that would get her back to the Bozovics.

CHAPTER SIX

Wherever Jolie was, it was dark--dark, but not close. She had the impression of immenseness, the black nothing going on and on. This full black expanded into a darkness that held something--some secret of life. The black folded around the promise of a distant sliver of light.

From the shadows, thick stone columns too wide for four people to clasp hands around. Like stone trees, they supported the endless dark above. Jolie felt a glow she could not see drawing her, her feet wobbling on the rough stones beneath her chilled bare feet.

A lone candle alongside the path became pairs, then small groups, until the middle path she walked was the only clear way amid a river of small, bright, flames, the brave amber of their light giving off a sense of warmth and joy. The flames flickered at Jolie as she passed, inflections of respect like a greeting between honored friends.

As she walked on, the individual candle's columns melted, becoming two pearlescent streams of wax, one on each side of the stone pathway. A grounded energy came up from the undulating stones through Jolie's feet caressing and massaging her bare soles. She noticed that--here in this place--she felt no fear, no sadness, no loneliness.

"Where am I?" she asked.

Then she woke up.

"You were out too late last night," Tulip declared as Jolie came down the stairs for breakfast.

"I got the job," Jolie said. "So, I worked a shift, then stopped by the school to let my friends know I'm okay since I don't have a cell phone."

"It was *too* late," Tulip repeated, tight-lipped. "You should not be out in the city that late at night, Jolie. It isn't safe."

"I didn't mean to make you worry, but there wasn't a way to let you know I was working." Tulip made a point of looking at the wall phone and Jolie made a point of looking chastised. It was a common argument for her generation. It wasn't like landline phones didn't work. "I'll ask about getting an earlier shift," Jolie promised. "But I'm not sure it's an option. I'm new and I must take the shifts they give me. If there's a chance to make money, I feel like I should take it."

Tulip sniffed. "I don't know why you can't work closer to home."

"This is where I got hired," Jolie pointed out. "It's just for the summer, Tulip. Once school starts again, I'll be focused on that." She did not say that she had no intention of still being with the Bosovics by then and hoped she would be nearer her job and the Kung Fu school rather than clear across town. "Are you ready to come down, Luce?" she called up the stairs.

"Yes," Luce answered.

Jolie helped the frail girl down the steps one at a time, ready to catch her if she lost her balance, still letting Luce use her own strength and balance as much as possible. This was why Tulip had convinced Reuben to bring in a third, older, foster child; she needed someone to help Luce on the stairs now that she couldn't. There were a half dozen reasons that Reuben stepping up to help wasn't going to happen, but no one voiced them.

He'd probably get stuck in the stairwell and Tulip would have to call the fire department to get him out, Jolie thought, smiling at the picture that put into her head.

"Careful now," Tulip hovered like a mama hen as Jolie helped Luce off the last step.

"Loooose!" Gerith raced into the room, wrapping his arms around the girl's legs.

"Gerith be careful! You'll knock her over," Tulip scolded. Luce sat down on a low step and opened her arms for the little boy.

"Okay, come on. I'm ready for my Gerith hug." He threw himself into Luce's arms, both making grunting noises as they swayed from side to side. There was genuine affection in this family. Affection that neither Reuben nor Jolie was part of.

"Stop with all the racket, for God's sakes!" Reuben shouted from his recliner in front of the television.

Everyone cringed and looked sheepish.

"Breakfast is on the table," Tulip announced. Gerith unwound from Luce, and Jolie shadowed the girl as Luce made her way to the table.

"You could use your wheelchair, you know," Tulip pointed out to Luce. "It's right there and God knows it cost enough."

"I'm having a good day--feeling strong and I need to walk as much as I can when I can."

There were pancakes, scrambled eggs, and bacon, which Jolie did not eat.

"Just more for The Mister," Tulip added the three slices of bacon to Reuben's plate before delivering it to him in his chair.

"You're chipper today," Jolie noted as she forked a partnered pair of pancakes and a few spoonsful of eggs onto her plate.

Tulip beckoned Jolie over to peek inside a kitchen drawer. An open box containing a set of calligraphy pens, notebook paper, and a cardboard card with swirly letters drawn on it.

"I did a little shopping on my own while Luce was at her doctor's appointment yesterday." Tulip's eyes danced with delight. She glanced toward the television room and held a finger to her lips before carefully closing the drawer. "I think I've already got my first job--a small one." She looked down at her feet as if the act made her less visible and would hide what she was about to reveal. "I took some samples to the beautician around the corner, and she said she does hair for lots of women planning their weddings, engagement parties, and baby showers. She hears about them from relatives and friends too, and she thinks if she shows samples of my calligraphy work to them, some of them will want me to write invitations or cards for them. She said I could charge for every item I made. The shop owner who made the contacts and arranged the deals would take some of the money for helping me out, a commission she called it, but I'd get the rest of the money--my own money, that I earned, myself."

"You do all the work taking care of us," Jolie pointed out. "Isn't that your money, Tulip?"

"Heavens no." Tulip shook her head, shocked. "That's the household money. That all goes straight into the bank."

"So you can buy groceries and stuff," Jolie figured.

Tulip again shook her head. "I never touch that account." Jolie frowned. "My name's not even on it."

Jolie was more than perplexed. "Then how do you buy groceries?"

"Reuben gives me an allowance for small things that run out during the week, like milk and beer, but for the rest, he takes me shopping so he can keep an eye on the budget."

An eye on what you spend, Jolie figured. "Wouldn't it be more convenient to just put your name on the account so you can use it when you need to, and he doesn't have to be bothered?'

Tulip's eyes flew right, then left, then right, as nervous, and jittery as a rabbit being questioned by a coyote. "Reuben wouldn't like that."

"Right." Jolie gave Luce a look that said, *this is so wrong.*

"Besides, I don't drive," Tulip added.

"What? So Reuben has to drive you?" Tulip nodded. "Everywhere?" Tulip nodded again, looking as if she had just confessed a sin.

"Sometimes, he's too busy so someone from church picks me up. He's usually busy on Sundays."

"Because there are games," Jolie muttered quietly.

"He wants to go to church, he really does, but he's tired a lot on Sunday mornings. I don't need to drive. I don't need to go anywhere anyway, except the store or church."

Jolie wanted to ask Tulip who told her she didn't need to go anywhere, but she knew the answer.

"DHS picks Luce up and takes her to most of her appointments, and I can go along if I need to."

Sheltered as she was--and must have always been-- this all seemed normal to Tulip. It was like she and Jolie had been raised in different worlds--or at least different centuries. Jolie had never felt more grateful to Jessie

Lynn for her unconventional views. It must have taken a lot of courage for Tulip to buy the pens, and then take the initiative to approach the beauty shop owner.

"That's great, Tulip. We're very happy for you," Luce said, sharing a silent agreement with Jolie for support without further comment.

CHAPTER SEVEN

JJ's Auto Towing was in an industrial part of south Las Vegas near the intersection of the I-15 and the Pahrump Valley Highway-- known as "the widow maker". During the real estate bubble of the new millennium, Pahrump, Nevada experienced a hot market moment. Housing was cheap over the "hump" in Pahrump, the Nopah Mountain Range that separated the Vegas Valley from the high desert that bordered Death Valley to the East. Benefitting from the bidding wars and years of equity in a suddenly volatile market, seniors living in Vegas found they could turn their city houses into new stick-built homes in a planned development in Pahrump--for less money--buy a manufactured home, plop it on an acre with a well and have enough left over to do some traveling. Those who acted early were buffered from the bubble burst that left Pahrump with the real estate version of all dressed up with no date for the prom.

Residents of the smaller nearby Tecopa and Shoshone had a good laugh at their over-fed neighbor's expense. The wave of new arrivals--mostly military retirees--who were used to giving orders, not taking them, unpacked the notions they had collected over the years about what a town should be trying to shape their new hometown into everyone's different versions of their old hometown, and trampling the old guard ranchers and desert rats who had moved there decades before to be left alone.

Jolie left a scribbled note on the kitchen table at the Bozovics saying she was going to work and with training and maybe an extra shift after that, she didn't know what time she'd be back, pointing out that if she had a cell phone, she could call them and let them know her plans. She told herself she would call them when she found someplace to do that, then forgot about it as she focused on the logistics of getting across town on the city's transit system.

Getting to JJ's Auto Towing took the last of her pocket money, her stomach protesting her decision to pay for transportation rather than food. More than food though, Jolie needed to get to Tecopa, gather her clothes, and financial documents then get back to town without the Bozovics noticing.

JJ's Auto Towing garage smelled like dirty automotive oil and cigarettes. As did J.J. The overall-clad mechanic eyed Jolie with suspicion, then demanded to see her driver's license. She didn't have one yet, so she stared him down and pretended to call Brett, threatening to tell her "Uncle" that JJ had been rude and refused to return the truck and suggesting he sue JJ. Las Vegas was a litigious society. Everyone was always threatening to sue. The less educated a person was the more likely they were to threaten a lawsuit or to believe the threat of one. Most people didn't seem to have the slightest idea how the law worked, aside from what they saw on television. They only knew what they heard from disgruntled friends, which was: that the system was rigged against the little guy.

"Oh, and I'll need five gallons of gas," Jolie added after JJ caved to her request for the keys. "Uncle Brett won't want to risk me running out of gas on the way home, which means you don't either. Just add it to his bill. He'll pay it."

JJ had one of his guys grab a couple of gas cans and pour them into the old Ford's tank while Jolie took the keys.

She yanked the door of the primer-gray tank of a truck open. The door always stuck, and it took some muscle to get it open. Someone at the towing shop fished the window on the driver's side up from of the bottom of the door well, but when Jolie yanked on the door, the window fell back down.

The outside of the old truck was a nineteen fifty-seven Ford. It was someone's half-finished hobby, with a raised rear end, glass packs, and an oversized V-8 engine under the hood. The customizing on the inside had progressed only as far as having a glossy, teak steering wheel and a shiny chrome footprint gas pedal added. The original bench seat had not been replaced and decades of butts had worn a hole in the driver's seat which now offered a dissected view of the old straw and horse-hair stuffing common to vehicles of the time, all of it pushed in around some old, rusty, springs.

Behind the seat, Jolie found the blanket she left in the truck the last time she slept there. She draped it over the driver's seat hole, climbed in, and inserted the key.

Memories of when she had sat in the truck last leaped at her like a sneak attack.

Bodhi had just died, and Remy was in the hospital with Hoke on the way to stop his parent's pulling life support. Jolie's mom's spirit had answered the Ridge Walker's call to cross over and Jolie had taken the truck, trying to reach her mom's body lying on the side of some road in Tecopa. Then the truck ran out of gas.

Jolie had abandoned the truck and, caught up in visions, wandered the pine forests of the Nopah Hills, distraught and getting more and more dehydrated. Somehow, she had walked down the East side of the mountain range and into Red Rock, where Remy's Aunt Rose found her.

Only she hadn't walked. The old, black, jack burro who led the Red Rock burro band had found her in the mountains and brought her down. But who was going to believe that part?

Jolie bit her lip, straightened her spine, and raised her chin. She needed to hang on to this bitchy girl attitude long enough to drive off the auto repair lot. If JJ or any of his drivers got a whiff of fragility, she was done.

It took a few turns of the key and some rambunctious foot-stepping on the chrome pedal, but the old Ford fired up, rumbling like thunder.

"Good truck." Jolie patted the spray-painted dashboard, then pulled out, turning west up the Pahrump Valley Highway toward the Spring Mountains.

Tecopa, California was a small desert hamlet of less than two hundred souls in the Mojave Desert, an inconvenient hiccup along the offbeat path from Las Vegas to Desert Hot Springs Resort or the more touristy Scotty's Castle in Death Valley. The landscape was flat, brown, and barren, and most of what grew here had spikes. But there were patches of Joshua trees, sagebrush, creosote, or desert willow snuggled like little girls at a slumber party in gullies where rain puddled after a storm.

Desert, punctured by stark rock features demanded you notice them in their singular settings. It was easy to believe the formations were something more than rocks. If you looked away and caught one out of the corner of your eye, they transformed quickly into reclined, gods, totem faces, or the mythically sized skeletons of prehistoric creatures.

White, puffy, clipper-ship clouds sailed through the brilliant blue sky, while taloned predators rode the air currents that dipped and fell, following the curves of the rolling desert.

Tecopa wasn't much of a town and the standard of living was far below the norms of Las Vegas residents where your house, car, clothes, and income defined your worth as a human being. Tecopa, by contrast, was open-hearted. Driving from Las Vegas to Tecopa was like going into a time warp. Desert folk lived quiet lives, preferring their laid-back "nowhere" to the hectic "somewhere" of the city just over the hill. They knew Las Vegas existed. They picked relatives up at the airport and shopped there for the holidays, but they avoided interacting with it any more than necessary.

Tecopa folk had flexible categories for their population. There were cowboys, ex-military--mostly enlisted types, old-timers who had been raised in the area and perfected a low-impact lifestyle requiring little money. Reliant on barter long before anyone thought it was hip, Tecopa had hippies, old and new varieties, along with a number of "Burners" who had left the playa at Black Rock after Burning Man, run out of gas in Tecopa and never left.

There were spiritual and political outcasts who lived off-grid and held interesting theories about the country, humanity, and the world--with personal stories to match--but you needed a good bottle of whiskey or some mind-altering substance to pry those out. With Area Fifty-One a few hundred miles up the road to the North, more than a few locals had stories of being abducted by aliens. Eighty percent claimed to be hiding from dark agents of the government, and yet they still offered a stranger a cup of coffee, a sandwich, and a tank of gas if needed. It's just the way they were. Whether a story was true or not didn't matter as much as it was a good story. Tecopans didn't judge. Residents earned their creds through their actions, and everyone filled a necessary role in the community.

Jolie and her mom were living in a long-abandoned shack that Brett's friends inherited but did not use. Jolie hated leaving school before the end of the year and living so far away from her friends, but it was better than living with her school friend, Becca's uptight, hypocritical family, and Jolie had a few good memories of cleaning the old place up and making it their own. What she remembered best though was the dark, soft, warm nights, sitting on the porch, everything so quiet you could hear a lizard sauntering through the sagebrush, or the porch door closing at the friendly rancher's house a quarter of a mile away.

But Jolie was not going back to Tecopa to relive memories. She was going back to close the chapters of her life she had shared with her mom.

Crossing the Spring Mountain Pass, she passed the sign indicating the dirt road to the boy scout camp where she had turned off on her way to the Ridge Walking ceremony continuing to drive West, then North as the highway curved.

There wasn't much traffic now. The Pahrump highway was only busy during commuting hours in the morning and evening, or on Friday nights when Pahrumpsters made an exodus for the weekend to go play in Las Vegas.

Turning off the highway onto The Old Spanish Trail Road going West, Jolie entered that other world, everything slowing to the speed of a Tortoise crawl.

The warm desert wind stroked her cream and cocoa-colored cheek like a length of silk--the good kind, like the scarves Iris kept from her New York fashion days.

Life on the edge of the Mojave didn't shout. It didn't ask to be seen. It was shy and subtle. Most people, impatient and moving too fast, dismissed the desert, calling it "lifeless". But it was not lifeless. Tiny flowers grew in the hidden crevices of rocks where the rare dew collected, nurturing the resilient roots of species found nowhere else in the world. Small animals, snakes, bugs, scorpions, and Tarantulas hugged the shade of the rocks, hiding from the sun, and people; either of which potentially meant death to their kind.

Once Jolie left the Old Spanish Trail Road and turned onto the Tecopa Road she began to count dirt roads, looking for the rusty evidence of humanity's invasions. In a landscape that shunned street signs, once you were off the highway, the term "road" became relative with most looking more like dirt paths. Directions here were given in the language of abandoned markers. "Turn left at the rusty red truck," or "watch for the third dirt road after the rock that looks like a witch's hat." "It's at the foot of the sleeping giant with the big nose."

Everything Jolie had done today had taken longer than she had expected, and the sun was low in the sky by the time she turned down the packed-dirt driveway that led to the old cabin. Unexpected tears blinded her vision, but the old truck kept to the ruts like they were a railway.

Joyriders had visited the property since the monsoon, making circles in the mud in front of the cabin. The rancher next door, Ward Colton, had probably run them off, but the damage had been done. Nothing would grow where those wheels had driven for over a decade.

As Jolie drove toward the house, imagining going inside alone, she considered going next door and asking Ward if he would come with her, but he and his wife were probably just sitting down to dinner, and she didn't want to be a bother. They would ask her to stay and no matter how often she said, no, they would set a plate for her because that was the way folks were up here.

Jolie's stomach growled its approval of the idea. Heck, they'd probably make up a bed and ask her to stay the night, but that was not what she had come for. She needed to get some things and let go of some things and get back to the city and the life she was working to rebuild.

What she needed to do here was not a group activity.

Unsure how mucky the yard's muddy clay might still be, Jolie edged up alongside the house where there was a little gravel mixed into the well-packed ground. She put the keys back under the visor and climbed out. The sound of the truck door closing was violence against the virgin quiet.

The humidity from the rains had burned off, leaving the air light, dry, and scented with sage. The woody smells of desert willow skipped over on a breeze from the nearby Amargosa River.

Jolie hoisted herself up the two feet to the weathered gray planks of the front porch.

The beer bottles from Jessie Lynn's get-to-know-you with the cabin owner's friend had tipped over and rolled under the rickety chairs that Jessie Lynn had dragged out onto the porch. They looked like defeated chess pieces and in this game, the Queen had been sacrificed, the game lost. Jolie wished she knew who this guy who helped pull her mom off the sober wagon was, and where she could find him. She'd like to give him a piece of her mind and a good punch in the face, but she had never seen him, only the evidence left behind. The discarded props of Jessie Lynn's last evening were a signpost indicating the direction of her final path: a time capsule into her final hours. Like so many other nights, she had been hanging out, having a few beers, laughing too loud and flirting too much. It should have been so innocent; just a chance meeting with a friend's friend, a few drinks in the shade of a porch at the end of a hot day. But Jessie Lynn's past had a powerful, destructive pull, and this seemingly simple, social connection had restarted a downward cycle the woman had been trying to escape for years.

The wooden floorboards complained as Jolie crossed the porch. She paused to take a steadying breath, then opened the door.

The twilight inside quivered like an eager lover awaiting the coming dark. The white spaces of Jessie Lynn's disturbing art glowed in the late light, contrast revealing the character of the dark charcoal shadows and deeply sad blues. The scattered, no-pattern hanging of the pictures amplified their tortured whispers.

"*You did this.*" Guilt drove a blade into Jolie's newly orphaned brain. "*You were weak and could not control these demons, so they were unleashed on the world. Your mother is merely one in a long history of forgotten victims.*"

Jolie reached out to turn the lights on, hoping electricity would banish her guilt along with the shadows. But there were no lights. The electricity had been turned off.

She went to a drawer and pulled out the emergency flashlight she had stowed there. A box of matches sat beside it. She pulled it out as well, setting it on the table.

In the bedroom that had been hers, Jolie retrieved her "go" bag, filling in the spaces with whatever caught her eye that she thought she might need: the most irreplaceable and used clothing for summer and winter. When the bag was full, she filled her backpack, then found two pillowcases and filled them. Unpacked boxes from their move here were stacked against the walls in some rooms. Jolie dumped out the contents of one and began filling it with items she knew she couldn't carry now, but hoped she'd be able to retrieve later. Maybe Ward would store a box or two for her until she got more settled.

The stuff she didn't need, Jolie threw into a pile in the middle of the floor.

When she was done, she filled whatever boxes were available with stuff from the "discard" pile and drug them out to the porch. The light was gone now, the sky dark, with only a bare hint of color.

Jessie Lynn's room was next. Now the task became a guessing game. Where was the address book with the Boulet family's contact numbers? Where was the check account register, and the bank paperwork? Jessie Lynn's "go" bag should have all the grownup stuff. Jolie searched the unpacked boxes stacked around her mom's room, looking for the bag. Any box with clothes, she pushed to the wall. Anything specific to Jessie, her brand of lotion, her brush, got tossed on the bed. Jolie wiped tears away more than once, pausing her sorting to blow her nose on a ragged T-shirt—Florence and the Machine. One of her mom's favorites. She finished her search through the boxes and made for the closet.

Under a box of shoes and work clothes from the casino Jessie had been working at when she was shot, Jolie found the bag. She brought it to the bed, unzipped it, and ran the flashlight over the contents, rummaging until she found the check register. If it was correct, there were almost three hundred dollars in Jessie Lynn's account. Jolie wasn't sure if she would be able to access it, but she was going to try. She found another hundred seventy dollars in cash stashed in the bag's inner pocket. Checking the other pockets, Jolie pinched her fingers along the bag's lining. There should have been more. There just wasn't.

Jessie Lynn must have been dipping into their emergency getaway stash for a while. Digging deeper, Jolie found a crushed cigarette pack with only one cigarette in it. She stuck it in her jeans pocket and kept searching until she found the cracked leather address book. Stuffing it, the check register, bank papers, and the cash into a zippered pocket in her backpack, she pounded the bag flat and zipped it shut.

Putting her go bag, backpack, and two pillowcases into a pile on the edge of the porch, she went back inside for one last look.

Jessie Lynn's artwork screamed like children sensing their impending abandonment.

"They are all that is left of your mother, a final expression of who she was," a voice accused her.

"No," Jolie disagreed, assuming the voice was the demon's. "They are an expression of the misery you and Axel made of my mom's life when you possessed her. They are not *her,* they're the worst of you and him. *"* She began ripping the drawings off the walls, crumpling them into balls, and throwing them across the room.

The last one—Jessie Lynn's final drawing, was a sketch of Jolie herself. It was good--emotionally raw, but it showed talent. Jolie's sadness was there, but also something of her spunk and determination. The artist's affection and admiration for the solitary woman-child sang in every line.

What might have become of Jessie Lynn Figg if the events of her life had been different? What might she have accomplished if she had been born to a supportive family who had encouraged her talents? What if she had not met Lucian Boulet and taken him to her bed, or if she had decided to get an abortion instead of going to New Orleans where her dead lover's family made her feel second in importance to the child she carried? Had there been some intersection of the stars that Jessie Lynn had missed that might have resulted in her pursuing her talents, altering the outcome of the life that drugs had ended?

Jolie sighed. What was done was done. There would be no more chances for Jessie Lynn this time around.

With the stack of wadded pictures stuffed under one arm, Jolie grabbed the matches off the kitchen table and strode from the cabin, leaving Jessie Lynn's portrait of her daughter on the wall, a question undecided.

A few dead twigs, a little dried grass, and Jolie had a fire.

A freckling of stars began to blossom from the deepening blue above, the brilliant oranges, pinks, and lavenders a wash on the far side of the Colton ranch to the West. Jolie took a deep breath, releasing the armor of business she was protecting herself in, inviting the moment to approach.

Tentatively, as if uncertain of its reception, the moment slipped in beside the woman-child. Side by side they stood by the fire in stillness.

Jolie fished out the crumpled cigarette removing the crumbling paper cover, she closed her hand over the tobacco shavings, turned to face the West, and began to make a prayer, slowly making a clockwise turn.

"Hau Mita'kuye Oya'sin." She placed her hand on the ground, then held her offering to the sky in her closed fist. "Spirits of all Directions, it is me, Wincincala Witko, the Girl Who Knows Nothing. I ask you to bear witness to the prayer of this small, humble person. I want to honor the woman who brought me into this world, my mother, Jessie Lynn Figg because whatever people say about her, she was brave enough to accept love when it was given, even though she barely recognized it. Even braver, she chose to become a single mom, and because of that choice, I live. Her life was never easy. She had no one to guide her in how to raise a child better than she had been raised." Chaos had been Jessie Lynn's natural state. She had been born into it.

"But flawed as my mom was, and as I am, she deserves to be honored for what she did. So, I ask you to carry my words to her spirit, wherever that is, because I need her to know that she matters…to me." The words choked Jolie's throat and she paused, before going on.

"Mom, wherever you are, I hope you've found the peace you kept searching for." Emotion coated Jolie's tongue. "But if you haven't, don't give up. You will-- eventually, you will. And don't waste energy worrying about me or feeling bad about our lives. You did the best you could. I know that. So did I.

"I just wish we had more time." Jolie licked the tears from her upper lip. "If we'd had a few more years, I would have been grown up and I could have helped you more and then maybe things wouldn't have ended like this." Jolie broke down and gave in to her tears, struggling for breath against the wracking sobs. "I just miss you so much, Mom. I'll be okay, I will. I *am* okay.

Even if it was mostly by accident, you raised me to be tough and resilient. I can go on."

Tears streaking her face, Jolie began to feed Jessie's nightmares in charcoal to the fire. The fire ate pinprick bright embers in the paper, red-hot mouths framed by images of dark screams, the edges curling as the paper burned the images to ash, their anguish released.

"I will always love you, because you're my mom, and everything I am, and everything I will be, is because you set your dreams aside and took a chance on me."

A figure appeared near the ring of the fire's light.

"A touching tribute." Yanna Maria's image wavered with the breeze, but her smirk, like the Cheshire Cat in Alice in Wonderland, remained unsettlingly present.

"What are you doing here, Yanna?" Jolie demanded, smudging the tears from her face. "We have nothing to say to each other."

"You cannot speak for others, Jolie. Certainly not for me."

"I don't have what you want," Jolie declared.

"But you do."

"I have not bonded the demon."

"It follows you like a puppy," Yanna Maria said like it was an accusation.

"It's free to go where it wants and do what it wants," Jolie argued.

The Santeria's eyes were banked coals. "It is a demon. It has less will, understanding, or direction than a toddler. Its whole existence is tied to being told where to go and what to do. You are only confusing it. If you will not bond it and direct it, you must send it away, Jolie. Send it to me. If you tell it to, it will go."

"Jolie? Is that you?" Ward Colton walked from the desert darkness into the firelight and Yanna Maria's image blew into tendrils of smoke. "I saw the fire and thought I'd better check up on the place. There were some kids here the other night." He indicated the tire tracks. "They were just fooling around. They didn't go into the house or anything, but I didn't want them to think this was a place they could use for partying." He came up alongside her. "I wasn't sure you'd be back, kid."

"I'm not." Jolie wiped her face with her sleeve. "But I brought back the old Ford for Brett." She tossed her head toward the house driveway. "And there were a few things I needed, clothes and stuff. The rest… I'm burning my past--not everything, just the pieces I don't need anymore." Ward nodded. He was the kind of man who spent words as thriftily as he spent money, always considering the expense, never wasteful. What Jolie said required no comment. "The stuff I want is in a pile on the porch," she went on. "But there are still some boxes inside with clothes in them. I figured I could burn them but maybe they're useful to someone?"

"The school's got a secondhand closet out back. I can take them by."

"If it's no trouble," Jolie agreed.

"No trouble. How long will you be here?"

"Until the fire's out. I have a new job in Vegas, as long as I don't mess it up by missing a shift my first week, that is."

Ward looked around, scratching his neck. "'You alone?"

"No. You're here," she teased, but she knew what he meant. Voices carried in the desert. He heard something. "I was making a prayer for my mom," she admitted.

Ward nodded. "I understand. Hoke's been helping me with horses for a long time. We've been through quite a few births and deaths together and some ways of looking at things kind of rub off."

The Moment lingered in the transparent twilight: palpable, private. Dressing up a moment with words cheapened it, like trying to define something that exists beyond definition. The place for words was far away. A true moment exists beyond words, the memory of it a marker rich in textures, visuals, and scents--those senses most closely connected to the brain's memory centers. Ward felt it, too.

He pulled a log up by the fire and sat alongside Jolie in silence.

The embers winked at them like fireflies slowly growing a deeper red, blanketed beneath the dark ash leftovers. Without a word, Ward rose and walked off.

The demon appeared, faintly visible through the flames and smoke. *"Your mother is gone, Jolie. But you are not alone. I am here."*

"I don't need a demon," Jolie whispered. "I need my mom."

She didn't know how a gray blob could look dejected, but it did. The demon's image faded into the heat waves and smoke rising from the fire's coals.

Yanna Maria was right about one thing, the demon did not have enough experience with freedom to desire it or value it. Could demons become attached to people outside of the archaic bonding of slave to master?

A truck started up next door at Ward's place. Soon it was rolling down the driveway, its headlights cutting off abruptly as it stopped beside the cabin, returning the desert to silence.

When Ward came back to the fire, he had a bucket of water in each hand. He sat them down and waited until Jolie looked up, acknowledging him.

"How are you doing?" the old cowboy asked.

"I'm okay." Jolie realized that oddly enough she meant it. She felt more clear-headed and peaceful than she had in a long time.

"Are you done?" Ward indicated the fire. "I'm not trying to hurry you."

"Yeah. I'm done." Jolie picked up a bucket and poured it carefully around the perimeter of the fire, walking clockwise. Ward stepped back to let her finish.

"There's two more in the truck," he said. "I brought four. I know Hoke likes to do things for each of the Directions. So, I figured North, South, East West--that's four."

"There are six Directions actually if you include up and down," Jolie indicated the earth and sky.

"Right." Ward smiled sheepishly. "I should have paid better attention, I guess."

"Four buckets is good," Jolie assured him.

"I just figured if you were putting things down—I mean trying to put them down in a good way, as Hoke says, then putting out the fire that burned the symbols of those things is part of the ceremony, so you'd want to do it right. I'm going to go now in case you need more time to say whatever it is you need to say." He walked back to the truck and returned with the other two buckets.

"Thank you, Ward."

"No thanks needed." He took a long pause, maybe studying Jolie, maybe trying to decide if he should say more. "You're a good kid, Jolie—a good person." The words decided for him. "Don't let anybody tell you different. People will try and mess with you because everybody's got stuff hanging on to them, and if they can't get rid of it, they want everyone around them to be saddled with it just like they are, so they won't feel so alone, even though they know it's terrible and it's eating them up. People are just so afraid to be alone."

"You're talking about addiction," Jolie surmised.

"Addictions wear a lot of disguises. Hoke says his people believe that tobacco, alcohol, or whatever it is 'knows your name' and it's always calling you, pretending to be your friend. Only it isn't. I'm going to go load up your stuff now, then I'm going to wait in the truck. And when you're ready, we'll get you back down to town. But take your time. I got nothing to do until tomorrow morning when the animals need to be fed."

"You know it's a felony to move a ward of the court across state lines," Jolie warned him.

"I guess it's good that I just found you hitchhiking then." He winked. "And I'm not taking you *out* of Nevada, I'm taking you back in. That's got to be different, right?" He walked back toward the cabin, leaving Jolie alone with the stars and the night, and the ashes of her past.

Jolie picked up the second bucket and began to pour. As the steam rose, she thought about all the baggage from her past that she wanted to leave behind, wondering who she would be when it was gone.

CHAPTER EIGHT

"**Y**ou really messed up," Luce informed Jolie when she returned from Tecopa. Reuben had even gotten up out of his chair, regaling her with every belittling name and loser's future scenario his micro-brain could think of and assuming every nasty, underhanded, criminal motive he'd seen on television until he'd blown off enough steam for Tulip to intervene shooing Jolie upstairs and out of sight. Now it was just Luce and Jolie, and the hooties.

Jolie didn't think she'd done anything wrong, but she did feel bad she'd stirred Reuben up knowing his bad moods endangered everyone in the household.

"If they helped me, I wouldn't have to go by myself." In Jolie's mind, the Bozovics needed to own up to their responsibility for the situation. But she knew that was not going to happen. "Did he mean it?" she asked Luce. "Will he send me away?" She didn't care. She hated being here, but as bad as it was here, it could always be worse. Reuben did not privately visit the girls' room at night and Tulip was not cruel.

"I don't know. We'll see tomorrow." Luce rolled over and fell asleep.

Hours later Jolie was still awake thinking over the situation and trying to figure out what she should do. How had Yanna Maria known where to find her? Would she come after Jolie now? Would she show up here at the Bozovic's? Yanna was not backing off her determination to get the demon. What was she willing to do to accomplish that?

Her inner voice answered: *"Anything."* She hoped it was wrong.

She was still worrying when the blobby gray creature appeared.

"You are not helpless," his sudden arrival gave Jolie a start.

"Don't do that," she muttered, knowing she could not afford to wake Luce.

"Do what?"

"Tell me what I'm feeling."

"I care what happens to you, Jolie. I feel angry when someone threatens or hurts you. You act as if there is nothing you can do about these situations but there is. It does not have to be like this. *I* can help you. I could kill"

"No!" Jolie said too loudly shrinking down into her covers as Luce stirred. "That is not going to help," she whispered once she was sure her roommate had fallen back asleep. "You can't murder your way out of every problem."

"That has not been my experience," the demon replied.

Jolie grunted. "Because the people who controlled you were psychos. Isn't there some kind of code they teach you about this stuff?"

"Who are *they?*"

"The demon teachers, or the demon council, or whoever teaches you about being a demon."

"I do what I am commanded to do. If I learned anything, it was from observing the behavior of the humans I was bonded to, and the reactions of those around them. There was never any teaching."

"That's terrifying." Jolie sighed. "Didn't you ever serve anyone who wanted you to do something good?"

"No."

Luce rolled over. "Did you say something, Jolie?"

Jolie closed her eyes and pretended to be asleep. When she opened them again, the demon was gone.

Jolie looked across the desk at a new counselor. "What happened to Ms. Lee?" she asked, evaluating this new opponent.

She was an older woman, likely near retirement, a grandmother. Family pictures with stair-stepped children crowded the peach-colored walls. The woman's sweater was the same color. The girlish barrettes in her gray hair were frighteningly close to the same peachy hue. It was tempting to dismiss the woman for her color choices but though everything in the room had been chosen to declare maternal caring, the face across from Jolie had sharp curves and brittle edges. There were thorns among these rose petals.

"Your session today requires a counselor with a higher degree of credentialing. I am Doctor Helene."

Jolie nodded. "I know why I'm here, Doctor. I probably shouldn't have hitch-hiked to Tecopa. It was impulsive and dangerous, and I might have gotten hurt," Jolie made the mandatory statement of responsibility, hoping to short-cut the interview.

"If you knew it was wrong, why did you do it?" the Doctor asked.

"I needed underwear," Jolie answered bluntly. It sounded sarcastic and snarky, but it was the truth.

"Underwear?" The Doctor looked quizzical.

"Yeah, you know the small clothes you wear next to your body, panties, bras, chemises? I asked the county, and they wouldn't take me back to where I once lived to get my things. Then, I asked the Bozovics, and they wouldn't do it either. So, being a resilient and self-responsible person, I did some problem-solving and took care of it myself, like I always have. It was more than clothes. I needed my mom's important papers, bank accounts, our social security cards, bills, and her address book. I need that information and I don't want it to get into the hands of someone else."

"I can't speak for the county regarding why no one saw to this detail." She consulted Jolie's file. "It looks like you weren't at Child Haven very long. And as for the Bozovics, well, maybe you just didn't give them enough time to comply with your request. You haven't been there long either."

"Long enough," Jolie responded quickly.

"What does that mean?" the Doctor prodded.

"I've been there long enough to understand that if it's inconvenient or costs anything Reuben Bozovic isn't going to do anything to help me. His parenting style leans toward the "do as little as possible" zone.

The Doctor sat back, her hands knitted together, the fake nails on her index fingers making a teepee.

"The Bozovics report that you are not adapting well to the foster home environment." Jolie did not disagree. "You won't follow the house rules or respect their authority." She opened a folder with notes stapled into it and flipped through the sheets of paper. "You are prone to extreme highs and lows, show signs of being emotionally unstable, and have frequent emotional outbursts. You question everything they tell you, sneak out when you are told you can't go somewhere, and use offensive language in front of the other children even though you know it's against house rules." Helene folded her arms on the desk and focused on Jolie. "They say you are a very unhappy young lady."

"My mother just died."

"Unhappy with your placement in the foster home," the doctor clarified.

"That's fair."

"They're concerned you are depressed and at high risk of harming yourself."

Jolie thought she might have to pick her bottom lip up off the floor. "I'm not. They're lying. I never said that. I never did anything to make them think that." *If anything, I'm likely to harm them.*

"You hitch-hiked out of state," Doctor Helene pointed out. "Technically, that made you a runaway."

"I came back. I would never have had to go to Tecopa if someone had just given me the help I asked for. It isn't much to expect to get your family papers and some clothes, so you don't have to hand wash your unders every three days."

"You accuse the Bozovics of lying. Let's look at that a bit closer. What would be their purpose in doing that, Jolie?"

"I don't know," Jolie clammed up.

"But why do you *think*?"

"Because I'm not like the other kids who live there? I'm not afraid to speak out about what I see that's wrong and that threatens them?"

"So, you don't think it has anything to do with any of these other things they've mentioned, the bad language, the disrespect, the outbursts or mood swings?"

"Those things didn't happen," Jolie informed the Doctor.

"You don't curse?"

"Not in front of Gerith or Luce, and I've never disrespected Tulip." *Not to her face anyway.*

"So, you are not unhappy there?" the Doctor probed.

"I didn't say that."

"You *are* unhappy living there, then?"

Oh God, yes! Jolie took a breath. "I'm just unhappy, Doctor. My mom just died and it's changed my whole life. I'm working on adjusting," Jolie defended herself.

"That's only natural." Jolie ground her teeth at the condescension in the Doctor's smile. "So, what kinds of things have you seen at the Bozovic house that are so concerning to you?"

Jolie thought about what she could say that would not get Tulip in trouble and maybe split up Gerith and Luce. "Nothing." She bit her lip.

"No, please speak freely, Miss Figg. It's important if you believe you're witnessing something inappropriate in the home you feel you can share that. But your accusations need to be specific and verifiable."

Reuben was a lazy slob and an abusive misogynist, but that wasn't going to bear any weight. Jolie tried to consider Reuben's end game in making the accusations against her. What was he trying to do?

If he wanted to get rid of Jolie, she was still in a probationary position at the house, so he didn't have to go through any of this. All he had to do was say she wasn't a good fit for the family. So, if getting rid of her was *not* the goal, then what was? Reuben wanted something else.

"Have you witnessed any physical abuse by Mister Bozovic?" Jolie shook her head. "Then what? What am I supposed to write on this form?" The woman looked at the clock on the wall. She was losing patience.

"He's prejudiced and derogatory. He belittles us kids all the time. We're all afraid of his temper, even his wife."

"The Bozovic's marriage is not the subject here," Helene declared as of bounds. "Have you ever witnessed him strike his wife or one of the children?" Jolie shook her head.

She was making a list of her complaints: Reuben and Tulip wouldn't let her get a cell phone, they monitored her calls, and they wouldn't do anything that could help her. None of that was any different than what a dozen kids she'd known in poor or dysfunctional families experienced in their own homes. There was nothing the Bozovics did that the county was going to do anything about.

"The Bozovics are very concerned about you, Jolie."

"I haven't done anything. They just need to let me be."

"Well, like most parents, they have rules. As I understand it, you had a lot of 'freedom' when you lived with your mother--perhaps too much freedom for a girl your age. It's understandable that adjusting to the boundaries a normal child has would present some challenges for you. But you are still a child, Jolie, and children require boundaries. You may not appreciate that now but someday you will.

"The Bozovics have been fostering for us for years. They have experience and they've done a lot of good for a lot of kids. They are a good, solid, foster family. I understand you've had a hard time lately, but everyone is not out to get you. You don't need to keep fighting the whole world." The Doctor opened her desk drawer and pulled out a bottle of pills. Setting them on the desk in front of Jolie.

Jolie looked at the bottle like it was a scorpion.

"The Bozovics have requested that we try putting you on medication to help you calm down and even out your moods so you're less anxious."

Jolie was aghast. "You want to drug me? What is this the nineteen-hundreds? I'm independent, not having a mental health crisis."

"We'll monitor your progress and see how you progress. If it looks like it's necessary, we can change the dosage when I see you again next month," the Doctor explained how things would be going forward.

Jolie felt like someone had gutted her open like a fish and stuck a bowling ball inside her.

"I want to see Wrangler," she managed to choke the words out.

"Okay." The woman punched in an extension. "Cliff? It's Helene. Jolie Figg is here. She's asking if you could come by for a minute. Yes, we've just finished. She's headed back to the Bozovics. A few minutes would be great." The Doctor hung up the phone.

Jolie fidgeted until Wrangler knocked and peeked in.

"Hey, Jo," he greeted her cheerily. "How are you doing?" He exchanged a look with Helene.

"I'll just step out for a minute," the Doctor excused herself.

Jolie pointed at the bottle of pills on the desk. "Did you know about this?"

"I'm part of your team, and we've discussed the Bozovic's request, yes."

"There's nothing wrong with me, Wrangler, and you know it."

"You've had a rough time, Jo, and frankly you've had a less than solid home life. It's amazing you're as together as you are, your team recognizes that, but we also see that you've never had the advantages that access to proper mental or behavioral health might have provided. We have the opportunity to fix that now. This could make a big difference for you, but you'll never know if you don't try. Testing, and a proper diagnosis could be a game changer for you, Jo."

"Our problem was we were poor, Wrangler. Do you have a pill for that, because if you do, pharmaceutical companies could make a fortune. Oh wait--they do. It's called Oxycontin. Give it to as many struggling people as possible and they'll keep taking it until they die. It's a great plan for controlling the poor."

Wrangler shook his head. "I understand you're upset, Jo, but--"

"My mom just died of an overdose, and you want to put me on some starter drug like it's as harmless as giving a twelve-year-old a training bra?"

"Just try it," Wrangler refused to be baited.

"I'm not--"

"Kids who run with a crowd that smokes think everyone smokes. We see it all the time. It seems normal to them because they're surrounded by it. Have you ever considered that these visions you have are like that? Maybe they're a reflection of your upbringing. It's what you know. Your mom was hanging out with a pretty out-there bunch last winter when that thing happened on Solstice."

Jolie finally understood. "You think I'm pretending."

"No, I--"

"Yes, you do. You think I'm faking that I see and hear this stuff? Crap. Why would I want to do that? I'd give anything to be normal, Wrangler--anything!"

"Great. Then try this!"

"What about Rose, and Sifu, and Hoke? Are they all imagining their experiences too? Are they all mentally unstable? Gee, if only they knew better," her words dripped sarcasm. "A third of the people in this country follow some dude who claimed he had visions from God. Maybe you've heard about it? It's been a pretty big deal for a couple of thousand years now. Maybe you should give them some drugs to stop their hallucinations." She threw the pills on the floor at Wrangler's feet.

"The medications are just a trial, Jo--to see if anything changes for you--if you feel better," Wrangler kept trying to bring the conversation back to a more even tone and make his point.

She glared at him. "I won't."

"You don't know that. You can't know until you've tried," he reasoned. Jolie's arms stayed crossed over her chest. "The bottom line is this is a condition of your returning to the Bozovics, and of you being allowed to hang out at the temple school."

And suddenly Jolie understood. "That's low."

"If you go back to the center, you won't be able to socialize with your friends at the school. The system doesn't allow for exceptions, but your team realizes that you're in a vulnerable place and you need support right now and Sifu's school does a good job of that. I didn't want that to be taken away from you. I fought for it." Wrangler picked up the bottle of pills. "So, take the pills, and let's see if they help. Unless of course, you're afraid to find out that there is a real world, and you haven't been living in it?" he tossed out the challenge.

"I thought you were better than this, Cowboy," Jolie used Wrangler's nickname from the sweat lodge circle. "I thought I could trust you."

"And I value that trust. I did the best I could for you," Wrangler assured her. "Now I'm asking you to give this a chance. No more running off, no more disrespecting Tulip and Reuben. If you're respectful and cooperative, you'll keep the privileges of working and hanging out at the school. I'll see you again in a week or so."

Not of I see you first, Jolie retorted silently.

Tulip held a glass of water out toward Jolie. Jolie stared into the small paper cup that held her meds.

"You've never seen "One Flew Over the Cuckoo's Nest," have you?" Tulip's blank face said she had not. "So, you will not understand the brutal irony of this situation."

"Take the pill, now, while I watch," Tulip commanded.

"Right." Jolie pretended to take the pill, miming swallowing while stashing the hard, slick pill in her lower cheek." Tulip was satisfied.

Gerith ran by, giggling, headed for the kitchen. He peered into the dusty dark alleyway in miniature alongside the refrigerator.

"What are you doing, Gerith? Come away from there," Tulip snapped.

"Hooties!" Gerith pointed into the dark crack.

"There are no hooties." Tulip chased him away from the fridge.

"Did I hear that little halfwit say the H word?" Reuben hollered from the TV room.

"Now you've done it," Tulip scowled at Gerith. "Go!" She spun him around and slapped his butt once while shooing him out of the kitchen. But nothing crumbled the little boy's joy. Jolie could complain and count all the bad things that happened to her and it was a pretty high count, but then there was Gerith, browner, naïve, an innocent with no family, psychically gifted, or cursed, depending on your opinion, and still open and happy and making his life situation work.

"Why does Reuben hate hooties so much?" Jolie asked. "Letting Gerith have his little world doesn't hurt anything."

"Believing in imaginary things is the devil's doorway," Tulip declared firmly.

"Imaginary things like Santa Clause, the Tooth Fair…the Great Pumpkin?" Jolie asked cautiously.

"Just because stores and advertisers make money promoting those things does not make them harmless. Gerith needs to understand there is a real world and there are rules he has to follow to successfully live in that world. If he can't do that, he'll live on assistance and in homes for the rest of his life."

"He's four," Jolie pointed out.

"It's wrong," Tulip repeated her position. Reuben had hauled himself out of his chair and was headed their way. Jolie and Tulip could hear the floor vibrating under his heavy footfalls.

"I'm sorry, Tulip, I didn't mean to question. I just want to understand."

"Go upstairs--or anywhere, Jolie, but go!"

"I need to go to work?" Jolie offered.

"Then go on and go! Hurry!" Tulip turned back to the kitchen when Jolie looked back. "I feel like some cookies, Reuben. What about you? Do cookies sound good?" she distracted her husband.

Jolie paused on the porch, listening. Tulip was working to keep Gerith from Reuben's wrath. The woman had some warped notions about the world, but she did care. Jolie had seen abusers before and once they got going, anything and anyone could feed their violence. The trigger didn't need to be real. It didn't need to make sense. Logic took no role in an abuser's outbursts. They were white-hot, emotions, and anger chemicals flaming through the body and brain in a dangerous, habitual overload.

It would be better for everyone when Tulip could keep Reuben in a neutral zone.

The floor stopped trembling at Reuben's footsteps.

"Here you go, honey," Tulip purred sweetly, handing Reuben a beer. "Ice cold, just like you like it." Jolie heard a pull tab being peeled a beer can followed by the sizzle and spit of carbonation exposed to the rush of air. "I'll bring you cookies as soon as they're done." She encouraged Reuben back to his chair. In a minute he was back watching TV, Gerith, and hooties, and punishing the four-year-old for seeing things he did not understand completely forgotten.

As soon as she got out of sight of the house, Jolie spit out the pill Tulip gave her and tossed it away.

Gerith's "sins" of course were far beyond Tulip or Reuben's understanding. The little boy wasn't mature enough to pretend he didn't see things most people thought weren't real. If he didn't learn, he would be a target for every bully he met, starting with Reuben.

Growing up in her grandmother's, Mem's, household, Jolie had a broader view of what other people called "extrasensory" perceptions. She saw how this supported Wrangler's premise that Jolie had always hung out with people who saw the world the way she did, but she couldn't help also seeing that this was what everybody did. People bunched into herds based on beliefs, cultures, or race, so they felt safer. People needed to feel like they belonged somewhere. It was when you didn't have a place in a herd--and were exposed--that thing got dangerous.

Working the dishwashing station in the kitchen at the Chinese restaurant was hot, hard, and humid, but there was a rhythm to it, and the mist clouding off the dish sprayer kept Jolie's discomfort to a tolerable level.

The manager, Mister Meng, was all business, stern with staff, he was all smiles and obsequious bowing with customers, but Jolie had no expectations of better. She just kept her head down and worked.

Moving quickly, Jolie continued to spray off the dishes, stack them into the washing trays, and slide them into the automated washer--like a carwash for dishes. The machine moved them out on the other side but she still needed to remove the strainer tray to a portable trolley so there was room for the next one to come through. The process took just enough attention that she could avoid thinking. Which was good.

From her station, she could see a sliver of the dining room. Sifu and many of the older students were regulars catching a late lunch, early or late dinner. The gray-haired Chinese businessman, Mister Yinchen was frequently around and Jolie got the sense there was a business relationship between him and Meng. Yinchen, clearly owned at least one of the shops in the mini-mall. Jolie had seen him through the floor-to-ceiling windows of the indoor part of the mini-mall, downstairs from the restaurant. He had been locking up the gifts and art shop as she was leaving for the night. He had not seen her that night but this night as she was leaving after her shift this night, their paths brought them together.

"Good evening, Miss." Yinchen inclined his head politely.

"Good evening, Mister Yinchen." Jolie was about to hurry onto her bus when he spoke again.

"I have noticed that you are a student at the temple school."

"No, I am not a student. I just go there to see my friends."

The man considered this. "You do not study?"

"No. I can't. I work," she gave the lame excuse, but it was less embarrassing than admitting she could not be a student because she could not afford to pay the school fees. Though she worked, she was secretly saving all the money she could, so she could become emancipated and get out of the Bozovic's.

"Forgive my boldness in voicing my humble opinion, but you should study, Miss Jolie. There are many things the school can teach you and you need to learn to protect yourself." Jolie just looked at him. "Spiritually" he added, oddly.

Jolie blinked in surprise. "That's not what they teach at the school."

"Again, I beg your forgiveness for disagreeing, but it is the most important thing they teach," the old man disagreed. "Most important for you. On Wednesdays, Sifu holds Spiritual Warrior class. You should go."

"Thank you," Jolie said politely. "I'll consider it." She felt him watching her as she walked away. *Las Vegas is the oddest place*, she mused.

CHAPTER NINE

The stone surfaces radiated a calm that affected Jolie like the cool trickle of a stream in a shaded grove. The middle path she walked was lined with the familiar, huge columns she had seen in this space in other dreams. On either side of the open pathway, small candlewicks floated in the lustrous wax-like liquid of pearls-- thousands of them in parallel rivers of warm amber light.

Distracted by the glowing beauty, Jolie stubbed her foot against a slightly raised stone.

"Ouch! Damn," she swore. Immediately she regretted it. This was not a place for frustration or anger.

"The Way is not always smooth," a voice commented. "There may be challenges. There often are. A person not minding their steps, may stumble, perhaps even fall." Jolie thought she recognized the voice.

"Where am I?" she asked.

"Here."

"Where is here?"

"With us, of course." Jolie detected humor in the reply.

"You play games."

"I like games. Don't you?"

"No," Jolie admitted. "The kind they wanted us to play as children were pointless and lame, and the ones older people play are cruel." She took a moment. "Who is 'us'?"

"Those you see here." The flames flared.

"And who are you?"

"No one."

"Can I see you?"

"If it helps." An old thin, bald monk appeared at the end of the candle-lined aisle. He was seated on a pillow on the floor, cross-legged. His body was wiry and slight. Orange cloth wrapped his waist, draping over one shoulder, leaving the other bare.

"You are a monk." The slight man bowed his head toward her once and smiled. His eyes widened as his eyebrows arched. "And who is this?" Jolie glanced down to find the demon peeking out from behind her. "Ah," recognition changed the ancient monk's face. "It has been a long time, Jing Ling." The old man's skin folded into tightly woven wrinkle and shadow patterns, quilted by centuries of smiles.

"How do you know me?" the demon asked.

"How do you not know yourself?" the monk replied. His continued study of the demon caused the creature to shudder, and he scrambled back into Jolie's shadow.

"It seems you have found a protector," the old monk said. Jolie was uncertain which of them he referred to, herself or the demon.

"Is it true, he was created to be bonded to someone else's will?" Jolie asked.

"A complicated question, requiring a complicated answer, but there is this truth I may share: spirits have free will which means they are accountable for their actions."

"But what if others commanded him? Is he still responsible?"

"Another good question," the monk nodded thoughtfully. "But we choose our masters, just as we choose our path." He paused long enough for Jolie to consider this. "Spiritual beings learn not only from the beauty of a butterfly but from facing the ferocity of the

tiger. If we lock away all tigers to avoid the fear of facing one, we remain unaware whether courage exists within us or does not, rendering us unable to face the conflict and chaos of the natural world." He shrugged. "Not all help we might give is helpful."

Jolie frowned. *"That's not very monkish."*
The monk shrugged. "But it is true."

Jolie was well into washing the dishes from the dinner rush at the restaurant when old Mister Yinchen approached her.

"Remove your apron," he commanded.

Jolie stared at him, not understanding. "What?"

"Remove your apron, please Miss Jolie."

"Are you firing me? What did I do? Wait, how can you fire me, you don't even work here."

"You are not being fired. It is Wednesday and Spiritual Warrior class is about to start."

"I'm still doing the dishes," Jolie stuttered gesturing to the stacks of dirty plates and cups.

"They will wait."

"You don't understand, Mister Yinchen, this is my shift. The rest of the crew needs clean dishes tomorrow morning. This is my responsibility." The old man was an adult--he had a business. How could he not understand?

"And it is admirable of you to hold to your responsibilities, but you have others that are of greater importance, Miss Jolie," Yinchen countered.

What was he talking about? She did not want to disrespect an elder, but she could not afford to lose her job.

"I'll get fired," Jolie protested.

"You will not. I will talk to Manager Meng."

He seemed confident that Meng would not object to her leaving. Jolie was far less confident.

"I'm sorry, Mister Yinchen, I appreciate your willingness to help, but I cannot just stop working. I don't do this for pocket money. I need my wages to live."

The old man considered this. "When Spiritual Warrior class is done, you will come back here and take the orders of the students who come over after class. There are often quite a few and the restaurant is low-staffed during those late hours. You will make more in tips waiting tables than you will lose in two hours of dishwashing wages."

"So, I'm a waitress now?" Jolie scrunched up her face.

"We will see. Go to class." Yinchen turned and walked away.

"A bodhisattva," Sifu explained, "is a soul that has reached enlightenment allowing it to rise to a higher plane of existence but who has instead vowed to remain here on this plane being reborn until all humanity has reached enlightenment and can rise together."

Spiritual Warrior classes were given at the end of the mid-week evening classes that were the bread and butter of the school, a variety of Kung Fu forms, Chen Sword, Broadsword, Qi Gung, Chen, and Yang Tai Qi styles for the older set.

The crowd was mixed, more of the older Tai Qi and Qi Gung students attended than the younger Kung Fu kids, but the more dedicated mid-level students understood that if they wanted to be seen as truly serious, they needed to learn the philosophies behind the Internal forms and practices as well. Hugo, Brutus, and Jiu hoping to one day be among the school's teachers, all attended.

The younger students sat or reclined on wrestling mats in the front rows, near Sifu, reserving the chairs in the back for the older students who were less flexible and could no longer comfortably sit on the floor.

"Taoists also believe that groups of like-minded souls are born and reborn in different roles, moving around together. You may have experienced this, meeting someone here at the school who you were strongly drawn to. There may be people you feel like you've known forever, even though you have known each other for only a short time. These ties go beyond one lifetime and create strong connections, which is why so many of you feel you are part of a family here.

"Within these spirit-family groups," Sifu went on, "there are roles. One may have the role of being the group's Truth-Keeper, the one who remembers the philosophies and stories. Others may take on the role of protector for the Truth-Keeper, so the truths are never lost but are maintained and passed on."

When Sifu caught Jolie's eye, she felt a jolt of electric energy. Unnerved, she looked at the floor. Despite their brief interaction on the mountaintop during the Ridge Walking, and him tending fire for her return after her informal Vision Quest, Sifu had never paid any attention to her here at the school. Why was he targeting her now?

"Stop!" she demanded silently. *"I don't want to stand out or be different. I just want to belong."* She did not realize that until she said it, that it was true. That was what she wanted; someplace to truly belong, not as some watered-down version who hid her true self, but all of her,

as she was and that meant not hiding. Not even from Sifu. She raised her head, ready to look him square in the eyes next time he looked her way.

The front door opened and some of the students glanced back to see who had arrived so late. Jolie felt a prickling warning like a hundred insects with needle-sharp feet were crawling on her.

"She's here!" the demon shrieked into Jolie's mind. *"Yanna Maria is here! She's come for me!"*

Jolie turned. Rance was politely giving the Santeria a chair.

Yanna's eyes found Jolie's. There was no kindness there. The woman turned to Sifu and gave him a warm nod and smile.

Does he know her? Of course he does, Jolie chided herself. Sifu did sweat lodges at Roses and so did Yanna. But how could someone like Sifu know Yanna and not *see* her for who she was? Rose was such a nice person she just assumed everyone else was as nice as she was. Obviously, neither of them knew Yanna or they would not be letting her into their spiritual circles. But how was that even possible? Sifu was supposed to *see* things--to understand people. He was the Truth Keeper in the temple school's family of reborn souls, wasn't he? How could he not recognize Yanna Maria's self-serving manipulations and wickedness?

Jolie snuck a peek at Yanna Maria. The Santeria's face was set, her mouth grim. Suddenly, she rose and went for the door.

"I have to go," Jolie followed, nearly tripping over the students scattered around the mat.

"What's going on, Jo?" Hugo asked.

Jolie did not have time to answer. She pushed through the glass door to the front courtyard. Yanna was creeping around stealthily in a dark corner, stalking her prey.

"Leave him alone," Jolie warned. Yanna's focus remained on the darkness.

"Shut up. You have no power over this creature, or me. Unless, of course, you've changed your mind?" She turned to Jolie. "I thought not." Yanna turned back, continuing to search the dark. "Where are you, little devil? Why do you play games? You cannot escape me forever, so why make me angry? It is not a good beginning for our relationship. You need me and you know it. You need a mistress who will give you direction and purpose, and I can do that for you. I know how to use your skills, demon."

"He doesn't want to be your creature," Jolie declared. "He doesn't want any part of you, Yanna. He is free now--free to make his own decisions."

"You call this thing *he?* It isn't a *he*. It isn't anything--just old energy held together by past deeds," Yanna Maria's voice scratched like a cat's claws. "Take your naïve notions and put them back inside that book of myths you checked out of the library." Yanna spun around. Swooping out one hand, she made a grasping motion in the air as if she'd caught something.

"She has me, Jolie! Help!"

"Don't do anything she tells you to," Jolie shouted. "Refuse her. You do not have to give in to her."

"But I do. If she controls me, I have no choice," the demon wailed.

"Remember what the old monk said, you always have a choice'." Jolie insisted.

"Stop interfering!" Yanna shouted at Jolie.

As if on cue, Jolie's Kung Fu friends spilled out of the temple's front doors, stacking up behind her.

"What's going on, Jo?" Brutus asked in a threatening singsong picked up from an old Western.

"Class is over," Hugo addressed Yanna Maria. "You should probably be going now." His tone was polite but with a firmness that warned if she did not comply that could change.

"You're Carmen's boy, aren't you?" Yanna Maria's teeth were a white glow framed by her dark hair and skin. "I told your mother you were in trouble. Now I see why. Good Catholic boys do not help foolish girls playing with dark spirits." Hugo's eyes flickered to Jolie; a quick question telegraphed in the connection. "Oh, you didn't know? She didn't tell you," Yanna Maria's voice slid over her insinuations like treacle. "Surely, you've noticed how trouble follows her. This sort of creature must be handled by someone who can keep the spirit's power under control."

"And that's you?" Brutus looked Yanna Maria up and down, flexing his muscles for effect. In the young martial artist's eyes, this woman was someone who had just showed up off the street for Spiritual Warrior class: a short, round, aging looky-loo. The school got dozens of them every month, looking for something they could not understand and would never spend the time trying to master, but thought might make them feel the vigor of youth, as if the skills of a Taoist Adept could be learned in an eight-week course.

Yanna's chin went up. "Do not underestimate me, young man. Just take the crazy girl back inside, let me do what needs to be done and no one needs to get hurt."

"I'm not crazy!" Jolie shouted.

"You know she is on medication for mental instability, don't you?" Yanna countered. Jolie wondered how the Santeria knew that, but that was not the most important issue right now.

"He doesn't want to go with you," she insisted.

Brutus seemed uncertain what to do but Jiu was not. "This woman was there at the Ridge Walking Ceremony," he informed his friends. "I remember seeing her. I don't know what she was doing there, but she was not helping."

"I was trying to control this spirit," Yanna defended herself. "It was a dangerous time. The spirit was in transition and needed guidance."

"That's not what she was doing," Jolie said between clenched teeth.

The boys took a step toward the Santeria.

"Like Hugo said Ma'am, class is over. It's time you left," Jiu restated.

"'You think I am afraid of a bunch of silly little boys?" Yanna Maria shot back. She raised an arm, preparing to cast something when the door to the school opened. A woosh of humid air preceded Rance's exit from the temple into the dark courtyard.

"You didn't have to wait, guys--" he stopped midsentence. His focus tracked from the kung fu students to Yanna Maria, power swirling around her, her arm raised to strike. "What's going on, boys?" he asked coolly.

Yanna Maria dropped her arm, instantly altering her physical stance and reducing her presence to a harmless old woman who had come to check out Spiritual Warrior class.

"Thank you. Good night," she sang out with false cheer as if she and the young people had just finished a conversation about where to find the best Chinese food.

Rance took in the student's guilty expressions, the re-set shoulders, and defensive body language.

"I guess whatever that was you'll tell me when you're ready. The weirdest people come to Spiritual Warrior class. Don't they? Anyway, who's eating?" He indicated the groups starting toward the restaurant across the street and began to follow.

"I could eat." Brutus jogged to catch up with the older student.

"I need to go home," Jiu muttered his face wan, his eyes over-bright.

"I'll walk you," Hugo offered. "You okay, Jo?" He squinted into the dark. "What about that thing, is it still here?"

"We're both fine." Jolie had a tether on her emotions, but the adrenaline of the incident was still rushing through her. "She's lying, you know, Hugo. I'm not working with any dark forces."

"Good, because I am a good Catholic boy, and that would be something I couldn't be okay with."

"I'm trying to get it to leave me alone and move on," Jolie defended herself. "Look, I promised to help at the restaurant in trade for coming to class. I've got to go."

Jolie took off crossing the street at a jog.

CHAPTER TEN

"**Y**ou are too soft with these kids, Tulip. They need a strong hand…"

"The *Lord's* hand, Reuben, not a *backhand.*" Tulip's eyes widened realizing what she had said. One of the teams on the TV scored a touchdown and Reuben either did not hear her sassy retort or it did not register.

Was something changing? Jolie glanced toward the recliner in the TV room.

Gerith interrupted the moment shouting, "Look, hooties!" He began pulling something the size of a twig out from under the table. It had bright blue hair.

Tulip snatched the little boy's hand out of the air.

"There's no such thing as hooties!"

Gerith's little boy's face fell, his eyes pooling with tears as he swayed back and forth caught in the ripples of the anger rolling off his foster mother.

"Hooties?"

"No! No hooties!" Tulip pulled him to the door at the top of the basement stairs that led to Gerith's room. Jolie wanted to run over and rescue him from Tulip's angry grasp, but Gerith looked back at her and shook his head, "No". Winking, he mouthed *hooties* as he was dragged away, grinning. He and Tulip could be heard clomping down the wooden stairs.

Jolie's cheeks burned. She clamped down hard on the fury flaring in her gut, the heat rising to her brain, burning logic like it was combustible.

Tulip reappeared, carefully closing the door behind her. Reuben was up out of his chair now. Had Tulip seen this coming? Had she removed Gerith from the circle of wrath she expected her husband to bring down?

"Look at the little mongrels, Tulip," the fat man sneered. "I know why you're always trying to cover for them. It's because you see yourself in them. After all, they're just like you," he accused his wife. "I see the weakness in them, just like I see it in you. None of you will ever amount to anything. You've got tainted blood. And you!" Reuben targeted Jolie. "You're going to end up just like your mother, overdosed in a ditch."

"You shut up about my mother!" Jolie exploded. "You didn't know her, and you don't know me."

"Don't raise your voice to me, little miss high and mighty," Reuben shouted back. He looked like a beet feasted on by bugs with his bald head and chewed-out face. "This is my house!"

Jolie ignored him, all the words she had bitten back over the last few weeks crawling over each other in their hurry to get out and be heard creating a traffic jam at her lips.

"People don't just get up one morning and decide to mess up their lives!" she shouted. "It takes years and years of poor choices, being beaten down over, and over, again until you believe that it doesn't matter what choice you make, it's going to turn out bad. My mom wasn't a bad person. She got a crap hand at birth and some mistakes have consequences that are so final you can never reverse them, even if you realize the second after you made them, they were: wrong because by then it's already too late." Jolie was trying not to cry and failing.

Reuben was about to bust out, but he didn't have the words to fight her. Words were not his thing. His hands closed into fists at his side, shaking in rage. Jolie prepared herself for the violence she knew was coming, then Tulip stepped between them.

"In this house, we follow the Lord, and we trust him to keep us from such mistakes," she said, facing her husband down. She glanced at Jolie. "You will learn to do the same."

Jolie doubted it.

Nothing was working out. But then that was the problem with expectations; they left you open to disappointment. For Jolie, a retreat to her protective blanket of indifference boosted her confidence, reminding her she could get by. She always had. Like an old baby blanket, even with its lingering smells of sour milk, lonely tears, and dust-covered rememberings, it provided the comfort of familiarity. Memories connected to lilacs and roses were not hers.

Jolie looked around the little attic room. There was nothing she would miss here. What she needed was a way out, but the one small window had a swamp cooler in it. It made the room barely habitable, but it took away the only useable window. Jolie kneeled on her bed and peered through the two inches of glass above the cooler. The height to the ground was too far to jump, but the way the roof met the carport meant a person could get from the house roof to it and from there to the ground. But to do that she would have to remove the swamp cooler and that required tools, time, and privacy, none of which she had. But she could not keep living with the Bozovics.

The little demon appeared, not saying anything, just staring at her. What Jolie assumed were eyes, rolled around the slimy-looking gray ball that was his body. The gelatinous mass had the appearance of a brain or cellulite on a butt. When he moved, he slid like a slug, leaving a translucent slime trail that no one except Jolie seemed to see. Mostly, the creature just disappeared from one spot and reappeared in another.

"No, you can't kill them," Jolie told the little guy with a sigh.

"Some people deserve to die."

"Maybe, but in this time and culture, there are consequences for things like that. When people die, other people come and investigate. They ask questions and check facts to figure out what happened. Then the person they think is responsible gets put in a dark dungeon for a long time."

"I could not be confined within such a space, and they would never figure out I had done it," the demon reasoned.

"But I could. Someone would get blamed, and that someone would probably be me, since Reuben and I just had a fight, giving me a motive to want him dead, and no one is going to believe me when I tell them a demon did it."

"What about Tulip?" the demon asked. "She wants him dead."

"Does she?" Jolie asked.

"She should."

Jolie studied him. "Why do you think that?"

"He treats her badly. He is cruel and unjust. Her life would be much better without him."

Jolie smiled. "She can have a better life without killing him. In our time, she can just divorce him. It's like unmarrying him."

"I do not think that would help. I have seen people who un-marry before. They can be so angry that the only way for them to go forward is for one of them to die."

"That's not about love. That's about control," Jolie explained. "Some people need to control others to feel good about themselves."

"Like Reuben."

"Yes."

"My former masters and mistresses were like Reuben. What Reuben does--how he treats you, and Tulip, and Gerith, and Luce, is wrong."

"Are you asking or saying that is what you believe?"

"It is what I believe," the demon replied.

"And if I told you that what Reuben was doing was right--that it was okay…"

"You would not, because it is not," the creature interrupted her.

"Then you've decided on your own that you think something is wrong," Jolie congratulated the demon. "I know it has nothing to do with me, but I'm proud of you."

"It is confusing. I am slow to learn. If what Reuben does is wrong, then why would it not be better for everyone if I removed him?"

"It wouldn't necessarily be bad if he were gone, but we can't always know the consequences of our actions. We can hope for a certain outcome, but we can't know. The truth is that the outcome may be something else entirely."

The demon remained thoughtful. "You are the only one who has ever talked to me about these things, Jolie. Please, teach me, so I can understand."

Jolie thought of how a young Obi-Wan Kenobi believed he could teach Anakin Skywalker as well as Yoda. It took five movies to work through that mistake. She shook her head.

"How can I do that when half the time I can't get it right myself?" The demon looked disappointed. "I'm not going to pretend to know something I don't, or that I'm someone I'm not. I'm just a kid, struggling to make my way. There are a lot of people who know more about this than I do, trust me."

"It is because I trust you that I ask, Jolie. I never felt trust before. It is new to me. I never trusted any of the masters or mistresses I was bonded to."

"Trust is a rare thing that has to be earned," Jolie agreed. "I worry that you ask me to teach you about these things, but what you are asking me to do is to tell you what is right and wrong, and if I did that you would still be relying on me to decide for you. And that seems dangerously close to bonding. Which is how you got into this mess in the first place. But I believe you can learn to decide these things for yourself--that you must if you are going to stay independent and not rely on someone else for direction."

"You wish me to become something other than what I am," the demon surmised. "That is my wish too, now, but you say that I must learn how, but I do not know how to learn that alone, without help." The demon jiggled like Jell-O.

Jolie side-stepped the offer. "You need a real master."

"Damn! You are such a confusing human," the demon declared. "How can you say I need a master when you are always telling me I should not bond because I do not need a master? And now you're laughing at me?"

"I'm sorry." Jolie chuckled. "I've just never heard you swear before."

"You swear! Apparently, swearing is not a sign of being a bad person."

"For some people it is, but that's not something you need to worry about. I don't mean to confuse you. What I mean, when I say you need a master is not a master to bond you but a master teacher."

The demon perked up. "A master teacher? Someone who has thought about this a lot. A philosopher, like Lu Dongbin?"

Jolie guffawed. "Sure, like the Taoist master Lu Dongbin. He'd be a great teacher, except he's dead, so I wouldn't get my hopes up if I were you."

"Dead in this world, not all worlds," The demon's voice lingered a moment longer than his image.

Jolie packed the essentials she would need most while living without a base into her two backpacks, then slipped into bed, fully dressed. Pretending to be asleep, she waited for the other occupants of the house to retire for the night, listening during the intermittent cycles between the swamp cooler's working drone and dripping silence.

She wondered how Gerith was doing alone in his little basement cubby. It wasn't much more than cardboard walls held together by flimsy, one-inch lumber. Had Tulip screwed it together herself? Probably. Reuben would never have gone out of his way to do anything for the little boy, but Tulip would.

Tulip would also have found a way to sneak downstairs and tuck him in, apologizing without words for her earlier anger. She might even read him a story, knowing Reuben's weight would squeak the floorboards if her husbandly behemoth got out of his chair, giving her a chance to scurry back upstairs.

Tulip was not a bad mom. She was not a bad person. She had just made bad choices. Different bad choices than Jolie's mom had made, but bad, nevertheless. Jessie Lynn's choices had been fearless, impulsive, reckless, and ultimately destructive. She lived with little thought for consequences, determined that despite her habit of magical thinking; making the same mistakes and getting the same negative outcomes something would change.

Tulip made her choices from a position of near-crippling fear--the nearly part being significant because, despite living imprisoned in the victimhood of her past, she was alive, often kind, and sometimes even brave, making the outcomes of her life undecided.

The cooler cycled through, the noise of the fan blocking out the rest of the sounds in the house but once it hissed, sighed, and resumed its slow, internal drip, Jolie could hear what was happening downstairs.

Tulip started the dishwasher, closed the kitchen down, then began sweeping the floor while the television blared the white noise of wins and losses that meant more to her husband than she did. Jolie had watched Jessie Lynn go through the same longings, the determined search for love everlasting, the narrow framework of happily-ever-after lurking in the back of her brain, coloring every decision. Jessie Lynn thought all she had to offer a relationship was sex. Tulip relied on service and obedience. They were both wrong, and both suffered for it.

But there were good relationships. There were people who loved each other and stayed together, positive and supportive of each other's growth and independence. It was possible to make a different--better choice, wasn't it? Maybe it was the romantic in her, but Jolie wanted to believe there was.

She thought about Sean who she had seen in his role as her mate in visions of past lives. She could not deny she missed him in this one, but he had made other choices, less brave, more convenient.

And then there had been Remy, who Jolie thought might be the one, but who loved someone else. Without anyone to anchor her, being alone meant more than the absence of other people, more than the completeness of silence without the breath or heartbeat of another living being nearby. It was the absence of any living person to whom she mattered more than someone else did--a person who would think about her even when she wasn't there. Someone who cared enough to drop everything and rush to her side to be with her.

Hugo's face bloomed in her mind's eye. *No. Hugo is a friend. A stalwart, loyal friend.*

She must have drifted off during a chilling cycle, the fan flickering her faded pink hair against her cheeks, cool and luscious in the heat of the attic, but when it stopped to wheeze and sigh, she realized it was now quiet downstairs.

Jolie slipped quietly out of bed and tip-toed to the top of the stairwell. Except for the plug-in nightlight that lit the way to the bathroom, the house's lights were off. Jolie caught up her backpacks and crept down the stairs one step at a time, her hands pushing against the stairwell walls to reduce her weight and the chance of creaking.

Leaving was a big decision--a dangerous decision, but she was suffocating here, and she wasn't sure how much longer she could take it before she exploded, creating a scene with Reuben that would most certainly have a bad ending. She needed to be away, to breathe again…to think straight.

She almost made it to the door when Reuben stepped between it and her.

"Where do you think you're going?"

"It's too hot to sleep upstairs," she improvised. "I thought it would be cooler on the porch, or in the yard…?"

Reuben took in the two bulging backpacks. "You're sneaking out to meet some boy…or girl. Who knows these days with you sickos."

"Reuben didn't want you," Tulip had said. *"I fought for you to be here."* If Reuben didn't want her in the house, what was he willing to do to get rid of her?

"You're going to end up just like your drug-addicted mother," he had said.

"I'm not meeting anyone, Reuben. I'm just leaving," Jolie informed Reuben, tired of his bull.

"What? Tulip didn't wipe your butt fast enough for you?"

"You're such an ass." Jolie tried to get by him and continue out the door, but his large, fat, body stopped her.

"I play the bad guy so Tulip can play 'mom'. Everyone's happy. It works…most of the time, but every once in a while some smart ass like you, raised without morals, comes along determined to mess things up." He pulled out the bottle of Jolie's meds. "That's why we need these." He rattled the bottle. "What have you been doing, pretending to swallow them then spitting them out? Tulip is so trusting. Not me though. And since they aren't helping your behavior improve, we're gonna up your dose."

Jolie backed away. "I'm not taking those."

"You think you have a choice? You don't." Reuben fished something out of his pocket and lunged forward as Jolie again tried to dodge around him. She felt a hard grip on her arm. Reuben whipped her around, grabbed her other arm, and pinned them both behind her back. Jolie kicked and wriggled, but Reuben was not just fat, he was big, and he had a big man's strength. In seconds he had her handcuffed and was dragging her to the old radiator in the living room. He released one cuff, enough to attach it to the radiator, then stepped away.

"Let me go, Reuben," Jolie demanded.

"No. Act like a feral animal and you get treated like one."

"You can't do this."

"It's done." Reuben grabbed Jolie's head and yanked it back. Squeezing her cheeks, he forced her jaw open and pushed a pill down her throat. "Swallow," he commanded. Jolie tried to spit it out, but he stuck his hand in her mouth and pushed it back down.

She bit him.

"You bitch!" Reuben slapped her hard enough that it whipped her head to the side, and she saw stars, nearly blacking out. She was not surprised that he knew how to brutalize someone weaker than himself.

She was still dizzy and disoriented when her mouth was forced open again and water poured down her throat. She spluttered, nearly choking, but swallowed.

Reuben dropped her head, releasing her. Her body flopped to the side like a rag doll.

"I'll see you in the morning." He stepped away, brandishing his height advantage. "You'll be calmer by then. Your friend, Wrangler, will be so disappointed in your choices. He believes you can beat the odds of growing up with a druggie mom, but I know better. And just so we're clear, you won't be trotting off to see your friends at that school anymore." He pulled a tiny baggie out of his pocket, glanced at the contents then slipped it back into his pants. Jolie closed her eyes to the pain in her face and the dizziness.

When she opened them, Reuben was gone.

Jolie leaned heavily over onto one side, her right shoulder stabbing with the strain of the long-term stretch of taking the weight of her upper body. She had probably passed out. For how long she didn't know. A sense of helplessness swelled over her like a King tide. Like her mom, Jessie Lynn, she never seemed to catch a break, born to a crap hand.

Well, that was not entirely true, she was not only a Figg. Jolie was also a Boulet—maybe more a Boulet than anything else. When her mom removed Jolie from the natural habitat of her New Orleans roots, Jolie had become a displaced person, a foreigner in the country of her birth.

Her face hurt. Her shoulders and arms hurt. Her throat hurt, but what hurt most was her pride.

She did not want to cry, but there was no point in stuffing emotions. Better to let them flow and then try to put herself back together. Jolie moved her legs, shifting her position to relieve the strain on her shoulder socket. Rubbing the old carpet brought up the rotting smell of the disintegrating pad underneath, combined with the sick-sweet cover-up powder that Tulip sprinkled on it before vacuuming.

"Where are you?" she called out to the demon. *"I need you."* But she had sent him away. How stupid. He had gone somewhere to find a teacher, somewhere far away, maybe another world, or another dimension, or wherever demons and incorporeal spirits went, but he was not here, and he could not help her. She was on her own…again.

This was what she'd been hoping for--what the demon needed, but the timing sucked because now she was handcuffed to a radiator and drugged half out of her head. She was not just listless, she was starting to see images, like an aurora borealis in the Bozovic's living room. Whatever Reuben had given her, was not just regular meds.

What had been in that little baggie? Jolie's instincts kicked in. What had he given her? She pulled her legs back so she was on her knees and bent over as far as she could get. Whatever Reuben had put into her she didn't want, and she needed to get it out. She tried to force her stomach to convulse, gagging, and gagging again. But trying to make yourself vomit was not as easy as it looked in the movies.

Blinking, Jolie tried to clear the dense cobweb bearing down on her.

"Come back," she whispered to the demon as she began to shake uncontrollably. She put her head between her knees and tried to find something inside herself to hold onto.

It was a charming courtyard, the broadleaf trees pruned so they provided beneficial shade to the subtropical bushes and flowers, each a perfect companion to its neighbors' color and height. Within it was a small pond, the scales of colorful fish sending flashes of light from the water's surface.

The house surrounding the courtyard was well-kept, with a tiled roof with pleasing curving lines. Sliding doors framed in delicate scrollwork opened onto patterns of decorative paving stones. A half dozen silent servants dressed in dark blues and grays were at work, maintaining order for the honorable family.

The young master stood in the courtyard, looking self-satisfied and proud. He enjoyed eating, his full face and plump figure a sign that the family could afford sufficient food and the cook was good.

Any stranger would know First Son was important just by looking. The cloth of his generously cut clothes was of good quality and there was a swagger of importance in his walk. The servants who passed by him never failed to offer a sign of their deference.

He, of course, ignored them, and their deference. As First Son, deference was his due.

"Little Sister," he shouted, scattering birds and butterflies from the garden in a cloud of wings.

A young female, older than a girl, but not yet a woman, slid open a door on one side of the courtyard.

"I am here, Older Brother Ling. What is it you want?"

"I have news." He puffed out his chest, rolling back and forth from toe to heel.

"Shall I call for tea?" Little Sister invited him into the cool comfort of her room. He ignored the invitation.

"You know our esteemed uncle has been most worried."

"Because our crops have been poor and some of our investments have failed," Little Sister said. First Son worriedly bundled her into her room, sliding the door closed behind them.

"Why would you say such a thing? And out in the courtyard for all to hear?" he demanded in a harsh whisper. "The servants in this house are nothing but gossips. You should not listen to uneducated people who know nothing. If it gets out that our family is in financial distress, we could lose everything. You must never say such a thing again."

"I will not, Older Brother. I promise. What is your news?" She tried to placate him with her sweetness and grace. It was hard not to respond to her. She was not only a beautiful girl but had a peaceful, loving nature that never failed to make Jing Ling feel better about himself and the world.

"I have solved our problem. I have arranged with a powerful person who will lend our family enough money to keep us afloat until we can recover from these unfortunate losses."

"News indeed. And who is this esteemed benefactor?" Little Sister asked.

"Zhibo Shang," Ling pronounced proudly.

Little Sister's face drained of color. "Shang the Silk Bearer? Brother Ling, I hesitate to speak ill of someone you have been seeing socially, but the Silk Bearer is spoken of as a person who cannot be trusted."

"Who has said such a thing?" First Son Ling demanded. "You are full of opinions today, but none has any merit."

Little Sister lowered her voice. "I beg forgiveness, Older Brother. I should not have spoken so to you. But this person you ask me not to speak badly of is said to be aligned with the Qin who are trying to overthrow the Tonghou, our Lord, the Jade Scepter Bearer. Stories of the Qin's deeds show them to have questionable honor and no compassion. The Silk Bearer, Shang, is known to make arrangements without any intention of keeping them."

"He will keep this one." Ling did not like having his decisions questioned. He had never liked it. Even as a small child, he had been certain his way was the correct way, and he had frequently made the household miserable until they gave in to him. "This time, things will be different. This time, Shang wishes for something we have in return, and I have promised him he may have it."

"What could we possibly have…"

"You!" Ling informed Little Sister triumphantly.

Little Sister's face, body, thoughts, and every emotion froze. "This cannot be, Older Brother."

"Of course, it can. It will be." Ling's face was becoming red. "It must be. I am First Son, and I have agreed. You should be grateful, Little Sister. The entire household should be grateful for what I have done by making this arrangement as I have saved our family from

ruin." Ling brought his voice to an intimate whisper. "If Lord Zhiqui's household is attacked, our family will not be harmed. It has been agreed."

"And what of our family's honor? What of the loyalty we owe our Lord after generations of patronage? What of my honor, and the loyalty you owe to me, brother? Shang does not care about us. We are nothing to a man like him--I am nothing. He will not keep this agreement, but he will make sure people know you have made it. Everyone will know you betrayed The Jade Scepter Bearer."

Little Sister's distress made Ling angry. She should be blushing and flustered with happiness at the match he had made for her, proud of her part in saving their family.

"You should not have done this, Ling," she scolded him instead, as if that were her right, which it was not. "You have destroyed our family. You have destroyed our name." Her eyes sparkling bright with tears, she added, "You have destroyed me."

"This is what I get for allowing you to have tutors and be educated! Do you think your opinions are better than your older brother's? Do you think you are smarter than me? Your opinions are of no consequence. I am sorry my indulgences have encouraged you to think otherwise. I cannot believe I have raised such an ungrateful sister," Ling derided her. "This agreement gives you, Little Sister, a purpose. It is your only purpose." He huffed out of her room, leaving his tea cold in its cup and his sister crying.

Swift fingers moved at Jolie's wrists, a quiet click, and the pressure from the cuffs fell away. Jolie lifted her heavy head groggily to find Tulip holding them. The woman put a finger to her lips, glancing toward the bedroom she shared with Reuben. The door was shut, but the walls were thin. Tulip motioned Jolie to get up. The teen tried but her legs were as wiggly as red vines. She shook her head to let Tulip know she could not stand. Another swell of the drug rolled over her like a tsunami.

"What's wrong?" Tulip knelt beside Jolie, helping her keep sitting upright.

"Reuben forced something down my throat," Jolie muttered. "I thought it was my meds, but it feels… different."

"You need to get it out of your system. You need to vomit," Tulip advised.

"I tried. I couldn't."

"You didn't have your hands then. Put your finger down your throat now and try again. Come on. It's important."

Jolie struggled to her knees, then stuffed her fingers into her throat to trigger her gag reflex. The first time she vomited it was mostly bile.

"Again," Tulip urged. Jolie did, gagging until the dissolving pill swam in the puddle of sick on the carpet. Jolie looked at the mess knowing Tulip would be the one who had to clean it up.

"I'm sorry."

"Don't be. I hate that carpet," Tulip replied. Jolie sat back, exhausted as Tulip fetched her a glass of water from the kitchen. "Here, drink this. Then you need to get out of here, fast." She found where Reuben had stashed Jolie's backpacks. "Can you stand now?"

"I have to, don't I?"

Tulip helped Jolie to her feet, then helped her load the backpacks onto her shoulders before walking her to the door. A car waited at the curb.

"I can't get caught, Jo--not yet. Not like this. So, you need to stay out of sight and not go anywhere they'll think to look for you." She shoved some bills into Jolie's hand.

"What about you, and Luce, and Gerith?" Jolie asked, worried about the repercussions of escaping, particularly if Reuben had any suspicion about Tulip's part in it.

"You focus on not getting caught. I'll manage the rest. I've been doing it for years."

"You shouldn't have to…"

Tulip cut her off. "I know. But I need to do this in my own way, Jolie, in my own time. Gerith and Luce need me. This is their home--*our* home. I can't risk losing that for them."

Jolie frowned. "Reuben drugged me, Tulip. He said Wrangler was going to be disappointed in me, but he was setting me up so it would look like I had messed up like my mom. He's dangerous. How can you stay with him?"

"In my own time, my way," Tulip repeated. "I can protect them, Jo, but I can't protect you. He sees them as children who don't threaten him, but you see through to the truth of things, and you make others see it too, and Reuben can't handle that. I'm sorry, Jo. All I can do for you is help you leave."

The screen door squeaked behind them. Gerith was on the front porch wearing jammies and a sleepy face. Tulip flinched Jolie a tearful smile with an apology, and so much more woven into it, scooped Gerith up, then hurried back into to the house. As the cab pulled away, the two of them waved goodbye to Jolie from the doorway. Hooties peeped out from between the porch rails.

"Hooties." Jolie smiled to herself.

CHAPTER ELEVEN

The sun was coming up over Frenchman's Peak to the East of Las Vegas when Jolie's ride dropped her off on the North end of The Strip. She considered other destinations, Iris's, if she was back, Tru and Marty's, if they were back, Mickey's, Rose's, or the cabin in Tecopa. She decided against them all. Those were all places Wrangler would look for her.

Her heart told her to run to Red Rock where the peace, spiritual richness--the very air would feed her, but having a hired car drop her off anywhere near Calico Basin would strip Rose of any deniability she might have over Jolie's whereabouts, and Jolie did not want to get her friend in trouble...any of them.

The Las Vegas Strip was a late-night-party venue, its inhabitants slept in until after noon, restarting each day with lots of coffee and long showers. At this hour, only hotel housekeepers, maintenance people, and landscapers were up and around, sweeping away the traces of last night's party before Mom, Dad, and the kids headed out to breakfast, supporting the masquerade that this was a family-friendly destination.

Despite long, triple-digit summers, the city had a large, houseless population, the casinos generating so much waste it was possible to live on the abundant buffet food discards, sleeping on the streets, or in the flood control tunnels beneath the city.

Jolie found a shaded park bench and sat before checking the Charleston Line bus schedule which would get her to Summerlin, an upper-class suburb of Vegas connected to what had been the city's Northwest edge before the latest spurt of suburban expansion. After what she had been through it was a relief when the demon arrived in all his gray blobbiness.

"So, what are we doing?" the demon asked.

"Leaving Brozovic's and the foster care system," Jolie informed him.

"I like this plan."

"Because you don't have to sleep, or eat, or poop or any of the inconvenient activities humans need to do that get complicated without a place to do them," Jolie countered. "You *don't* poop, do you?" The demon's round body shuddered. "That's what I figured. So, I was thinking about our last talk when you said your past was so dark and it got me wondering what about *before* you were bonded? Are you sure there was no before? I mean, you must have some memories from your life before?"

"No," the demon replied. "I was summoned to serve from the beginning."

"You had no life before?"

"No."

Jolie found this hard to believe. "What's your earliest memory?"

The demon perked up. "My master ordered me to get rid of a rival. He hated the man very much and wanted-- not only him dead, but for the rival's entire family to be publicly humiliated for generations. I arranged a very public display where the man was pulled apart by horses."

Jolie blanched. "Whoa. You understand we don't do that sort of thing anymore, right? That is definitely on the 'bad' list."

"Having someone pulled apart is wrong." The demon nodded. "I will remember."

"Good." Jolie took a deep breath. She was not good at this. She had done a bit of babysitting, what teen hadn't, but there was a big difference between making a mistake where a four-year-old stomped their feet and wished you were dead, and a demon who wanted to kill anyone who crossed it and could.

Her "Spidey" senses began to tingle.

"We're being watched," she muttered, and the demon disappeared.

A street kid with his hair twisted into shoulder-length dreadlocks, wearing torn jeans and an I Love Las Vegas T-shirt, was pretending not to be scoping Jolie out. The teen looked a little older than Jolie, but she suspected he was older than he looked and used his youthful appearance to lower the tourist's guard; an advantage useful to a thief, or recruiter, tasked with bringing in runaways to work for prostitution rings or to sell to human traffickers.

It was odd to see a street kid out so early but with her double backpacks, and disheveled appearance Jolie probably looked exactly like what she was: a runaway.

The kid sauntered up to the bench and gave Jolie a good look over before asking, "Can I sit?"

Jolie shrugged. "It's not my bench."

He sat a bit too close, failing to estimate the correct distance required between them for her comfort. She scooted to the very edge of the bench and turned away.

"Going somewhere?" The invader tossed his chin at Jolie's backpacks. She gave him a cold look that said the answer was too obvious to warrant a reply. "What I meant was, are you traveling…visiting?"

Jolie indicated the backpacks. "Not suitcases. And not interested."

"In what?"

"Whatever you're selling."

The kid raised his hands in a defensive gesture. "I'm not selling anything. I'm just sitting here making conversation."

"Not for long." Jolie checked her phone and got up. The "kid" stood as well. "Don't get up. I don't need an escort. I know my way."

"But you're not going home," the kid suggested, reading her. "Are you?" Jolie didn't even know where home was, but she knew it was a mistake to answer. As nonchalant and harmless as this guy was trying to appear, she could feel the need radiating off him. He was a user, mainly of drugs and people.

"Look, if you need a place to stay…"

"I said, I'm not interested," Jolie reminded him.

"There's no charge. I'm just saying I could show you a place and you could stay there for a while if you need to."

"Look, I don't have money or anything valuable. I'm not open to selling or doing drugs or screwing anyone for favors, so just move on. There's nothing for you here."

The kid's eyes tracked to the larger of Jolie's backpacks. "What a person considers valuable depends on how much they don't have." He moved a knife in his hand, holding it low by his pant leg. The blade glinted in the morning sunlight. Things had progressed and he wanted her to know it. "Give over the backpacks."

Jolie shook her head, no. The kid sprang like a coiled rattler, grabbing the larger pack before bolting. Jolie grabbed the smaller pack and hit the pavement running right behind him.

No one paid any attention to two teenagers running through the empty streets.

The kid who wasn't a kid was thin but not weak or underfed and his adrenaline was spiked. He also knew the terrain flowing through the cityscape like a parkour athlete.

"Give me back my stuff!" Jolie shouted, unable to keep up. She was going to lose him and everything in that pack--mostly clothes, but clothes are hard to replace when you don't have money.

Running full out through an open area, the kid tripped without any visible reason. Tumbling to his hands and knees. He barely broke his stride, running a few steps on all fours before scrambling back to his feet, but the stumble bought Jolie a gain of a few feet. She grabbed the strap on her backpack and yanked it from his grip. He was reaching out to pull it back when the demon appeared, bumping the kid on the back of his knees. He fell over backward.

Sprawled on the pavement, he scowled up at Jolie.

"You're a damn nuisance and a thief," she scolded him, "stealing from someone like yourself who has nothing. A respectable thief at least steals from people who can afford it."

"I'm not frigging Robinhood, bitch. I steal to live, and I guarantee I need whatever's in that pack more than you do."

"Really?" Jolie unzipped her backpack, pulled out a bra, and threw it at him. "You think so?" It hung draped over the boy's head, hiding one eye. He pulled it off, glaring at her. Jolie's hand wrapped around something else in the pack and threw that at him, too.

A pair of white polka-dot panties with pale pink elastic around the legs and top landed on the kid's chest.

"You need 'em? Keep 'em," Jolie taunted. The boy grinned insolently.

"I think I will." He jumped to his feet stuffing the panties into his pocket as he jogged off.

The demon was quickly beside Jolie. "Do we pursue?"

"No, let him go. We're better off rid of him."

The demon smirked. "I thought I detected a limp."

"You should have broken his legs."

"I would have loved that, but I didn't think you'd want me to do that sort of thing anymore."

"I don't. I'm just mad. Thanks for showing up," she added, the sarcasm thick.

"You're welcome?" Sarcasm confused him. Apparently, demons were literal in nature and sarcasm was difficult.

"You tripped him?"

"Both times," the demon said proudly.

"See, now that was helpful, and you didn't have to have him drawn and quartered."

The demon looked surprised. "You know that phrase?"

"It is a horror that has survived history; a remnant of humanity's violent past."

"I do not think your violent past is very past," the demon suggested.

"Maybe not," Jolie admitted, "but don't think because I'm glad you helped me, that I'm going to bond you."

"I did not think that," the demon assured her. "You have made your stand on the subject very clear. I am working on acceptance."

"That's good," Jolie assured him. "Where have you been?"

"Finding a teacher."

She could hardly jump down the little guy's throat for not being around when she was the one who sent him away, but what good was having a demon hanging around if they weren't there when you needed them? Getting angry about your failures was the sort of thing rooky parents did. Was that what she was now: an inexperienced single parent with a demon child? She consoled her feelings of inadequacy by reminding herself that demon parents were probably pretty crappy at teaching healthy self-esteem, so the bar of expectation for her was going to be low.

"Was it bad getting out of the Bozovics?" the demon asked.

"Bad enough," Jolie admitted.

"I'm sorry I was not there."

"Me too. But Tulip came through. Who would have thought?" Jolie hitched her backpack onto her shoulder and began to walk back toward the bus stop just before she fainted, collapsing onto the pavement.

When she opened her eyes, someone was bending over her, blocking the sun, their face in shadow.

"There you are. Take it easy and drink some water," the voice was low-pitched and textured, like a shallow stream rippling over gravel. Jolie hesitated. "It's just water. I'm not trying to roofie you or anything."

"Which is exactly what a kidnapper would say," Jolie muttered.

"True." The stranger sat back, giving Jolie some space, and allowing the sun to reveal their face. "I guess you'll have to rely on your judge of character to decide whether to trust me or not."

Jolie was having a hard time concentrating on the young person's words. All she wanted was to lie back down on the warm pavement and wait for her head to stop spinning.

"When was the last time you ate?" her would-be rescuer asked. Jolie couldn't remember and said so. She'd had a shit of a time the last few hours, adrenaline racing and dropping, then racing again. She hadn't slept much, and some of the drugs Reuben had given her had made it into her system. She was played out and there was no one around to help her but this person.

Like Jolie, it was impossible to figure out the cultural or racial mix of the stranger. Their hair had been recently shaved and was now a short, dark stubble: texture unknown. Their brown skin marked them as having some African DNA somewhere in their family tree, but the scattering of freckles dotting their cheeks and nose like a confab of ladybugs suggested European ancestors had infiltrated the dark continent DNA—that and the pale blue cat-eye marble eyes.

The hang of the stranger's safari outdoorsman's vest covering their black tank top revealed no clue as to gender. Jolie risked a glance at the crotch of their baggy army surplus pants.

"Careful there." Frost chilled the crisp edges of the stranger's British accent. "I gave you permission to decide *who* you thought I was, not *what*."

"Sorry," Jolie apologized. "'Just part of my threat assessment."

"That's fair. Apology accepted." The stranger looked up coyly through thick lashes. Their full-lipped smile lifted slightly on one side. "I'm Oz." *And I'm not in Kansas anymore*, Oz thought

"As in the entire land of?" she asked.

"No, Oz as in the Princess Ozma of that fictional land," Oz added a toney, upper crust flavor to her accent, "or the Wizard of," she dropped it. "Take your pick."

"I don't know you well enough for that," Jolie rebutted. Offering a stranger to choose to see you as either a fictional princess or a wizard was very left of center, which Jolie usually liked, but a chance meeting with someone this attractive and charismatic under her present circumstances raised Jolie's storm warning flags.

She had just been drugged, handcuffed to a radiator, robbed, passed out, then woken up to this extraordinarily interesting-looking person. It seemed…convenient. How did she know the new person wasn't part of the same group trying to lure her into a dark alley? By design, none of her friends, or enemies, knew where Jolie was. If she disappeared now no one would know. Being pickpocketed was practically a right-of-passage for a Las Vegas tourist, but even worse than losing your stuff was losing your freedom and your life, and Las Vegas was the number two city in the United States for human trafficking.

Of course, most teenagers did not have a demon following them around, so she did have that advantage. Where had the little guy gotten to now? She hoped he had not gone off again to do more searching for a teacher.

"So, water or no water?" Oz held out the bottled water. Their eyes met Jolie's, daring her to look inside and decide who she thought they were, little knowing how far such an invitation could go for someone like Jolie. Still, there was only so far you could delve into a person's private thoughts before it became an unforgivable breach of trust. Jolie wanted to trust. She accepted the bottle and drank.

"Keep it," Oz suggested, standing. Slender and graceful as a dancer, they looked like an elf from The Lord of the Rings, without the obvious pointed ears--Jolie had checked. Oz's were just pointy enough to be charming and a little fey.

"So, you're a girl," Jolie said clumsily.

Oz cocked one eyebrow. "Unless we're planning on making babies--which we're not, I don't see that has any relevance."

"You're right. Sorry." Jolie blushed. "Thank you for helping me. I know you didn't have to."

"'Got everything you came with?" Oz indicated Jolie's backpacks.

"Yeah. I chased down the kid who stole my pack just before I…"

"Fainted? Collapsed?" Oz offered.

"I'm dehydrated, I guess. I probably haven't been drinking enough water."

"An easy mistake to make."

"Look, I don't have much, but I'd be happy to thank you by treating you to breakfast if you know somewhere that's cheap and vegetarian?" She dug in the side pocket of her smaller backpack and pulled out the small dollar tips she had stashed there, hoping her hormones weren't tipping the scales toward a bad decision.

Oz tilted their head to one side, shrugging one shoulder. It was charmingly theatrical.

"I can help with that."

"So, do you want to tell me about yourself, or is it your plan to stay all mysterious?" Oz prompted as they enjoyed breakfast burritos from one of the trucks in the food court off Freemont Street.

"It's not so much about being mysterious as it is about being safe," she said.

"You're on the lam."

"On the lam?" Jolie laughed. "Who says that outside of Humphrey Bogart or Edward G. in some old gangster movie?"

Oz shrugged. "Film people. Theater people. It's a good word, lam: underused. It is our duty as human beings with actual vocabularies to use good vocabulary, so the words remain in the human consciousness and don't die slow, sad deaths of neglect." Jolie chuckled. She couldn't get enough of Oz's British accent. "You laugh, but there are reasons these words were created. They were necessary for expressing a very particular feeling or action, each unique with a very specific nuance."

"Nuance: another good word," Jolie pointed out.

"Noo-on-sss," Oz repeated slowing the word down so that her lips caressed the changing vowels, kissing the air. Jolie's head swam, imagining being on the receiving end of that kiss. She wanted to say the word back. She wanted to breathe it into Oz's mouth lip to lip. *Jolie Figg, you are in way over your head, and completely out of your league,* she told herself.

"Which are you, a film person or a theater person?" she asked to cover her lapse during her kissing fantasy.

"Both. Not professionally, but by birth. My parents are "in the business" --one in each, actually--with an occasional crossover. They're not posh stars or anything, just normal working artists. Professionally, I am the family's black sheep. Film and theater people are snobbish about "circus" folk," but that's my gig. I'm a circus nerd--an acrobat." Jolie almost choked on her bite of burrito. "You think I'm joking? I'm not. As soon as I turned eighteen, I came to the States with a friend for the Cirque De Soleil auditions."

Jolie waited for more. "And?" she prompted.

"My friend started shagging someone else. Obviously, I couldn't stay at our apartment anymore, so I moved out."

"I meant what happened with your audition?"

"They cast a different acro duo for the spot. I'm waiting for the next auditions.

"And your parents have had a change of heart and are being supportive?"

"Oh God, no. They're mortified. An acrobat is not even a dancer. They tell their friends I'm taking a year off to travel and find myself--so trite." Oz made a flamboyant gesture of dismissal. "I have learned a few things though. Like how bad some countries treat their artists. It is so backward here." Jolie blinked, trying to keep up with the change of subject as Oz's mind flipped from subject to subject. "There are no national training schools, no state-supported identification projects to help young artists-- nothing. One of the richest countries in the world, but if you are not fortunate enough to be born into a family of means who believes a career in the arts is worthwhile, which most do not, you're completely on your own, on the streets, or living in your parent's basement if they'll allow that. Sorry." Oz winced. "It's a sore spot among my friends. I live with a bunch of artists, an Aussie, two Germans, a Parisian, but the Yanks have it the worst."

"People aren't keen on *different* here," Jolie explained. "There are pockets of culture founded on celebrating individuality: New Orleans, New York, San Francisco—cultural and artistic centers, but most people are nervous about different. They want to change it, form it into something familiar, control it, or wipe it out so they don't have to deal with it."

"And yet they idolize artists who are successful and treat them like we treat our royals," Oz added. "It's mind-boggling."

"My name's Jolie, by the way. Jolie…" Jolie paused, "Boulet. My family is from New Orleans."

Oz settled their shocking blue eyes on Jolie, waiting for more. It didn't come.

"You're rather an old soul, aren't you?" Oz asked when they realized Jolie was not going to share her life story. Jolie shrugged; her mouth full of the last bite. "But you're very young to be on your own, Jolie." The statement was tender, not judgmental.

"Life doesn't always offer us good choices. Sometimes you have to pick the best option in the moment, and right now, I need to get going. I've got another few hours, and a long hike before my head can hit a pillow."

"My place is close," Oz suggested. And there it was. Jolie needed to decide absolutely whether she was willing to trust this person or not. "No strings. Like I said, there's a bunch of us who live there together, but we each have our own little spaces and we're selective about who we let in, so there are no creeps. It's not fancy, but it's safe. You can get some rest, then head out to wherever you're going when you're ready."

"Safe is a relative term," Jolie pointed out.

"It is," Oz agreed. "But I wouldn't put you in harm's way, Jolie Boulet."

"Good, because I've got friends who would kick the ass of anyone who messed with me." Oz raised one eyebrow. "Your friends are artists? Mine are martial artists, Wiccan, and Red Roaders."

Oz laughed. "Every time you say something I have a dozen more questions. Please, come and stay with me. You look exhausted." She put her hand on Jolie's. "And I'm not ready to watch you walk away."

Jolie bit her lip. It was a great line.

Oz tossed away their empty burrito wrapping. "Do you need to call someone, maybe someone special, to tell them not to worry? If I were your friend and I didn't know where you were, I'd worry." Oz tilted their head in that charming way, their full lips twisting up on the side again. There was no makeup on those lips--no makeup or artifice anywhere on that pixie face. It didn't need it. It was perfect: uniquely beautiful as it was.

Jolie was about to skirt around the hinted question about her romantic relationship status but looking at Oz she decided to be daring and honest and shook her head, no.

"Just checking." Oz smiled.

Jolie smiled back, shyly, feeling incredibly awkward. She was having the most terrible day, then this amazing person appeared, sparking a light inside her, and suddenly everything was bright and possible again. *This was what Mom felt over and over again.* It was why Jessie Lynn had kept trying, despite her many misjudgments, continually hoping for another person who, like Lucian Boulet, could make that feeling last. The possibility of love had been Jessie Lynn Figg's strongest addiction, and Jolie was her daughter. Despite all the promises she had made to herself, Jolie was letting her guard down again.

It felt amazing.

Oz's place was in Las Vegas's fledgling Arts District off the northern end of the Strip, their personal space defined by boho-style cotton wall hangings strung with Christmas lights in an abandoned building connected to a soon-to-open art gallery and sometimes yoga studio which the tent people accessed by a person-sized hole in the common wall. A mattress and lots of pillows were the focus and living area. A battery-powered lantern with a colorful scarf tossed over it gave the space additional ambiance.

"Sorry, there's no fan," Oz apologized. "No electricity. The lights are battery-operated. Technically, we're squatters, but nobody knows who owns the building and no one seems to care, so for now, it's ours."

"Great." Jolie put her backpacks down, uncertain what to do next.

The other "villagers" had their tents inside the warehouse and the artist renovating the studio on the legitimate side of the wall let them use the bathroom and kitchenette in trade for helping her with her renovations or any unique "found" items they brought her that she could use in her remodel. It was a barter system that worked, at least until the fledgling district became financially successful and the missing owner of the abandoned side re-emerged and kicked the artists out.

"Just make yourself at home. You can sit, or lie down, or whatever."

"What are you going to do?" Jolie asked. "I mean, what would you do if I wasn't here?"

"I am going next door through that hole in the wall to help my friend, Ava, and finish painting the kitchenette in her studio. After that, I'll take the yoga class her friend runs there, then I'll probably take a nap. You should fast forward to the nap part. You look like you need it. When you wake up, I'll be here, or there." She pointed toward the studio. "Don't worry, no one will bother you." Oz left, dropping the curtain behind them.

Jolie flopped back onto the mattress and closed her eyes with a sigh.

"I'm here," the demon whispered into her mind.

It was the last thing she remembered.

CHAPTER TWELVE

The semi-communal living situation in the warehouse tent village was a strange sort of private non-privacy. It was like living next door to an ongoing party: spur-of-the-moment dinners, cooperative artistic happenings, and philosophic discussions that went on late into the night. Oz and her friends were accepting of Jolie's presence, but it was clear they viewed her as someone passing through. She always felt like a guest.

Oz was happy to include Jolie in most of her activities, pulling her guest into dumpster diving expeditions, parkour sessions run by one of her roommates as a way to keep in shape, or the "donations only" yoga classes, which Jolie found she liked. The stretching and strengthening felt good, and there were a surprising number of similarities between the meditation practices incorporated into the class and the teachings at the temple school.

But though Oz invited Jolie along, the British acrobat firmly established her independence. They were not a couple, and Oz didn't want anyone to think they were. Jolie reminded herself that both she and Oz knew Jolie was not staying, so Oz's insistence on defining their relationship as a friendship might have been the British acrobat's way of protecting themself from getting hurt, or maybe it was just only a passing friendship and nothing more to Oz. However strong their chemistry was and however interesting Oz found Jolie, the homeless teenager did not fit into Oz's new adult world.

Though Jolie found herself smiling more than she remembered smiling since Faith died, the first in the domino collapse of losses that defined her life over the past few months, her thoughts often returned to questions about where she was, and where she needed to be.

The outcome was Oz's life was not hers and she needed to leave. Red Rock was calling.

Jolie entered the open space of the next-door art studio, her backpacks already slung over her shoulders. In paint-spattered clothes, paint dotting their brown skin, hands, and stubble hair, Oz was texturing a section of one of the studio's walls.

"Hey, Oz, I think I'm going to take off now." Jolie shifted her weight from one foot to the other. Oz stopped painting and turned around, trowel in hand.

"You think? You're not sure? Say what you mean, Jolie. It's simpler and more honest."

"I need to leave," Jolie clarified.

"Okay." Oz's face remained blank, but their body language revealed an inner battle the teen found confusing. Oz had made it clear; they were not a couple, and they were not going to be a couple, and yet the deep longing Jolie saw in their eyes tugged at her loneliness.

"I'm sorry," Jolie stuttered. "You've…." She didn't know how to finish the sentence.

"I've what?" Oz demanded. "Been busy with my own life? Didn't ask you to go steady? What?"

Jolie pulled back into her shell. "You've been great--all of you, and it's been fun, but I've got things I need to take care of. So, thanks for everything." Jolie remembered sleeping next to Oz, smelling the scent of her, like vanilla beans--her breath, her skin. Jolie had been careful to avoid casual touching, even pseudo-sisterly hugs, unwilling to risk knowing things about Oz and their future that would complicate Jolie's life even more, but when they were together the space between and around them vibrated. Oz must have felt it, but their response had been to amp up their general, non-specific flirting with everyone, their statement declaring they would not be heartbroken over some stray who strolled into, then out of their life.

"I don't know what I would have done if I hadn't met you," Jolie added in an impulsive show of emotion. "I don't know what I'll do now that I have."

It was as close as either of them had come to declaring they had feelings deeper than a brief proximal acquaintance.

"You *could* stay," Oz said, their face vulnerable and childlike. Jolie closed her eyes.

"I can't. I'm a complication you can't afford right now, Oz, and you getting sucked into my problems wouldn't help either of us." Along with the countdown to the next Cirque auditions, Oz was in the United States on a visitor's visa that was running out. "The only way I can get my freedom back is by proving I can make my own way. I know you understand because I've seen how much you value your freedom."

"I've been hurt," Oz said.

"Me too," Jolie admitted. "Timing, right?"

"Yeah, it sucks. Where will you go?" Oz asked.

"A friend's. It's better if I don't say, in case Juvenile Probation comes looking for me. But it's a good place. I'll be safe there."

"You think they're going try and track you down? Who are you, Jack the Ripper?"

"No. Nothing like that, but my life is…." Jolie searched for the right word. "Complicated." It wasn't the right word, but it would do as a placeholder.

"I hate you going and not knowing when I'll see you again, or *if* I will see you again. Will I?" Oz said.

"I have your number. I'll text when I can," Jolie promised. "Things will settle down and get straightened out for both of us and when they do, everything will be different."

"Not everything, I hope," Oz said.

"No, not everything." Jolie smiled shyly. "Hey, and if you want to learn some different meditation practices, try the Kung Fu school in Chinatown. I have friends there. I think you'd like them."

Oz started to stumble forward for a parting hug, but Jolie stepped back, stopping her. Trying to save Remy's life from the accident that she had foreseen when he bumped into her had been the start of months of hell and ended for Jolie in heartbreak. *Knowing* was just too hard. By its nature, uncertainty held a space for the possibility that knowing shattered. Right now, Jolie needed the hope of uncertainty and possibility.

"I'll see you." She did the right thing and walked away.

CHAPTER THIRTEEN

Summerlin, a planned patchwork of middle and upper-class housing developments, only went as far as the newest neighborhood west of the beltway that surrounded the city, and there the Charleston bus line ended. After that, the terrain turned into sagebrush and cactus, creosote, and Joshua trees.

As it left the city suburbs, Charleston Boulevard became Red Rock Highway and Jolie followed it, veering from the paved highway as she reached the utility road that eventually would lead her into Calico Basin from the East. It was an unofficial thoroughfare, unsanctioned for public use, but it was the shortest route for someone traveling on foot. Midday, she stopped to rest in the shade of a big rock beside a creosote bush before tackling the last leg of her sweat-bath hike.

By the time Jolie finally made the gravel road that ran in front of Remy's Aunt Rose's house, the sun was leaning on the red cliffs to the west of the basin that separated it from Red Rock's scenic loop.

Cars and trucks lined the rutted road by Rose's, the smell of five-finger sage, incense cedar, and sweet grass, wafting from the lodge grounds. It was the Saturday closest to the full moon. Rose would be holding a

Women's Full Moon Sweat. Jolie smiled. Now, it really felt like a homecoming.

She knew better than to knock on Rose's door on a lodge day. People would be coming in and out and Rose would be juggling the details of preparing for the ceremony and the feast to follow.

"Rose?" she called out as she stepped into the homey log cabin. The inside walls had been left rough, the large windows and sliding doors placed to invite the outside in, giving you the sense that you were in an oasis among the Desert Willow and Mesquite trees.

Brightly colored Native American blankets were tucked neatly over the two lodgepole pine couches that faced each other in the main room. The unfinished wood floor was freshly swept and the scent of the food for the potluck feast made Jolie's mouth water and her stomach growl.

"She's out back," a voice answered Jolie's call. "Checking on the fire tender."

Remy! Jolie's heart jumped. The last time she was at a women's lodge, Remy tended the fire. Her adrenaline plummeted as she remembered Remy was at Pine Ridge so he could not be here.

The sizzling of frying oil coming from the kitchen crackled like cicadas. Jolie stepped further into the room.

The woman reigning over the kitchen had a round, comforting face, and curly, graying hair poofed out around her head like a round-bristle brush. Her sweat dress was a Hawaiian Mumu print that required sunglasses to look at--no rings or earrings, and no makeup let Jolie know that the cook was a lodge participant.

"Do you like frybread?" The woman flattened a ball of dough between her strong, brown hands and dropped it into a wide, shallow pan of oil. "That's a dumb question, everyone likes frybread, especially mine. This is not the white doughy crap they sell at fairs and try to pass off as traditional frybread. Oh no. Auntie Thea's frybread is the real stuff, made the old way like my grandma's and aunties showed me, with prayers and healing worked right into the dough."

"That sounds wonderful." Jolie smiled. "Thank you for doing all that."

"It's no trouble." Thea's gesture allayed any concerns. "But I do need to pee. Hydrating before the lodge, you know." She grimaced. "Come watch these for me a minute, will you?" She stepped aside to make room for Jolie at the stove. "If the edges get golden brown before I get back, flip them." She handed Jolie the pancake turner and headed for the bathroom with a rolling gait.

Rose walked in the back door and stopped, her face lighting up. "Jolie!" And in that moment, the teen knew she had not made a mistake in coming. With a swallowed sob, she crossed the room and threw herself into Rose's arms trusting the Spirits had nothing terrible to tell her about Rose. "Wincincala Witko," the Native woman whispered the Lakota name that Remy's Uncle Hoke had given Jolie. "What a wonderful surprise. Welcome home." They both held on tight.

Thea came out of the bathroom, shaking her hands dry. "Your little hug-fest better not have ruined my frybread," she teased. Jolie got back on task.

"It looks perfect."

Thea looked from Rose to this new woman-child.

"Thea, this is Jolie, Wincincala Witko," Rose introduced them. "She's the amazing young person I told you about that Remy brought us."

"The ex. Don't feel bad, honey. We're all a little in love with Remy. Those two-spirited boys are just so hard to resist. But 'Girl Who Knows Nothing'?" Thea snorted. "Did that old fart, Hoke, name you that? I don't want to spoil this wonderful frybread by putting any negative energy in it, so I'm not going to tell you what a bunch of masculine warrior bullshit that is."

"I don't mind," Jolie said. "I probably deserved it."

"Well, don't forget that among our people, names are fluid and can change as you do, or the way those around you see you." Thea gestured with the turner. She flipped the frybread. "People can call you anything, but you decide whether you accept it or not. Look at me, I've called myself Princess Thea since I was three, but the rest of the world insisted on calling me Timothy. They were slow, but they're finally catching up." Thea grinned.

"You're staying, for the sweat, aren't you?" Rose asked Jolie.

"If it's okay."

"Of course, it is."

"Uh, has Wrangler been here looking for me?" Jolie asked hesitantly.

"Been and gone," Rose replied pulling a cotton sweat dress from a closet whose door was a faded sheet. "I told him I hadn't heard from you." Rose's look held a scolding as she handed the dress to Jolie.

"I'm sorry, Rose. I didn't want you to worry, but I also didn't want you to have to decide whether to lie to Wrangler or not. That, and I needed some time to work through what happened at the Bozovic's." She glanced at Thea.

Rose noted the look. "We can talk about that later. Have you left for good then, or are you expecting things to cool down so you can go back?"

"I'm not going back," Jolie stated decisively. "I'm done with them--with the whole system, the meds, the counselors, they lied so they could put me on drugs--all of it. My Mom died, leaving me on my own. That doesn't make me mentally or emotionally unstable."

"Speak your truth, girl," Thea cheered her on.

"Well, you're here now and I'm glad," Rose reassured Jolie. "We can talk about the rest of it after lodge. Maybe things will seem clearer to you then."

Jolie went to change into the long, cotton, sweat dress in the little side room where Rose put guests and other extra stuff that showed up at her house. The addition felt like a lean-to with walls and a bank of horizontal windows facing west. It couldn't have been built to any codes or with permits. The sloping ceiling was so low that by the time it got to the outer wall you had to hunch over to look out the windows.

This was where Remy brought Jolie the night Axel-
-the possessed man whose apartment was above Jolie and
her mom's--had died. Jolie tried to stop him from beating
his wife when he had started on the teen. Jolie pushed him
away with such force that when he stumbled against the
chair behind him it broke his back. Axel's wife hurried
Jolie out and Remy had taken her away, bringing her
here. Jolie knew it was an accident, but it was the kind of
thing that stuck with you. That night had felt like the start
of Chapter Two of her troubles.

The second time Jolie came to Rose's, it was again
Remy who brought her. Jessie Lynn had been shot by her
ex-boyfriend and was in the hospital and Jolie was under
a constant onslaught by the demon and Axel's spirit
trying to possess her. Barely lucid, Remy and Rose had
tucked the exhausted girl into the bed in this little room.

Remy had sat beside Jolie all that night but,
sometime during those hours, Bodhi had come. And that
was the night Remy realized it was Bodhi he loved.

There were holes in Jolie's memories of that night,
but the picture of Remy and Bodhi crying in each other's
arms, the ache of their longing for each other, and all the
pain they had endured, remained vivid.

The third time Jolie had been brought to Rose's it
had been the old, black jack--the lead burro of the local
herd--who had found her, lost and confused in the
mountains, and carried her on his back down into the
basin.

Now, here she was again in Red Rock, in trouble,
and uncertain of what came next.

She peered out the narrow windows at the summer twilight. The sun glowed behind the basin's western wall outlining the rounded rim that looked like a woman's breasts.

Rose told Jolie how the burros came and slept on the lodge grounds after every ceremony. Would they come tonight? Were they out there now in the red-tinged gloaming, waiting? She went outside, slipping around the south end of the house as the cloak of night settled. Cicadas buzzed among the feathery leaves of the mesquite trees. Crickets rubbed out their songs. The voice of the owl in the cliffs to the North cut through the insect orchestra like a French Horn, brave and triumphant. Somewhere to the southeast, a burro brayed. It didn't matter if it was the black jack calling to her or just one of his band braying into the night, it said "I am here". And she was too. And that was enough.

Worry slipped from Jolie's shoulders like a summer shawl. She felt still, like the waters of a summer lake at sundown once all the fishing boats had beached and the fishermen had retired for the night. At this moment, nothing she worried about over the past few weeks seemed important. It had all worked out and those troubles were now behind her, or ahead of her, but not present. She was in Red Rock. She absorbed the feeling like your skin absorbs steam in a sweat lodge, filling herself with peace and gratitude.

When she joined the other women around the fire, she was ready to begin the ceremony.

They filed into the lodge and were sitting in the darkness waiting for the first stones to be brought in when truck lights flashed through the bushes separating the lodge grounds from the driveway.

"Were you expecting someone else?" Thea asked Rose.

"It's Wrangler." Jolie knew.

"Go," Rose urged her.

Careful not to cross the spirit path, Jolie slipped out of the lodge door and into the bushes.

The heavy blankets covering the opening of the lodge were drawn closed and the Spirit Calling song began. Cliff Wrangler could not interrupt the ceremony now until the lodge was over.

The demon appeared in the bushes beside Jolie.

"I couldn't get in," he complained. "Those poles with the funny colored dolls on them wouldn't let me pass."

"The flags," Jolie explained. "They make a protective boundary."

"Protection from what? Me? You don't need protection from me," he protested. The fact that the flags did not let him pass brought that into question.

Wrangler's face turned, squinting into the darkness at the bushes where Jolie and the demon were hiding. Jolie backed up slowly, turned, and fled into the desert, her bare feet feeling for the sandy paths.

Climbing onto a large boulder among the field of boulders scattered in the flat ground near the base of the pink mountain, she sat, listening to the prayer songs sift through the night air. The demon joined her, but she kept her attention on the songs and prayers. Each round had a different focus: West for setting an intention, North for introspection and self-honesty, East for healing, and South for completion and new beginnings.

"Look into my heart, Grandmother," Jolie whispered to the Earth, "and take away this anger I have toward the man, Reuben. Whatever he did, holding onto anger only hurts me. I know that I have carried a lot of anger in me over the years, and I have done some stupid things--maybe even some bad ones, but I want to do better. I want to be a better person and focus on the good things that have happened *for* me, not the bad things that have happened *to* me. I don't want to be a bitter, angry person, so help me find a good path, Grandmother, one that moves me toward a future where I make Mem, my dad, the Boulet family, and mom, proud of me. I've fought against the gifts I've been given. I know that was ungrateful, but they felt so heavy and I'm just a kid. Help me learn how to embrace my gifts now and use them in a good way to make the world a better place so other kids don't have to struggle like I have. I just need a little help…please."

The drumming and singing stopped. Jolie could hear the women greeting each other as they came out of the lodge, muddy, sweaty, and glowing. It was a beautiful tradition, the lodge goers lining up to greet their lodge sisters in an open-hearted sharing that was special because of how clear, clean, and raw their fierce prayers had left them.

The glow from the lodge fire dimmed and the house lights came on, light laughter drifting from the house out into the desert. The smells of food and sage and cedar were strong in the air.

"You must be hungry." The demon sounded worried.

"No. Not really," Jolie replied quietly. "This is what I needed." She indicated the desert. "The evening, the energy--it's better than food."

"For beings of spirit, it is," the demon agreed. "Energy is what we live on, but I did not think it was like that for humans."

"I guess that depends on the human."

The black jack brayed, his trumpeting bouncing off the horseshoe of rock walls that made the protected basin. His herd would sleep on the lodge grounds at Rose's tonight. Maybe she could slip in long enough to say hello.

"Oh, and Grandmother, please help Tulip find a safe space for herself Luce, and Gerith," Jolie added to her prayer. There was a part of her that wished she could have fit in with the small, tight, family. Maybe that would have been possible without Reuben. Maybe she should have stayed and fought it out with him. Had it been cowardly to leave? At the time, it had seemed like the only option, and Tulip had agreed. There had been a lesson in Jolie's confrontation with Axel. She intended to stop him from hurting his wife, but in the end, the woman had lost her husband and had no one. It was not for Jolie to say how that trade-off had turned out. Had she helped, or had her interfering only made things worse?

I need to stop stumbling around, she told herself. *I need to understand my abilities and train to use them.* Experience was a teacher, but it had proven to be a costly one.

Jolie looked at the red desert, sensing the richness of spirits attached to the ancient sacred space. She would begin here.

The muddy-faced women made a pathway for the man dressed like a cowboy.

"So, have you seen Jolie yet?" Wrangler asked Rose.

"Yes." Rose had washed some of the dirt off her hands and face, but her skin was still flushed and glowing, her bare feet caked with red mud, her long salt and pepper hair rippled and coated from the dust-laden steam of the lodge. One of the women handed Wrangler a plate of food and a fork.

"So, she's been here." He accepted the offering and dug in as he continued to interrogate Rose. Women's lodges always had the best food. "When?" Rose did not answer. "Is she here now?" He looked around.

"You know she's not, Cliff. You've been sitting in your truck, watching, and snooping around the yard for hours now. Did you see her?"

Wrangler frowned. "Where is she, Rose?"

Rose shook her head. "I told you; I don't know."

"You realize that she's all alone now, right?"

Rose scoffed. "Jolie was 'alone' long before her mother died."

"Except for all you women trying to mother-hen her," he pointed out.

"Except for that," Rose agreed.

"She's a smart kid, Rose, and because of what she's been through, she seems older than she is, but she's still a kid. She needs our help."

"Locking her up right after her mother died and forcing her to talk to people whose only definition of someone like her is that she's broken and wrong in the head doesn't sound very helpful to me, Cliff. Neither does putting her in the care of people who think that because she's got a little fire in her she must need to be medicated into numb submission. Jolie lost her mom and several close friends. She did not lose her mind. Drugging her isn't going to make her losses magically disappear. That will take time and making her look to substances as an answer is not an answer."

"Is that what she told you happened?" Wrangler asked, alarmed.

"She didn't stay long enough for me to get more than the highlights."

"Just help me find her, Rose. There are nice foster families out there," Wrangler kept on.

"Families who understand what Jolie needs? Who she is? She doesn't understand that, Cliff. What would a 'nice' white family know about raising a girl like Jolie?"

"It's dangerous for her out there on her own," Cliff argued. "Living in some spiritual bubble doesn't make real problems go away, Rose. Not everything can be solved by climbing into a lodge."

"Good choices require perspective and a firm foundation in grounded truth. A lodge is a good place to find those things," Rose disagreed.

"Some say the same for a church."

"In church, they tell you what to think and how to act. In a lodge, you do the work yourself. There's no one between you and Spirit."

"Great. So, you can imagine that God tells you whatever you want him to and no one can call you on your bullshit," Wrangler countered bitterly.

Rose turned away. "This is not about you being disappointed because you trusted the wrong people, Cliff. Your mistakes are not Jolie's."

"You know where she is, don't you, Rose? Just tell me." Rose's silence was insolent and stubborn. "Dammit, if I find out that you, or any of the other ladies, are hiding her…"

"You'll do what, Cliff? Wouldn't it be better if the girl was safe somewhere--anywhere? Or are you more concerned about getting the paperwork right? She's a kid not an illegally parked car."

"You know what happens to girl runaways here," he argued.

Rose's lips tightened. "Jolie is not most girls."

"No, she's tough and spunky, but she's also more vulnerable than she lets on. She has strong notions about right and wrong and believes that good people stand up to protect those who can't protect themselves from the bullies of the world. How do you think that's going to play out on the streets of Las Vegas? She's going to get on the wrong side of someone the first time she opens her mouth."

"Is that what happened at the foster home?" Rose demanded. "She spoke up because she saw things were wrong, and the foster parents couldn't handle it?"

"We're still investigating the situation," Wrangler dodged.

"And where were you, Cliff?" Rose studied the man she thought she knew, and the officer whom she did not, comparing them. Both men stood in front of her. Both believed they saved kids--that the work they did was right and just, but neither knew the system from the inside and they sure as hell didn't know it from the point of view of a female from a minority culture or one who was severely psychically gifted. Cliff Wrangler had never experienced the rotten heart hidden at the core of a system based on the philosophic foundation that beating every spark of independence out of a kid to make them better servant-class workers who would grow up to have no voice, to take up no space, and whose entire existence would be an apology--people who accepted every authority outside their own, was a good way to go.

Rose knew there were good people in the juvenile probation system, but history had proven that predators and bullies were also drawn to positions of petty power, people   who   saw   financially   underprivileged, marginalized kids as something less than human and made it their job to shred the last remnants of vulnerable young people's unraveling lives, layering on more abuse over what they had already survived.

Some kids needed the system to help them gain a foothold and find their way. Jolie Figg-Boulet was not one of them.

"Pick a side, Cliff," Rose told him. "You either believe Jolie, or you don't. You believe Hoke, and Sifu, and me, or you don't. There is either an active, tangible spirit world, or there isn't. Walk the Red Road, Cliff, or don't, but you can't keep jumping back and forth across the line."

The moon had climbed the sky over the Eastern ridge of Calico Basin, darkness resting lightly over the red rocks and sand, completing their nightly transformation. If you looked up, the stars winked back. They were so far away they gave little light.

The silhouette of a man walked the path between Rose's and the boulder field where Jolie lay on the top of a rock looking up at those stars.

"Someone's coming," the demon warned. Jolie rolled over keeping her belly flat against the warm stone.

"It's Wrangler, looking for me."

"What should we do?"

Jolie scanned the landscape. There was a lot of wilderness around them: boulders, caves, sunken bowls of land submerged below the desert's surface, and aside from the rising moon, not a light to be seen. Cliff Wrangler was not going to find Jolie here unless she wanted him to. And she did not.

"Let's go." She skittered off the top of the boulder, sliding down the far side toward the pink mountain. She leaped over the desert floor, light-footed as an antelope. She had never moved so certainly, trusting the land to guide each step. It was like running with the wind, and it felt right.

CHAPTER FOURTEEN

"**T**hen Reuben shackled me to the old heater and forced some pills down my throat," Jolie explained to Rose as she refilled her water bottle adding it to the sleeping bag and camp mattress she was borrowing for her stay out in the basin. "I'm sure he planned to tell Child Protective Services that he caught me using—which, if I had stayed, would have been proven by a drug test because of what he made me take."

"Cliff would never believe that," Rose assured Jolie.

"Cliff agreed to them putting me on meds, Rose! He said I should at least *try* them to see what it was like to live in the real world as if I don't, and all it would take to fix my life was some pill. A pill isn't going to bring my mom back, or Faith, or solve the hundred problems my mom left me to face alone." Jolie dashed tears from her eyes, hoping Rose hadn't noticed.

"What happened to your friend Iris?" the older woman asked. "I thought you would stay with her after your mom crossed over."

"The state's approval process takes time and Iris had to leave town to deal with a family emergency." Jolie shied away from saying any more. She hadn't known Iris had family back East. Iris had never mentioned it. So, where had that come from? Rose must have caught the uncomfortable look on her face.

"But it's going to get worked out, right, Jo?"

Jolie shrugged. "I guess."

"You know you can stay here," Rose offered. "Not just for now, but long term if you need to."

"I appreciate that, Rose, and I sort of am staying here. Just not in the house." Jolie kept scarfing down the quinoa and corn salad leftovers she had scrounged for breakfast.

"But you could."

"And you'd have to lie to Wrangler every time you saw him," Jolie pointed out. The smile that seldom left Rose's face lost its lilting curves.

"I don't care about that."

"Right now, because you're mad at him, but I don't want to be responsible for getting in the way of your friendship."

"Cliff's responsible for his own choices."

Jolie took a deep breath, then let it out, shrugging off the stress that had built up in her body during this discussion.

"For the last six months, Rose, my life's been one long angst-riddled, teen, horror film. I need time to work stuff out and the basin is a good place for that."

"It is," Rose agreed. "But you could do that without sleeping on a rock. I'd give you as much space as you need, Jo. I wouldn't bother you."

"I know, but I need to do this my way. Would it be okay if I still came to the house to touch down, use the facilities, get water, and maybe get something to eat now and then?"

"Whatever you need. If I'm not here, I'll leave the courtyard door in the back open so you can always get in."

"Thanks, Rose. Oh, and one more thing, could you text someone for me and let them know I'm, okay?" Rose raised an eyebrow. "It's just someone who helped me after I left the Bozovic's before I came here."

"Sure. Just give me their number." The returning curves of Rose's smile indicated she was thinking there was something more to this new acquaintance than Jolie was admitting to.

"Don't get ideas. It's not like that," Jolie protested the thoughts not being said. "Oz is an artist—an acrobat from London. They're going to be in one of the Cirque shows here on the strip."

Rose frowned. "And they are living on the streets?"

"No, she--they live in a warehouse in The Arts District with a bunch of other artists. They were nice and let me stay with them there. I said I'd let them know when I was safe so they wouldn't worry."

"Oh, so they would worry, huh?" Rose's smile twinkled up into her brown eyes. "That sounds pretty serious for a two-day acquaintance. It's not like you to be impulsive about people, Jo."

"I wasn't…I'm not," Jolie spluttered. "But they helped me when I needed it. Don't tell Wrangler, please, Rose. I don't want to get Oz in trouble. It could mess up their visa."

Rose laughed. "You never want to get anyone in trouble, but somehow it just keeps happening."

Jolie made a face. "I don't mean to."

"It's all right, Jo. I won't say a word." Rose made a gesture like she was zipping her lips together. "I look forward to meeting your new friend though. Maybe at the next Women's Lodge?"

"Maybe." Jolie wondered where she would be and what her life would be like by the next full moon.

There was a perfect sheltering spot around the east side of the pink mountain a half mile from Rose's house. A path defined by the regular use of rock climbers hiking to a popular cleated climb in the canyon between the pink mountain and the one behind it. The path followed the curve of the mountain's east end.

Hundreds of years ago, a thick slab of rock had fallen off the mountainside and landed with one end wedged against a cottage-sized boulder. The space beneath was cave-like with a front and back exit, though the back one was complicated by boulders requiring some climbing. Jolie ruled that out. It was too close to the popular path.

She looked around her, feeling the breeze, the sun, the quiet, relishing how it settled her insides. Her attention was caught by the ruffled sandstone terraces on the pink mountain's east end above her. Climbing up, she explored the ledges and caves carved out by the wind and rain until she found one that was not too difficult to climb, but hard enough to get to that not many people would try.

The sandstone ledge outside was just wide enough for her to sit with her legs stretched out or to do some of the practices she had picked up at the temple school. Inside the cave, there was a flat rock she could use as a sleeping platform. It wouldn't stop snakes or scorpions from trying to share her sleeping bag if it got cold, but Jolie felt more secure being up off the ground.

She would have a roof over her head to keep out the sun or rain and three walls she could retreat into that would shield her from view and the harsh winds. One natural window faced south with a view of the path that started at the gravel road running past Rose's. Here she settled in. Stashing her backpacks at the base of the stone sleeping platform, she unrolled the sleeping bag and mattress, spreading them out on the top, then wadded up a winter hoodie for a pillow before lying down to try out her new sleeping situation.

From this high on the mountain, the tip of the Stratosphere Tower was just visible to the east outside the cave's opening.

Jolie let the barriers she protected herself with fall away with a sigh--a relief like taking off too-tight shoes and feeling your feet relax and stretch back to their natural shape.

Finally, time to think. It was quiet up here--quiet enough for Jolie to hear her thoughts without the taint of anyone else's intruding. Sometimes these thought-intrusions felt like someone trying to kick down a door into her brain. Others, it was like an insidious sliver of foreign thoughts trying to slice through her boundaries.

The late afternoon breeze hummed through the sandstone, licking its soft curves like a fastidious cat cleaning its fur in preparation for its afternoon nap. When the breeze paused, the silence was so intense that Jolie's ears strained for proof of life outside of her heartbeat.

A nap sounded good. What was her plan going forward? Drifting off, she felt her spirit floating.

"You do not need a plan."

Jolie did not know if the voice was hers, or someone, or some*thing* else's. Or maybe it was just the wind.

"Does it matter?" the voice asked.

"No," Jolie decided.

"Plans give the illusion of control--a habit based on the lie that a person can predict what is to come, which most people cannot. Such skills are possible to attain with great discipline and a true master to instruct the student, but once the student practiced enough to gain the skill, they would no longer have any interest in such use.

Spending time planning for a future that is constantly changing, encourages frustration and feelings of failure. It is wiser, and in greater harmony, to live each moment as it presents itself."

The wind whistled and hummed over, around, and through the cave's sandstone curves, rattling the dried seed pods on the creosote bushes at the foot of the mountain, lulling Jolie to sleep.

Shang was not an important man in the region, but he wished to be. As a merchant of questionable repute, however, his standing would only change when the quality of his wares reached a standard that gained the attention of the Tonghou's household, and this required connections and influence he did not have.

The silk merchant invited the young Jing's scion, Older Brother, Ling, to dine, entertaining him with fine dishes, courtesans, and the best rice wine. He flattered the vain young man, fanning the youth's resentment of his uncle, who was the second son of the previous generation, brother to Ling's deceased father. When Ling's father passed on, Uncle stepped forward to run the family because Ling had been a mere boy. Now however, Ling believed himself to be a man-grown, and he was sure his time to take his rightful place and be in charge of the family had arrived. His uncle did not agree, causing a rift between the two generations of Jings that Shang could leverage to benefit himself.

Along with the exotic dishes and drink, the silk merchant fed Jing Ling's ego, promising him support and loyalty within and without the family once he had married into it.

After a dinner of many courses and much rice wine, Ling had agreed to the match between Shang and Ling's younger sister.

When Ling woke the day after the dinner where he sealed Shang's agreement, he had a historic hangover. Uncertain of how events had progressed, Ling tried to remember what had been said and agreed to, beginning to question the promises he had made. Little Sister was precious to him, and though Shang had entertained him lavishly, the silk merchant's reputation was not that of a good man.

Ling was not, however, the only one having second thoughts about the arrangements that had been made.

Shang was not a patient person. Being the husband of the daughter of the Jing House would provide him with connections to society and additional wealth through the girl's dowery, but it did not give him the kind of power or wealth he craved. It was a step, but not nearly enough. But these were times of unrest in the region and another option had presented itself.

A change in the region's leadership could give the silk merchant the opportunity he sought, but he desperately needed to prove his value to the Qui, who were looking to replace the current Tonghou with their candidate but to earn a place of importance within the new regime once the old Tonghou fell, Shang needed to make himself invaluable. The problem was that he had neither sufficient wealth nor position to gain the rebel leader's respect or attention.

Once again, he invited Jing Ling to dinner.

"Outside the cronies within his court, this Tonghou has no support," Shang told Ling as if sharing a great confidence. "He has lived in the palace his whole life, and his father, and grandfather before him and he is out

Jolie opened her eyes, remembering her dream about Jing Ling and the silk merchant, Shang, Uncle Jing, and Jing Ling's Little Sister.

The old monk in the temple had called the little demon, Jing Ling, challenging him by asking why he did not recognize himself. There was only one explanation: Jolie was seeing visions of the demon's human life--a life that the demon did not remember--or did not want to admit to remembering.

But why was she being shown these bits of his former life? Was what the demon said about not being able to pass the protective flags around the lodge grounds a message that he was not as contrite and changed as he pretended? Under all the talk, was the little demon playing her? Maybe the flags had rejected him simply because he was still a demon. Maybe working on being reformed was not enough to be viewed as being reformed in the spirit world and it would take something more before he was cleansed enough to be recognized as a positive spirit. Jolie certainly did not know how it worked.

Yanna Maria had been to lodges at Roses though and the flags had let her in. Yanna had come into the temple school and Sifu had not stopped her or confronted her. He accepted her, as he did everyone who came through the school's doors. If Sifu was the protector of the school and its students, how could he be so lax? Jolie had a lot of questions.

She got out her journal and began to sketch, using the manual focus as a distraction while her unconscious mind worked on her questions.

By evening's fall, the east sky over the strip had become a golden glow wiped in a haze above the city, the color intensifying as the sky darkened. She sensed the demon nearby, but as usual, he did not interrupt her journaling. He was just there, maintaining a silent presence.

After a while, Jolie put away her notebook and joined him on the ledge. They were in the blue shadows here on the East end of the mountain, a pre-twilight shadow while the sun was still a brilliant gold on the West side of the distant Sunrise Mountains.

"What are we doing here?" the demon asked, after some time in silence.

"We are not *doing*. We are just *being*," Jolie replied.

And so, they sat in silence, just *being*, alone together.

Jagged fingers of bright flame leaped into the night sky surrounding the Jing family home. The house servants clung together in the shadows. Outside the walls, the neighbors, and the town burned, screams blistering the air, scaring the minds of those forced to hear their death cries.

"Do not fear," First Son Ling said, trying to reassure them. "You are safe here. We will not be harmed. We have protection."

"How do we have protection?" Uncle appeared in his armor. The boiled leather suit's once vibrant colors had faded, the surface crisscrossed by the scars of blade slices and axe hacks from battles fought before Jing Ling was born. The leather straps extended and stretched over the elder Jing's large, barrel-like body. He was not the warrior he had once been.

He is not the man he had once been either, Ling thought. That is why I had to make this decision to save our family. If he was not so old and frightened of the world, my actions to save our family would not have been necessary. If Uncle respected me, as I deserved, we might have made decisions together. But he never listens to my ideas--never agrees with my decisions, always claiming I am too young and inexperienced to take my father's place as head of the family.

"How do we have protection from this attack, Ling?" Uncle repeated.

Ling lifted his chin, looking down his nose at his father's younger brother.

"I have made an arrangement." Uncle's angry silence demanded an explanation. "With Shang, the silk merchant. He agreed that if there was violence against the Jade Scepter Bearer, our property would not be harmed."

"Why would the silk merchant make such an agreement with my nephew?" Uncle demanded.

"He recognizes it is not in his interest for our family or property to suffer in this time of turmoil."

"Not in his interests? You borrowed money from the silk merchant without discussing it with me?"

"I am First Son. It is my right to make such decisions."

"He will take all of this away." Uncle's hand swept around to indicate the house and courtyard, but Ling knew that his uncle meant more; the orchards, the fields, the rice paddies, everything the Jing family owned.

"I tell you, Uncle, Shang has no interest in separating us from the sources of our power and wealth," Ling said, clinging to his newfound superiority. Uncle's eyes grew smaller as his suspicions grew larger.

"A man like Shang does not make agreements that do not benefit him. What did you offer him in return?" Ling did not answer, trying to keep the paper dragon he was riding on from crumbling. "What did you promise him, Ling?"

Jolie did not hear the answer because the dream ended, but the dream stayed with her all day.

Standing outside her cave retreat, Jolie had sung the sun up and was now focused inward. She practiced the three Qi Awakening forms that opened all classes at the temple school, moved on to the Taoist Seed Sounds that Sifu had given them a chart of, imagining her major chakra points growing larger and more open, cleared of life's emotional baggage.

The waterfall meditation, another simple practice she remembered well enough to be confident of, was next. Sifu's instructions were to sit in front of a source of running water for at least twenty minutes every day for thirty days, observing what you learned.

There was a creek flowing through the desert oasis at the foot of the basin's west cliffs. Early and late in the day, a chorus of frog song ratcheted above the desert grasses and small catches of water. Bighorn Sheep with their gold-marble eyes hugged the rocky mountainside, playing at being statues. Tortoises measured the meadow with their slow, steady, steps.

Here, Jolie began her thirty-day practice. She would be somewhere else before she finished, but it was a good start.

The final practice Jolie wanted to incorporate was a meditation Sifu called the Microcosmic Orbit.

"That's not its real name," the master teacher had explained. "It's a Westernized label given to the practice when the immigrant Taoist teachers decided that so much of the old knowledge had been lost in the political and cultural wars in China, that they needed to teach to a broader population. That is when they began teaching this rare practice to outsiders. Before that, many practices had not been openly taught outside the temples of China. Some had only been taught to high-level initiates. We have been given permission to teach them now."

Sifu himself had only been accepted by his first teacher because of the master's compassion for a poor, sickly, mixed-heritage boy growing up in a tough neighborhood. That boy had gone on to start one of the most prominent temple schools on the West Coast, his students spreading across the country.

Often, during the day, Jolie thought about the demon and wondered about his past as Older Brother, Jing Ling. He claimed not to remember having had a name before, or a life, but Jolie could not imagine the old monk being wrong. Was the Ling in Jolie's dreams the demon she knew? The creature insisted that he and the Jing Ling the monk spoke of, were not connected. He got twitchy and disappeared when she tried to talk to him about it. But if there was no connection, why was she having these dreams?

Flickering torchlight cast splintered light over men stealthily approaching the base of a hill below an elegant palace. Creeping silently through the forest, two dozen men followed Jing Ling to a vine-covered entrance. Seeing it, Jolie's breath caught. It was a secret entrance, known only to the Tonghou, and his most trusted allies-- the old families who had been loyal to the Jade Scepter Bearer for generations. Observing the dream, Jolie could not say how she knew this, only that she did.

When the vines were cleared, the entrance to an underground tunnel was revealed. Old tunnels, beneath the oldest sections of the original structure above. Ling knew of them because the Jing family had been among the Tonghou's retinue for as long as they had ruled the region.

Standing in the carved tunnel listening to the cries of those in the palace above, Ling felt ill. Shang had promised his men would avoid shedding the blood of innocents in the palace.

"What I am hearing is merely a skirmish," Ling made excuses. "The palace guards have attacked Shang's men, and they were forced to defend themselves." But Ling's confidence in his judgment of this new ally was dying alongside the palace servants.

"I should not have trusted Shang." He pushed away the memory of how he had spoken harshly to Little Sister for saying these same words. "I should not be here. I cannot be." Ling ran from the sounds of clashing swords, and the screams of women and people dying in the palace above. "Because of what I have done."

Hurrying from the tunnels, through the forest, then through the city streets, Ling closed his fears and shame behind the heavy wooden gates of his family's estate. His mistakes felt like a heavy rock in his stomach.

"I will not tell Uncle about this," he promised himself. "I will not tell anyone. Ever."

Precious days passed. When Jolie was not practicing meditation, she was hiking the basin, drawing, writing down her thoughts, or just sitting and letting the stillness fill the empty places that so many losses had left within her.

Sometimes the demon would appear and they would talk about questions or philosophies that helped answer those questions. He was learning very fast now.

"I study when you are asleep," he explained. "And I am not confined to teachers alive today in this realm. You were right. Lu Dongbin is a very good teacher," the demon Jolie thought of as Ling proclaimed proudly.

"Now, I learn from you," Jolie teased him.

But she continued to wonder about what she was being shown in her dreams and what, if anything, this story had to do with the little demon. If the Jing Ling in her dreams was the demon, how had he been changed? And why could he not remember?

Thoughtfully chewing the cut-up vegetables Rose had left for her, Jolie asked one night, "Do you think you are a Hungry Ghost?"

"What is this Ghost who is hungry?"

"It's a belief some Asian cultures have. People make offerings to their deceased relatives, so their spirits feel cared for and don't get angry and cause the family harm."

"I am not a ghost at all," the demon replied, offended.

"But are you actually a demon, or is that just a label someone gave you?"

"You ask strange questions, Jolie Boulet. I have no family and I have no longing for a human life."

"But what if you did have a family and a life once, a long time ago?"

"I think I would remember," the demon replied stubbornly.

"Maybe you wouldn't. You had a name, and you didn't remember that. It only makes sense that you had a life to go with it."

"I did not," the demon insisted petulantly.

"But isn't that what the old monk was saying?" Jolie persisted.

"No."

"Well, not exactly—not in words…"

"If he did not say it in words then he did not say it," Ling made his position clear.

"But it's what he was inferring when he asked you 'how you could not know yourself'…"

"I. Never. Had. A family," Ling said, separating each word to make this meaning perfectly clear before he disappeared.

"Right." Jolie was sorry to upset the little demon, but she was increasingly convinced that there was a purpose behind her dreams, and it had to do with the demon's evolution. He needed to remember the circumstances around how he came to be who and what he was, recognize the mistakes that got him here, and come to terms with them.

A breeze tickled Jolie's cheek.

"It is attached to you, this spirit," the whisp of air tonged wisdom into her ear. Was it the voice of the old monk or some spirit of the basin? She was not experienced enough to know. Just to be safe, she drew up energy from the stones beneath her and drew a circle of protection around her before answering the spirit's question.

"No. The spirit is free--free to make its own choices," she informed whatever was attached to the voice.

"And it chooses to follow you."

"Because freedom is new for it and it doesn't yet know where else to go," Jolie explained. "But in time it will grow braver and wish to explore. Then it will leave." She had never raised anything before--except a stray cat that had left after a few days.

"The lad is rich with memories here," the gentle voice pivoted. *"The echoes of many prayers… the shadows of a host of ancient spirit-beings."* Jolie felt a tingle climb her bones as the disembodied spirit on the wind's focus returned to her. *"I hear you sing the sun up*

and down. It is good. It pleases our dragonfly friends as well."

When she sang at sunrise and sundown the dragonflies came, circling her head, as if her song had called them. Sometimes they came when she meditated too, landing nearby and resting, soaking in the waves created by the meditation.

"I don't know why I sing. It just feels right," Jolie explained with a sigh.

"You sense what is right, and by observing, and trusting your instincts, the spirit who was Ling gains confidence to do the same, rediscovering the strength of his own heart."

"So, it is Ling's life I've been seeing in my dreams? Older Brother is Ling?"

"Does it matter? The past is gone," the voice sidestepped answering.

"But the stories of our lives shape who we are," Jolie disagreed.

"Do they? Your history with this demon might indicate his spirit to be of questionable intent. How is it you are you not frightened of the demon?"

Jolie shook her head. "I was once, but he's changed, and I see who he's become--who he is becoming."

"So, though you believe our past molds your character, you also believe that change is possible, even for the most misguided?" Jolie frowned but she had to admit she agreed. *"Your dreams have shown you Ling's past so you can better understand his challenges and help him. In time, regaining his memories will either awaken him completely or destroy him like a poison fog. Either way, he will need a true friend.* The spirit changed its focus. *"Ah, look, the sun is going down. Time to sing."*

The dragonflies began to arrive, and Jolie took up her drum.

CHAPTER FIFTEEN

Once again Jolie fell asleep and became witness to the Jing family's tragedy.

The fire, the smoke, the terror felt as real as if she were there. From whose perspective was she seeing this story? A servant? A disembodied spirit? She saw what Ling did, and felt what he did, but she also saw things Ling was seeing; the silk merchant Shang's plotting, the way the villagers reacted to the ambitious silk merchant, and now, how they reacted to Ling as well. Jolie, the dream observer longed to warn Ling of Shang's avarice and unreliability, but she could not speak to him. He could not hear her. Her role was to observe, not to become a player in the game.

"What did you promise the silk merchant, nephew?" Uncle stood in the courtyard like a warrior, feet planted wide apart. Behind him, fires scorched the night sky, the smoke of neighboring fires rolling over the Jing estate's stone walls. He could have been the model for the General Tsao statue at the temple school.

Ling's lower lip trembled; all his certainty shattered.

"Tell me, nephew!" his uncle bellowed.

Shame slipped off Older Brother's shoulders onto the ground. "I promised him Little Sister."

Uncle shook his head. "You must have given him more than that. Shang would not make such an agreement over a woman, even one as accomplished as Little Sister. What else did you give him?"

Ling had justified each action leading up to his betrayal of his lord, but those justifications dissolved, unspoken. His actions had been without honor.

"I am disappointed in you, Nephew," Uncle said as if he knew what Ling had done.

The bitter words gouged wounds in the raw scabs of Ling's self-doubt.

"We must leave here. We will go to the country house," Uncle raised his voice to command the household's evacuation. "Pack the wagons with what food and necessities you find near at hand and take anything you might use as a weapon. Warrior or not, we will fight for our lives tonight. We leave immediately."

"We will not leave!" Ling grasped at the tatters of his failing plan. "We do not need to go. You are not listening to me, Uncle. You never listen to me. We are safe here. Promises have been given."

Little Sister's handmaid screamed from the door of Little Sister's rooms.

"She is dead!" the woman wailed, wringing her hands. "My mistress is dead. She has killed herself!"

Uncle and nephew ran to Little Sister's open screen door.

Her delicate body hung from the rafter lifeless, like a silk banner on a windless day. A black lacquer chair with embroidered pillows lay sideways on the floor beneath her perfectly curled rose-bud feet.

"Little Sister has had her say on this matter. I hope you have heard her at last." Ling's uncle's face was a map of despondency. "An agreement is only as true as the men who make it. She would not sully her innocence and honor by becoming the wife of a man like Shang. I

tried to teach you this, nephew, but I failed. It is my shame as well that your sister has paid the price." His gaze ran over the disarray of the courtyard. "As have we all."

The shouting outside the house's confines was explosive, scrapes and thumps pulsing against the Jing House's thick wooden gates.

When the gates split open, men with weapons, blood staining their hands, faces, and clothing came in like a sewer, spreading through the courtyard, cutting down any member of the household they came across.

"You must run if you would live, nephew," Uncle cautioned Ling. "You are the last of our line. If you do not live, there will be no one left to honor our ancestors."

Uncle prepared to fight the attackers, knowing he would not live, knowing his sacrifice would save nothing but the ragged remnants of his honor.

But First Son Ling could not run. His legs would not carry him from the shame of his decisions.

"Little Sister." The stillness of her blue dressing gown and long, dark hair hanging limp and lifeless was an accusation of the brother she had held so dear. "My little sister, who was ever my joy and comfort. You warned me, but ego stopped my ears and I refused to hear your honest words," Ling confessed. "I wish I had listened to you, to Uncle, to anyone other than my foolish self. I have caused the ruin of our family. Our name will be cursed as betrayers for all the years we are remembered.

"And more, I have caused the deaths of those whom I love best and should have held most dear. I alone am responsible for this unthinkable tragedy." He ripped open his shirt. "I renounce my position as First Son, as Older Brother, as a member of the Jing family." Ling pulled the dagger from his belt. "This chest does not hold the heart

of a man. It holds the heart of a demon. I am not worthy of life as a human being. I must never be allowed to make decisions on my own again. From this day on, I will exist only as a lowly demon, subject to the will of others." He stabbed the knife into his chest slicing through the flesh and cutting out his heart.

Jolie sat straight up on the stone platform, screaming into the night, trembling with adrenaline from witnessing the horror in her dream.

Instantly, the demon was there.

"What is it? What is wrong, Jolie?"

"A dream." Tears burned her sunburned face. She could still feel Little Sister's spirit leaving the body hanging from the rafter, the unnerving weightlessness of suddenly becoming incorporeal, the pain of her brother's betrayal mingling with the love she still bore him. As her brother opened his chest, making his terrible vow, Little Sister wailed from the depths of her being, in an empty spirit's voice, and Jolie felt the dead sister's agony as her brother died, his spirit released from the flesh, dissolving as it entered the demon world.

"Don't leave me, Ling," Jolie begged the demon, wondering if the words were hers or Little Sisters. "Stay close, please."

"I am here, Little One," the demon promised. "I will always be here." He planted himself at the cave's entrance.

Jolie's wracking hiccoughs became fewer, her sniffling ending. She stopped shaking, but sleep remained a far distant thing.

I was Ling's Little Sister, she realized.

Sometime in the wee cold hours before dawn, her breath smoothed, falling into a restful sleeping pattern.

When Jolie woke to sing up the dawn, her eyes and lips were puffy and swollen, her heart heavy and filled with miseries borrowed and her own. If the demon, Ling, wondered what dream she had dreamed, he did not say, keeping silent vigil as he had promised.

Wraiths of confusion and despair born of a thousand questions haunted Jolie's mind. She had met the demon leading an ant-army of black urchin-like spirits summoned by a fool who had promised it a feeding feast of human energy. Jolie was not responsible for the death of that man, but she had played a part. She had played a part in the death of the demon's next host, Axel. It had pursued her for weeks, trying to force her to become its next master, finally taking Jessie Lynn instead. Then Jessie Lynn died, and Axel finally crossed over.

The demon left a trail of death behind it, but it was not only his trail. It was Jolie's as well.

And now he was trying to become a better being and beginning to remember his past. What did reawakening mean for a spirit who made such a terrible vow? Was it possible to come back from such guilt and shame? Would remembering help the demon, or finish him?

Once her daily practices were completed, Jolie finally broached the troubling questions circling her mind.

"You said you don't dream. Is that still true?" she asked.

"I do not lie to you, Jolie." He looked suspicious, but the answer was not a 'no.' "What makes you ask this question?"

"You used to chase me in my dreams."

"They were not dreams to me."

"So, you have no dreams? Not even waking visions of things that aren't happening where you are, but you still see them?"

"No." Ling was shocked. "This happens to you?"

"Sometimes," Jolie admitted.

"Humankind has many problems."

"It doesn't happen to all humans," Jolie clarified. "Some of us are just luckier than others."

"That was sarcasm?"

Jolie nodded. "Philosophers say that what we think of as our real lives, is only an illusion. That idea seems even stranger when you claim that what I experienced as a dream was not a dream for you."

"*The way of learning is none other than finding the lost mind,*" the demon quoted.

"What is that?"

"Meng-Tzu," the creature replied without hesitation.

"Who is Meng-Tzu?" Jolie asked, carefully.

The demon's strange little face went blank. "I do not remember."

"Do you come into my dreams now?" Jolie prodded.

Ling was offended. "Of course not."

"I ask because I think I've seen you there."

"It was not me."

"Or maybe it was a different you," Jolie suggested.

"There are not multiple me's, Jolie. There is only one," the demon insisted.

"I'm not sure the Taoists would agree. Last night, I had a very vivid dream--part of a dream I have been seeing pieces of for weeks now. In the dream, there is a brother and a sister." She told the story she had seen in her dreams, linking the episodes together to complete the full picture as she was given. "It is the oddest thing," she finished. "But the brother, Ling, feels so familiar--like I know him. Like I loved him. It feels like he was you."

"He could not have been," the demon declared quickly.

"I know. It seems impossible. He was a human who lived centuries ago, but his sister called him by the name Jing Ling, just like the monk."

"Then perhaps that is his name and not mine," the little demon argued. "The old monk said he liked to play games."

Jolie frowned. "You weren't in the dream with me when the monk told me that."

"I am always with you," the demon declared. "Where else would I be?"

"So, you *are* in my dreams then?"

The demon did not answer, but after some time he asked. "What did the boy call the girl?"

"Little Sister," Jolie replied.

The demon let out a heart-wringing wail, his round body collapsing over itself as it melted down into the sandstone. The rock swallowed his tortured cry.

Jolie sighed. There were some kinds of pain you had to work out alone.

Making choices requires that we accept responsibility for what we say and do," the wisdom voice whispered to Jolie. *"Some pieces of our lives are unbearable burdens. Some spirits, unable to carry the consequences of their choices, seek a path that relinquishes their free choice, giving all the responsibility for their actions to another, then another,*

*and another, lifetime after lifetime, until they forget they
ever lived any other way.* "

"Ling had a life, once," Jolie said. "He made terrible
mistakes, but given the chance, I know he can change.
With time and better people around him, he could have a
life again, couldn't he?"

The wisdom voice did not reply.

Jolie crawled up onto her bed, took up her journal,
turned on her flashlight, and began writing.

It was the end of the next day before Ling returned.
Jolie had climbed high up on the pink mountain, hiking
to a scouting point where she could see from Turtlehead
Peak in the northwest to the small township of Blue
Diamond in the southwest. Las Vegas Valley lay to the
east, its lights just beginning to hold their twinkle against
the blinding heat of the Nevada summer.

She was waiting for the sun to near the western
horizon, singing any tune that came into her head, an easy
vocable from the sweat lodges, all the lyric's heys and
yahs, the meaning of the prayer carried by the singer's
intent.

The dragonfly brigade frolicked in parade ribbons
around her head, riding the high mountain's air currents.
The last in line flicked its tail at the girl as if inviting her
to catch hold and Jolie reached out to catch the
dragonfly's tail, but it was too far away. She looked down
to the rocks below, feeling death's breath on her face.

"I can't fly with you," she told her winged friends.
"I'm human and I'll fall." Part of her wanted to believe
she could fly if only her belief was strong enough. Part of
her recognized the ease of giving up the struggle that was

her life. She held both truths simultaneously within her, with just enough reason remaining intact to keep her feet on the mountain.

"I would catch the dragon's tail, but I do not want to die," she said softly.

The demon appeared, waiting in expectant silence before finally speaking.

"You feel different here; calmer, clearer," it noted.

Jolie nodded. "There is something special about the energy of this place. Important truths seem so close I feel like I could pluck them out of the air, but maybe it's that we understand better when we stop all the noise and take time to listen." She held out a finger and a dragonfly landed on it.

"You should not listen to strange bugs," the demon cautioned her. "You never know who may have influenced them."

Jolie lifted a questioning eyebrow. "Influenced them?"

"Insects and small animals are very malleable."

A burro brayed far below. Jolie smiled, not pressing the demon, who was Ling, and therefore perhaps not a demon at all. She had learned this skill of silent-waiting from him.

"I am afraid, Jolie," he said finally.

"What are you afraid of?" His pause was so long she thought he had said all that he was going to, but he had not.

"I am afraid of remembering," the statement sounded like a doomsday prediction. "I am remembering--getting glimpses of a life I both do and do not recognize. Uncertainty makes me feel like vibrating glass about to shatter. For hundreds and hundreds of years, and through many masters, Certainty has been my armor, because certainty repelled the hard truths. It made me feel strong and invincible."

"Even though it was a lie?"

"The armor concealed the lie, so I did not need to face the truth."

Jolie smiled. "That's very philosophic for a demon."

"How many demons have you known?" it countered.

"I'm not sure. The one beside me does not seem much like the one I met at Solstice or who chased me through my dreams insisting I belonged to it."

"That was wrong of me."

"Yes, it was, "Jolie agreed. "How do *you* feel here?" There was a significant delay before the demon replied, the falling night stretching time to make space for honesty.

"Lonely." The demon's reply sounded like it had been dragged from the bottom-most mud muck of a graveyard.

Jolie felt a twinge of guilt. "But you're not alone. I'm here."

"For now. But you have a life before you. You have seen my life—who I was, what I did even before I had a master to blame for my actions. You know why I am what I am now, Jolie. You know how I betrayed you when you were my Little Sister. Why would you allow me to stay near you?"

"I don't think there is anywhere I could run where your demon powers couldn't find me," Jolie teased.

"You could banish me."

"You mean like, 'I banish you from my kingdom,'" Jolie played the role of a self-important royal making a decree. "You know I can't do that, don't you?" The demon said nothing, allowing Jolie to hear the answer he could not bear to speak aloud. "I *can?* But I wouldn't…Ling," the name felt right but the standalone promise of what she had just said might require some qualification. "I wouldn't unless you did something so terrible that I had to protect someone, or myself."

"I will never again knowingly do anything to hurt you, Jolie Boulet," the demon promised. "Not of my own free will. But what if I hurt you—or someone else by mistake? I have made so many mistakes." Jolie thought he was crying but she did not look, allowing him the dignity of privacy.

"You're not going to do that, Ling." It was hard for Jolie to think of a demon feeling fragile or frightened. What could possibly frighten a demon? She knew her refusal to bond him had challenged him, but she did not realize how hard his struggle for independence would be. Did parents go through this watching their children try to grow up? It seemed like the harder Ling struggled, the more Jolie wanted to jump in and fix things for him. But that felt like dishonoring his struggle and all the progress he had made.

"I am a spirit who for centuries has had one purpose, to be bonded and follow the will of those who held my bond. I can no longer be that. I don't want to go back to being that. But I do not know what I am now, or how to be something else."

"I don't know who or what I am yet either," Jolie confessed. "That's what growing up is all about. It takes time to learn about ourselves and how things should work. But at least we're not alone. We've got each other, right, my friend?"

The demon rolled back in surprise. "We are friends?"

"I guess… maybe." Jolie suddenly felt embarrassed. "It's not something one person decides for both."

"I have never had a friend before."

"Well, I haven't had very many," Jolie commiserated.

"You have lots of friends," the demon protested. "At school, and the Kung Fu boys at the temple place." He stopped, realizing that was the end of the list.

"There's a difference between people you hang out with and a true friend though," Jolie explained. "A true friend is someone who stands by you."

"Like the students from the school," Ling suggested.

"Yes, but there are a lot of things I wouldn't feel comfortable talking to the boys about. They don't see the world like I do, and that makes a barrier between us because not talking about the things that are important to you is a lie by omission and a person should feel like they can tell a true friend anything, even if it's weird or confusing. A real friend sees your strengths and weaknesses and doesn't judge you. They're patient with you while you're sorting things out, and they won't stab you in the back, I don't mean literally with a knife, though they wouldn't do that either, I mean they wouldn't try to do something hurtful on purpose."

"The Kung Fu boys do play with a lot of knives," the demon commiserated.

"And of course, if you want to have a true friend, you have to *be* a true friend and tell the truth--not just when it's easy but even when it's hard. You might have to tell your friend they're headed down a bad path and they might get mad at you and say you're not friends anymore, but you still have to do it."

"So, a true friend might hurt you?" the demon looked concerned.

"They might have to for your own good. Not everyone is brave enough to do that."

The demon thought about this. "That sounds very difficult."

"It is," Jolie agreed. "That's why most people only have a few true friends over a lifetime."

"I would like to have a friend like that. I would like to have you for a true friend, Jolie."

"I would like that too, Ling," Jolie agreed. It felt good to use his old name. "Is it okay to call you that?"

"I am trying it on, like a pair of new pants in the store dressing rooms."

"What do you know about store dressing rooms?" Jolie demanded, laughing.

"I find clothing to be an interesting phenomenon," Ling replied. Together they sat on the ledge as the night wrapped the basin in a soft, satin stillness.

A demon on a leash, Jolie chuckled to herself. Only there was no leash here, no master, and no slave, only the trust building between two friends.

CHAPTER SIXTEEN

With her sudden departure from Bozovics, Jolie needed to work out an unexpected absence at the restaurant extending her days off, but the time had come for her to leave Red Rock and return to the world.

Knowing Rose would try to talk her out of staying in the city, Jolie left her friend a note beside the sleeping bag and camp mat thanking her for everything and letting Rose know that if she needed to get in touch, she could contact the restaurant.

Leaving Calico Basin before the day's temperatures rose into the triple digits, Jolie got back to town well before her shift. With nothing else to do, she went by the temple school on the off chance that one of her friends would be there.

The front door was locked but mellow jazz trickled out of the back-alley door like sun-warmed honey.

"Hello?" Jolie called out. "Is anybody here?"

No one answered, but the music kept playing. Someone was inside.

It was strange to be at the school when there were no classes, and it was not filled with the boisterous energy of students. Oddly though the building did not feel empty. History emanated from Taoist and Buddhist statuary, pictures, and spiritual items on the large altar. Jolie walked the walls looking more closely at the traditional weapons and tapestries, straining her neck to look up at the ever-present paper mâché lion heads--retired from use by the Lion Dance team --hung from the loft's edge.

Being at the school off-hours allowed her to casually explore areas she had never been in, the small kitchen adjacent to the larger crafting and dining area. The walls here had low cupboards with counter space on top. Three long tables filled the open floor space. Every flat surface had a lion head in some stage of repair on it, along with tools to make those repairs: wide paintable tape, paint, brushes, and glue.

The Lion Dance team represented the school, performing at celebrations, cultural events, traditional Chinese holidays, and festivals throughout the Las Vegas area and into California. They also helped train and support a sister school in Mexico. Their efforts were a major source of income for the school and generated a lot of goodwill within the community.

As Jolie came around the end of a table, she discovered a large, red, lacquered, Chinese drum weighing down spread-out newspapers on the floor. There was a chair in front of it, paints and brushes arrayed on the end of the table near at hand. Half painted on the leather drumhead was a golden dragon, the original artwork on a sheet of paper on the floor beside it. It was very detailed with a lot of flowing red, green, and white lines in the design. Jolie was admiring it when Rance came out of a back storeroom and stopped, startled.

"Oh, hello. Sorry. I didn't realize anyone else was here."

"I just--the back door was open so…. I just stopped by." *So lame.* "I work at the…across the street" Jolie indicated the restaurant.

"Right. You're Remy's and Hugo's friend, Jolie? I've seen you. I'm Rance."

"I know." Of course, she knew. Everyone knew Rance. Next to Sifu, he was the most well-known face at the school. "We haven't exactly been introduced, but we have sort of met, on the mountain at the Ridge Walking Ceremony," Jolie reminded him. Rance had been in charge of security that night, overseeing selected Kung Fu students tasked with keeping outsiders from climbing the mountain and getting in the way of the ceremony. The Kung Fu kids had all been dressed in black pants, shirts, and hoods with glow-in-the-dark skeletons painted on them, but even in that costume, you couldn't miss Rance's thin six-foot-plus frame and confident air. Sifu counted on him. The younger boys idolized him.

"I remember," the martial artist replied simply. Jolie didn't think she'd ever heard him say more than half a dozen words at a time, except when he was teaching.

"Is this your work?" she asked, indicating the dragon on the drum. Rance nodded. "You're good. But why does the dragon have antlers?"

"It's a Chinese dragon." Rance resumed his seat at the drum. "That's how you can tell a Chinese dragon from a European one."

Jolie gave him a skeptical look. "Antlers?"

"They're not literal antlers. They're symbolic. Have you ever watched a deer jump over a fence? They go almost straight up like they're defying gravity." He took up his paintbrush and a pallet of paints and started painting in the penciled sketch on the leather. "The old Taoists *saw* that energy and recognized it as Qi. Deer shoot Qi up through their bodies and out their antlers to make themselves super light. The antlers on a Chinese dragon represent Qi rising through it. Watch a deer sometime and you'll see. But, of course, to *see* the energy like the old Taoist Masters takes practice."

"Got it." Jolie tried to brush off the young man's condescension. If she had not been fresh from days of meditation in Red Rock, she might have resented it, but as it was, she just smiled.

"Did you ever see the old Kung Fu television series?" Rance asked. Jolie shook her head. "There are some weird things about it because, you know, it was made in the 70's and even though Bruce Lee started the project he was pushed out and the people who took over didn't know what to do with it. But politics and prejudices aside, there are some good teachings in it. That guy up there?" Rance pointed to one of the pictures of the school's lineage masters. "He trained the lead actor and choreographed some of the fight sequences. If you know who you're looking for, you can see him in shots or watch for his name in the credits. The master didn't much like the lead actor--a white guy playing a half-Asian monk-- and when Bruce Lee was pushed out of the project there were a lot of bad feelings as you can imagine. But Sifu was the guy up there's student at the time, so he ended up being the one who taught the actor most of the time." Rance continued to paint smooth lines on the leather hide as he talked.

"Sorry, that must have seemed like a big sidetrack but there is a connection. In the opening of the TV show, the character, Kwa Chang Kaine, walks barefoot over rice paper without leaving a trace. You have to use Qi to make yourself light--like the deer--to do that. There are forms we teach here at the school that teach you how to do that but...

"It takes a lot of practice," Jolie finished his sentence.

If this was Rance's version of a pickup line, it was pathetic, but Jolie didn't get the vibe that the young man was interested in her that way. What did he know about her? Anything? What had Sifu said? Nothing probably. Sifu was another one who did not talk much.

Jolie walked around the room, trying to shuck off the nerve tickle that had come with remembering the night of the Ridge Walking Ceremony. Empty beverage cups, dishes, and take-out containers littered the kitchen.

"You spend a lot of time here?"

"I live in the loft--the room across from Sifu's office." Rance tossed his head toward the loft above. "It's as close to temple life as I can get right now. In return, I teach classes, clean, answer phones and texts, maintain the website, and the demo gear--whatever the school needs."

"That's cool." Jolie crossed off the school as a potential place to crash.

"If you're interested in knowing more about the school's lineage and the principles it's founded on, there's a library just outside the office door. There's no manga or graphic novels, just old-school philosophy books. I know a lot of you kids don't read these days, but it's what we have."

More condescension. "I read," Jolie said.

"Great. Well, help yourself." Rance continued painting.

Jolie meandered a bit then took the stairs to the loft.

The small bookcase beside the office door was full of thick books on philosophy, martial arts, history, and religion: "The Autobiography of a Yogi", "Tibetan Yoga," and books on Taoism and China. Jolie chose a book on Buddhism, plopped down in the bean bag chair beside the bookshelf, opened the book at random, she began to read.

"When I speak of the 'initiated, I do not mean the dogmatically initiated, those who are initiated as priests

of a sect. I refer to the naturally initiated, artists, and those who are creative, who know how to open up and listen to the wisdom of the natural world."

Jolie felt struck by the idea. The philosopher was saying that he believed creative people heard and accepted spiritual teachings and enlightenment more readily because of how their brains were wired. It was a unique intersection of philosophy, new science, and Jolie's own experiences.

She kept reading.

Much of what was in the book was hard to understand the first time you read it, but the depth of the ideas was far beyond the pop culture versions Sifu had been doling out in Spiritual Warrior class. Jolie understood the teaching strategy; Sifu used pop culture references to make the information more relatable to modern students which kept them coming back. Eventually, if they stayed long enough, they would seek more serious information. But Jolie was not looking for spiritual mini-bites. She was starving. What she needed was a banquet. She continued to read as students began arriving for class. Their chatter barely pierced her awareness as she focused.

She was still reading when it was time for her shift. "Can I keep this until I'm finished?" She held up the book for Rance to see.

"Of course." He stood, taking off a paint-spattered overshirt, revealing his Kung Fu uniform beneath. "Come back tomorrow if you want and I'll show you a few practices to help with meditating."

"I will," Jolie promised. She did not know where she would sleep tonight, but she would be back. There were things at this school she glimpsed and she wanted more.

It was not difficult for Jolie to find someplace to sleep, though she knew none of the options could be permanent. The first few nights she pretended to leave the restaurant after her shift, but didn't, waiting until the manager locked up before curling up on the vinyl bench seat of the large corner booth. When the manager returned in the morning she hid until she could slip out, then headed across the street to the school.

A week was as long as she felt safe gambling on being discovered, so after five days, she began to scope out a new place finding a cozy, girl-sized space behind the large Buddha statue on the ground floor of the mini-mall. It was not as private as the restaurant, but the lobby area where the statue was placed was large and had little traffic, and once the doors were locked there was no one there until morning.

Mister Yinchen was in charge of opening and closing the mall's doors, though Jolie thought he might have noticed her one morning when she peeked out from behind the statue, he said nothing to reveal her.

Life fell into a pattern. She ate on her breaks at the restaurant, took extra shifts whenever she could, and spent as much time as she could reading texts or studying at the school with Rance. She had never been very physical and Rance's lessons were demanding, but she was too excited by what she was learning to let fatigue and sore muscles slow her down.

She was not Rance's only private student, however, and while he taught others, she listened in, worked around the school, read, or sometimes caught a nap on the bean bags pushed together to make a bed.

One day she noticed a middle-aged student give Rance a wad of bills and realized she should be paying him for all the time he was giving her. Her lack of any means to do that raised red flags for her. Did Rance have expectations that would come into play once she felt deeply indebted to him? She did not like the thought.

"I can't pay you, you know," she faced the issue head-on after one of his private students left. "Maybe I could save up something if I make enough tips but--I don't know how much I owe you."

"Our lessons are not that kind of arrangement," Rance informed her, unconcerned.

"What kind of an arrangement are they?" Jolie asked, not satisfied by his evasive answer.

"Our own kind."

Jolie stared him down. "I don't like owing people."

"You don't owe me anything, Jolie. I offered to teach you knowing you could not pay."

"Why?"

"Because I heard you knock on the door," he replied, cryptically.

"I don't know what that means."

"Traditionally, in China, students presented themselves to the temple they wished to join and knocked on the gates to request entry. If a student was from a wealthy family, it was easier to be accepted because someone would pay the temple for the privilege of the student being there, but those students were often light on commitment and lacked natural ability. Still, the donations they brought in helped feed the temple community, so the arrangements had value.

"Common folk, however, could not pay like the wealthy. So supplicants without wealthy families approached the gates, knocked, and waited. Sometimes they waited for days, through rain, wind, snow, or heat. The temple elders observed the supplicants, evaluating their behavior while they waited, and marking their character, patience, compassion, and commitment. If it was decided they were worthy, eventually the gates opened for them and they were invited in, but only if they passed the test."

Jolie frowned. "I wasn't knocking."

"I think you were," Rance disagreed.

"But if I didn't know I was knocking, how could I have passed any test?"

"You try hard not to be seen, Jolie, but for those who can *see*, you shine like a full moon. You have a great thirst for knowledge and understanding. So, I opened the gate."

A few days later Rance left the costume room at the school open, and Jolie got a peek inside. There were two rows of racks along each wall, old wood chests of drawers along the walls behind them, and stacked totes full of costume trims, paint, and sequins. A large pile of yellow satin lay on the floor under some of the costume racks. The room smelled of stale sweat, dry cleaning chemicals, cheap satin, and dust but the room was quiet, seldom used, and luxuriously private.

Jolie watched Rance put the key away and that night, as classes ended, she returned to where he had hung it and pocketed the key. After opening the door, she replaced the key before sneaking back in and locking the costume room's door behind her.

Jolie piled the yellow satin material tossed on the floor under the costume racks, tucking the green, white, and red trim along the dragon's serrated spine under the softer parts before crawling on top. She snuggled down with a sigh.

"There are lots of pretty clothes in here," Ling's voice commented from the darkness. "Are we going to stay?"

"Maybe. If it's safe and works out." She could hear him nearby rustling among other bits of satin material. "Would you like that?" she asked him sleepily.

"If it's safe and works out," he repeated her words back to her. "I do like it here at the temple school though," he added. "The spirits are friendly, and they know things."

Jolie smiled in the darkness. "You're making friends?"

"Maybe. I do not know yet if they are true friends or not. I will have to wait and see how they behave, but they will never replace you, Jolie," he said as she drifted off.

It was weird, but what Ling said made her feel good--mostly. He was growing up so fast and making new friends. Soon he would outgrow her and leave to follow his path. And why wouldn't he? That's what she had been telling him to do for months now. Still, secretly, she just wasn't sure that was what she wanted anymore. What she did want was not to be alone.

What would it be like to be loved, protected, and supported, like other kids? But other kids had families. All she had was a demon.

CHAPTER SEVENTEEN

Recognizing that Jolie's interests leaned toward the spiritual and energetic practices of Taoism, Rance began his third week of Jolie's instruction with a seldom taught practice: Bagua.

Beginning with the footwork used for stepping the Bagua circle, a pole was set up in the center of the circle to represent the Tree of Life. Rance modeled the eight Mother Forms that a practitioner cycled through while tracing the circle around the tree, reviewing what he taught Jolie to check for understanding, repeating the process until he thought she had it. Finally, he announced she was ready to put all the pieces together. Rance took up a position opposite Jolie and both began to slowly circle.

Within seconds, Jolie's consciousness whooshed out of the top of her head like some cosmic hotel maid had vacuumed up her brain.

Rance and the practice room disappeared.

Jolie was in a moonlit courtyard dominated by an ancient, gnarled tree so broad its branches shaded the stone pavement beneath it from the moonlight.

The skinny old monk from her dreams was tracing the circle around the tree, his arms extended in the first of the Mother Forms. After completing the circle, he began the second of the eight forms, stepping up into the air and circling over the top of the tree. Continuing, he moved down and disappeared beneath it, reappearing on the opposite side, repeating the cycle. A silver, glittering substance lingered in the air where the old Wisdom had passed, glimmering lines shimmering around the tree like a snow globe.

"The Bagua is not just a circle around the trunk of the tree. It's three-dimensional--a circle in every direction," Jolie realized.

"Jolie! Jolie! Are you alright?" Rance's worried voice shattered the vision. As abruptly as she had been swept away, she was dropped back into the school's practice room.

Jolie wavered on the circle's outline, then melted to her knees, her mind a dizzy fog. Rance was beside her.

"What happened?" he demanded.

After a few false starts, Jolie replied, "I was in a courtyard in a stone temple," her voice sounded faint and far away. "It was night, and an old man--a monk whom I'd seen before in my dreams, was doing Bagua around a huge old tree. Only he wasn't just going around it walking on the ground, he went up, and over, and under it—showing me that the circle was three dimensional." She turned to him. "Did you see it too?" she asked.

Rance sat back on his heels. "No. I couldn't see anything but you going Zombie," he admitted.

The way the young martial artist was looking at her made Jolie wonder if there might be negative consequences to her sharing this vision.

Too late.

"You're not going to tell me I imagined it?" she asked.

"Would you believe me if I did?" Rance asked.

"No."

"Then there wouldn't be much point unless I was going to try and undermine your confidence and keep you from trying some practice I didn't think you were ready for, or I wanted to establish my greater knowledge so you would defer to my wisdom. I'm not that kind of teacher or person. But I have to say, Jolie, that I am beginning to question my ability to teach you."

That was not an outcome Jolie anticipated. "Please don't stop teaching me, Rance. It's been helpful, and I am so grateful. I've felt lost and alone most of my life, trying to find some version of the world where I fit--some explanation that includes me as I am, but experiences like mine have been kept in the shadows and shoved into dark cracks between places for centuries. Most of us never find a genuine teacher. Finding someplace like this school is a gift--not the kicking and punching so much, but the spiritual stuff--it's rare and special."

Rance stood. "I can share the forms and practices that the Taoists have developed to access and deepen abilities that people call 'psychic', Jolie, but your skills are quickly going beyond what I can teach you. You already do things I can't."

"Is that a problem? You do things I can't," Jolie announced straightforwardly.

"You're going to have questions I can't answer. I don't want you to get disillusioned because I can't give you the answers you need."

It sounded like Rance was channeling her talking to Ling, and she finally understood Ling's need for support and his frustration with her refusal to give it, because she thought perfect understanding was the prerequisite of having anything to offer.

"I won't," Jolie agreed. When she needed answers, she wouldn't go to Rance.

"Okay. We'll try Bagua again tomorrow." Rance turned his focus to the students just coming in. "Okay, let's line up for Damo's Temple exercises."

"Are you awake?" Ling woke Jolie.

"No," she mumbled. "That's usually what it means when it's the middle of the night and my eyes are closed. What's up?" She sat up, rubbing her eyes.

Ling shrugged his shoulders. He had shoulders now; arms and legs too, becoming less blob-like by the day.

"I have made a decision," the demon declared.

"What's that?" Jolie yawned.

"I love you and I want to spend this life of yours by your side."

Wow. Jolie was stunned. She had admitted to herself that she didn't want him to leave her alone, but she had not said anything to him, and she certainly had not expected this.

"This isn't Buffy the Vampire Slayer. There's no future in us, Ling. We've talked about this, and I think I've been clear; I won't bond you," she chose her words carefully.

"Don't belittle my feelings to avoid your own, Jolie," the demon chided her. "I am not talking about bonding or a romantic attachment. This is about friendship and more, it is about the kinship between us. I care what happens to you. Not in the self-serving way that Axel cared what happened to your mother because she provided him with a body to work through but because your existence in this world matters to me."

Jolie blinked. "That's…sweet."

Ling clutched his chest as if there was a physical heart there and it ached. "With the return of my memories has come *feelings,* shame, self-anger, fear, guilt, loss

…and I do not know what to do with them," he whispered, his voice a tortured gravel.

"A lot was going on there at the end before you and Little Sister died.

"I *could* have protected her," Ling flared "I should have, but I did not because my thoughts were selfish. Everything I did as Jing Ling was based on my stubborn pride. I was twisted by my desire for recognition and Little Sister's life was sacrificed."

"Ling's as well," Jolie said quietly.

"No punishment could ever be enough for such a betrayal."

"I think hundreds of years in bondage, forced to do another's wills might be," Jolie suggested.

"Robbing Little Sister of her life cannot be balanced out by robbing more people of their lives."

"They were not all good people."

"And they were not all bad ones," Ling countered. "If I could, I would have cut my soul out like I cut out my heart," Ling declared.

"And instead, your soul is rediscovering itself, learning to take actions that are helpful instead of destructive. Little Sister loved Older Brother," Jolie said gently. "She would not want him to keep on suffering."

"The pain will never leave me."

"Probably not, but you can use it to inform who you become, Ling. Little Sister forgave you before she died. Isn't it time you forgave yourself?"

"I do not know how." The little demon sniffled.

"One step at a time," Jolie said. "I don't know how any other way unless you give up." That was not Jolie's way. Ling looked at her with trust and determination. It was not his way either.

CHAPTER EIGHTEEN

Jolie was coming down the stairs from the school's loft when a half dozen teenage boys and a couple of twenty-somethings swaggered through the main doors. They were followed into the main practice room by two middle-aged male Latinos. Something about their energy made Jolie stop. One of the adult men looked strangely familiar.

"Where's your Sifu?" the other older man demanded in a booming voice. "I want to talk to him."

The younger temple students looked around at each other, alarmed by the clear aggression in the declaration.

The temple school's older teens reacted by sauntering forward and placing themselves several lines deep between the younger students and the intruders. All of them parted for Rance as he strode forward. The movement of his tall, muscular frame was a declaration of command.

"Sifu isn't here right now," he spoke politely without being deferential. "But you may speak to me. I will pass your message on to the Master." The contrast with the older man's rudeness immediately cast the uninvited guest in a poor light.

One of the teens in the intruders' group snorted. The older man used a cautionary hand on the youth's arm to stay his volatile temper.

Rance's eyes went to the cocky teen, staring him down with his cool strength. Eventually, the boy looked away, unable to bear the silent humiliation.

"We're here to declare a formal challenge between our schools," the short, muscle-bound Latino announced.

Rance's eyebrows rose. "A traditional formal challenge? Lion Dancers, swords, staves, iron fist…dragons?"

The other man's eyes bugged.

He can't afford all the equipment for that, Jolie realized. She did not know where this other school had come from. She had never heard it mentioned. Whatever its roots were, it appeared to have gone completely under the temple school's radar.

"We are not…"

"A traditional school?" Rance finished for him. "No, you are a new school, small and just starting, set up in a storefront. It is a good place to start though. Did you get the welcome gift we sent you for your opening?" Rance knew of the new school's existence which meant Sifu did also.

"We did." The man once again looked shamefaced.

"What are you talking about, Rance?" Brutus pushed forward. "They're luring gullible kids by promising to teach them stupid stuff like 'poison thumb'."

The man in charge of the rival school glanced nervously back at the students behind him.

Rance gave Brutus a look and made a subtle hand gesture warning him to back off and be quiet.

"This school *is* a traditional school," Rance pointed out. "Perhaps, after thinking about it, you might reconsider the wisdom of such a challenge so soon after opening? We are well thought of here in Chinatown, recognized regionally and internationally. There is a reason masters from other countries visit here. There is no shame in recognizing such a challenge might be premature in timing."

"Your reputation is based on doing splashy demonstrations, that's all," the cocky kid who spoke up before blurted out.

"Your school is old and tired, like your Sifu," the other Latino adult who looked familiar to Jolie added. "You don't teach real fighting, only Wu Shu."

"We follow the lineage passed down to us from masters who learned their art at Won Lung Kwan and Wu Dong temples." Rance indicated the wall of lineage pictures to his right. "Our school, our Sifu, and our lineage are well-known and respected. But though your school's lineage is not equal, and we hate to embarrass you before your students, we will not turn away from a challenge if you are determined to go forward. Please understand that such an event is a combat on every level, spiritual and physical, external and internal, and you cannot defeat us."

The energy in the room pulsated testosterone rioting among the young men on both sides, aggression about to be loosed. Tempers were being held back, but barely.

"Anyone can hang pictures on a wall. After we win, we will see who the community supports." The banty rooster leader of the rival school planted his feet and thrust out his chest. "In a year this school won't exist." The stocky man turned and reversed his entrance, his students folding in their ranks as they followed him out the door.

"Wow. Was that for real?" Brutus said as Jolie joined her friends on the practice room floor. "That was like something out of an old Kung Fu movie." He puffed himself up and used a silly voice, imitating the leader of the challenger's group. "Our school is better. Fight us and be shamed."

"Who cares about that stuff anymore? If you like a school, you go there. If you don't, you go somewhere else," Hugo said.

"Sifu and the Board of Directors, that's who," Jiu piped up. "We're in a huge space in the middle of Las Vegas' Chinatown, Bru. Think about it. The school can't afford the rent on this building." The other kids looked to Rance for confirmation.

"It's true. The school has been here for years because of the goodwill of the Chinese community and the downtown merchants. They pay the rent as cultural support and to help the kids and families who come to study here. Sifu is very involved with local Prevention efforts for youth, the Youth Task Force, and the Juvenile Probation Department."

That's his link to Wrangler, Jolie realized.

"He also takes care of the community in other ways-spiritual ways," Rance went on. "Half the students here can't afford class, but we never turn anyone away." Jolie felt like he looked at her when he said that. "Why do you think we do so many Lion Dance blessings at Chinese New Year--and any other time the community asks? We perform at every store opening and cultural event. Those contracts, and the merchant's generosity, are what keeps the school open, not class fees."

"So, what does that mean with this new school moving in?" Jolie asked.

"Nothing?" Rance shrugged. "These small schools come and go. Someone gets excited about what they've learned and opens a school. Then they find out how much work it is to keep the doors open, and they close."

"But they're dissing us, Rance!" Brutus declared. "They're trying to cut us out, and themselves in by showing the community we're not as good as we once were. But we are."

"We are," Rance agreed.

"Is there really something called poison thumb?" Jolie asked.

"No! Yes!" different students declared simultaneously, their declarations overlapping.

"That dude's a pretender," Brutus insisted.

"I remember him," Jiu said. "He was a student here for a while last year. He told Sifu he came here because he had taken martial arts training in the military and studied in different places where he was stationed, but he never got any of the internal stuff."

"Without it, you can never really be a top-tier fighter," Brutus declared.

"So, this guy doesn't teach the spiritual side?' Jolie asked for clarification.

"No, just kicking and punching," Jiu answered.

"Which is why we're the best school," Brutus boasted. The three friends did an elaborate hand, arm, elbow, belly, boys club secret greeting.

"Okay, the excitement's over," Rance announced. "Line up for class."

That night Sifu gave a lecture at Spiritual Warrior class about Taoists and their demon-allies, complete with pictures of old wall hangings and paintings of The Eight Immortals and other famous sages being followed around by monsters looking like they had been plucked out of the children's book, "Where the Wild Things Are".

"Flipping a demon spirit from an evil nature to becoming an ally, focused on acting for the benefit of humankind and enlightenment, is considered the highest level of achievement for a Taoist," Sifu explained.

Did Sifu know about Ling? Had he seen the little demon lurking about? Was he saying that Jolie should be making Ling into an ally? That sounded awfully like bonding him and she could not believe Sifu wanted her to do that. So, what was he telling her to do?

She cornered Rance as soon as class ended.

"I need to talk to Sifu."

Rance gestured to the man. He was surrounded by parents and students all wanting a moment of his time.

"Privately," Jolie insisted.

"Good luck. Everyone wants to see Sifu privately."

"Does Sifu know you are teaching me?" she asked Rance.

"I assume so. Not much goes on here that he doesn't notice."

"What you've been teaching me is great, but I need more." Rance looked at her questioningly. This was probably the moment she should explain about Ling and the weird history of what had been happening to her over the past seven months--what was still happening with Yanna Maria and her efforts to capture Ling--but she couldn't get the words out.

"You do Bagua and get teleported into a vision. No one can beat you at Sticky Hands because you read them. I'm teaching you forms and philosophies I've never taught any other student. What more is it you think you need, Jolie? And why the sudden urgency?" Rance studied her and Jolie wondered what he read on her face. Did he know she was hiding something? Would he call her on it?

"I don't know," Jolie assured him, perhaps a little too quickly. "My mom and I moved a lot, so I've never been able to stay in one place for long, even if I wanted to. I guess I just want to learn everything I can in case I don't get this chance again."

It was the truth, if only part of it, but Rance accepted it, as she hoped he would. Like Sifu, the young Kung Fu master believed the best in people--all people. It took an obvious betrayal before either of them addressed it for what it was, and even then, their reactions were compassionate and forgiving, free of judgment and condemnation. It kind of drove Jolie crazy. In her mind, people who did the wrong thing needed to experience the negative consequences of their actions or they would never learn. Sifu's path of compassion gave transgressors a pass, and that seemed wrong to Jolie. It was, however, in line with what the great teachers and sages taught. Jolie just could not wrap her head around applying it so completely to the world they lived in.

"A teacher's purpose is to guide their students, isn't it?" she continued her argument.

"To guide them, Jolie, not to give them the answers to the test."

"I'm not asking for the secrets to the universe!"

Rance cocked his head to the side. As if to say, "Aren't you?" but he did not say the words aloud. He was too careful and controlled for that. Instead, he said, "Sifu is not going to give you the answers you're looking for because he doesn't have them. Someone else can't tell you *your* truth, Jolie. Everyone thinks that if Sifu would just give them the key to life it would fix everything for them, but he can't do that. He won't do that. It's a false promise.

"And I understand how that can feel like he's saying you're not worthy of the secrets he knows, but that's not it. It's not that he's withholding information because you're not good enough, it's that he refuses to pretend he knows something he doesn't, because that would be unethical. We all look up to him and it would be an abuse of power for him to take advantage of that and make us reliant on him and his interpretation of the universe's truths. Spiritual leaders do this all the time. It's a major pitfall of being in a position of leadership in a spiritual community. Sifu is very careful not to let that happen here.

"It is one of the things that makes him a great man. He is a complex character, but at heart, he is a simple, humble man who understands sharing *his* truth with others in the guize of being *the* truth would be as much a lie as any other dogma."

"That sounds like a lazy man's philosophy. 'Sure, *I* know," Jolie put on a pompous male voice," but *you* can't know until you finally do decades from now. Meanwhile, just go struggle. And why do we have to struggle so long *not knowing*? Because 'I don't want to share.' Maybe the truth is, he doesn't know at all and if he tells someone anything, we'll see through his bullshit."

Rance reddened. "Don't ever speak about him that way. Sifu is a good man."

"Sorry, I have a problem with authority, especially when it makes rules that make no sense and only seem to be effective for…well, no one. The world doesn't have different rules for different people, Rance."

"Doesn't it?" he shot back. "I've worked hard for years to get even a glimpse of the spirit world while you walk in and out of it like you're crossing the street. You have all of it, but you're so selfish and wound up in your crap, that you don't see how you could use your talents to help people. The rules you've been given, Jolie, are not the rules most of us have to live by."

It felt unfair for Rance to judge from his place of ignorance, as if Jolie had been hiding out, refusing to use the insights that bombarded her.

"You don't know anything about me, Rance, what I've been through, or what I've done," she defended herself.

"I know a little. I was there at the Ridge Walking. You were invited right up into the thick of it. None of us were."

"That wasn't Sifu. Remy's grandfather asked me to come up," Jolie explained.

"I've been hanging around those guys for years. You show up, hang around a few weeks, and suddenly you're given a hand-written invitation into the front doors of the club."

Jolie thought about how she had been pursued by a demon for the past seven months, then her mother was shot, and a few weeks later she died. Jolie had been assaulted by her foster father, run away, and now she was trying to make it on the streets. And during all that, Rance had been sleeping nice and cozy in his little room at the school, eating at restaurants, playing monk, and teaching Kung Fu.

"Yeah, I feel really special," she spat back. "If you say I have a gift, Rance, I'm going to punch you."

He smiled. "You can try, but then you'll be on my turf, and you can't beat me."

Jolie wondered what Rance would say if she told him she accidentally killed someone with Qi before she knew what it was called. She wanted to say so badly, "Oh, by the way, I have a pet demon." But she didn't.

"Like I said, you don't know anything about me," she repeated spinning around to leave.

"What was that all about?" Hugo intercepted her.

“Nothing.”

“It didn’t look like nothing…”

“Mind your own business, Hugo,” she flung herself through the front doors.

Class was over and Jolie spent some time cooling off by the time Hugo tracked her down sitting out back in the alley.

“Are you okay?”

“Sure,” she replied sullenly. “I’m sorry I snapped at you.”

“I knew it wasn’t about me.” He didn’t pry. “Look, after we eat, some of us thought we’d hit the arcade at the New York, New York. If you’re up for it?”

“I’m on shift until the restaurant closes at 10:00, or whenever you clowns get done stuffing your faces.”

“That’s cool. So, you’ll come?”

“Sure.” She could use a change of focus.

CHAPTER NINETEEN

As much as Jolie complained about Las Vegas since she and her mom moved here, it was not all bad. It was, after all, the *other* city that never sleeps. You could never claim there was nothing to do.

Back when it had still been a toddling-resort town, it had built its reputation around being a playground for Hollywood celebrities, and those who wanted to pretend they ran in those circles. In the '60s, Vegas was the hip place to see and be seen by the sexually liberated adult who read Playboy "for the articles". The big-top themed casino, Circus Circus, was the first to dip its toe into the "family friendly' vacation market, and by late 1989 Steve Wynn had expanded on the notion opening The Mirage Mega-resort complete with the pirates and a British clipper ship that sank twice a night.

Other venues on The Strip rushed to compete with their family-themed vacation spots, further expanding the city's appeal, or ruining it, depending on your point of view.

But if visiting juveniles were excited by all the options the new Vegas offered, their excitement paled to the enthusiasm of the local teens who lived there. Too young to drink or go to a nightclub, an open buffet of activities was now spread before them seven days a week.

Jolie, Hugo, Brutus, Jiu, and two new student tag-a-longs entered the New York-New York, and headed for the arcade: a kinetic bunch of kid energy ripe for release.

The New York-New York casino's interior was dark and gritty, with inner-city grunge that Vegas itself lacked.

New York City had pulled down Gilded Age billionaire mansions built by steel magnates and robber barons, leveraging the valuable blocks of real estate into skyscrapers that quadrupled their owner's profits. Riffing on that trend decades later, Las Vegas imploded any property no longer living up to its full potential, building a shiny new casino and resort hotel in its place, in a constant loop of urban renewal. Nothing was around long enough to get a patina of age, forget about New York grunge.

So, the designers of the New York-New York Casino painted all the patina and grunge on, emulating the look of aged brick walls and cobbled streets down to putting in manholes with steam rising from them.

"Boy, would I love to do a parkour run in here," Brutus said wistfully, looking up at the fake tower skyscrapers pointing to a fake sky only a few feet away.

"The Luxor is better," Jiu argued.

"What about The Paris?" Hugo asked. "The Eiffel Tower? Come on that has to be the best."

"You can't climb anywhere near The Paris," Brutus warned Hugo. "Their security is seriously serious. I'm talking mean dudes with no sense of humor."

"That sucks," they all agreed, even the new kids who probably had no idea what the older boys were talking about and would never dream of climbing on something they were not supposed to. They just wanted to belong.

"Did you decide about doing Golden Bell?" Brutus asked Hugo. "I think Jiu and I are going to go for the whole thing, not just Iron Body--the whole thing, lifting weights with your balls--all of it." Jolie jabbed him with an elbow. "What?"

She gestured toward the youngest tag-along. She thought his name was Sammy. At the mention of lifting weights with your balls, the kid's eyes had gone as round as quarters and the whites showed all the way around.

"Well, that's what you have to do," Brutus defended himself.

Hugo's eyebrows scrunched together in the middle of his face. "I don't know, Bru. That sounds weird."

"And painful," Jiu added.

"And Sifu warned us if we weren't ready that it could be dangerous," Hugo took Jiu's remark as if it made them allies.

"It's only dangerous if you stop in the middle," Brutus insisted. "If you do the full one-hundred-eight days and never miss one, you're good. Bodhi did it, right?" He tried to get Jiu to join his side.

"I don't think that's much of an endorsement. Sorry Jiu," Hugo apologized.

"Bodhi didn't stop in the middle of Golden Bell if that's what you're thinking," Jiu cautioned his friends. "That's not what messed him up. It was drugs and all the crap at home. Dad wouldn't accept him for who he was, and then Mom left. He didn't have any support except me and Remy."

Except Remy. How could a former rival's victory still hurt so much even after they had passed?

"He had the school and us," Brutus pointed out.

"Yeah, I know," Jiu agreed. "But…" He shrugged.

As the Kung Fu kids moved through the casino, headed for the arcade area, Jolie noticed a teen hanging out nearby who watched them as if they were somehow worth watching. Had she seen him before? She and her friends walked on and the question faded from her mind until she noticed him again. He was still watching her and her friends, but now there wasn't just one watching. There were more. And they all looked familiar.

They're kids from the school that challenged us.

Jolie aimed the heavy wooden ball at the top circle of the game she was playing, hoping for a high score. "Don't be obvious but look over there." She indicated the direction of their observers with a roll of her eyes. "Isn't that some of the students from the school who challenged you?"

"Where?" Hugo spun around without the slightest subtly, scanning the arcade.

"I said, don't be obvious, Hugo," Jolie protested.

Jiu did better. "Over there." He flipped his head, indicating the direction of their stalkers while not looking at them. "They've been trickling in for a while now."

"That older one--I've seen him before," Jolie muttered. She hesitated before adding, "He was at Yanna Maria's fortunetelling store."

Hugo's head whipped around. "Where? Who is he?"

"I think he was a landscaper or a gardener," Jolie remembered him because he had lectured her about being respectful toward the Santeria. "Someone Yanna Maria was teaching. What's he doing hanging out with those kids?"

"What's he doing hanging out watching us?" Jiu asked the more pertinent question.

"What are any of them doing here?" Hugo's voice was half an octave higher than normal. "What do they want?"

"Probably to intimidate us," Brutus said. "But we won't be intimidated." He started to strut toward the challengers' group. Jolie grabbed his arm.

"Wait, Bru." A dark-skinned, older, Latino woman wearing a thick rope of necklaces just joined the gardener.

Yanna Maria did not search the arcade. She knew exactly where Jolie was and she looked right at her, tossing her chin as if giving the gardener directions.

"Shit," Jolie mumbled as Yanna began to walk down the faux cobblestone street toward Jolie and the Kung Fu boys.

"Where is your little friend, Jolie? How does one find a babysitter for a demon?"

Jolie felt the boy's eyes all turn to her.

"That thing is still hanging around?" Hugo hissed. "You didn't send it away?"

"Where would he go?" Jolie countered.

"And you brought it *here*?"

"What are they talking about," the older new kid asked in a reedy voice, looking worried.

Hugo pushed the kid toward the Arcade's exit. "Call your mom. It's time to go home."

"Me too?" little Sammy asked.

"Definitely." Hugo placed Sammy's hand in the older boy's. "Don't lose him." The two youngers began to shuffle away but Yanna Maria raised a hand, stopping them. They turned around once, twice; confused, the delay allowing the rival school's students to circle through a parallel row of games and surround Jolie and her friends.

"Leave them alone," Jolie growled through clenched teeth.

"Or you'll do what?" Yanna's chuckle was base-heavy, guttural, and feral. "You know what you need to do to protect them. You could protect them if you wanted to. Just give me what I want. It is no good to you. You don't even want it. Why be stubborn? No one has to get hurt."

"Except Ling," Jolie said.

"You *named* it?" Hugo said, in his too-high panic voice.

"That is pathetic." Yanna Maria shook her head. "It's not a puppy, Jolie."

"He is not a slave either," Jolie countered.

"But it is. That is what it was created to be. You fool yourself by thinking otherwise. What you fantasize will never happen. The demon will bond to someone, and you will whine and be morose because you failed, but it is the creature's nature to seek a bond and you cannot win against the inherent nature of such a thing. It is hubris to think you can. Give it to me and all these problems will go away."

"Is the old woman still talking about that thing that was following Jolie?" Brutus asked Hugo.

"Ling. His name is Ling," Jolie stood up for her friend. "And he's not here, Yanna. So go away and leave us alone."

"Why has she got a demon hanging around her?" Brutus demanded of no one in particular. "Why do you have a demon hanging around you, Jolie?"

"Because he has no one else."

"You have a demon?" little Sammy asked. "Cool. Can I see it?"

"Maybe later," Jolie tried to distract the little guy. "Right now, you need to go home."

Sammy tried to comply but could not move. That problem did not seem to be registering though, his mind still focused on the idea of seeing a real live monster. "Can I pet it?"

"Does it bite?"

"No! And no, Sammy," Jolie answered both questions.

Like the Tasmanian Devil in the cartoons, Yanna Maria became a tornado of smoke and whirled over to a dark corner at the end of the midway. Pulling her hand from her pocket, she tossed powder into the corner. The casino air bloomed with a heavy earthy scent as the powder dusted the demon, making Ling visible.

The Kung Fu boys took a step back as the Santeria rushed forward, throwing herself at the oatmeal-colored blobby being.

"Don't let her get me, Jolie!" Ling wailed, sliding away as fast as he could. Yanna Maria missed touching him by inches. Across the midway, Ling trembled like jiggling Jello, his back pressed against a new wall. Yanna glared at the demon from where she had fallen onto the floor when she missed grabbing him.

"Get it!" she commanded the rival school students and the gardener. "A hundred dollars to the one who brings the creature to me."

"Go Ling! Go!" Jolie shouted. But Ling did not go. He stared at Yanna Maria, frozen. Shit. What had happened to the wise and together demon who talked philosophy? That demon would not have frozen like a nerd at a Junior High School dance.

Jolie ran forward, hoisted the demon into her arms, and took off.

Following the simulated twists and turns of a New York City alley, she ran carrying Ling. Urged on by Yanna Maria's shouts, the rival school's students followed. If they thought fast enough and got organized, they could cut her off, but Jolie was banking that there were no strategic geniuses in the group. Running flat out, she kept her eyes open for an opportunity to do something to change the game.

There was a manhole cover up ahead. Was there anything more emitting steam other than a small tube? It would take too long to remove the cover and without a guarantee of human-sized access, she'd be caught. Anyway, her arms were full of jelly-roll demon.

She made a beeline for the casino exit, burst through the doors, and turned left.

The newer, more popular strip casinos were north of the New York-New York. So would the crowds be, and Jolie needed a crowd to lose her pursuers.

"You're heavy," she complained to Ling as she ran, her arms beginning to ache.

"I can make myself lighter if you want me to."

"You mean if I *command* you to, and then we're bonded? Pass. Make yourself lighter or not, Ling, it's your choice, but when I drop you, I drop you." Ling got lighter. "What else can you do that you haven't told me about?" Jolie asked, breathless. "Roll around at the speed of sound? Fly through the sky? I know you can disappear, so why didn't you just do that back at the arcade? You're a demon, with hundreds of years of experience. Couldn't you just have teleported somewhere? It's like you got scared and reverted to being three years old."

"That's what happens when I get scared," Ling pointed out. "With those sticky leaf bits on me, everyone could see me, and I couldn't disappear, or go anywhere." Ling shuddered, his squishy body leaning into her chest. "You will not let her get me, will you, Jolie?" Ling's assumption that Jolie could save him was sweet, but he had way more confidence in her than she did.

"I'm trying," was the most she could honestly promise.

The idea that getting into a crowd would help them escape was not working as well as she had hoped. The people they passed kept stopping and staring at her. Carrying a demon that looked like a giant jiggling brain with stubby arms tended to make you stand out.

"We're getting a lot of attention," Jolie shared. "It's making us too easy to follow." She glanced around, taking a quick inventory of the resources available: her backpack.

"Ling, can you shrink yourself small enough to fit inside my backpack?"

"Sure."

Jolie skittered from the middle of the wide sidewalk, angling toward the edge of the crowd. Once free of the slow flow of humanity, she dashed up the stairs to the broad piazza that previewed what could be expected inside the classically themed casino. Using a Roman statue with just enough strategically draped cloth to be child-friendly for cover, she set Ling down, swung her backpack off her shoulders, and began tossing out clothes.

"Tell me when there's enough room inside and I can stop."

"It's fine."

Jolie stopped. "It's fine now, or it was fine a few handfuls of clothes ago?" Ling did not answer. "How long has it been 'fine', Ling?"

"A bit." Jolie began to put clothes back into the backpack. "Not that one," he stopped her. "I hate that one."

Jolie scowled. "Now you're a fashion demon?"

"I seem to be recalling having had a certain sense of style when I was alive." Ling moved closer to Jolie's pack, extended one of his short arms, and picked up a sweatshirt from her discard pile beside the Roman god. The sweatshirt was blue and green with an Anime design on it. Ling put it back in the backpack. "You dress like a peasant," he noted in disgust.

Jolie added her Princess Leia "A Woman's place is in the Rebellion" T-shirt.

"Yeah, I guess you missed Mao Zedong and the Cultural Revolution. This is the uniform of our time, Ling. Jeans or shorts and a T-shirt." Jolie indicated the stream of tourists on the walk just below the stairs. It was summer and everyone wore modern uniforms.

Suddenly Jolie noticed one among the masses who made it look good.

"Oz!" Jolie held her backpack open. "Shrink and get in, Ling." He did and she drew the drawstring top closed. "Oz! Up here!" Jolie ran out from behind the statue and down the stairs.

"Jolie? Hey kid, how are you doing?" Oz gave her a quick once over as they got close. Oz hugged her. Jolie bit her lip and tolerated the contact, hoping she wouldn't "get" anything.

"I'm good. I can't believe I ran into you".

"Right? Well, I'm an understudy at Ka now." Oz tossed her head toward the nearby MGM Casino. "I can renew my green card."

"That's great, Oz. Are you still at the warehouse?"

"I put a deposit on an apartment today." Oz's pride in achieving this milepost of independence was clear. They glanced at Jolie's backpack and decided against asking the usual return question about where Jolie was living. That was okay with Jolie. The distressed teen was thrilled to see her friend, but this was not the time for a casual catchup. She checked the crowded sidewalk to her right. The rival school kids had come out of the casino and were scanning the crowd up and down the Strip. Jolie stepped behind Oz putting her friend between them.

Oz turned and looked south down the Strip. "What's going on, Jo? Are you in trouble again?"

"No," Jolie lied. The Kung Fu boys tumbled out behind Yanna's allies, tripping over each other in their re-enactment of a Three Stooges routine.

Oz smirked. "Well, that's one way to make an exit.

"Bunch of clowns," Jolie muttered.

Brutus caught sight of her and called out. "Jolie!"

"And they're calling your name. Friends of yours then?"

"They go to the Kung Fu school," Jolie admitted to the connection. But Yanna's boys now also saw Jolie.

"This way!" the gardener shouted, pushing north through the crowd.

"And that bunch?" Oz demanded. "Are they the evil clowns?"

"Maybe. Look, it was great running into you, but I'm kind of in a hurry. Sorry Oz." Jolie spun, crouched down, and began weaving her way through the crowd.

She wasn't losing them. She wasn't losing anybody because Oz was right beside her.

"What are we doing?" the acrobat asked, her voice excited and breathless.

"Avoiding the evil clowns." Yanna Maria's gardener acolyte was ordering the challenger kids to keep searching up The Strip.

Jiu saw Jolie's head, pointed to her and the Kung Fu kids were also in motion. Following Jiu, they slid through the manmade landscape like it was an oversized jungle gym, leaping over low walls and vaulting handrails.

"They're pretty good," Oz commented.

"Hey, you!" Jolie's friends began shouting to the challenger kids to draw their attention. "Hey! We're talking to you, loser dudes!"

"Oh shit," Jolie mumbled. "No, no, no, no!"

The gardener was trying to keep his kids focused on pursuing Jolie but the mix of school pride and male hormones was too strong.

Oz frowned. "And why are the evil clowns after you, Jo? Did you punch their red noses or deflate their balls?"

"You wouldn't believe me if I told you. Gotta go." Jolie resumed running north.

What she needed was to lose the clowns--evil or not. She and Oz, who refused to be left behind, reached the wide walkways in front of the Bellagio. The fountain show in the lake started and suddenly all foot traffic dragged to a stop. No one was moving, enraptured as they watched the four-hundred-sixty-foot high choreographed water spouts dance to music. Jolie slowed so she wouldn't stand out so much and swung her backpack around to the front. Digging inside, she handed Oz a bundle of clothes.

"Hold this and don't drop it," she commanded, digging out a T-shirt. Wriggling into it, she pulled out a scarf which she twisted and wrapped around her head, pulling her hair up to change the style. Oz was staring at the bundle in her hands.

"Jolie, your clothes are breathing. Oh, my God, they just wiggled!"

"Don't worry, it's fine." Oz began to reach inside.

"Please, you don't want to do that. Oz?" Jolie waited not breathing.

"What is this?" Oz pulled out an ornate embroidered satin Chinese doll--a perfect imitation of the human Jing Ling down to his brocade robe and black topknot hairstyle.

Jolie swallowed hard. "It's a doll. See? Not a baby, or drugs, or anything--just a doll." She took back her backpack.

"What's in the doll, Jolie?" Oz whispered. "Is that why those clowns are chasing you?"

"It is," Jolie admitted.

Oz stopped; her feet rooted. "My God, Jolie, what did you do?"

Jolie looked into the backpack and Ling, once again himself, looked back, his alien-looking "face" turned up to hers, his button-black eyes filled with fear, hope, and so much trust. The little demon was not just an inconvenient episode in her life. He had been her adored Older Brother who had stood up for her and taken care of her until he made a terrible mistake, but he had barely been more than a boy then. He was little more than that now. She needed to protect him.

Jolie looked back up and met Oz's eyes. "I didn't do anything. But I am going to do something," she declared.

CHAPTER TWENTY

"**T**here's someone I have to save," Jolie told Oz. "And I don't know the cost of doing it, but I know there will be one." She spoke to her friend with all the sincerity she could muster, longing to have someone she could rely on, but terrified Oz would agree to help and then something would happen to them. "I'm not asking you to get mixed up in my mess. You can come with me, or turn away and go back to your life, secure in the belief that the world is what you were told: there is no magic, and no other beings worthy of our notice inhabit the world. The choice is yours."

Her friend studied her carefully. "Wow. I knew you were weird, Jo, but not this weird. I love it." She broke into a grin. "I'm in."

"This isn't a game, Oz. I'm not playing," Jolie warned her. "Things could get dangerous. People have died; people I cared about…and some I didn't, but I was responsible. I'm warning you; you should probably just leave and go move into your new apartment, enjoy your new job, and make new friends--because the shit I'm involved in will change your life, and I can't say it will be for the better. In fact, most likely it won't."

Ling peaked up over the edge of the backpack, blinking his button eyes at Oz. Pocket-sized, he looked vulnerable and cute. Jolie felt like they were doing a revisionist homage to the movie ET.

"Get back down," she hissed at him. "Someone's going to see you." She pressed Ling's head down, pulling out a pair of unders and tossing them over him.

"What is that?" Oz asked. "The real story this time."

"It's my friend, Ling," Jolie replied. "He's not actually a doll, but he is what the evil clowns are after. I'm just in the way."

"Huh. So, kind of a save the Baby Yoda thing? Cool. Come on. I know a place we can lose them." Oz turned West on Flamingo Boulevard.

Leaving the cover of The Strip to cross the eight lanes of Interstate Fifteen--that funneled people through the city to their destinations--was risky because, while they were crossing the overpass, there was nothing to hide behind. There was a sidewalk with a high wire fence on one side, six lanes of traffic on the other, and eight lanes of highway raced below. But once they got across, there were casinos, parking garages, railyards, a large industrial complex, and within a few blocks, suburban housing. Taking this one risk broadened their options and as long as their pursuers did not see which direction they went, there was a good chance they could lose them. Jolie hoped she would also lose the Kung Fu boys and they would give up and go home.

Oz led Jolie across the overpass at a jog, crossed the street, and began to weave through the east-end parking lot of the Rio Casino.

"There's an interactive alternative circus doing a limited engagement here." Oz pointed to a strange-looking big top with bright squares painted with confetti and stars covering its top. "I met some of the aerial artists a few nights ago and they gave me a tour of their setup. No one's going to think of looking there."

"Isn't there security?"

Oz shrugged. "Security is about keeping the audience and the general public out, not the performers.

There's always a back way for the talent to get in if you know where to look. Which I do."

Oz guided Jolie around the backside of the tent to where it bumped up to a service entrance for Rio employees. Pausing to make sure security wasn't nearby, she slipped in behind a collection of tour boxes and crates used for moving the traveling circus's set. Jolie followed.

Behind the crates and boxes was a concealed entry.

Inside, Oz hesitated before locating a plain wooden staircase pushed up against the tent's south wall. Moving quietly, Oz and Jolie climbed the steps and accessed another semi-hidden half door, stooping to crawl through it. On the other side was a maze of vertical crosspieces, horizontal spans, wires, clamps, rigging, and plywood walkways with an occasional pillow stack placed at intersections.

"What did you say this place was?" Jolie whispered.

"A traveling circus show." They crawled over the board walkways and through trusses as Oz explained. "It was created by a group of Brazilian experimental performers. Promotions to the public are deliberately mysterious but the audience comes in on the ground level, stands under the tent, and the aerial artists, concealed by the false ceiling, fly around above them, peeking down at them through little holes and giving them gifts. As an audience member, you feel uncertain and kind of like you're being studied, like bugs under a microscope, but then the artists start sprinkling glitter from the little holes. That's where they drop gifts from, too.

Oh, and then before it ends, it rains on everybody inside the tent. It is so cool. There's no warning or explanation--it just rains. There are no words, just music, and these strange, whimsical, and completely unexplained interactions between the aerialists above and the humans below. It is so charmingly weird. Are the aerialists supposed to be angels? Or aliens?" Oz shrugged. "They do not attempt to explain.

"And who are we--as the audience--supposed to be? The uncertainty the show creates does a number on the audience's heads, because we just don't know. But then when these otherworldly beings flying over your head unseen, except for an eye looking at you from the other side, start dropping these little plastic toys it feels like such a special gift. I wish you could experience it, Jo. It's absolutely brilliant."

Jolie and Oz continued to climb through the trusses until Oz got to a place where there were two pillows. Three boxes sat beside them. One box had glittery stars, moons, and planets in it. The other two had small plastic toys like kisses, hearts, airplanes, stars, Tao symbols, and little buddhas.

"After it's over, you feel like you've been touched by gods or had an alien encounter or something, but all you have are these odd little cheap toys. One part of you wants to hold onto the toy because not everyone gets one and somehow it represents something that has meaning, but another part of you says, hey, it's just a stupid plastic toy, completely meaningless.

"It's performance art on so many levels." Oz scooped a handful of the cheap plastic toys, then let them fall back into the box. They were the kind of thing poor and middle-class people used to fill kids' birthday party favor bags. How could they be imbued with something more than that?

Jolie looked at the holes in the false tent ceiling where the items were poked through, or artists peered down.

"As an audience member, the experience shredded our ideas about reality, at the same time helping us view the world with a fresh, childlike wonder. It was everything theater was supposed to be. At least that's the way it was for me. It's probably different for each person," she added suddenly embarrassed by her effulgent critique. "If I could, I would make theater like that for the rest of my life.

"Anyway, your evil clowns are not going to find us here," Oz declared confidently. "So, I think it's time you told me what's happening."

Jolie shook her head. "You're not going to believe me."

"That's so unfair. Have I ever not accepted what you told me as truth?" Oz defended themself.

"No," Jolie had to admit. "Okay." She started with her misadventures last winter on Solstice.

Sometimes Oz got teary-eyed. Sometimes Jolie did. Ling crawled up halfway out of the backpack and clung to his friend, reliving his own story as he heard her experience of their history together. Jolie narrated their tale, by silent agreement leaving out parts that were Lings and Little Sister's alone, providing the simplified explanation that though they had not seen or recognized each other for many lifetimes, their spirits had been connected for a long time.

"How will Ling ever be safe?" Oz asked.

Jolie did not know.

"But I do," Yanna Maria appeared, hazy and incomplete among the trusses. "The demon becomes bonded…to me."

Jolie leaped to her feet. "She found us. She's here,"

"No, look, Jolie." Oz pointed. "She's not solid. So, what can she do?"

"The woman is a sorceress." Ling shivered. "Do not underestimate her."

"Why are you afraid of her?" Oz demanded. "You are brilliant, Jo, and you have these amazing abilities. When we first met, you might have been a little desperate, but now you have the Kung Fu boys, a demon, and me."

Jolie snorted. "That's quite the pep talk, Oz."

"When I go in, I go all the way." The acrobat leaned forward impulsively and kissed Jo on the lips. As she slowly pulled back from the intimate contact, she turned to Ling. Before Jolie knew what was happening, Oz had Ling under one arm and was scrambling for the tent's outside wall. Dropping through a large hole in the false ceiling, her feet hit the ground and she kept running.

"What are you doing, Oz?" Jolie demanded. "Bring him back here! Dammit, if you try to make a wish or command him --don't do it, Oz. I warn you. Don't try and bond him. Oz? Oz!" Ling was screaming silently in Jolie's head.

Jolie made it to the hole where Oz had jumped down. The floor was at least fourteen feet down and she was no acrobat. She looked toward the stairs, then noticed a harness and rigging clipped to a nearby wire. Unclipping the carabiner, she climbed into the harness, buckled it, and slid the carabiner toward the hole. Finding the gizmo that would adjust the height, she released it. The floor seemed to rise way too quickly. Jolie pushed the release back just before she hit the ground, the harness yanking her hard. Climbing out of the harness without her feet touching the ground was next to impossible, but she knew that every moment Oz and Ling were getting further away and that motivated her.

Where would Oz take the demon? Jolie knew where the warehouse was but not the new apartment. If she staked out the MGM, she should eventually be able to catch Oz coming off work and follow them to their new place, but all that would take time, and by then, it would probably be too late.

Wait, too late for what? What did she imagine Oz was going to do with the little demon?

Make all her dreams come true. Unlimited wishes and commands were hard to resist. Someone as charismatic and attractive as Oz could go a long way with a demon's help. Ling would be unable to deny Oz anything they wanted. Money? No problem. They could work as an artist, produce, or do whatever they wanted to. Oz said her parents were in show business. With Ling under their control, they could win their parent's approval by producing plays, movies, and whatever projects they wanted. The lack of success their parents saw in their daughter would vanish.

It was not the worst option for Ling. Oz would not become a dictator or have their rivals drawn and quartered, but in time who would they become? Jolie had not thought her friend would do what she'd done: steal Ling. And once Oz's life was over, who would be Ling's next master? No. Jolie had to get him back before Oz bonded him.

Outside the tent, she scanned the parking lot. There was Oz, running away, not realizing they were running toward the rival school challengers.

The Kung Fu boys drove up in Brutus' old mini-pickup and piled out not far away.

"Hey, guys, grab them!" Jolie shouted.

They waved, smiling excitedly. "Hey, Jolie! We found you!"

"Grab them!' Jolie pointed frantically. The boys looked at the young woman running through the parking lot, their arms full of something, and just looked confused. Hugo leaped into action, spurring the others to follow.

Jolie and the boys were converging on Oz when a large black car pulled up in front of the challenger group and Yanna Maria stepped out, solid, physical, and menacing as hell.

"Stop!" she commanded, blocking Oz. The challenger kids moved in behind the Santeria, the gardener placing himself beside her.

He grunted. "I warned you that one was trouble, Senora."

"Give the demon to me and I will reward you," Yanna Maria addressed Oz. The young acrobat looked confused and disoriented. "You may ask any boon," Yanna crooned. "After you hand him over." Oz continued to stand in the parking lot, clutching the demon to her chest. Jolie thought Ling was speaking to her. Yanna raised her voice. "If I have to take the demon from you, you will get nothing," she threatened, "except pain." Her dark eyes narrowed, her full face scrunching into a mask that backed up her threats. She was perfectly capable of killing someone who stood in her way. She had tried before with Remy.

"Don't give him to her, Oz!" Jolie shouted.

"I'm not giving him to anyone," Oz called back. "I'll take good care of him. I'll be a good mistress, little guy," Oz tried to soothe the demon. "You'll like living with me."

"No! I want Jolie!" Ling cried, sounding like an emotional child.

"That's okay. Jolie can come with us," Oz assured the demon. "We can all three be together."

"I do not wish to be bonded to you, or anyone," Ling declared.

"He is a demon, many hundreds of years old. You will not know how to handle him," Yanna Maria warned, covetously drawing closer.

"Stay back, you," Oz warned the woman. "And tell your clowns to stay back too."

"Don't be a fool, girl. You are alone. There are too many of us for you to fight." Oz looked at Jolie and saw only the betrayal she had written there. "Your only choice is to give the demon up," Yanna continued her pitch. "Jolie will throw his abilities away. She will never let you use them. But if you give him to me, I will reward you with whatever you wish. Imagine my gratitude, and what you can achieve through this one act. A lifetime may be very long," her voice hardened, "or tragically short."

Indecision swirled across Oz's face.

Hugo, Brutus, and Jiu were closing in.

"Tell us what to do, Jo." Brutus cracked his knuckles, flexing pecks that strained his T-shirt.

"Take the demon," Jolie ordered them. "Sifu doesn't want them to have him," she lied. Directions were given in quick glances and nods as the Kung Fu boys prepared to strike.

Yanna's allies recognized that something was about to happen and took up fighting stances.

Disappear Ling. Just disappear, Jolie tried to send him her thoughts.

Oz held the little demon up into the air. A gust of wind swept through the parking lot, blowing the last of the leaf bits off him. He looked at Jolie over Oz's shoulder and she heard him think, *"I am free."* He would disappear and go someplace safe, and she would find him.

"Red Rock." Jolie pictured the cave above the slab cave. *"I'll meet you there."*

Hugo was within arms reach of Oz. Jiu and Brutus were preparing to leap in to stop Oz from escaping with him.

"Stay back! Don't touch me!" the acrobat screamed.

The boy's impending attack had taken the focus away from Yanna. Thrusting her hand into her pocket she tossed a second handful of glittering herbs onto Ling.

"No!" He froze, his face melting into despair.

Yanna pushed the gardener away. "Get back. The demon is mine!" Running forward, she wrestled Ling from Oz's arms, jumped into the car and it sped away, its doors closing as it moved.

Yanna's allies blinked confused, then began to drift away in small groups, throwing scowling glances over their shoulders at the Kung Fu boys and Jolie.

"We failed," Brutus said as if the Ring fellowship had just been broken and Frodo had traveled on alone. "We're sorry, Jo. We just weren't fast enough."

"It's not your fault," she tried to reassure him.

"No, it isn't," Hugo agreed. "We can't be expected to defend someone or some *thing,* if we don't know it needs defending." He stomped off.

Brutus made a face. "What's his problem?

"Where's he going?" Jiu asked.

"I don't know," Jolie muttered.

"Maybe back to the school?" Brutus suggested. "That's a good idea. We need to tell Sifu what's happened."

Shit, Jolie thought. She told the boys that Sifu knew about the problem between Yanna and Ling, but he didn't. How was she going to fix this?

Riding in the pickup, Brutus, Jiu, and Jolie caught up with Hugo pretty fast, but he refused their offer for a ride. No one spoke as they drove the rest of the way back to the school. Failure was something endured in silence.

It was after two o'clock in the morning and the school had long been dark and locked.

"We could wake Rance?" Jolie suggested.

"He's out of town," Brutus informed them. "He left after the last class to go see some woman in California." Brutus rolled his eyes. There was consensus among the younger Kung Fu students that females busted up the brotherhood and distracted martial artists. Aside from moving away for college or jobs, girls were the number one reason the school lost members.

Jiu went around the side of the building returning with a key. The others looked at him dumbfounded. "What? There's a brick. Don't you all know about the brick?" Jiu's family had been at the school since before he was born. His mother was one of Sifu's early students.

"No." Brutus looked surly.

Jiu opened the door and the three of them shuffled in, collapsing onto the mats. The adrenaline was fading fast, and they were finally feeling how tired they were-- too tired to turn the lights on.

"That was intense." Brutus lay flat out, one arm thrown across his face. "But it was cool, right? We showed those wannabe's whose school rules, didn't we?"

Hugo shuffled in not saying anything. He sat down near them, but not among them, still holding on to his disagreement with Jolie.

"You know how Sifu talks about how souls travel in groups like they have an agreement to meet up in each lifetime and that explains why you feel close to certain people so fast?" Jiu asked. "I think we're like that--us, and Remy." He did not need to add that his brother, Bodhi, had been part of the group before his death, but they all understood that. "He said those groups often have one of them who is their truth keeper, and the rest of them have vowed to protect that one so the knowledge won't be lost." He paused and looked at the faces around him. "I think Jolie is our truth keeper."

Jolie lay down, hiding her face with her arm. "You play too many video games."

"No, listen to me," Jiu protested at being dismissed. "You know stuff, Jo. You understand things none of us do, but we all knew tonight that whatever was going on with you, it was our job to protect you. Because you're our truth keeper."

"I'm not. But I am grateful you tried to help." She sat up. "I have to get Ling back."

"How?"

"I don't know."

"Do you know where that woman took him?"

"No, but she has a shop on Charleston."

True to his cautious nature, Hugo suggested: "We need to talk to Sifu."

"I'll do it," Jolie offered. "This is on me." She hoped she could cover her tracks and her lie about Sifu knowing about Ling.

"No," Brutus spoke up. "We all took part. We need to explain this to him together. It's the right thing to do." He looked up at the clock. "Crap." He jumped to his feet. "I've got to go before my mom gets home from her shift and sees I'm not in my room. See you tomorrow? We can take care of this then."

Only they couldn't. Jolie could not wait, hoping for Sifu's help. In her experience, when things needed to get done, grownups mostly just got in the way and Ling was living on a far tighter timeline. How long could the little demon hold out against Yanna? Because once they were bonded, there was only one way to break the bond: Yanna's death.

"Me, too." Jiu got up. "Catch ya' tomorrow."

And then it was just Hugo and Jolie.

"Are you staying?" he asked. Jolie nodded. "I figured. So, is it you and Rance then?" Jolie looked at him, frowning. "Romantically, I mean?" Hugo clarified.

"Oh God, no!" Jolie was shocked at the idea. "It's not like that at all, Hugo. Rance has just been helping train me, teaching me about Taoist philosophy and stuff."

"That's how it starts," the teen said cryptically.

"Didn't you hear the part where he just went off to see some woman in California? We're not a thing." Hugo shrugged as if the existence of the other woman didn't mean much. "Honestly, Hugo, I don't have any interest in Rance romantically. He's old!"

"In a few years, those years won't seem like anything. Girls always go for older guys."

"Only the dumb ones," Jolie defended herself. "Older guys who go for underage girls are skanks. Give me some credit. I'm way too smart for that." She leaned over and kissed Hugo once, good and strong on the lips.

"What was that for?"

"Why? Didn't you like it?"

"It didn't feel honest. It didn't feel like it had anything to do with me. It was kind of like being run into by a bulldozer with lips."

"Nice." They sat in awkward silence.

"Is what Yanna Maria said about you and that demon true? Are you controlling it now?" Hugo asked after a while.

"No. It just follows me around."

His eyes narrowed. "Why?"

Jolie cringed. "Because it wants to? It wants me to tell it what to do and not do, which I won't...mostly."

"It thinks you know what to do. Did you tell it you're a teenager?"

"It knows that, but it's complicated. Ling is a very old spirit but a very young soul."

"That makes all kinds of sense," Hugo complained.

"Ling didn't mature because he never experienced the consequences of his actions. Being bonded to one master or another and forced to do whatever they told him to, kept him from learning responsibility, values, or morals."

"And you're still letting this morally challenged demon hang out with you, why? Are you nuts, Jo? You should have gotten rid of it weeks ago like you said you were going to."

"I didn't say I was going to get rid of him. I said I was trying to get him to move on. Ling isn't evil, Hugo. He's confused. He just needs some guidance until he learns--like a toddler only with superpowers."

"Great power with zero sense of responsibility. There's no cause for alarm there," Hugo quipped.

"But he *is* learning," Jolie defended her supernatural friend. "He wants to do the right thing now."

"Now...." Hugo let the ramifications of the word simmer. At the very least Jolie's choice of words inferred that Ling had done bad things in the past. Hugo had not missed that. "Just how long has this demon been hanging around; the truth, Jo."

"Around me, or how long has it been around, like in the world?" Hugo pinned her with his dark-brown eyes, communicating his mistrust. Jolie knew answering truthfully would raise more questions than they answered, but her friends had been on the edge of the strange events that webbed around her, becoming caught up in them without understanding what was going on and it put them in danger. She remembered what she said to Ling about true friends and realized how many of her own decisions were based on maintaining her secrets rather than sharing them. If her friends were truly her friends, she owed them the truth.

"Ling's been around since Winter Solstice," she admitted reluctantly.

"All through that stuff with your mom and her boyfriend, and her getting shot, and you going wacko at the hospital?" Jolie nodded. "It had something to do with you showing up at the Ridge Walking ceremony, like Jiu said, then you running off and getting lost in the mountains?"

Jolie nodded again.

"What about Remy's accident and your mom's overdose? Was the demon responsible for those things?"

"Not responsible, but he was connected."

"Through you?" Hugo guessed.

"Yeah."

"What about what happened to Bodhi?"

"Bodhi's death was his own bad choice. Ling was in Tecopa with my mom when that happened."

"And Remy knew about all of this," Hugo stated. It wasn't a question, but he couldn't have known that Remy knew about the demon.

"And his Grandpa Hoke, and his Aunt Rose, of course," Jolie explained.

"Of course." Hugo turned his back to Jolie. "All of them knew, but you didn't think to explain it to the friends who stuck by you and didn't leave when things got weird and messy."

Hugo saw her actions of protection as a betrayal.

But you did know," Jolie tried to defend herself. "You helped save Ling that night after Spiritual Warrior class when Yanna tried to snatch him."

"No one thought you were keeping him. So, you just went on taming this thing, putting yourself and the rest of us in danger without letting us know anything about it? Don't you see how wrong that is?"

"It wasn't the sort of conversation that fit neatly between 'Where shall we eat dinner?' and 'What happened at class last night?" It doesn't fit into anything anywhere close to normal, but this is my life. I was trying to protect you."

"But you didn't," Hugo challenged. "Becca had a nervous breakdown and isn't allowed to see you anymore, Jo. That was because of all of this, right? She was *there* on Winter Solstice, and she saw something she couldn't handle. Remy was in a terrible accident and almost died. Bodhi died, your old lady friend died, your mom died. Do you see a pattern here? And what's the common denominator? You. And now, because I'm friends with you, this Yanna person has her claws in *my* family. What does she want with us? We're not part of this. We're nothing." He shook his head. "I don't think you were trying to protect anyone, Jo. I think you were protecting yourself like you always do. Don't let anyone get too close. Don't let them *in*. Don't trust them with the truth. Don't touch them, or let them touch you because then you might know something uncomfortable about them, and things might get too real."

Jolie looked away to hide the tears flooding her eyes. "I let Remy in."

"And look how that worked out. The one he loved, died."

That was like a punch in the gut--something Jolie did not expect from quiet, steady, Hugo.

"You know, I used to think you were so brave, but now I see that you're just in so far over your head that all you can do is hope to find a sandspit to put your feet down on the sand and catch a breath before you keep treading water. I'm sorry."

He pulled her over to him and kissed her--a real kiss, a gift that held within it everything he was or could be, promises unspoken but *there*; scrawled on his heart, firm and indelible. A sense of sweet longing spread through Jolie. Hugo was a good person.

Too good for you. You don't deserve a good person, some small, mean voice snarked at her.

Hugo released her. "Maybe you should reconsider your criteria for love interests. You're always going for people you can't have. It might make good fiction but in real life it sucks." He paused. "If both people don't feel love, is it really love? Nah. 'Probably just infatuation.'" Hugo got up and left.

Jolie's head was spinning.

Hugo had nurtured a crush on her since the first day she had shown up at Chaparral High, but he had never stepped out of the geeky friend lane. Even when he started to thin down, his features sculpting his broad face into early signs of Latino handsomeness, Jolie had refused to consider Hugo as boyfriend material. Was he right? Was it because he was available? Or was it that they were friends and romance ruined friendships?

"It figures" She grunted. "I tell the truth and he leaves."

CHAPTER TWENTY-ONE

Snowclad mountains peaked like fairytale castle turrets, paper-white cutouts against the starry sky. Tiny granules of ice nipped at Jolie's cheeks, the frozen wind trying to nuzzle under her clothes like a cat determined to explore what was hidden. She looked down from the back of the dragon, judging the fatal drop that would be her fate if her hands slipped and she clung even tighter.

"Come forward!" The old monk, sitting on the golden dragon's shoulders called back to her.

"No. I'm good here," Jolie replied with a tight smile, her eyes squinting against the gritty snow.

"Jin Long's spine is less wobbly up here," he encouraged her, patting the dragon's scaled shoulder.

"I'll fall!" Jolie squeaked, eyeing the stone needles and deep black crevices below.

"You won't though, because I will not let you." The monk was suddenly close. "Trust me. Take my hand." Jolie was terrible at trusting, but his eyes were earnest and kind. She took a deep breath and released the dragon's spine, trading for the monk's slender, wrinkled hand. "Open your eyes, Jolie." He chuckled.

She did.

Sitting on the dragon's shoulders in front of the monk, Jolie drank in the star-filled night…the world…the universe.

"It is…magnificent." She sighed, her heart expanding as if it could burst with fullness and that seemed fine because then it would be joined to the Everything.

The dragon's insides rumbled, its body vibrating beneath Jolie's rump and legs, its warmth warming its gold scales. She giggled.

"It's like riding a really, big horse...that flies. Or maybe an elephant." The beast's mighty heartbeat thumped against her thighs, its ribcage contracting and expanding with its breath. Its huge wings swept the crystalline snow toward it like a herd of glistening sheep, then pushed it away, scattering it to the wind as its wings pushed down again, as a huge sky-bellows.

Jolie could see that it was not only the air currents the beast used to fly. It also used the currents of Qi that wove the fabric of the universe together, even the little things.

Like me.

Jolie breathed in the night sky, the snow-bright mountains...the glittering universe. Ahead, a stone temple was perched on the side of a steep mountain, the torches in its windows winking at the travelers. Then she was once again standing on the center path marking the middle of the soul-flame river of candles carpeting the temple's stone floor.

Do I know any of these soul-flames in physical life, she wondered? Would we recognize each other if we met on the street? Maybe we would if what Sifu says about souls traveling together is true.

Jing Ling appeared in the path looking as he had as a young human man, dressed in rich, old-style, traditional, Chinese, layered clothing, a tunic, and robe with ballooned pants laced close to his calves above the ankles. His thick black hair was gathered into a twisted top knot, two long braids swooping from his temples down over his shoulders. Seeing the demon return to human form, brought tears to Jolie's eyes. The person she

Jolie awoke curled up on the mats where she had fallen asleep and instantly remembered that Ling was not there. She could not feel him. But something had awakened her.

Outside in the school's parking lot, a large pickup engine growled before rattling to silence as the engine was shut off. Jolie's alarm was immediate.

Breathing fast and shallow she scuttled away from any windows.

The front door handle rattled.

"Hey, is anyone in there?" The would-be intruder banged his fist against the glass. "Sifu? Someone? Anyone? Its Cliff Wrangler, Juvenile Probation? I'm looking for a lost girl." He rattled the door again. "I think you may have seen her, Jolie Figg? She's a friend of some of your students. Please, let me in. I just want to talk."

Jolie did not move. If Rance had been at the school, he would have answered the door, but he wasn't, and Sifu wasn't. It was just Jolie and the papier mâché' Lion's.

Jolie waited.

Wrangler waited, tense…listening. Both were stubborn. Neither would give in easily, but Jolie had nowhere to be while Wrangler had wayward youth to look after, all of whom might be up to mischief at any hour on any given day. Jolie closed her eyes and soothed her nerves by cycling energy using the Microcosmic Orbit.

After some time, the hard click, click, click of Wrangler's hard-soled boots on the pavement pierced her attention. Wrangler's truck rumbled back to life, growling as it pulled out of the parking lot into traffic, one more bass note in the city's street symphony. And then he was gone.

Jolie uncrossed her legs, massaging them to encourage blood flow. Walking to the center of the practice floor, she began Qi Awakening exercises.

"I'm here, Ling. Come find me," her mind called to the demon. *Oops.* She returned her focus to her breath and her practice. But her mind found it difficult to settle.

Did it mean something that Ling had disappeared in her dream? Had Yanna succeeded in bonding him and commanded him not to speak to Jolie? Had he been injured in his struggle against Yanna and was unable to respond?

Jolie re-focused and started the Chen Sword form, a fast-moving Tai Qi form that required her full attention and still, she felt distracted.

If Yanna successfully bonded Ling, would the little demon go back to being the creature he had been when Jolie first met him, or would he be forced to act at

Yanna's command even though his conscience was intact? Jolie almost hoped for the first. Having a conscience and being forced to do things you knew were wrong would be a spirit-warping torture.

I told him to meet me at Red Rock, she remembered. But if Ling could manifest in Red Rock, he could manifest here. No, wherever he was, he was confined, constrained, and not free. So, where would Yanna have taken him?

Somewhere she felt in control, Jolie answered herself: *her shop.*

Trying to coerce a demon into doing something it did not want to do was bound to be messy, maybe noisy, and Yanna's shop was in a mini-mall, wall to wall with other businesses. The sounds of demon incarceration were sure to be noticed. And if so....

Someone would call the police.

Jolie let herself into the school office and dialed 911.

When Jolie got to Yanna's shop four police cars were already in the parking lot, two blocking the shop's front entrance. They couldn't have been there long. Yanna was outside on the walkway wringing her hands while she spoke to the officers who were questioning her.

"This is all a mistake," the Santeria was insisting. "Some of my clients make unusual noises.... My neighbors have never complained." Jolie picked up a few words over the cacophony of traffic. "There is nothing to find here," she assured the officers in as many ways as possible, as if simply by rewording her pleas they would become more convincing.

Two of the officers went inside, presumably to search the shop, leaving one outside with Yanna who continued to pace up and down the walk, frequently looking in through the big picture window.

Jolie wasn't sure what outcome she was hoping for. Yanna would not have put her special leaf mixture on Ling to make him visible if she were trying to hide him but since it also kept him from transporting, she might have used it, which meant she need not have put him where he would be seen.

"Come on, little guy," Jolie whispered. "Give me a sign, a burst of light, a sneeze--anything."

A car turned into the parking lot then backed out, a second one repeating the action a few minutes later: the curious, or customers too worried about getting involved to keep their appointments with the Santeria. Yanna's scowl deepened. She was losing business.

Jolie felt the hairs on her arms stand up. *Yanna.* She was looking toward Jolie from across the street. The teen slipped behind a metal light post, concentrating on being nothing. When she looked out again, the Santeria was speaking in galloping Spanish to someone on her cell phone.

"Escuchan, Guillermo! Ya policia esta aqui! Yo soy..." the rest was lost beneath the sound of screeching brakes as someone, distracted by the police presence at the mini-mall, almost rear-ended the car in front of them. The cops gave the near transgressor the stink eye until the next turn of the traffic light let them drive away.

Walking half a block up the street, Jolie crossed to the side where the mall was, using the cover of the buildings to stay unseen. Keeping to the cover provided by the police cars, she joined the small crowd of the curious gathered there. A female officer headed for a squad car and Jolie moved to intercept her there.

"Did you find anything, Officer?" she asked.

"I can't say," the officer replied with an apologetic smile.

"Oh, sure. Of course. I just—my folks have the furniture store there," she pointed to one of Yanna's near neighbors, "and well, we've heard things, like people shouting for help or kind of moaning like they are in pain. Papa says that sometimes late at night when he's here after hours, he's heard pounding on the walls. I bet there's a hidden room or a secret basement in there. Maybe human traffickers work out of the shop!"

The officer scrutinized Jolie. "Did one of your parents make the call to the police?"

"No. Oh no," Jolie acted frightened. "They wouldn't do that. They couldn't…" she stopped herself, her eyes wide with pretended fear.

"Stay here. I'll be right back," the officer told her.

As soon as the woman's back was turned, Jolie was gone. With the police here, there was nothing more she could do right now to help Ling, but she hoped the official scrutiny would slow Yanna down.

News about Jolie and her friend's adventure on The Strip spread fast through the school, stoking student fervor against the challenging school, and infusing the desire to put their rivals in their place. It also revived old stories about Jolie's part in the Ridge Walking Ceremony.

Jolie had no control over this speculation-fed mythology. She hadn't been around long and had only begun taking part in public classes recently, yet suddenly, she knew half a dozen forms, was unbeatable at Sticky Hands, and was part of a mysterious chase that happened between some of the older teen students and the temple school's challengers.

Brutus looked to be enjoying the notoriety of retelling the story of the adventure on the strip—at least the part he knew. Jolie hoped he was not saying too much. True to their natures, Jolie, Jiu, and Hugo were focused on rumor de-escalation and avoidance of any discussion about last night's events. They had not been a cool adventure. They had been frightening. But no one who had not been there understood that.

Jolie wondered if the boys were questioning how much of what they remembered was real and how much was the power of adrenaline-saturated suggestion, wondering if they asked her, which way should she nudge them. It felt selfish to pull her friends into a world she could not explain, but Hugo's statement struck hard. Maybe her decisions were more about protecting herself than protecting them. It was a little late now, though. They were recognized and now potential targets for Yanna and her minions, their school rivals.

Jolie and her friends did not have the chance to confess their sins to Sifu and receive absolution yet. He had not been seen at the school since the adventure. With Rance away as well, everything felt off.

The students were lined up for class when Sifu came rushing in accompanied by a gust of one-hundred-degree summer. Taking aside a senior student who sometimes ran classes, he spoke to them in hushed tones before hurrying back out.

"What is he doing that's so important?" Brutus asked.

Jolie watched the Taoist disappear through the double glass doors. "He looks tired."

"He's working too hard," Jiu explained. "Sometimes things happen in the community, and he gets called in to fix them." Jiu looked out the window. A shiny, black limousine was parked at the curb outside the door. Sifu was disappearing into it.

Brutus made a face. "In a limousine?"

"I told you, Brutus, Sifu has a reputation in spiritual circles—not just locally, but all over the country," Jiu explained. "He gets calls from all kinds of people asking him to come and fix situations for them."

"What kind of situations?" Brutus demanded. The kids all waited for Jiu to provide more.

"Clearing out haunted buildings and houses, banishing spirits--stuff like that," he tossed off as if it were old news.

"Sifu's a Ghostbuster?"

Jiu cringed. "No, he's the real thing; a Taoist Master, but yes, he does clear out unwanted spirits, it isn't easy. It can take a toll."

Jolie was thinking about what Jiu said about how long his family had been involved with the school. She was still looking out the window when Cliff Wrangler's truck drove into the school's parking lot.

Wrangler. Again.

"Shit. You don't know where I am or where I've gone." She sprinted for the back alley door.

Climbing the roof ladder, Jolie lay on her belly to peek through a clerestory window to the practice floor two stories down. The senior student-sub was talking to Wrangler and nodding compliantly. The sub scanned the students scattered around the floor and pointed out Jolie's friends.

"Shit. Shit. Shit!" Jolie swore, scaring nearby roof pigeons into flight. Wrangler looked up. Instantly she flattened against the tarred roof. It was hot, and the warmed tar clung to the threads of her clothes. It smelled like dead dinosaurs. She had been to the La Brea Tar Pits once when she and her mom lived briefly in Los Angeles. There was no way Wrangler could have heard her, but logic didn't stop her heart from pounding out a drum solo. She waited for her breath to calm down before cautiously looking through the window again.

Wrangler was talking to Brutus and Jiu. Brutus was doing the talking. Jiu was standing by looking worried. Hugo was burning off nervous energy spinning, lunging, and striking the floor in a staff form. He had been quiet and distant since last night. Jolie knew he wouldn't want her to get caught, but Hugo was no liar, and adding lying to the authorities to the list of things he had done to help her that he didn't want to do was not going to reduce his resentment.

Jolie crept away from the window, taking up a new position, sitting with her back to the school's large AC unit where she could keep an eye on the alley and the ladder she used behind the school to climb up. She couldn't go back to class. Wrangler would have given the sub a card in case she showed up, and the sub would feel compelled to use it.

Of course, he knew where she worked. It would have been on her record. That would be his next stop. *Crap. I'm going to have to find a new job.*

"How did I get here?" she asked the sky wistfully. *And how do I get my life back?* The question inferred she had been living a better one at some time before, which was marginally true. Technically she was houseless, secretly sleeping in a costume closet, and living hand to mouth. But in truth, she was eating well at the restaurant, and the costume closet felt safer than most of the bedrooms she'd had when she'd lived with her mother. Life with Jessie Lynn had never been anyone's version of easy. It had always been about too little security, not enough money, and too many skanky guys hanging around.

What the end of this summer would bring was anybody's guess.

Jolie's plan had always been to go to college and earn her and Jessie Lynn a better life, but that pipedream felt like a straw dream now. How would she pull down the kind of scholarships she needed, save money for college while going to school and working, plus pay for all her living expenses?

It wasn't fair that Jessie Lynne's death would end Jolie's dreams.

"Whatever it takes, I am going to graduate," she promised herself. Jolie's friends had not meant to abandon her. Her situation was simply the outcome of a cluster of badly timed, poor circumstances and it would all get straightened out…probably…maybe.

She sighed, missing Ling. She would feel so much better if he would appear right now.

Where are you, Ling? Maybe she should have bonded him when she had the chance. She discarded the thought as it completed itself. She could not do that. She would not. Not now. Not ever. But damn, she sure could use a little help.

Someone will come back, she encouraged herself. One of her grown-up friends would resurface and offer a hand, and this time she would not be too proud to take it.

CHAPTER TWENTY-TWO

"**W**ake up." Sifu loomed over Jolie like a redwood over a patch of moss. Bedded down on the pile of yellow silks in the costume room, she had not heard the door open, and he did not turn the light on. She scrambled to her feet.

"I'm sorry, Sifu. I guess I fell asleep. Rance asked me to make a list of repairs for the character costumes…"

"I don't care that you're sleeping here, Jolie. Where's Rance?" the Taoist demanded. Even in shadow, his expression was a dark thunderstorm.

"In California with his girlfriend?" Jolie offered tentatively though she was sure Sifu already knew that.

"Oh, right." He turned and walked out leaving Jolie standing among the racks of brightly colored costumes. When she did not follow, he came back. "Come with me." He disappeared again.

Jolie grabbed her tennies and a summer hoodie putting them on as she tried to catch up.

"Where are we going?" He was opening small drawers in the altar, pulling out leather bags and glass vials. He handed what he had gathered to Jolie.

"We need a box." He disappeared into the kitchen returning with a small cardboard box indicating that Jolie should throw everything he had given her into it before shoving the box back at her so he could continue adding to its contents: a repurposed mayonnaise jar with red sand in it, half an abalone shell, the black and white feather of a large bird, matches. Sifu took his guan do staff off the wall and headed for the door, his black robes flapping behind him like a Raven preparing for flight.

Jolie stood by the altar holding the box.

"Come on," he called as he exited. "There's no time to…" His last words were cut off by the door closing.

Sifu seemed flustered. Jolie had never seen him flustered. What could do that?

You probably don't want to know, she answered herself.

He poked his head back inside. "Hurry up. The car is waiting." Jolie moved toward the door in stilted uncertainty. She was not sure she wanted to go wherever he was going, to do whatever he was going to do, but he had not asked. He had just assumed. She could take exception to that treatment.

On the other hand, Sifu was the only person she knew who might be able to help her untangle the problems of finding and saving Ling. Jolie followed.

Sifu was waiting to lock the school doors behind her.

"What exactly is it that we're doing?" she asked.

"I'll explain on the way." He opened the door of the black limousine that had picked him up earlier and ushered her inside.

But he did not explain. He mumbled. He sighed. He brooded; a wayward traveler mired in his thoughts. None of it meant anything to Jolie. The thing she did understand was that the school's head teacher was facing a problem he had not been able to resolve, and it had him worried.

"So, the problem…?" Jolie nudged him.

"It won't leave."

"It?"

"The spirit haunting a property down in the old Rancho area. It's made itself unwelcome and begun to endanger the people who live and work there."

"Are they ever welcome?" Jolie had her own opinion, but it had been evolving over the past seven months.

Sifu's casual shoulder shrug clashed with his Taoist priest's robes like the opposite ends of two centuries being shoved together.

"Some people don't mind as long as it doesn't become a problem. Honestly, most people don't even notice them."

"If they want to get rid of it, shouldn't they call a priest?"

"I am a priest," he reminded her.

"I mean like a church priest--like a Catholic priest or something."

"Watching The Exorcist a dozen times does not mean you know anything about exorcisms," the Taoist retorted. "Usually by the time someone calls me they've tried all that plus a few less savory options."

Ah. So, after all other methods fail, it comes down to the dude in the black robe who runs a martial arts school to chase the monsters away.

"And why am *I* here?" Jolie asked.

Sifu's attention turned and took a sum of her. It was a low sum.

"Because Rance is in California."

Great. I'm here because I was available. That's comforting.

"And what exactly do you expect me to do?" Jolie asked, trying not to sound defensive.

"Whatever I tell you to." He pulled back into himself. The conversation was over.

Jolie licked her lips. This was it: her chance to prove herself. If she performed well and did what he needed, she might earn the privilege of a few pearls of wisdom, or get his help with Ling. She was still trying to work out her priority list of questions as if she was going to be given three wishes by Sifu the djinn when the limousine pulled up to a property secured behind fancy new wrought iron gates. The limo paused and the gates opened, letting them pass.

The grounds were torn up. A newly built mansion sitting amid open irrigation trenches. Ridges of clay soil snaked like oversized worms around the property and along the newly paved driveway.

"Expensive taste for a ghost," Jolie commented.

"Don't make the mistake of thinking of a spirit as a person. It's naïve and dangerous."

Jolie didn't need him to tell her that, but guys from all religions and philosophies signed the "females don't know anything about spirituality" pact.

"Sorry. You're the expert." She shut up.

The limousine stopped and Sifu hopped out before the driver could open his door for him. The man looked resigned but awkward standing by, his purpose appropriated.

"Opening car doors; it's just one of the amazing things he can do," Jolie commented wryly as Sifu disappeared into the house, leaving Jolie behind like ocean foam drying on the beach after a wave recedes. Her continued presence kept the driver in limbo. Technically, she was a passenger and therefore a guest of his employer, but she was also a scruffy-looking, sassy-mouthed teen. She leaned against the car earning a glare equal to her having painted the limousine's black finish with fingerpaints. She rubbed the print of her upper arm out with her shirt.

"Don't worry about it," the driver said. "I polish it all out at the end of the day."

"It's clear you take pride in your work. It looks real…shiny." Her compliment had the intended effect. The driver almost smiled. "Do you know what's going on?" she tested her luck.

He shook his head. "I just drive." He hesitated before asking, "Do you?"

Jolie rolled her eyes. "I'm just here to do what Sifu tells me to."

"So, what exactly is it he teaches at that school?"

"Kung Fu, Tai Qi, Qi Gong," Jolie rattled off forms. "He's a Master of Shaolin Kung Fu." The driver shook his head, his palms turned up indicating that her descriptions had not helped. "Taoist martial arts?" She added. "Like the real Bruce Lee stuff."

"And he's here to take care of the Disturbance?" The driver frowned. "What's he going to do, karate chop the dam thing?"

Jolie played dumb. "The Disturbance?"

"Never mind." The man shut down. Maybe she played dumb too well.

"Have you seen it?" she asked after what she hoped was a reasonable reset.

"I'm paid *not* to see things," the driver countered.

"Oh, sure. It's important to maintain a professional 'don't see, don't tell' in your line of work. I get that. But I'm not a reporter. I'm with Sifu and we're here to fix the situation. He's the adult with the big reputation. Clients see me, immediately think 'kid' and dismiss everything I say. But you understand that. People treat drivers like that too, right?"

"Don't pretend you know anything about me," the man muttered.

Hiding the action behind her, Jolie pressed her hand against the shiny automobile, delving into the energy imprint the driver left behind during his many hours of taking care of the limousine.

"I know you're working on a master's degree in social advocacy," Jolie said. "You have two kids and you've recently become a single parent. I'm sorry about your wife." The driver's look was a mixture of anger at her invasion of his privacy and surprise that she knew what she knew. "I told you who *he* was," Jolie offered quietly. "Now I'm telling you who *I* am, and why I am here." She hoped it was true and the Universe had a plan beyond the happenstance of her being the only person around when Sifu came looking for an assistant. "So, do you know anything about this Disturbance, Mister...?" she waited for him to give her his name.

"Rufus Johnson. How come you know all that other stuff but not my name?"

"I was trying not to pry. Nice to meet you, Rufus. I'm Jolie...." She made an instant decision to leave the name Figg behind. "...Boulet. My family's from New Orleans." Pretending that meant something was a cheap shot but maybe her family origins would provide enough mysterious background for her unique gifts to give her an inch of credibility. "Anything you can tell me could be helpful, Rufus."

The driver rubbed his hand over his mouth and chin working on making a decision himself.

"Last fall some of the staff working here started seeing things; a glimpse out of the corner of the eye, a feeling of being watched--that sort of thing. At first, it was just that--things you think you *might* have seen, or an unsettling feeling. The workers who left first didn't tell the truth about why they quit, so things went unnoticed longer because of that. Getting labeled as being 'superstitious' is not a great job recommendation and the stories about what folk were experiencing didn't sound real. I didn't believe anything was wrong until it happened to me. So, it was a few months before anyone spoke up about the problem.

"That was about the time the house was mostly finished and the staff moved in. When some of the housekeepers mentioned they felt like they were being watched, we checked to see if someone was creeping around, looking for tracks and the like. We didn't find anything, but there were too many instances from too many different people to dismiss it as imagination.

"About this time, the encounters--I don't know what else to call them, took on a threatening tone. People reported having nightmares. They started walking off the job, not just house staff, but landscapers, too. They left and refused to come back." Jolie noted the dead and dying trees and plants in their wooden boxes and black plastic containers, left to shrivel in the sun. Rufus noticed what she was looking at.

"The pool was supposed to be done weeks ago, the landscaping finished, and the ditches filled in." Rufus waved a hand taking in both the front and back yards. "The contractor can't get the pool fence up, and the pool can't be filled until the fence is up and has been inspected. It's a code violation.

"Word was out that the property had a problem, and no one wanted to work here. The Missus finally decided she had to do something to calm people down."

"Had *she* seen anything?"

"If she did, she would never admit it, and the place was still under construction, so she wasn't here that often."

"Did you have nightmares, Rufus?" Jolie asked.

"Only if I slept over, which I hardly ever did. My sister helps me out with the kids, but I don't want to ask too much of her, you know? She's got her own life and her own family."

"But when you stayed over, you had them?" Jolie clarified.

Rufus put his hand to his chest. "Yeah. It's the same dream for all of us, you got jumped and stabbed in the chest, or the other one is you are drowning in really blue water--like Hawaii or the Caribbean, or someplace. It's so real that when you wake up it's hard to accept that you're not dead."

"So, what about the images you glimpsed out of the corner of your eyes? Did anybody ever see them clearly enough to identify what they were?"

"Sure. Once things started ramping up, the thing stopped hiding and started coming right at people. It's a really big dog--bigger than any real dog. It waits until you're alone then comes out, growling. It's scary as hell."

"You said things 'ramped up', Rufus. Can you remember when that was?"

"A couple of months ago. I remember because that's when they started digging the pool."

"Did this 'dog' ever hurt anyone?"

"Not yet." Rufus shook his head. "But it chased a few."

"Spirits can be dangerous, but mostly because they use our fears to affect our bodies. If they're *only* a spirit, it's nearly impossible for them to physically manifest enough to harm a person. It's like that game kids play

'Ghosts In the Graveyard', where you can do all kinds of crazy things to the person lying on the ground, shout, make faces, whatever to get them to break, but the one thing you can't do is touch them. That's the rule."

Rufus smiled. "My kids play that game at day camp."

"It's a classic," Jolie agreed.

Rufus scratched his head. "Well, the dog doesn't act like it can't touch us."

"Even if a ghost knew that—which I'm not sure they do, they're not going to reveal their secret. From what I hear, the 'rules' in the spirit world are more learn-as-you-go than Hogwarts Academy."

Suddenly, Sifu reappeared in the house's doorway, exiting as if someone had set fire to the hem of his robe.

"We're leaving," he announced getting into the limousine. Jolie shared a look of surprise with Rufus, then climbed in.

"Well? she asked the Taoist as the car drove away.

"Well?" Sifu countered, throwing a questioning glance at Rufus.

"Wait. You left me outside with Rufus on purpose? That was part of your plan?"

"Your dogged curiosity has not gone unnoticed," Sifu replied. "And the people who have been living and working here are bound to know more about what's been going on than an owner who has barely spent a week here in the past six months, and most of that time she was in denial."

"But wasn't the owner the one who called you in to deal with the Disturbance?"

"Reluctantly, at the suggestion of an acquaintance."

"So, you're not going after it?" Rufus asked from the front seat.

Sifu's thin lips compressed with a frustration foreign to his nature. "I'm sorry, but your employer refused every suggestion I made. I will not put people in danger and myself in the position of fighting on two fronts, the spiritual and the physical."

So, we are leaving. Jolie sighed.

Sifu's internal thunderstorm sharpened the silence like the threat of a freshly honed knife. Jolie wanted to ask him what she could do for Ling, maybe even get his help, but there was a long story going back to the events leading up to Winter Solstice that needed to precede that discussion, and in his current mood, the Taoist was not in the mood to listen patiently while Jolie stumbled through her convoluted history.

She did have him alone for a few minutes though. What should she ask? What did she need to know? And how could she approach the subject without him getting all suspicious and asking questions she didn't want to answer?

"Sifu, can I ask you something?" she ventured. He turned to her not saying yes, but not saying no. "You say Kung Fu was created to strengthen and prepare the monks for meditation but also so they could defend the peasants and people who were unable to defend themselves." There was nothing he could say about that. It was what he taught at the school. "But what about spirits? Are Taoists also expected to defend and protect them?"

"You were at the Ridge Walking Ceremony, Jolie. You saw what was being done there. We called the spirits and helped them cross over."

"Those spirits were lost and confused, not evil."

"A Spiritual Warrior stands on the line between Yin and Yang, maintaining the balance of energy. The nature of energy is fluid and ever-changing. Yin is not bad. Yang is not good. They are different, but both are necessary."

"But there is still good and evil," Jolie argued. "You're not saying there isn't."

"I'm saying, everything can and does change and the state of another's spiritual progress is not for us to judge," the Taoist clarified.

Jolie had struggled for a long time with believing Ling's protests about wanting to change, but he *had* changed, supporting Sifu's statement. But did Ling's ability to change mean every spirit or human possessed the same potential for positive change and therefore they should be given unlimited chances to do that? Wasn't there a limit to the non-judgmental rule? Surely, bad people or spirits could not be allowed to continue doing terrible things without consequences? There were rules, and rights that needed to be paid attention to.

"Then how do you decide when to intervene?" she asked.

"Mostly, I don't. I let things work themselves out." "You just ignore things and hope the problems will go away? Sifu, that's terrible!"

"It's not for me to intervene in another's life path," he stated, echoing what Rance had said about the Taoist Master.

"Then why have a school? Why teach anyone anything?"

"It's important to pass on what has been learned about how to lead better lives."

Jolie crossed her arms. "The word 'better' is a judgment."

"It isn't that there is no 'better', Jolie. There is, and humans need to understand how to make more positive choices because that will make their lives and our world a better, more compassionate, more peaceful place. Each decision affects the whole."

The Thousandth Drop lesson. The one the old monk had shown her. *"It takes many drops to make a lake but only one to break the dam."*

And I am only one drop in a vast pool of souls, small and unimportant, Jolie thought.

"Someone must be that thousandth drop, Jolie," she heard the monk's voice as clearly as if he was riding in the car with them. *"What if that drop is you?"*

"That's what we are trying to teach at the school," Sifu's statement returned Jolie from her thoughts.

"So, not kicking and punching?" Jolie recovered herself.

Sifu smiled. "It keeps the lights on."

"You're saying two opposite things though, Sifu, that we shouldn't judge, but that we should hold up and support this image of a better world. They can't both be true."

"Do you know how the universe has been woven together?"

Jolie wanted to say "yes," she had seen it in her dreams, but anyone could dream anything and wake up believing to have been given divine inspiration. Who was to judge whether it was true or not? Jolie remembered Rance telling her that Sifu kept silent about much of what he knew or believed personally to avoid setting himself up as a guru and he was very careful not to put himself in a position of telling another human being what is right or wrong for them. It suddenly occurred to Jolie how similar that was to her insistence not to become Ling's arbiter of right and wrong, because it felt like she would be setting herself up as an authority, expecting him to do what she said, and that was too much like a bonding.

We are alike. Somehow, she had stumbled on this core understanding that Sifu used to anchor his life, all on her own.

Sifu turned to her. "What was it you wanted to ask me?"

"Nothing." Jolie turned and watched the city go by outside her window. *Where are you, Ling? Where are you?* She wasn't praying for strength, or to find some part of her she felt was missing. She just wanted her friend to be safe and free.

CHAPTER TWENTY-THREE

That night, after class, a hoard of hungry students from the school filled the chairs around three large tables, ordering enough food to put the kitchen staff in overtime with Jolie as their waitress. It would be a good night for tips.

"He seems nice," a single male in a nearby booth indicated Hugo. Jolie stopped and looked. It was Sean.

Sean?

It felt impossible. Sean had left Vegas, abandoning his grandmother, Faith, and his friend, Jolie, for a coward's safe life, outside the world of spiritual realities, magic, and people who did unthinkable things for power.

"And he likes you," Sean added, showering her with his charming, boyish grin. How did a man in his twenties keep a boyish grin?

"And he's close enough to my age that it's not wrong for us to hook up, is that what you're thinking, Sean?" Jolie retreated into prickly sarcasm. She was not going to forgive him like he had brought the wrong brand of cookies to the party this time.

He chuckled, unfazed. "There's that combination of shaming, coercion, and conviction that you wield so well. Contrary to your juvenile beliefs, Jolie, I don't spend time fantasizing about you. You and I have a connection, but it's not that kind, no matter how much we flirted."

"No, we have the kind of connection where you walk in whenever you want something and walk back out when things get uncomfortable, and you might have to do something difficult. Why are you here, Sean?"

Resentment showed in every line of Jolie's body, every twitch of muscle.

"I came to find you. What else?" His smirk was as cocky as ever. He had been using charm to get what he wanted from the women in his life since before he could talk. "I talked to your friend Rose," he admitted. "She didn't give you up. She just hinted where you weren't, then mentioned this place would be good for dinner, so I took a chance."

Jolie scowled. "Where's the French pastry?" Last time Jolie had seen Sean he was engaged to a woman who had grown up in France. Instead of it making her cool though, she was ultra-conformist, and super uptight-- completely wrong for Sean. The woman had immediately started to reinvent Sean in her image of a fawning husband, pushing him to give up his motorcycle, and dressing him in designer polo shirts. Jolie hated her.

"We broke up," Sean replied.

Jolie made a face. "Oooo. She found some guy who actually enjoyed being told what to wear and how to hold his fork?" Back when Sean was a regular at Jolie and her mom's trailer, they shared a wicked sense of humor. She was testing to see if the French pastry had buried that along with Sean's motorcycle keys, black leather jacket, and blue jeans.

"I had a little bonfire before I left Washington." Sean grinned. "I burned all the clothes, and crap, that wasn't me. I'm back at the old house in Boulder City now."

The house where Jolie met Faith. It was because of Faith that Iris felt obligated to take Jolie in—which Jolie hated. She didn't want someone to pretend she was part of something that didn't exist.

"I was going to inherit the place eventually anyway, but Grace had her heart set on a new start in Florida, so we worked out an agreement that helped both of us."

It was surprising how relieved Jolie felt knowing that Faith's daughter-in-law was gone. Grace had been carrying some heavy baggage along with a dark side that was misguidedly criminal. "I hope you smudged the heck out of the place before you moved in."

Sean inclined his head. "You're not the only one Grandma Faith mentored in her Pagan ways." For a while, it seemed like Sean wanted to forget everything his grandmother had taught him. It felt like he was pretending he hadn't turned his back on Faith and Jolie, the two people closest to him at the time, and that none of his betrayals had happened.

"You weren't there for Faith when she needed you," Jolie declared flatly.

"No, but you were." Sean's sincerity was disarming. "When I faltered and lost courage, I did the best I could by bringing the two of you together."

"You think you get extra credit because you introduced us so that I was there when you weren't? That's so irresponsible, Sean."

"I agree." He sighed. "But it was the best I could do at the time. You two needed each other and I needed some space to get my head together--away from all the weird spiritual shit that was going on. Faith was always saying that we don't always see the effects of our actions, but when things get bad we need to have faith that something done with good intent will have a positive outcome. For a long time, I assumed Faith, Iris, and Grace's talk about magic and spirits was a harmless fantasy. Then you came along.

"The part of the world that wants to put you at its center is terrifying, Jo, and as much as I loved Grandma, and them, I wasn't ready for it."

"Rick and Rory were never harmless," Jolie reminded him of the cast of characters involved in the Winter Solstice debacle.

"No, and Grandma had me watching them long before you were in the picture. She knew things, my Grandma Faith did."

Jolie smiled to herself. "She did." Faith had been the first person since Jolie's Grandmother Mem to recognize Jolie's abilities and help teach her anything about using them.

"I have to ask, Jo, why haven't you signed the papers to finish setting up your trust fund?" Jolie stared back at him, her face a blank. "You should have the money. It's what Faith wanted." Jolie frowned, and Sean tried again. "Iris talked to you about this, right? It was in Grandma's will. It came out at the reading."

"I wasn't there. My life got complicated around that time and then the day after my mom's funeral, Iris had a family emergency and went back east."

Sean nodded. "Ah. Griffin, her grandson."

"Iris has a grandson?" Jolie had been sure the old woman, who never married, made the family emergency up to get out of becoming Jolie's foster parent.

"Not by blood. He's the son of a designer friend of hers from her days in New York. Griffin's father and mother never married. The woman gave birth to the kid, then left the baby with his dad. So, when Iris' friend died of HIV, she adopted Griffin." Sean shrugged. "Iris does what she can when he lets her, but you know, some people are just too proud for their own good." Jolie wasn't sure which of them he was talking about, this Griffin person, himself, or her.

"But you're avoiding answering my question about the college trust fund Faith left you."

Jolie felt like someone had punched her in the chest. "She shouldn't have done that."

"She thought it was the least she could do. She didn't want that amazing brain of yours to go to waste. You should have seen Grace's face when she found out. She was so pissed."

Jolie could imagine. Grace never liked her, mostly because Jolie had seen through the pretender Grace was holding up to the coven as a great leader, encouraging them to go along with his twisted notions. When Rory's pretenses were revealed and his plan unraveled, Grace's part in it went with it and she blamed Jolie.

"Faith didn't owe me anything." Jolie bit her lip so she would not cry. "I owed her everything."

"No one's keeping score, Jo."

"Grace is right though. She shouldn't have left me anything. I'm not family."

"You were to Grandma," Sean disagreed. "And to Iris, and me. You still are." His face looked so honest and open. His smile--Faith's smile, reminded her of his grandmother. He had Faith's long eyelashes, her wavy hair, and the same long fingers that Jolie always saw in other-life memories playing the piano. In this life, Sean didn't play piano. He was not perfect. Most of the time he was an idiot, but then so was Jolie, so who was she to judge? They shared memories: people they cared for, troubled times they had come through together, and that counted for something.

Jolie's mind went to Ling and her heart panged. It was hard not having a friend who knew her so well, had shared so many of her most pivotal experiences, and understood without explanation all the unexplainable weirdness that was her life. Harder still was knowing that friend was in danger and you did not know how to save them.

I promised myself that if someone reached out a hand again, I would stop being proud and take it, Jolie reminded herself.

She put her arms around Sean's shoulders and gave him an actual, unrepressed, hug. He smelled like the same aftershave he had always used, and he felt solid and present. He hugged her back like he could squeeze the loneliness out of her, but all it did was squeeze out a tear.

"I'm here, kid. I am." It was a simple promise. One that did not go beyond the moment. One that did not promise a future that he might mess up.

"I miss them so much, Sean," she sobbed into his shirt, "Mom and Faith." *And Ling,* she added silently.

"Of course, you do. I can't even imagine."

She had always tried hard not to let Sean see her weakness, afraid that if she was vulnerable, it would lead them to inappropriate intimacy and trouble, but maybe letting someone know they mattered wasn't a weakness. Maybe admitting you were vulnerable and needed help was its own kind of strength.

She had learned that from Ling.

CHAPTER TWENTY-FOUR

Despite her eternal worry over Ling and his welfare, Jolie's thoughts often returned to the disturbance at the Rancho estate, wondering what was happening now that Sifu walked away.

Rance returned from California, rejoining his and Jolie's practice sessions. After their disagreement over Sifu's stand on the guidance of others, Jolie sensed a new tension between them. Some things had changed at the school during Rance's absence: the rival school's harassment, Wrangler showing up at the school, and Sifu asking Jolie to assist him with a haunting. Jolie was suddenly no longer a satellite to a more accomplished student. She earned her position whether she wanted it or not. She didn't. Being so visible meant people whom she did not know had expectations of her, which made her very uncomfortable. To avoid her new notoriety and the chance Wrangler would catch her at a class, she stopped attending public classes, picking up shifts at the restaurant where it would be easier to slip away if he showed up there instead.

Jolie had the next day off, and after checking Yanna Maria's shop to see if any new developments could provide her hints about Ling's location and finding there weren't, she decided to walk down to Rancho Drive.

Rufus and his limousine were in the Rancho estate's driveway and the gates were open.

"Hey, Rufus, how's it going?" Jolie greeted him, casually strolling up.

"Jolie. It's good to see you. Better late than never, eh?" He shook her hand, not asking why she was there.

"Still being 'disturbed'?" she asked.

The driver chuckled. "That's an understatement. Sifu and that other guy are inside talking to Missus Macullen. I think she's finally willing to do something. It was nice of him to agree to come back." Jolie did not let on that she did not know about this.

"He's a nice guy," she quipped, scanning the neighborhood around them.

Rufus snorted. Calling Sifu "nice" was like calling a tarantula wasp "a bee".

A synagogue spike poked up through the dense canopy of old cottonwoods that shaded the neighborhood. Gated fences marked the driveways of older half-acre properties. By Vegas standards, this was an old-money neighborhood.

Rufus noted Jolie's study of the surroundings. "This was a sleepy, backwater town once."

"Did the mob moving in build it?"

"Officially, the mob was gone when most of the suburban buildup around here happened, but they were an influence for a long time. This was close to The Strip casinos, but still suburban enough to raise a family."

"You know, this haunting doesn't add up for me, Rufus. Spirits don't randomly move in. The house is new, so the problem has to be with the land. There's a reason this disturbance began when and where it did. Have the sightings been connected to any particular place on the property?" Rufus nodded. "Show me."

Jumping across open irrigation ditches and walking around the wilting boxed palms, oleander, and boxwoods, the driver led Jolie around the east side of the house.

Jolie stopped. "What's that?"

"The old house."

The property on the far side of a partially finished fence was vacant and neglected, there was no landscaping and there didn't appear to ever have been. Clumps of dead grass, creosote bushes, sage, and rabbit grass grew naturally around the adobe brick house covered by catclaw vines. A rotting veranda shaded the front of the faded, white-washed building. Barely visible tracks from an old dirt road dead-ended at the porch.

"Back in the day, there was probably a hundred acres or more attached to that old place," Rufus explained. "As the crow flies, it's close to the original Springs at The Meadows. Back then there wouldn't have been anything else for miles, except the seasonal shelters of the Natives who camped near the Springs."

"How long has it been since anyone lived there?"

"An old bachelor uncle of Missus Macullen's lived there until he had to go to a nursing home. He died a few years back and Missus Macullen inherited the place. For the most part, though, the Macullens left Las Vegas generations ago. They made some money here, then used it to build new lives in California. 'Least that's the story the Missus told me. Nobody's lived in the old house for over a decade, except scorpions, snakes, and tarantulas."

Jolie eyed him skeptically. "Tarantulas? You're making that up."

"No. You see them. They're kind of shy though." The man grinned, pushing back his billed chauffeur's hat. He looked ten years younger and a hundred percent more human.

"I look around the neighborhood though--how it's built up into big houses with larger lots, the Synagogue nearby--and can't help thinking how odd it is that this property was never developed."

"The old house and the lot the new house are on are both Macullen properties; all that's left of the larger acreage once connected to the old place." Rufus shrugged. "The bulk of the land was sold off to whoever built those houses and shops." He pointed toward the commercial sprawl by the freeway. "When the Missus inherited it, she didn't think much about it at first, then her husband passed and she decided to build a new house on this piece, with paddocks, a barn, and an arena on the piece the old house on it. She said she wanted her grandkids to have a true Western experience when they visited and learned to ride horses. She's lonely and likes to talk when I drive her." He pointed ahead to where the fence progress had stopped. "The sightings have mostly been over in that area."

"By the fence?" Jolie asked. Rufus nodded. Before Jolie could ask any more, Sifu and Rance came out of the patio door of the big house.

"I've cleared the house." Sifu tucked a sage stick back into a leather satchel slung over his shoulder. "Hey, Rufus," he greeted the driver. "Missus Macullen's going to need you to drive her and maybe some of the staff. I told her she needs to go somewhere else--it doesn't matter where as long as it's away from here. She's giving all of you the next few days off. It's important you all understand you can't be here. You'll need to leave as soon as you can and stay off the premises until we're done."

"What are you doing here, Jolie?" Rance asked a suspicious edge to his voice.

"I just stopped by to see how things were going..."

"Well, you should go now too. Sifu doesn't need distractions."

"He brought you," she shot back. "So, now there are two of us distracting him." She walked to where Sifu was looking over the crumbling irrigation ditches, dying boxed nursery items, and partially excavated pool.

"Should I be surprised to see you here?" he asked her.

"I can't ethically make that decision for you, Sifu." Jolie countered with a sly grin.

"You are a pain in the ass, you know that, Jolie Figg?"

"It's Jolie Boulet to you, and that's pretty damn judgmental for a Taoist Priest. Rufus says the problems started about the time they began excavating for the pool," she pivoted to the business at hand.

"Six months ago," Sifu confirmed.

There was a threatening growl from the area of the unfinished fence line and Jolie turned to see two red eyes grounded by a huge shadow-body rising from beneath the recently planted oleander bushes. It was not just huge, it was unnaturally gigantic, its musculature shaded in swipes of charcoal held together by a smoke-defined body.

"You said 'big', Rufus. Not the size of an elephant," she complained.

"What is that?" Rance demanded.

"It's the 'disturbance'," Jolie replied.

"But why a dog?" Sifu muttered. "This is a lot of fuss over a bone."

"Not bone, *bones*," Jolie corrected him. "The real bone of contention, forgive the pun, was the fence starting to go up in this back part of the property." Sifu looked at the faded fence line spray-painted on the ground. The standing finished fence ended at a bunch of posts dropped onto the ground like oversized pieces of a Pick-up Stix game.

"You're thinking an unmarked grave?" Sifu asked Jolie.

"I am."

Rance stood between Sifu and Jolie, looking uncomfortable. Apparently, he did not need to protect Sifu from her, but how would he have known unless Sifu told him, Sifu didn't tell anybody anything unless he thought about it, and they needed to know.

Sifu stepped toward the fence.

The spirit dog growled, crawling out from under the bushes, its head sunk between its shoulders. Sifu took another step and the growl got more intense.

Jolie looked around at the others. "You heard that, right?"

"Oh, yeah," Rufus confirmed. Rance had turned pale. Jolie remembered how hard it had been for her the first time she realized there were otherworldly creatures bent on doing ill to human beings. "It's okay, Rance," she tried to encourage him. "Sifu's got this."

"Get behind me," Sifu ordered the others. He took out his sage stick and then brought out the feather he had put in the box. Lighting the sage, he used the feather to waft the scented smoke toward the creature.

The Ghost-dog let out a long, anguished howl.

Jolie cringed. "Why is it doing that?"

"The sage is a cleanser. If a spirit is evil or has malevolent intent, the smoke will make it uncomfortable so that it will want to leave." He returned his focus to the dog, muttering whispered chants.

The ghost dog continued to whine and howl, rolling its head.

"It's not leaving," Jolie pointed out.

"I know you don't want to leave," Sifu addressed the spirit. "But you can't stay here." The dog barked at him. "You have died. This is no longer your place. This realm is no longer your home. You must move on." The ghost-dog barked again, and again, shaking its head as if to shake the Taoist's words from its ears. The pads of its paws began to glow, its skeleton popping bright against the black cloud of its unsubstantial body. "Heads up everyone," Sifu warned. "Something's going on."

"What…?" Rance's question was cut off as lightning sparked from the ghost dog's feet webbing out from it in all directions. "Shit!"

"Don't take the energy into yourself, but don't block yourself off either," Sifu shouted stepping over the crackling energy lines coming toward him.

"Taoist directions are for shit," Jolie grumbled. "Try that again."

"Don't let it *in,* but don't try to keep it out."

"What are you doing out there?" Missus Macullen called from the back door. "What's happening? Did you find it?" She clomped down the steps in her bejeweled sandals and sun dress onto the patio.

"Go back inside Missus Macullen," Sifu shouted at her. "Rufus get her out of here."

The woman marched down the pool deck toward them. "You can't tell me what to do on my property."

"You asked me to take care of this problem for you. Now let me do that. I can't focus on you *and* this creature."

The woman was upon them now and noticed Jolie. "Who is this?" she demanded. "If it's safe for this little girl to be here, it's certainly safe for me." She planted herself between Jolie and the bushes with her back to the fence.

"Missus Macullen don't..." It was too late, the growl, the attack, the scream, all exploded at once.

A funnel web of whirling blue clouds opened behind the woman. The ghost-dog leaped over her, placing itself between her and the people who might try and rescue her, barking as it backed her toward the funnel.

"Missus Macullen!" Rufus ran forward.

Sifu stopped him. "It won't help to lose both of you, Rufus. Jolie, quick, fetch my guan do from the limo."

Jolie shot like an arrow from the chaos, running for the limousine. But the chaos did not stay behind.

Something was following her, wheezing, and whistling in a high-pitched tornado-doom voice. Desert-hot winds flung bits of grit and rock chips at her face, her chest, her arms, and legs, forcing her to close her eyes. Stumbling blindly forward, Jolie reached the car, throwing open the door. Grabbing the poled spear, she spun around, holding the Taoist Master's weapon before her as a protective shield, hoping it had power of its own and not only if it was wielded by Sifu.

"Stay back! I don't want to hurt you," she warned the condensed-air figure. It shrunk away; anguished burn marks darkening the translucent fabric of its visibility. Its hollow, whistling mouth wailed with the heart-stricken mourning of a keening mother, twisting Jolie's heart. Compassion froze her.

"I don't understand. What are you trying to say? What do you want me to do?"

Blue energy fingers fluttered slowly toward her, begging permission to touch. Silently she granted it, standing still as half-seen digits brushed her heart center. Two words accompanied her as she was swept into a vision. *"See...understand."*

The weathered man set out food and water for his dog friend, a routine he followed every day. Plumping up a bed of fresh straw, its scent reminding him of his youth working on a plantation down south, he pulled over the cotton braided rug his sister had made him, draping it over the straw as a bed for the dog's old bones before pulling his rocker into the shade beside it.

After removing his worn army boots, he wriggled his toes inside the knitted socks the same sister had sent him at Christmas, another reminder of her goodness.

The ex-soldier-turned-rancher wiped his brow with a crisply laundered cotton handkerchief. It was cooler in the porch's shade but still hot. He did not bother wondering how hot. The weather was what it was. In Southern Nevada, mostly sunny and hot, but windy in the spring, and freezing in winter. Complaining about it didn't only make you more miserable, slowing your acceptance of the moment--like this one--taking time to sit on your porch with your dog, enjoying a cup of clean water and a breather.

The rancher had a kind face, light smile wrinkles carved deep into the dark skin near his temples pointing like arrows to brown eyes shaded by gentle humor.

The rancher took care of the dog, just as he cared for any neighbor or stranger who showed up at his door, though there were not many. And the dog took care of him: loyal friends and companions. He hoped soon to be able to bring his sister's family here to live with them. The boys would love to have a dog. They were old enough to help with chores and Mary had a pleasant temperament. It would be good.

Some women did not like the desert, but Mary loved it, and the plain adobe house. And the thirsty land would love her back. They could build a future here, leaving behind the pain of plantation life and the war between the states.

The land around the whitewashed adobe house was flat, except for the mounds marking where former inhabitants of the valley had encamped over many generations. It was flat all around the house--to the springs at The Meadows.

The dog stood under the shade of the porch, panting, his eyes watching the horizon. After some time, he let out a warning bark.

A man on horseback was approaching, his face and the details of his tack obscured by undulating heat waves and the lowering sun behind him. As the stranger drew closer the dog growled, the short hairs along its spine standing up like a ladder on edge.

"You're awfully quick to judge, my friend," the rancher chided his companion. "Let's you and I just wait and see what the fellow wants before we go growling at him, shall we? He probably just needs a drink of water and a sit-down out of the sun. Yessir, a cool drink and a sit down will soothe the burnout of most folk traveling through the desert." The dark-skinned man kept sitting on the porch and the dog kept watching, his suspicion's quiet, but sharp.

The rancher was still sitting on his porch when the stranger shot him, he barely had time to realize what had happened and thought "By George, the ol' dog was right about this one," before his heart stopped.

The spirit broke contact, and Jolie steadied herself. It was an eerie silence.

"You don't need to be afraid of me," she told the blue spirit--the spirit of the dead rancher, for that was who she knew it was; the ghost-dog's friend. "I am not your enemy, but the dog--he can't keep doing this. Sifu won't let him."

The bubble surrounding Jolie and the rancher's spirit vanished. The shouting and screaming at the fence grew louder. Jolie ran back.

Sifu and Rance were trying to distract the dog spirit, while Rufus tried to coax Missus Macullen away from the tornado funnel and toward him. The woman was gone now, no more than a shell, tears running mascara down her makeup-caked cheeks, the bald spots her carefully coiffed hair had been hiding revealed.

"Sifu!" Jolie tossed the Taoist his weapon. "The dog won't let her go?"

"I will make it!' Sifu declared, spinning the weapon and moving into attack position.

"Wait, stop!" Jolie shouted. "Don't hurt it."

"Are you kidding!" Rance exclaimed.

"I've asked it to leave, Jolie, but it's only become more savage," Sifu declared.

"Because it's afraid."

Missus Macullen screamed, and her body finally collapsed.

"Whatever you're going to do, Sifu, you better do it now," Rufus shouted.

Sifu pointed his weapon at the ghostly dog, energy crackling down the weapon's shaft. Behind Jolie, the Rancher's blue spirit wailed. Flying forward, it wrapped itself around the giant dog's larger bulk.

"Stop, Sifu!" Jolie placed herself between Sifu and the spirits. "Don't hurt them. Listen to me, please. Just listen. I understand what happened here. I *saw* it. Those spirits didn't do anything wrong. The dog is only trying to protect his friend's grave--and the rancher is trying to protect the dog."

"What did I tell you about projecting human emotions onto a demon spirit?" Sifu barked.

His judgment of her was there on his face. "I am not making this up. I am not unstable or imagining things. I know something about spirits, and not from playing video games or watching movies. I know because I know a demon, personally." She frowned. "I thought you knew about Ling and I. You can see him, right? Isn't that why you gave that talk about how changing a demon into an ally is a big deal?"

"I gave that talk because it was on my curriculum," Sifu said, his jaw tight.

Jolie shook her head, tears springing to her eyes. "I am not crazy. Don't dismiss me as if I am."

Missus Macullen screamed again, and Jolie spun to face the ghost dog.

Help me. You need to help me, Jolie pleaded with the rancher's spirit.

"He is a good boy. Calm him."

Stepping toward the dog, Jolies reached out a hand toward its muzzle.

Some part of her was aware of the three men shouting at her not to move forward, not to touch the spirit dog, but she could not think about them right now. She blocked out everything except the ghost-dog, clearing a quiet space within herself.

"Good boy. Good boy," she whispered.

The rancher's spirit also whispered; *"There's my good boy. See, she's just a girl. She didn't do this. She didn't hurt me. She won't hurt us."*

"Peace, my friend." Jolie gently tickled the dog's muzzle, working soft fingers beneath its chin, down its chest, and into the depths of its smoky form, working toward where its heart would once have beat. The dog relaxed and dropped down to the ground, resting its chin on its front paws.

Out of the corner of her eye, Jolie saw Rufus pull Missus Macullen's body from the tornado's mouth before another vision took her.

A black man with a weathered face smiled down at the dog. The dog had never worn a collar, been fenced in, or tied up. He stayed with the man because he chose to, and he could leave whenever he decided to. Neither one belonged to the other, but they belonged together.

The dog smelled his friend's scent—clay dust, sweat, the lye soap the rancher washed his shirt in last week, the smell of bacon and eggs he had made this morning. The man pulled straw from a cracked bale on the porch, the golden smell of the dry grass stalks a late summer perfume that coated the hot air. The man covered the pile of straw with a cotton braided rug still scented by the woman who had made it—a woman who shared his man-friend's blood but whom he had never met. The dog knew her scent though from the packages of jam and dried fruit that came during the short days of winter, along with a pair of knitted socks.

They were sitting on the porch in the shade of the veranda, the same as they did at the end of most days when the dog saw a stranger approaching--a stranger wearing a false smile, with no water in his canteen, and no kindness in his heart. The dog tried to warn his friend, but his friend's heart was so bright it never saw the darkness in others. Before the dog could make his friend understand, the false stranger shot a dark hole in the bright heart of the good man. Then he shot the dog.

The dog lay bleeding into the dust where the false man tossed him as two more men of the same make appeared. They dug a shallow grave and threw the bright-hearted rancher into it. Having no reverence for the dog's kind, they left him to rot in the desert sun. But though they had mortally wounded the dog's body, they had not killed his loyalty. It dragged itself to the fresh burial mound where his friend's body rested and lay down, guarding it as his heartbeat faded. Sometime after the stars came out, it stopped.

And still, the dog stayed, its body desiccating in the sun.

The ants came, nibbling at the feast of meat. The wind came, blowing away the tufts of his fur. The rain came, washing his bones clean. The bones broke, slivered, scattered, and were ground to dust, and still, the dog remained, guarding his friend.

For decades the ghost dog stayed in that spot—his spot, on top of his friend's bones. No one paid him any mind. No one came near.

Eventually, people built houses around the rancher's house. The landscape changed from virgin desert to a neighborhood with streets, backyard pools, green lawns, and water-guzzling sprinklers.

Someone moved into the rancher's old house, but they left the bushes and the dust as it was--as it had been, and never visited the grave, now almost flat. The wind and sun shriveled everything, except the ghost-dog's loyalty.

Then one day, big machines ridden by strangers came and began pushing the dirt around.

The dog watched, and worried. At first, that was all he did, hearing the rancher's calm voice saying "Let's not be too quick to judge. Let's just wait and see." But when the men and their machines began to come close to the rancher's resting place, the dog pulled back together what it remembered of having bones and a dog's body, rose from the ground, using the dirt to make itself more solid, and growled from the depths of its long-harbored mistrust.

That growl said, "Do not come closer."

It did this every time one of the strangers came near, and for a while that kept the Destructors away. Then one day they stretched a string from a post at the front of the property to the back, the line going right over the rancher's bones.

Despite his growling and prowling, posts were pounded into the hard clay along that line, each post bringing the strangers and their destruction closer to the rancher's grave until they were right up to where the ghost dog's friend's bones lay beneath the ground.

The dog had been growling and howling more and more with every passing day, but no matter how it carried on the Destructors did not seem to hear his warnings over the noise of their machines. Until one day they walked right up onto the dirt covering the rancher's bones, ready to place a post right through where his big, bright heart had been.

The dog grew from the ground like a weed in monsoon season, pushed the post-pounding man away, and tossed the post toward the new house, breaking a window.

The men left after that.

When the dog went to investigate, he found he could walk right into the new house, as easily as if he had been invited. The stranger's fear was salty and good. From then on, he went inside whenever he wanted to.

The Destructors replaced the window and tried to resume putting up the fence, but the dog would not allow it. He had given them fair warning, but they had not listened. They were not respectful. They needed to go away.

The dog butted Jolie's hand away, tossing her back with enough energy that she fell to the ground.

"Are you alright, Jolie?" Sifu asked, gently helping the teen sit. "The ambulance will be here soon."

"I don't need an ambulance." Rufus and some woman from the house were tending to Missus Macullen. Sirens were approaching in the distance. Jolie stood and brushed herself off.

"Don't be stubborn. Sit down before you fall down," Rance said. She was shaking uncontrollably.

"What were you thinking putting your hand inside that spirit like that?" Sifu demanded.

"I wasn't thinking."

"Clearly," Rance commented. Jolie glared at him.

"I was *doing*. The rancher who owned the old house was murdered. There was never an investigation. No one was ever punished. The murder was just covered up and forgotten by everyone, except the dog. The dog stayed, even after the rancher was dead--after both of them were dead--guarding his friend's grave."

"It's a touching story, Jolie but you can't know…" Sifu started to protest.

"I can," Jolie disagreed. "When I touch someone or sometimes just get close to them, I know things about them and their lives, Sifu. It's who I am. I hate that people call it a gift, but maybe that's what it is." She could see the disbelief and it felt like it sliced her open, bleeding out all her hard-earned confidence. "You don't believe me."

"She knew things about my life that she couldn't have known, Sifu," Rufus stood up for her.

The Taoist remained silent.

Jolie turned to Rufus. "Can we go now?

"We're not done," Sifu said.

"*I* am." She looked at him dead in the eyes, matching him stubborn to stubborn. She was not faking it. She had not imagined what the spirit had shown her. What she saw was real. He could accept it or not, but she was not backing down.

The chauffeur shot a questioning look at Sifu but got no reaction.

"As soon as EMS gets Missus Macullen off safely, I'll take you wherever you want to go, Jolie," Rufus assured her. She went to wait by the limousine.

Driving back to the school, the silence in the car could have been sliced by a knife.

"They didn't do anything wrong," Jolie muttered finally.

"I understand that," Sifu agreed.

"The crew was about to put a post right through the rancher's heart," Jolie directed the disclosure to Rufus.

The driver nodded. "Like in the dreams I had."

"Like in the dreams," Jolie agreed. "The dog couldn't let that happen."

"The contractor never said anything about a grave," Rufus shared.

"Not even to Missus Macullen?" Jolie asked.

The driver hesitated. "I don't know."

"If he had, what would have happened?"

Rufus knew the answer. "They would have had to shut the project down until it could be assessed for archeological significance."

"So, he didn't report it and tried to cover it up. Or she did."

"And the disruptions escalated," Rufus muttered.

"But it was the people who were doing the wrong thing," Jolie pointed out. "Not the ghost-dog. The people were wrong--going back to someone murdering the old rancher."

Sifu shook his head. "They're spirits, Jolie. and they're dead. They don't belong here. They need to move on. It's the natural order of things."

"That land belonged to that rancher," Jolie insisted. "If he hadn't been murdered and the land hadn't been stolen, it could have provided security for his descendants for the last hundred years and more. His people would have had financial stability. It would have changed their lives, Sifu, and someone took that away from them, covered it up, then hid the crime; twice, and now they have to be punished by being sent into oblivion?"

"That's not what I do," the Taoist defended himself. "But we're not the police and ghosts can't own the deed to a property. Someone is going to build on that land."

"Not if we stop them," Rufus spoke up.

"Rufus is working on his Master's Degree in social advocacy," Jolie explained.

"How could it be stopped, Rufus?" Sifu asked.

"Well, it's possible that all we'd be able to do is slow things down, but if formal papers are filed reporting the grave, it will halt any more excavating until the gravesite is analyzed for archeological, or cultural significance."

"I don't think the rancher was Native American," Jolie said. "He looked African American."

"They'll test for DNA," Rufus assured her.

"Good luck with that with that dog standing over the bones."

"That will need to get figured out, but Black or Native, there are protections now that there weren't before," Rufus pointed out. "Filing will get the site official notice though, and that will buy some time."

"Let me know what you need us to do," Sifu offered.

"If you would sign the filing, I might be able to keep my job."

"Of course, Rufus."

"It will give us time to investigate the original deed as well and see what happened after the rancher's death, look for surviving family--draw attention to the case. There's a real interest in Las Vegas's early history these days, and a rise in the national will to address the wrongs done to people of color around issues of property that was stolen from them."

"You don't know it was stolen," Sifu objected.

"I *do*," Jolie declared. "You think I can't know because I haven't been studying for twenty years, but Padmasambhava said there are people who are naturally initiated who don't have to struggle with understanding and disbelief because they're naturally open, so they just get it. Well, *I* get it, Sifu. That's why I'm trying to help these spirits, and why I'm trying to save my demon friend, Ling from being forced to bond with Yanna Maria who kidnapped him--or demon-napped him, or whatever that would be. I don't know if I'm doing the right thing half the time, but I am trying." Jolie wiped the tears from her face with the back of her hand. "I'm sorry. My life has been a real shit-show lately."

"You tamed a demon?" Sifu repeated.

"Tamed is probably a strong word, but yeah, pretty much."

"I've driven some weird folk," Rufus muttered, "but you two have to be the weirdest."

"The ghost dog is only trying to protect his friend, Sifu. You can't just banish him," Jolie pleaded.

"You need to get some rest. We'll talk about this tomorrow," was his reply.

Jolie recognized it as a typical grownup way to end the conversation on their terms.

When they got to the school, Rance and Sifu got out, but she remained huddled in the far corner.

"Could you take me to my friend's in Red Rock?" she asked Rufus, quietly. "I don't feel much like camping out in a closet tonight."

"I'll come out tomorrow and we can talk." Sifu headed for his car.

Rance let himself into the school and the limo pulled out and headed west.

Jolie texted Rose. Rose would be waiting up for her.

CHAPTER TWENTY-FIVE

The smell of toast and coffee spiked the summer morning air. Rose had started her day already. When the sun hit the red, western cliffs of Calico Basin, it was hard to stay in bed unless, of course, you were exhausted by attempting to understand the emotional baggage of haunting spirits while searching for a captive demon. But waking up at Rose's in Red Rock had a texture of memories for Jolie.

Key events in her time in Las Vegas tracked back to this place, this house, this room. How different might her life have been if Remy had not bumped into her at school last winter, pushing her, stumbling into a vision of his death that set into motion a string of events still playing out today? If that night after Axel died, he had not brought her here to Rose's, how might things have been different? In Red Rock, Jolie had discovered a magical place that grounded her spirit--a place where the Earth's life radiated so close to the surface you could feel it vibrating through the soles of your feet, reverberating in the air, echoing through the chambers of your heart.

It was here, at Roses, in Red Rock, that Jolie spent the night after Jessie Lynne was shot. She went into her first sweat lodge here. This was where the black jack brought her after finding her lost in the mountains.

Not having packed for an overnight, Jolie slept in her unders and tank top. She wriggled into her shorts and padded barefoot out to the main room, which was both the living room and the kitchen with a breakfast bar that doubled as a preparation space separating the two.

"'Morning Rose." Jolie eyed the beginnings of breakfast, her stomach grumbling. "That's a lot of food."

"Sifu is coming, and I never know how many will come with him." Rose continued cutting veggies, a basket of eggs sitting at the ready.

"I don't think there will be that many," Jolie replied. "This isn't a group discussion. Do I have time to go out for a quick run?" Rose knew it wasn't about running. It was about Jolie having a chance to get out into the desert and connect.

"Sure." Rose smiled. "Anything you want to talk about between us girls before Sifu gets here?"

Jolie wondered what Sifu had already said to Rose. Would he have told her about Ling? Not sharing that your demon friend would be hanging around with you when you were at someone's house was probably a breach of etiquette.

"When I get back. I promise." Jolie hopped on one foot as she slipped on a tennis shoe, changing to hopping on the other to get the other shoe on before she reached the door.

The morning was waiting. She took off at a jog.

If Ling was here, where would he be, she wondered? Was there someplace he might have left a message or a clue? Was there a place in the basin where the veil between the worlds was thinner and her pleas and promises had a chance of reaching him and giving him hope to hold on?

She jogged to the east end of the mountain, climbing to the high cave where she had spent her retreat.

Everything was as she left it. No tracks, no evidence of an intruder. Not even coyote scat. She sat cross-legged and breathed in the warming day.

"Ling, it's your friend, Jolie," she started. "Wherever you are, whatever Yanna is trying to force you to do, don't give in to her. Hold on, and don't give up. There are hundreds of paths you could choose. Only one leads to you being enslaved. Refuse that path, Ling. You're strong enough."

Jolie rose, removed the prayer beads wrapped around her wrist, reached up, and hung them on an outcropping. "I'm leaving these as a spiritual torch, to light your way back to safety from wherever you are."

"Thank you," she muttered to the mountain before climbing back down.

Jolie reached the door to Rose's. The smell of spiced eggs and hash browns skipped from the kitchen to her nose on a sizzle.

She took a slow sip of fresh, hot coffee, followed by a bite of buttered toast, savoring the classic American breakfast, something she missed eating only at the Chinese restaurant.

"What you need to know before Sifu gets here...." She paused for another sip. "First of all, I'm not sure where Sifu's coming from--like what he's thinking. He's kind of an enigma to me. So, I might need some support there, because I don't know how much he's willing to accept about me. It doesn't seem like that much." Rose waited, holding her pancake turner at the ready. "Okay, here goes," Jolie explained her history with Ling and how he fit into events Rose already knew about.

"I'm sorry about Oz," Rose said when the teen was done. That part came out too. "I know you liked them."

"I guess I didn't know them as well as I thought."

"Even people you know well can make choices that disappoint you," Rose replied.

Jolie wondered if Rose meant her. "I'm sorry I didn't tell you before about Ling. I kept thinking he was about to move on and if he was just going to disappear one day then what was the point in trying to explain it all? That's what I was trying to get him to do for the longest time, leave, but he just wouldn't. For a long time, he kept insisting that I should bond him. When he finally gave up on that, he started badgering me to teach him right from wrong. I tried to explain I wasn't the right person to do that, but he wouldn't listen."

A smile tugged at the corners of Rose's lips. "I think I'm with Ling on that one. I'd trust your compass. You believe Yanna Maria is holding him prisoner?" Said like that, it did sound far-fetched.

"I *know* it," Jolie insisted even so.

Rose shook her head. "We weren't friends, but she seemed nice enough--helpful, harmless."

"Please. You've got to believe me, Rose."

"Oh, I do, Jolie. I do."

"I'm not sure Sifu does. That's the part I might need help with."

"Sifu doesn't know you like Hoke, or Remy, or I do. He was around the edges of last spring's events, but he wasn't part of them." Car tires crunched the gravel on the road. "That'll be him." She turned off the stove, put down her pancake turner, and went to greet her latest guest.

"I need to finish up at the Rancho property today. Will you come, Jolie?" Sifu asked Jolie once breakfast was finished. "You seem to understand these spirits. I could use your help negotiating a truce."

Jolie glanced at Rose. Maybe he believed her after all, or maybe sleeping with his doubts had changed his mind. She wondered if Sifu went to the same temple she did in his dreams and if he knew the old skinny monk. Had the old man spoken to Sifu for her? There was no point asking. Responding to a direct question with a direct answer was not a Taoist thing.

"Moving the pool and the fence would go a long way toward settling things down," Jolie suggested. Sifu raised his eyebrows above the rim of his coffee cup.

"Do you know what moving a pool and all its plumbing would cost?"

"How much is not being haunted worth?"

"I'm not saying it isn't the right thing to do," Sifu clarified. "But Missus Macullen has been reluctant to do what I've told her needs to be done and she's even more reluctant when it comes to spending money."

"But she hired you to fix her problem, didn't she?" Rose asked.

"She asked the school for help. We're obligated to respond. The donation she gives in return, however, is her choice and frankly, once the threat has been handled, the white community is not usually very generous in these situations."

"That doesn't seem right," Jolie protested.

Sifu shrugged. "It's not a commercial transaction and it wouldn't be right to turn it into one."

"People don't pay to go into a sweat lodge either," Rose pointed out. "Or at least they shouldn't. If someone wants you to buy a ticket to go into a sweat lodge…"

"Run," both Rose and Sifu finished the warning together, laughing afterward.

"The authorities may tell her she has to move the pool or the fence," Sifu pointed out. "And then she'd have to do it, but she doesn't have to listen to me--or us." He smiled at Jolie. "So, until the authorities step in, we need a more immediate short-term resolution to at least settle things down. Got any ideas?" he asked Jolie.

"If Missus Macullen would agree to put up at least a temporary protective fence around the gravesite, maybe the ghost dog would not feel like his friend's grave was being threatened?" Jolie suggested.

Sifu nodded sipping his coffee. "I think I can get her to agree to that. I'll have Rance gather a few of the Kung Fu students. They can meet us at the house with some supplies to build a temporary protective barrier. Now, what about the other thing?" He glanced at Rose, uncertain how much to say.

"I know about the demon," Rose said. "And as far as I'm concerned, he was a perfect house guest." She began to clear the table. "I never even knew he was here." She winked at Jolie.

"You know Yanna Maria, too, right, Rose?" the Taoist asked. "She's been to Women's Lodges?"

"She came a few times, but I never realized there was any connection."

Jolie grunted. "Because she threatened that if I told anyone anything she wouldn't help me, and I thought she was trying to do that back then. She made a huge deal about me not questioning her over anything. I had to do exactly what she said."

"I can't imagine why she would say something like that." Sifu smiled, wryly.

"You know why, Sifu," Jolie argued. "She wanted to get close to Ling so she could bond him, and she thought she could get to him through me."

"You don't think maybe you misjudged the woman's motives?" Sifu suggested.

"Absolutely not. Yanna Maria nearly killed Remy last spring, and she would have if I hadn't stopped her." Jolie saw surprise on Sifu's face. "For months I tried to figure out how to change the outcome of the vision I had of Remy's death. Hoke had premonitions too, and he was hanging around trying to protect his grandson. Just ask them. They'll tell you."

"It's true, Sifu," Rose said. "She saved Remy's life. When she sinks her teeth into something, this girl can be a bit of a bulldog."

"I've noticed." Sifu offered his small, wan, half-smile. "So, because you were a bulldog, Remy lives. The question is what action do we take now?"

Hope fluttered in Jolie's chest. "We need to find Ling and free him."

"There's a woman on the Women's Lodge call list who Yanna gave a ride to a few times. She might know where Yanna Maria lives." Rose went to a drawer and took out a well-used piece of paper then went to the landline phone.

Jolie hesitated. "Sifu, how would a person know for certain that a demon had changed and was good?"

"You think your demon friend is not being truthful?"

"No. I just wonder if there's a way to know if he's been turned or bonded, or if there's a way to protect him from that happening."

They could hear Rose talking on the phone in the other room, but minutes slipped away before the Taoist replied.

"He could take Refuge.

Jolie frowned in confusion. "What does that mean?"

"It is a Buddhist ceremony of commitment, a way to connect to a lineage founded on Buddhist precepts of non-harming. It would bond him to those precepts as opposed to bonding to an earthly master."

Rose rejoined them. "We struck out. She's got no idea where Yanna is. Why don't you just send some of your kids over there and let them go all ninja on her until she releases the demon?"

"I would never put my students in danger physically or with the law, Rose." He had such a dry delivery it was hard to be sure, but Jolie thought there was a bit of sarcasm behind his words.

Jolie was sitting by the Chinatown fountain grabbing an early lunch before returning to the Rancho house when Mister Yinchen unexpectedly joined her.

"May I sit?" he asked, always the gentleman.

"Of course. I would be honored." Jolie bowed her head respectfully, offering him to share an egg roll. Smiling, he accepted.

"A bit too much garlic for my taste, but I give Mister Meng credit. He delivers a fine egg roll."

"You are not here to discuss egg rolls," Jolie said.

Yinchen chuckled. "No. I am here to discuss how Spiritual Warrior class is going for you?"

"Slow," Jolie replied without thinking. Yinchen cocked his head to one side: a silent question. "Don't get me wrong, I am grateful for the opportunity to learn, Mister Yinchen," Jolie replied more carefully. "Thank you for arranging it."

"But?"

Jolie sighed. She had been caught out and it was her own fault. "My questions are different from the other students, and it doesn't seem like this class is going to answer them. I'm sure it is a failure in my character. I need to learn patience, but…" She shrugged. There was a long pause before the elder spoke again.

"I have not seen your little friend lately."

Jolie looked at him. "My little friend?" Yinchen gave her a knowing look. "You see Ling?" He nodded.

"I suppose he must be allowing it."

"That's interesting. I wonder why?"

"Maybe he thinks I am so old it does not matter because no one would believe me anyway." Yinchen chuckled.

"I think he is kinder than that. He's not a bad spirit," Jolie defended her friend. *At least not anymore.*

"I did not think he was." The elder man sat calmly watching the cars go by on Spring Mountain Boulevard. "Is he all right do you think?"

"He's in trouble. That's why he hasn't been around. I've been trying to look for him--trying to get Sifu's advice on what to do."

"Ah, and what will you do then?" Yinchen asked.

"Anything I can. Whatever I have to," Jolie answered, her determination clear.

"Then he has a good friend in you. I have found that sometimes when answers in the physical world are hard to come by, I have better success leaning into the spiritual world: visions I am given during meditation…dreams. Often, they provide insight that my conscious mind has yet to grasp. Of course, that is just me, and each person is different. I do not mean to try and tell you what you should do." Yinchen rose and gave Jolie a small bow. "Thank you for the conversation, and the egg roll."

My dreams, Jolie thought. What had her dreams been showing her that could be important? And then it came to her: *The Thousandth Drop dream.* What did it say to her?

I need to stop waiting for someone to show me what to do and do something. Because it was just possible the dam was about to break. It only needed one final drop.

CHAPTER TWENTY-SIX

Sifu was finishing cleansing the area with sage, preparing to engage if the ghost dog became aggressive when the Kung Fu boys and Rance showed up at the Rancho house. It was the usual group: Brutus, Hugo, and Jiu, with Rance playing shepherd.

Hugo gave Jolie an uncomfortable glance, then avoided meeting her eyes. Jiu paused as he walked by Jolie.

"He's been raised South American Catholic, Jo," the young martial artist explained. "He's been warned all his life to watch for demons because they'll try to take you over."

"And there was a time I would have agreed with him," she admitted. "But Ling's not like that anymore. I wish Hugo could trust me on this."

"Accepting isn't easy, it's so different from how we were brought up. Taoist philosophies can be challenging for some Christians."

"I get that, but that doesn't mean I'm apologizing. I haven't done anything wrong," she said loud enough for Hugo to hear her.

Rance organized the Kung Fu boys to build a split rail fence that sat on the ground rather than required posts dug into it. When they were done, they fixed a temporary sign onto it cautioning against trespassing.

Everyone stood by respectfully as Sifu offered tobacco and whispered to the Six Directions asking for protection of the sacred ground.

"And now we wait on the Archeological Society," the temple's master instructor said after thanking the students for their help. He and Rance walked off together, talking about the upcoming school challenge, and organizing what needed to be done to be ready.

The Kung Fu boys seemed reluctant to leave, loitering, uncomfortable, near the gravesite.

"I heard Rance talking to Sifu, Jolie," Brutus said. "He said he was going to go talk to that woman who stole the demon thing."

"His name is Ling," Jolie helped him.

"Right, Ling."

"Why does he have a Chinese name?" Hugo demanded.

"It's the name he had during his last human incarnation. It seemed better to call him that than to keep calling him 'Little Demon Dude'." Jolie's cell phone rang. It was a number she did not recognize so she almost ignored it, but something told her not to. "Yeah? Who is this?"

"Miss Boulet," Singh's distinctive East Indian accent identified him immediately. "It is Singh. I think you should come to the shop. I may have seen your 'Mister Whiskers'." Singh knew there was no Mister Whiskers and Jolie was about to say that when she realized he was speaking in code. He had seen something out of place at Yanna's shop.

"I'll be there as soon as I can, Mister Singh. Thank you, and please, don't do anything dangerous, like try to go near my 'cat' or confront it or anything. He's been hanging around with some very bad 'cats' lately and I wouldn't want you to get hurt."

"I will keep an eye on things but try not to bring attention to myself," Singh promised.

"Perfect." Jolie ended the call. "I have to go," she apologized to the boys as she headed for the front gates. Sifu and Rance were being driven out by Rufus.

"You're going there, aren't you?" Hugo said. "To the fortune teller's shop, to find the demon."

Jolie considered lying to keep her friends from jumping into events she could not predict the flow or outcome of, but remembering what Hugo said, she chose another way: the truth.

"I've been watching it, but I haven't seen anything useful yet. That call was someone who has been helping me and thinks they saw something."

"You should wait for Sifu," Jiu said.

"I can't," Jolie declared.

"Okay, then let's go," Hugo surprised them all.

"Seriously? I thought you…"

Hugo interrupted. "Do you want the help of your friends or not, Jo?"

"I do. I absolutely do."

"We can call it a skills practice session," Brutus suggested, obviously excited by the prospect.

"Except it isn't," Jolie pointed out. "This is not a video game, or a movie, Bru. If we get caught, we could get in trouble--not only with Yanna, who seems to have no problem hurting people but with the law if she thinks she can make that work for her."

The group exchanged looks, coming to a quick consensus. "Then we won't get caught." Brutus took in his friend's clothing, light, summer wear. None were ninja-worthy. "We're not exactly dressed for a stealth mission though, guys. We need to go to the school and gear up." They all crammed into Brutus's old Toyota pickup.

Rance and Sifu were not at the school, so Jiu fetched the key from its secret hiding place. The door to the costume closet was open. Jolie and Sifu had left in a hurry. Had that only been yesterday morning? It felt like longer.

"We're looking for anything black or dark blue." Jiu began to sift through the racks passing up articles of the wrong color, that wouldn't fit any of them or were made of too delicate a fabric for their purposes and tossing those that might work onto a pile on Jolie's yellow satin fabric bed.

"Hey, guys, look what I found!" Hugo pushed a box out from under the back rack by the wall. He lifted an item from it. The black pants and long-sleeved shirts with white skeletons painted on them that the Kung Fu students running security for the Ridge Walking Ceremony had worn.

Jiu looked skeptical. "Skeleton costumes in July? Yeah, that'll blend in."

"We could wear them inside out," Hugo said, holding up a fully black long-sleeved T-shirt.

"That works." Brutus pounced on the box, digging through it and tossing aside the costumes too small for his muscular frame. "Hey Jiu, look. This one was Bodhi's." He displayed a shirt bearing the initials KB, for Bodhi Ke, in black permanent marker on the tag. "It should fit you, or is that too weird?

"It's a costume, Bru, not a death shroud." Jiu took the shirt and pants and held them up against his small frame. He was the younger brother, with a similar slender build. Although he was slightly shorter than Bodhi when his brother passed a few months ago he was catching up quickly.

It did not take long for each of the young people to find a black costume, even Jolie. They quickly put them on behind the racks.

"We can use this to darken our faces." Brutus held out a tin of dark eye makeup.

"We're not Navy Seals," Hugo protested.

"Long sleeves, long pants, full-on black in one hundred ten-degree heat? Blacking our faces is going to make us even more suspicious," Jolie added.

"I'll take it along just in case." Brutus stuffed the makeup into his pants pocket. "I think we're ready. Let's go." They scrambled back into the pickup.

The first thing Jolie needed to do was to check in with Mister Singh and find out what it was he had seen.

"I have been making quite a nuisance of myself with Missus Yanna," the merchant confessed when Jolie arrived at his furniture shop. "Dropping in every day to visit, saying that after the police were called to her establishment, I realized I did not know my fellow shopkeepers and needed to do better. This afternoon while I was there, the postal person delivered a package to her. She was outside speaking to me--she does not seem to like people coming into her shop—which I find to be very suspicious because why do you have a shop if you do not want people to come inside and see the things you wish to sell? But she grabbed that package quick as a cobra, holding it to her chest as if it were a precious child. Then she shooed the postman and me away and hurried back into her shop.

"I pretended to have forgotten to tell her something and returned and saw her inside opening a hidden room in the left side wall behind the beaded curtain that leads to the back room. I saw no people, Miss Jolie. No metal rings on the wall. No mattresses on the floor, but she did close it very quickly, as if she were most anxious that I should not see it. Do you think this is of any significance? Could this be helpful in your search?"

"I hope so. Thank you, Mister Singh."

He scrutinized her friends in the pickup. "Are your friends performers? Is that why you are all wearing matching uniforms?"

"We belong to a dance and acrobatic team," Jolie offered an improvised half-truth. "They've agreed to help me look into what you found today."

"Ah. Despite the dangers, you warned me about. They must be very good friends indeed, Miss Jolie. You are fortunate to have such good friends; loyal, good boys, and good sons, I see."

"You can see all that from here?" Jolie laughed. "You must have incredible eyesight."

"There are things we see with our eyes and things we see other ways. I have seen how important your missing friend is to you—how determined you are not to let their disappearance go unresolved. Being such a good friend to others can only draw good friends to you in return. I have met few such young people since coming to this country. I wish my daughter had found such friends here." He gave a small, respectful bow. "Let me know if there is anything more I can do to assist."

Jolie left Singh's furniture shop. Brutus moved the pickup to the far end of the back alley where it would be out of Yanna Maria's sight. Mostly what they needed to do now was wait for darkness, which--at this time of year--was always a late arrival.

"This is taking too long," Jolie grumbled. She looked at the sun, still an hour from sliding down behind the Western mountains. "What is she doing in there?"

"We can't do anything until she leaves."

"And it gets dark," Jiu added.

"Whatever was in that package she got this morning is important to her. It must have something to do with Ling. I know it. She could be doing anything to him-- torturing him!"

"How would a person torture a demon?" Brutus wondered.

Jolie scowled. "I don't know."

"Would they scream, or groan, like a person, or just get pissed off?"

"It's probably a bad idea to piss off a demon," Jiu said.

Hugo looked at the sky. "Maybe they would call down a lightning storm?" It was clear, without a sign of inclement weather, now dark clouds were grouping over the mini-mall. "You said Yanna Maria wanted the demon for his power. How much power does she already have?"

"I don't know. Some. She did manage to nearly kill Remy, and she did make Ling visible and keep him from disappearing." Jolie looked up at the storm clouds.

Brutus paled. "She was responsible for Remy's accident?"

"Well, she set it up," Jolie explained. "She's a bad person. That's why she can't get control of Ling--aside from it being wrong for one being to enslave another."

They fell back into silence.

"I could go into the shop, pretend to casually browse, and secretly scope out the door to the secret room," Brutus suggested.

"Like she's going to let you get anywhere close to it," Jiu contradicted his friend.

"Maybe two of us should go. Then I can keep her busy in the front of the shop while the other one of you checks the back room," Brutus tried again.

"It can't be me," Jolie pointed out. "She knows I'll be trying to get Ling back. She'll have set wards to keep me out. The minute I cross any of the shop's thresholds, she'll know I'm there."

"I should go," Hugo said. "Yanna's been working to get to me through my mom for weeks now. I've got the best chance at keeping her distracted. I'll go into the shop and talk to her while, Bru and Jiu, you slip in the back door from the alley and search for a way to get through the hidden door." Hugo looked at Jolie. "You can be the lookout."

"She's going to know you're there," Jolie groaned. "She's going to catch you."

"Not Jiu and me," Brutus boasted. "Little brother here is as silent as a cat and as sneaky as a shadow."

"What about you?"

"I'm his backup--strong as a bull. That old woman does not want to mess with me."

"You can't beat up an old woman, Brutus," Hugo said shocked.

"Stop," Jolie interjected. "You can't think of her that way. If you do, she'll take advantage. She's not some frail old grandma, Hugo. She's messed up and twisted."

"Sifu says we shouldn't judge."

"If this makes you uncomfortable, you should go home. There are energies focused on good, and energies focused on evil, and if you sit down to tea with evil, you're probably going die of poisoned tea."

"What if you're wrong, Jo?" Hugo asked.

Jiu answered, "If Jo had wanted to, she would have already taken Ling and been controlling its power for weeks now. It would have been a lot easier for her if she had, but she didn't. She thought the demon might have been responsible for killing her mom, but she still taught it about friendship. I don't know if I could have been that forgiving. As Spiritual Warriors, we do the best we can, making the best ethical, compassionate, choice we see in the moment. If the other option is leaving this demon and all its power to Yanna, knowing how she's acted in the past, I'm with Jolie and I'll accept the consequences of that decision."

Brutus wiped damp eyes. "That speech was effing awesome, Jiu. I wish your big brother had been here to hear it. He would have been so proud." The boys made a circle, wrapping their arms around each other's shoulders and pulling together until their heads touched. Brutus motioned Jolie to join them, and she did. Standing together, the excitement and fear in their breath mingling, their quickened heartbeats found a common rhythm.

"I'm with you, Jo," Brutus muttered emotionally. The others repeated the promise. "Now, let's get to work."

Hugo lingered as the others headed down the alley toward the fortuneteller's shop, then he walked around to the front.

The back door was locked but Jiu deftly picked the lock.

"That's handy. When did you pick up that skill?" Brutus asked.

"It was a game Bodhi and I played at home," he explained.

"We need to talk about your home life, dude."

Jiu's expression said that he would rather not.

With the back door cracked, the Kung Fu boys could hear when the front door shop bell rang, announcing Hugo had entered.

"He's in."

Jolie could not hear what her friend and Yanna were saying, but it seemed to start with Yanna not recognizing him and thinking Hugo was the casual shopper he was pretending to be. Hugo did not hurry her discovery of his connection, drawing out their encounter, buying his friends as much time as he could.

Jiu, then Brutus, slipped inside the back storage room while Jolie waited outside, cautious of the shop's threshold.

There was a brightly colored, Mexican-print, wall hanging over the hidden doorway. An extra challenge that gave them no cover. It would be impossible for anyone opening the door to the hidden room not to be exposed from the front door or center section of the display portion of the shop. If Yanna looked back while within sight of the curtained entryway, she would see them.

Hugo called Yanna to the south wall of the shop's display area and Jolie could hear him speaking to her earnestly. *She recognized him.* How long could Hugo keep Yanna's attention without her getting suspicious or pissed and kicking him out?

Jolie's heart was beating like a heavy-metal drum solo, and she was sure the whole neighborhood must be hearing it. She did not know anything about the Santeria religion, but she was sure that, as a traditional old-world practice, it was not normal for its adherents to be trying to do the evil, vindictive things Yanna had been trying to do. Whatever religion a person ascribed to, human beings were subject to their baggage and false notions. It felt unfair to blame an entire religion for the choices made by a few individuals.

Jiu and Brutus slinked behind the corner that abutted the wall with the hidden door, trying not to make the wall hanging flutter as they examined the corner for clues as to how the door worked. Somewhere, there had to be a device to open and close the wall.

Hugo's voice suddenly became louder. He was trying to keep Yanna close to him on the south wall where she would not see the trespassers, but the woman had a fiery nature, and when she was upset, walking turned into stomping. She was stomping now.

Brutus and Jiu flattened their backs against the wall, throwing themselves under the wooden storage shelves stacked with trinkets and self-help books as Yanna's voice and heavy footsteps drew closer.

I need to get her out of the building. Jolie pulled out her cell phone and called Mister Singh.

"Mister Singh, could you find a reason to call Yanna outside, to the front of her shop?"

"I was just there a few hours ago. What reason could I give?" he asked dismayed. "She would most certainly become suspicious."

Jolie got an idea. "Give me a minute. Brutus!" she hissed. "Brutus!" She motioned wildly to the boy to throw her the truck keys.

His head appeared beneath the shelving.

"Throw me your truck keys!" Jolie mouthed, motioning as if playing charades. She hated the game. She was terrible at it.

Brutus finally figured it out and tossed her the keys just as Yanna stomped back past the archway on her way to the North end of her shop.

"Yanna Maria!" Hugo shouted so she would turn away from the back room. Brutus shrunk back under the shelving.

Jolie ran to the pickup, keys in hand. Driving it around to the front parking lot, she hopped out and raced back to the alley before calling Mister Singh back.

"Do you see the beat-up Toyota mini pickup in the front?" she asked him. "Call Yanna outside and ask her if she noticed it being there yesterday and whether she thinks you should have it towed. But please don't have it towed. It's my friend's. Maybe you could complain about how it makes the parking lot look bad because it's such a junker and it's bad for business. Just keep her distracted as long as you can." She ended the call before Singh had a chance to respond. Either he would do it or not, but she thought he would. She was right. Within a minute Singh was calling out to Yanna as he strode determinedly down the front walk toward her shop.

"Can you hear me, Ling? Do something to let me know you're here, please."

"Your friend, Singh, lost her. She's coming back!" Hugo hissed toward the back room.

"Hugo, get out of there, now," Jolie commanded. With a look over his shoulder, Hugo went for the door. The moment he was clear, Jolie leaped through the alleyway door and sprinted for the shop's front door. Turning the lock, she ducked down below the window, out of sight.

Instantly Yanna turned and reached for the door handle.

It did not open.

She rattled it, cursing under her breath, then put her face up to the glass, peering inside.

"Is something wrong, Missus Yanna?" Singh asked.

"I have locked myself out." She checked the pockets of her gathered skirt and frowned. "Maybe I left the back open." She started to walk around the building.

"It is too hot on the west side of the building this time of day for a lady like yourself. Stay here in the shade and I will check the back door for you. If it is open, with your permission, I will step through and unlock the front door for you. If it is locked? Well, perhaps we must call a locksmith?"

"That won't be necessary, Mister Singh. I have a spare key at my house. I will simply have to go get it. Oh dear. My car keys are inside as well."

"Then I will drive you," Singh suggested helpfully. "But first let me check and see if the back door is unlocked."

"I never leave it unlocked," Yanna groused.

"Nevertheless, we would feel foolish if we both had to close our shops only to find the back door unlocked." Singh quickly walked back to his shop and took the shortcut through it to the alley.

Yanna Maria's back door was softly closed but not latched and Jolie watched it move ever so slightly before hearing the latch click.

"I know you are in there, Jolie," Yanna hissed through the crack between the glass door and the doorjamb above the teen. "I knew you would come, but it will do you no good. I have control of the demon. His power is mine."

Jolie wanted to jump up and declare to Yanna's face that she was a liar, but she stayed where she was, breathing slowly. Yanna could believe what she wanted but that did not make it true. The Santeria was desperate to get Ling's power because she did not have enough of her own. But why did she need it so badly? What had made this hole in the woman, and why did she think filling it with Ling's power would ease her pain?

Jolie did not think that even Yanna knew the answers to these questions, but given time, perhaps she would find them.

That's what Sifu would say. And maybe it was true. Maybe given enough time, anyone could evolve into someone better, and wiser. A law of the Universe could not be true part of the time, or it was not a law of the Universe.

"I am sorry Missus Yanna...." The rest of Singh's out-of-breath apology was lost to Jolie's ears.

Jolie took advantage of Singh's arrival to skitter away from the front door and out the back. Hugo was there, waiting.

"Is he in there?" Hugo asked her.

"If he is, he's shielded by something--layers of magic, or some special metal she's used to keep him from using his power to free himself."

"It's been days," Jiu said soberly.

"But he doesn't like to eat or poop anything, right?" Brutus asked. "I mean he's a demon. Maybe he's just hanging out."

"She's not feeding him bonbons, Bru," Jolie argued. "If Ling were fine, I don't think I would feel so worried about him."

"You care so much for this demon?" Hugo did not look pleased with the idea.

"I care for all my friends." Hugo took that like a stab, though she did not mean it that way, but this was not the time or place to clarify definitions and types of love.

"Your friend, Singh, just pulled out with Yanna Maria in his car," Jiu announced as he came around the north corner of the building.

"Let's go." Brutus pushed inside and led the others to the door. Jiu ran his hands over the wall.

"There's no break in the face of the wall," he informed the others. Hugo stepped forward fingering the ninety-degree corner where the short entry wall met the longer one. "Here." He scratched at a lip edge. "It's an invisible hinge--that's what my dad calls them."

"How do we open it?" Brutus asked.

"There'll be a pin latch somewhere." He continued sliding his hand along the edge of one side and then the other. "Here it is." He picked at the top of the L-shaped metal bar until he could swing it out from its flat position, enabling him to lift it and free of the hinge locks. Pushing once quickly on the door surface, something popped, and the door opened.

Inside were more boxes of supplies, all in wooden crates, none of them labeled. A sleeping cot with a Mexican blanket and a pillow was pushed up against the inside wall.

"Well, someone's been sleeping in here."

"Ling doesn't sleep," Jolie informed her friends. Her eyes moved to the old trunk sitting at the foot of the crates. It was about a foot wide and two feet long, too short for a steamer trunk, but whatever was meant to be contained in it had to be of some significance. The trunk itself was a work of ancient art, its exterior ornate, worn leather alternating with vertical wooden strips, and stained a deeply, faded red. Decorative, brass nails had been set in swirling patterns. Even the hardware was ornate, stamped with unfamiliar symbols, though some with a religious feel to them.

"Look at this." Jiu lifted a primitive Mezo-American sculpture, a mask with very large circular earrings and a feather headdress from one of the crates, shucking off the straw protecting it.

"That belongs in a museum. It's probably not even legal for it to be in this country," Hugo remarked.

Jiu lifted a second sculpture out. This one of a kneeling woman, the primitive red and indigo coloring of her dress and shawl, made by natural mineral or botanical compounds, giving her clothing a patina of history and grace not replicated by louder more modern pigments.

Jolie's eyes returned to the antique trunk.

"Are you going to open it? Hugo asked quietly. Jolie continued to stare at the object. "Do you want me to?"

"No. I can do it." Jolie leaned down. It was locked.

"Okay, so we take it with us." Brutus tried to lift the small trunk but couldn't. Even with all of them taking a side, they couldn't. "It's either got something super heavy in it or it's attached to the floor," he announced.

"So, we have to open it here," Hugo said.

"We need a key." Jiu stepped over to look at the old lock. "An old skeleton key. Help me look." He disappeared into the front display room.

"There's a bunch of them in a basket under the window," Hugo shouted after him. Jiu returned quickly. Metal grated on metal as he tried one after another.

Jolie put a hand to the trunk trying to feel the presence of the demon. "Please be here, Ling. Please," she whispered.

"None of these will work," Jiu complained. "They're all from cheap molds--not remotely like the real thing." He disappeared back into the display room.

"Do you feel anything?" Bru asked Jolie.

"If I did, I'd be afraid it was only wishful thinking."

Jiu came in holding up a separate skeleton key. "On a shelf under the cash register," he announced. This time the key fit, moving a mechanism within the lock. Jolie worked the buckle hinges on either side, then opened the lid.

The insides of the trunk smelled like time; memories long abandoned to dust and decay. It was covered in brittle, yellowed paper, curled at the edges where it had been cut off to match the trunk edge. Three burn spots marked the paper at three points where a round tripod urn squatted. Perched solidly atop the clay urn, its handlike claws gripping the bottom half of the pot, an unidentifiable hybrid creature of some fierceness perched.

"I think they're trying to let you know you shouldn't open that," Brutus muttered.

"Which is exactly why we need to," Jolie replied, lifting the heavy urn. She tried holding it with one arm and using the other to jostle the clay claws that held the two pieces together, but it was awkward and heavy. She put it back down in the trunk and leaned over the object trying to work out how to get it open.

"Here, let me help." Hugo lifted the urn holding it against his chest, the sculpted creature's head pointed toward Jolie.

Its eyes came alive, glowing a hot coal amber, followed by its mouth brightening to the same. Jolie caught a flash of a shriveled gray blob lying like a desiccated leaf in the bottom, its veins were fine skeletal lines hatching the bag of skin holding it together. Then a scream punctured the world.

The pot lid's head fell open in three pieces. The creature inside turned to dust, its remains swirling from the urn, enveloping Jolie, before evaporating in the air. Its shriek shattered the guttered gasps as it fluttered to the ground around the young people.

"What was that?" Brutus demanded breathlessly.

"A demon screaming." Hugo looked to Jolie for confirmation.

"No, that thing inside."

"The demon."

"Ling," Jolie clarified. She leaned over to peek inside the empty urn, stretched and became thin then vanished.

The three-part lid flew back together with a sucking noise as the urn slipped from Hugo's grip, landing in the trunk. The trunk's lid snapped shut with a thud.

Outside, a car door slammed shut in front of the shop.

The three boys stared at each other.

"Yanna Maria's back."

"I feel this is my fault, Missus Yanna. If I had not called you outside to consult with me about the ugly truck…," they could hear Singh saying.

Hugo kneeled before the trunk desperately, and unsuccessfully, trying to open it.

Brutus pulled at him. "Leave it! We have to go!"

"We can't leave her!" Hugo argued.

Yanna was turning her key in the lock at the front door. Mister Singh was speaking loudly as if to warn the young people they were about to be intruded upon.

"I am ashamed, Missus Yanna, that you have been so inconvenienced by my foolish worries, please let me…."

"She's coming in. We have to go!" Brutus hissed.

"Jolie's in there!" Hugo argued.

"And we'll come back for her, but we can't help her if we get caught!" Brutus dragged Hugo away. Jiu reluctantly followed, the three boys emptying into the alley, then scrambling up and over the far wall.

Leaning against it, they panted, listening for signs of pursuit.

"Go quiet, Ninjas" Brutus commanded. The three Kung Fu students closed their eyes and tumbled into an instant calm. "We're not here. We're nothing, just three grasshoppers on the wall."

The world around them grew quiet, the city slowed, its metal noises softening. The slipstream of the traffic became subdued, the cicadas stilling in the mesquite trees.

No one followed them.

"We left her behind," Hugo whispered in anguish.

"We'll get her back," Brutus declared.

CHAPTER TWENTY-SEVEN

Yanna Maria's eye pressed against the opening of the Urn Guardian's mouth looking like a giant's.

"It was not so easy for your little friends to save you, after all, was it, demon?" the Santeria chuckled, pleased with herself. "You cannot die, but you can become so weak and lonely that you wish you would. You are going to stay in there though, all alone, until you give in to me."

She thought Ling was still inside the urn.

Whatever she sees when she looks inside, it is either not clear or it's not a physical replication, Jolie realized. *We did it. We freed Ling!* Success warmed a spot in her nervous belly. This was progress. It meant something.

Except you're trapped in Ling's place, an inner voice scolded. When Yanna realized Ling was free and all she had was Jolie, she would be livid. Would she be so angry that she hurt Jolie?

No. What Yanna wanted was Ling and Jolie was leverage. Would Ling give himself up to bondage to free Jolie?

Yes. He would not abandon "Little Sister" again.

Jolie thought back to the flashed image she saw of Ling just before he vaporized and escaped the urn. He looked so weak…so ill. What was it about the urn that kept him imprisoned and unable to escape?

Jolie began to explore her surroundings, walking around inside the rough clay walls of the urn, touching the surface smoothed out by some ancient artisan's hands, the widths of their fingers preserved in the faint raised ridges where they pressed in to make the pot become their vision.

Had the urn always been destined to be a spirit prison or had that been something added to the original creator's design--an added desire.

Perhaps, like an add-on to a house, an add-on to such a vessel would also create a weakness that could be exploited. It was an odd thought, and yet if the rule of "as above so below" were true....

Jolie sat cross-legged in the center of the pot's floor, her palms connecting to the clay beside her, and thought about the clay's history, its purpose.

She saw the clay being dug and plopped into a twig basket, the young woman working and refining lumps of it until it became warm and supple in her hands, its texture fine and smooth to the touch. Jolie, the observer, saw the young woman molding the pot with her hands, hollowing out the middle, rounding the walls to look like her older sister's belly, full with child. She saw the features of the character on the pot's lid pressed and pinched, and scribed into a mother's placid mien.

Then the vision shimmered and faltered.

The young woman had gone back to the cliff in the forest to dig more clay. She was alone, singing to herself as she worked, when a man came upon her quiet bliss. A man without kindness or compassion, he assaulted that bliss, crushing it, and the young woman's innocence as well, beneath his desires.

When the young woman returned to her family home, her cheeks stained with tears and dirt, silently she resumed making the pot, pressing, and scratching the creature on the lid into a being of vengeance and retribution.

When it was finished, she took the urn to the hut of a bruja, begging the bruja to place magic symbols on the vessel so it would capture and hold the spirit of her enemy. The bruja agreed, but the price was high: the young woman's happiness.

But the young woman did not believe she would ever have happiness again; that was lost to her, and she wanted to make sure no other young woman in her village, none of her sisters, cousins, or friends, ever had to endure the twisted affections of her attacker.

When the bruja finished the job, the young woman placed the urn in her basket and carried it to the cliff in the forest where she gathered clay. She returned every day throughout the summer, certain that one day the man she hated would return.

And he did.

The sad potter was ready for him and when he came toward her, she drew him closer. Pulling the urn's lid off, she pointed its open mouth toward him, sucking him into it. Replacing the cap, she returned to her village and put the urn on a shelf near her family's fire. When asked about it, she said it contained the remains of the man who would have been the father of her child.

Her belly swelled and she bore a girl child.

When she was in labor, the urn danced and trembled on the shelf, and forever after, when the child cried, the urn shivered, dancing toward the edge as if trying to fall off the shelf and go to the little girl. In time, the fierce head on the top of the urn took on an added aspect of anguished sadness alongside its fierce expression.

When the potter died, so did the story of what she had done.

But the urn itself was passed down to her daughter, then another, and another, gathering its tales of strangeness until a powerful wizard heard of it and came to examine it.

When the wizard heard the stories and saw the symbols on the urn, he knew more than anyone had since the bruja who had etched them into the clay.

Taking the urn for himself, he used it to capture a demon he had been hunting, imprisoning the demon in the pot and keeping it there for all the years of his life and the years of his son's as well. But by the time the urn was passed to the third generation, people no longer believed in such magic, and they did not hold the vessel in any esteem or keep it anywhere special. One day a child in the family was playing with it and they disappeared, releasing the demon the wizard had captured back into the world.

The demon kept the pot as a memento of its past, unconcerned with the spirit of the child within it, who, not being a demon, died.

No longer of any importance to him, somewhere during the demon's travels, he lost the urn.

Still seated within the urn, Jolie opened her eyes. She could feel the poison of hate that had permeated the clean clay the young woman had dug from the Earth. She sensed the grandmother's sadness at what had been done to her daughter, the sad potter. The young woman's pain had combined with the twisted desires of the man who had wronged her then been set in the clay by the symbols of permanence upon it. Neither spirit had been able to evolve into forgiveness, compounding through future owners driven by fear and bitterness until it saturated the clay itself, tainting what it touched.

Jolie could feel the hate surrounding her and understood how if a spirit were to live inside the vessel that hate would eventually saturate and become part of them.

The thousandth drop. The concept was present in every change, and everything changed, each day, each year, each life. Our stubborn insistence that we could hold it off and deny this truth caused us untold layers of anguish--self-inflicted because we kept clinging to a static point of view as if it were our lifeboat when it was the thing causing us to drown.

She closed her eyes again imagining the great weft and weave of the world, its threads alive and glistening, the singular colors, aware with life, standing out against the black background of The Nothing. She knew now how to use these threads to travel in the spirit world. Her spirit recognized itself now as a part of it all, and not separate--even here in this ancient urn. Jolie could feel the heart of the urn, the piece of the grandmother that had been separated and changed to become something questionably evil itself, simply by how it was used by others. It mourned its path and felt it had been forced to do what it had done at the behest of others, without choice.

We always have choice, the old monk had said.

At heart, the urn remained a simple clay pot, a small piece of the Earth formed into a vessel for use. But there was not only a Thousandth Drop of Water, but a Thousandth Person, a Thousandth Bit of Earth, and all things changed.

"What do you want the direction of your change to be?" Jolie asked the urn.

"I wish to go back to The Grandmother," its essence whispered.

"Then break." Jolie drew bright colors of energy from the world, gathering a ball of it within herself. When she expanded the ball, the clay burst apart, becoming shards that would be returned to the Earth, and once again become dust.

She was free.

She knew Ling was as well.

"Ling, where are you, Brother?" she called out to him. She felt the demon's essence, trembling, and weak, but palpable, and she followed it to a nest woven of the glistening threads, a small gray creature curled at the center of the tangle.

"Little Sister, you've come."

"I said I would," she assured him, gathering him into her lap.

"People often say things they do not mean," the demon wheezed.

"Not me," Jolie reminded him. *"We are true friends. I will always come."*

As she spoke to the demon, its form began to fill out, its image becoming stronger and more robust, not as a gray ball of jiggling flesh, but a more human-like form, with arms and legs, a head, and neck, but also wings and eyes with long lashes that held the glistening dust.

"You look different," Jolie said.

"I am experimenting with who I wish to become as I change into a free being," Ling declared. *"Will that make you sad?"*

"No." Jolie shook her head. *"Be whatever you wish. You have eternity to explore. Whatever you do--whoever you are, you will still be my true friend."*

Ling frowned. *"I was in a terrible place."* The demon shuddered.

"It was just a place," Jolie pointed out. *"Neither more nor less terrible than any other. It too was ready for a change."*

"And I could not get to you--or you to me, but now I can, and you can, and we are together again."

"Yes."

"You look different too," Ling told her.

"I suppose I am growing up--changing." Jolie smiled.

The little demon snuggled down into Jolie's arms and fell asleep.

The glistening weft and weave wove a ball around them, dewing on the demon's skin and clothes, though neither of those things existed until the demon spirit was covered lightly by the dust of the world, settling over it like frost as it slept, gently dreaming of the new self it would become and the new world it would live in with its friends of good intent.

Jolie looked around, remembering the path back to her world. It had not been a short climb, but it was there for her when she was ready.

In the distant black Nothing, a sinuous gold thread moved freely over the world-weave, drawing closer.

"Welcome Jin Long," Jolie greeted the Golden Dragon.

CHAPTER TWENTY- EIGHT

Jolie woke up lying on the yellow satin material that made the body of the Golden Dragon puppet in the costume closet at the temple school and remembered.

"It's good to be home." Ling came out from under the costume rack. His features still had an Asian influence, but Jolie would have described them as pixyish. His skin, or whatever a demon had, was an ever-changing array of swirling rainbow colors and his hair was bright, spring green--a nice contrast to the pink satin smock that had fallen off a hanger and onto his shoulders. He had shoulders now. He did not move the material, allowing it to rest on him, like a shawl. The look on his face--he had one of those too--dared Jolie to say something.

"You look great," Jolie complimented him.

"You look like shit," Ling countered.

Jolie grinned. Yeah. She was back in her body; Ling was free, and things were back to normal.

Over the next few weeks, volunteers worked for many hours repairing and refurbishing lion heads, or character heads that represented happy children, and silk costumes heavy with sequins, trim, and tassels. The army of volunteers sewed new pennants and replaced the scarves tied to the pommels of swords. They sanded and burnished weapon handles and blades and repaired the leather straps on the cymbals--everything needed to help the school shine on the day of the upcoming challenge.

Students who had taken classes at the temple school in the past, weaving what they had learned into their lives but no longer actively attending, were asked to return to help with the challenge.

The Lion Dancers practiced tumbling skills and choreography, doing strength and agility training so they could hold up their lion's head, or their partner if they were the support person. It took great athleticism, skill, and a tight partnership for a lion dance couple to create a lion of dynamic personality.

"We have a whole backstory for our lion," Butus bragged. "We filled it all out just like we do when we create a Dungeons and Dragons character."

Jiu shrugged. "It's probably overkill, but it works. The crowd loves us."

"I'm sure they do." Jolie's smile said she did too. Jiu's smile said the feeling was mutual.

The school's drummers worked out dramatic rhythmic patterns practicing until their hands bled and new calluses healed over the wounds. Cymbal players planned their timing within the dramatic melee of sound.

The final, most impressive character in the school's arsenal--brought out only on important occasions--was the Golden Dragon. Stretching three hundred feet from head to tail, the giant puppet required a hundred people to animate. Rance had been on the phone contacting alumni he hoped still felt connected enough to the school to come and help make the dragon come alive. The best version required people of descending sizes, beginning with the tallest working the head and shoulders, descending to the shortest who would flick and tease the tail.

This challenge was more than a public questioning of the temple school's educational quality. It was a test of the very essence of the school's foundation and lineage in traditional Chinese Kung Fu and the stakes were high.

Every aspect of the school's performances had to be memorable, displaying the importance of using both internal and external aspects of Kung Fu.

It was not enough to instruct students in forms. Temple students were encouraged to look at life in new ways and commit to a daily practice that helped them maintain a compassionate view of life and the world, but how did you prove that had happened to a team of judges?

Tru and Marty returned from their cruise, and not having a new gig yet, started showing up at the school. At first, the excuse was they wanted to spend time with Jolie, but soon, they, too, got caught up in the excitement and camaraderie forming among the volunteers, young and old. Mickey and her girls came, promising to bring Sean to the event.

"He's fixing up the old house. No more mauve walls, wall-to-wall carpeting, or floral curtains." Mickey made a shocked face.

"As long as he doesn't make it into a man cave with Metallica and Grateful Dead posters it will be an improvement." Jolie rolled her eyes.

She looked over the crowded main hall as volunteers were organized into groups and given rehearsal assignments.

"So many have come to the school to learn," Jolie marveled, feeling a twinge of wistfulness that Oz was not among them. But the Oz she remembered was not the Oz who had revealed themselves when they stole Ling. One more piece of the relationship learning curve. Still, everything changed, even people.

And we can learn to become better.

"Sifu has been building this dream for a long time," Rance said, joining Jolie and her scrutiny of the busy room of volunteers. "Starting in his garage with a handful of students. We don't often get a chance to see the foundation of what he built like this though, seeing the old students and hearing their stories." The challenge brought people together who had not seen each other in years. "They come to the school, get what they need, then move on, replaced by new faces. And so, the river grows."

"That challenging school are idiots," Jolie declared.

"Or perhaps they are being used by the Universe to make a point we need to see, and, in an odd way, they deserve our gratitude." Rance smiled.

Jolie laughed. "Rance, you are more like Sifu every day."

Rance bowed. "A compliment indeed. I saw Ling playing in the costume closet a bit ago. He was wearing a silk dress and a feather boa. There might have been a tiara involved."

It was Jolie's turn to smile. "Ling is a very old demon, but a very young personality, and is actively exploring who he wishes to be. Arms, legs, clothing, hair, and colors have become a huge distraction. One day Ling looks like a punk Peter Pan, the next it's Dame Edith, the British drag queen."

"Whenever the volunteers are getting tired here comes Ling to brighten the mood."

"Do you think they have any idea what he really is?"

"Do any of us?' Rance chuckled. "Some mysteries are better left mysterious, Jo."

"Jolie, could you come up here please?" Sifu called.

"What is it, Sifu?" Jolie asked entering the Taoist Master's office.

"I would like you to stand beside me in the front line when we approach the challengers. If you're okay with it? Rance will be on my other side."

"I--I'm honored, Sifu, but I'm sure there are more deserving students. I don't need...."

"But *I* do," Sifu stopped her. "The school does. Centuries ago in China, when the Taoists were still recognized by the leaders of the great houses, and in demand for their skills, when two armies approached for a battle, they would line up facing each other, their Taoist wizards by their side. In the front lines were colorful pennants, representing their houses. The stories are that the armies would wait and watch to see which direction the pennants went. Whichever side could blow the other side's pennants back was predicted to win because they had the greatest Qi. Sometimes the armies didn't fight because the outcome was so obvious.

"I want you in the front line putting out all the Qi you can manage, Jolie. Will you do that?"

"You have given us a home. We belong here. Of course, Sifu."

"And Ling, will he stand with us?"

"He is his own being and makes his own decisions, but you can ask. I expect, however, that he will stand with his friends."

At the end of most days, Hugo drove Jolie out to Rose's, or Rose picked her up, taking her home to sleep so she no longer needed to sleep in the costume closet. Wrangler dropped by several times a week on the excuse that he was checking up on how Jolie was doing, but he did not interfere with the living arrangements. Rose and Wrangler were getting close, Jolie had support and protection, her future was in a holding pattern.

"Are you happy?" Ling whispered to Jolie in the night, snuggled into the little bed in the lean-to room at Rose's.

"I think I am. I'm not sure how happy is supposed to feel, but I think this is it. What about you?" Jolie asked. "Are you still worried about Yanna? Do you think she realizes you escaped?"

Ling thought about that. "I don't know but she hasn't given up. I'm not worried about her forcing me to her will anymore though. I'm much too stubborn--like you."

"I'm not stubborn," Jolie protested.

"You are," Ling insisted. "You know what you believe, and you stick to it."

"That's not stubborn, Ling. That's having clear values."

"It seems like the same thing to me." The demon shrugged because he could.

"Remember what I said about gray areas having to do with the words we choose?" Jolie asked. "This is a good example. Sometimes a particular word means nearly the same thing as another one, but there's a subtle difference in meaning that makes people feel better or worse about what you're saying."

"It is a very imprecise and ineffective language," Ling complained.

"I stubbornly agree." Jolie teased. "Good night, Ling." She pulled the cover up to her chin. "What do you think about Sifu's idea about taking refuge?" she asked as she drifted off.

"I'm thinking about it," Ling disappeared, gone off to follow his nighttime adventures while Jolie slept.

The day of the Challenge finally arrived, a strong dawn, the sun rising in a clear, desert-blue sky. The courtyard and parking lot at the main entry to the

Chinatown Mall had been fenced and blocked off. Dignitaries, judges, and honored guests from Las Vegas, the Chinatown community, and beyond, were seated on the second-floor balcony where they would have an unobstructed view.

Students, former and current, young, and old, were tucked in along with their assigned groups, nervous and excited, but ready to do their part. Jolie could not see her friends, but she knew that Rose and Wrangler, Marty and Tru, were among the hundred people who committed to working the Golden Dragon.

Hoke sauntered toward Jolie, a path through the crowd clearing before him as he walked.

"That's a neat trick--like the parting of the Red Sea," she teased him.

He grinned. "An old story, and an even older skill."

"It's good to see you, Hoke."

"Sifu asked, and it is the least I can do to support the school that gave so much to my grandson. My arms are too stringy to hold up a dragon's back, but I can still make wind--and not just with my butt."

Jolie laughed. She was sure Hoke could gather an impressive amount of qi. "How is Remy?"

"He is doing good work. He may even have found his heart again."

Jolie felt a twinge in her heart, but she did wish her friend the best. "He deserves to be happy."

"As do you," the elder said tenderly.

Jolie heard her name called and turned to see Sifu leading a group of people toward her.

"You have guests, Jolie." Sifu gestured. As he stood aside there was Iris... and Topi.

"Oh my God, you're here!" Jolie ran into Iris' arms, crushed into the familiar perfume that connected her to the good times she had spent with Iris and Faith.

"Dear girl, I am so sorry it took so long for me to get back," the white-haired fashion icon whispered.

"It doesn't matter. You're here now." Jolie pulled away.

And there was Topi, the graceful, kind South American man who had been an invisible lifeline lingering in the background of possibility, keeping her a half breath from despair just because his affection for her lived in her memory.

"Topi." His name filled her heart like a sonnet. "What are you doing here?"

"When you disappeared, we were worried about you, Tessa, and I, and Grand Mere and Grand Pere Blancflor. We searched and found your friend, Iris, who led us to other friends, which brought us here." His warm laugh was a honey balm, soothing the hurts she had endured over the past year. "What a community you have gathered around you, Jolie."

"It's not me, Topi," Jolie explained. "It's Sifu and the school. I'm only a student here--not even a very good one, but I do love it."

"I want to hear all about it."

"And I want to tell you." She turned to Iris. "Both of you, but I can't right now. The Challenge is about to start."

"We will talk later, then," Topi offered.

"We will." Jolie hugged him again and squeezed Iris' hand. "Later."

"Yes, later."

Jolie knew when she touched them what they had each come to offer her: a home, a place to belong, where she would be cared for and supported in her exploration of who she wanted to become, but had their offers come too late. Didn't she already have those things? Hadn't she already found them for herself?

Mister Yinchen blew a conch shell, the sound growing rounder and fuller as it expanded across Chinatown calling the people and the spirits to take notice. The time had come. Something important was about to begin.

Jolie shivered. The conch was a primal call, harkening back through human history, present at countless moments of significance now lost to history, but the conch's call seemed to touch that older, deeper understanding, drawing people to join in this moment, in this time, on this day, to witness what would be.

The time had come.

On every side, throughout the challenge grounds, people stood, silent, and focused. Jolie looked up to the balcony. Even the dignitaries were standing, honoring the solemnity of the event.

Air--that was not wind--was stirring, lifting people's hair, their hearts, their expectations.

"Who is the distinguished-looking Latino standing beside Mister Yinchen?" Jolie asked as she took her place beside Sifu.

"Mister Orlan Xiu, the head teacher at our sister school in Mexico. He is one of the judges."

"How is that impartial?"

"Mister Xiu is well known and respected for his character. The committee suggested him, and the challengers approved him," Sifu explained.

"And the man beside him?"

"Mister Alvaro Cocom, a guest of Mister Xiu. I had not met him until last night when Master Yinchin invited us to dinner. I think you would find Cocom's spiritual background interesting."

Jolie knew better than to ask what that meant.

The temple school and their challengers moved forward in lines entering the staging area, Sifu's school coming from the West, the challengers from the East, until finally, the two groups faced each other across the staging area in the parking lot. The groups were not the same size, the challengers being the smaller, newer school, but the difference was not as obvious as it might have been. Sifu, with his usual compassion, held back many of the volunteers, including the hundred who would animate the Golden Dragon, awaiting their cues in the parking lot on the backside of the building, an unseen horde.

The challenger's core group was uniformed. Not entirely undisciplined, Jolie could feel their chaotic energy, resentful, aggressive, and barely contained.

Sifu's students, except the dancers, were all dressed in plain, black cotton pants, gathered at waist and ankle. Initiates wore long coat-like tunics over their blacks, everyone else wore black T-shirts with the school logo in white on the backs.

The temple school approached with a measured pace, confident and in control. When they reached the edge of the staging area, they stopped, as did their opposition.

"Now," Sifu said quietly. Rance, Jolie, Hoke, and other senior students began gathering qi as the command was passed through the ranks.

A chorus of humanity stepped out to the right and a wave of soft arms began to rise, one row after the next beginning the first qi opening exercise, arms drawing energy up from the Earth, then down from the heavens, combining before settling among the generations of students stacked behind Sifu.

The temple school's pennants whipped into horizontal arrows pointing at the challenger school, their pennants slapped back, before the wave of energy.

The challenger's teacher's eyes widened, and he looked around as if having lost track of what he was doing.

"He doesn't know what just hit him," Rance chuckled.

"I think he suspects it's not good though--not for him anyway," Jolie added.

"Do not lose sight of your compassion today, my young padawans," Sifu cautioned playfully using the Star Wars term. He often talked about how The Force in the science fiction classic had been modeled on Taoist philosophy. "The people who made this challenge were not entirely in charge of their own decisions, and they did not fully understand."

"They're about to find out," Rance muttered.

The temple school drummers began signaling the youngest group of performers. The little ones, some as young as four, ran forward, instantly planting their little post-toddler bodies in formation and beginning the Five Family's Salute Form accompanied by the pounding bass rhythm of the temple school's drummers, the energetic wooden clicks of drumsticks, and the sharp staccato of the sticks hitting the drum's wooden edges, in a complex rhythmic counterpoint.

As the beginning students finished, a second wave of more advanced students replaced them, launching into a new form, the pattern mirrored, less adeptly, on the challenger's side as their student groups, fewer in number, and less accomplished, presented their forms.

Some of those students were so unfamiliar with the form they were performing, they struggled to follow the teacher's lead.

Nevertheless, the crowd applauded as the size, skill, and number of students grew, until Ling, in human form and dressed very like the Ling of his past incarnation appeared and began Bagua as learned from Lu Dongbin.

The crowd stilled, watching the graceful, yet powerful, movements as Ling walked a glowing circle created by his energy, spinning, and disappearing during the spinning 'changes' that connected the Eight Mother Forms.

Then suddenly he did not disappear and reappear. He was just gone, his demonstration ended.

The big drums slowed their beats and the other instruments dropped out, leaving the single, strong dramatic beat.

A champion from either side stepped from among their peers.

As they did, Jolie saw Yanna Maria standing among the challengers. Jolie's heart felt like it was trying to crawl from her throat. How long had Yanna been there? Did she have something to do with Ling's disappearance?

"She cannot force me," the demon had said. *"I have become stubborn, like you."*

Ling reappeared in the open space between the two champions. Not all formal challenges included hand-to-hand martial combat, but the nature of this challenge and its claim that the temple school only taught forms for show, meant that this one did.

Ling, in human form, a small-boned, muscular, male practitioner, walked slowly toward Yanna. With the speed of a snake, he leaped forward landing in a wide, and extremely low Horse Stance. His right hand extended toward Yanna, two fingers standing like blades of grass tied together, the other fingers tucked in the classic Chen gesture of warding and warning. A spin of air encircled the demon. It compacted into him, then burst out from him pushing back the challenger's front rows so that they stumbled over each other.

Yanna looked up from the concrete at the being of radiance he had become, forced to cringe away, and shade her eyes.

It is over. Yanna would never have Ling. She could never control him. He had grown far beyond her.

Ling turned and walked back across the open circle toward the temple side of the crowd which opened then closed in around him.

Jolie felt Sifu's gaze and turned to him, sharing a smile.

"Do you feel like a parent watching their child walk across the stage at graduation?" he asked.

"I'm not sure because I haven't graduated yet, but I think I do."

The students who would not fight, faded back to form a half-circle backdrop on each side as the audience strained for a better view of the fighters who would face off.

Jolie frowned. "I think I know their fighter," she said. "He's one of Yanna Maria's students. He was with the guys who chased us the night Yanna kidnapped Ling." She realized that Rance was no longer standing on Sifu's other side.

He was the temple school's champion, now taking his place, preparing to fight and her friends were filling out the ranks of senior students backing him up.

"Sifu, the boys…"

"They are only there in case the challenging school breaches etiquette and attack as a group."

"Do you expect that?"

"I don't expect it, because that would indicate I lacked confidence in my fellow human's good nature. So, I will say it is better to be prepared than to be surprised. A lack of discipline creates problems of its own. That's why our students--who study the more aggressive martial arts forms--are required to meditate a significant amount of time to balance the hours they spend training in those aggressive forms. Without this balance, some forms can have negative effects on a practitioner's health."

Jolie watched the sparring session, wincing at the violent impacts of punches, kicks, and throws, but it was soon clear who the more controlled and stronger fighter was: Rance.

In the crowd, Yanna Maria's trainee's frustration and anger were building.

The challenger's champion started landing kicks he had not been able to land before, accessing a physical intensity he had not shown earlier in the fight. Jolie noticed him throw a glance at the crowd.

Yanna was at the front of the half circle on the challenger's side, her dark eyes focused on him, her fingers moving in quick symbols and shadow movements of the movements the challenger was using.

"Yanna is using magic to help the challenger, Sifu," Jolie protested. "They're cheating!" Jolie looked over at the Taoist Priest. "You don't seem surprised."

"Cheating is what people of weak character do when they cannot face losing."

"How do we stop them?"

"We don't." He turned to Jolie. "I believe that with or without magical assistance Rance can take this opponent."

The battle between the champions began to take on cruel undertones, morphing from a technical show of precision and skill into a personal vendetta. Yanna was frustrated and getting sloppy, her puppet challenger focused now on doing Rance harm and the rules be damned. She knew she had lost, and her anger demanded someone pay.

The challenger's fighter looked alarmed by the power and intensity of his strikes as if he had lost control. He looked over at Yanna and scowled. Jolie thought he was saying something to Yanna, but she could not hear what. Whatever it was, it was not nice, it only made her angrier and more determined.

Sifu looked up at the dignitaries on the balcony. Sifu Xiu and his friend, Mister Cocom, looked at each other, then at Sifu, silent messages being exchanged.

"I yield!" The challenger's champion threw himself to the ground. "I yield!" He glared barbed arrows at Yanna.

The big drum stopped, the air slowly becoming calm, then silent.

Sifu gave a silent command and the entire traditional percussion orchestra started up again as six Chinese Lions leapt forward. Gold, green, red, blue, orange, and black, the sequined and tasseled characters wiped away the somber mood left hanging by the combat. Charging the staging area's center from multiple directions, the Lion Dancers leaped and tumbled, swooping through the crowd, feet and bodies moving in coordination.

The people clapped and cheered as the dancers supporting the heads, climbed their partners like ladders to make the Lions stand tall, each team striding forward like a colorful giant.

And leaping and tumbling through the air beside them was Ling.

Disguised as one of the masked "human" dancers that accompanied the Lions, their fans flickering and flirting, Ling teased and taunted Lions and dancers alike, delighting the audience, who seemed completely willing to detach from the realities of physics to be entertained by the demon's mischievous charm.

Scanning the challenger's front line, Jolie saw Mister Cocom standing by the challenger's confronting Yanna Maria, his stance reminiscent of a scolding father.

Jolie frowned, her brows wrinkling. "What's going on, Sifu?"

"I believe Mister Alvaro Cocom is chiding his old student for poor behavior and a lack of judgment. Cocom was Yanna Maria's teacher before she left Mexico and under the rules of their religion, he is responsible for her actions, and the actions of the students she trained--whom she was not supposed to have." Yanna looked like a toddler pretending to be contrite, her face contorting between rage and embarrassment, her jaw set. She knew she had been caught doing something wrong. She was not sorry for doing it. She was only sorry she had gotten caught.

"He told her she was not to teach. He did not find her to have the correct temperament for starting others off on the path of their religion. I don't think you and Ling will be bothered by her anymore."

Jolie smiled. "Cool."

Once again, the conch sounded from on high announcing the imminent entrance of the Great Dragon.

It stood, its magnificent head regal with its red cutout scales that arced above it like a crown. The head moved slowly taking in the crowd, waiting for their attention. The Las Vegas sun sparkled across the three hundred feet of gold sequins, the dragon's center spine curving like a perfect wave, suspended at the most picturesque moment before it crashed. The huge, animated beast raised its nose into the air, opened its mouth, and shot fire out of its throat. Jolie wondered how until she saw Ling.

Popping out of the air, Ling appeared, leaping from the dragon's head to dance and twirl on the tips of the flames, making faces as if they burned his feet to make the audience laugh.

Once its entrance was sufficiently climactic, the dragon began to undulate forward to the center staging area, shoulders and upper body moving sinuously, the many volunteers perfectly coordinating their sticks, so the huge puppet appeared not only alive but to possess great power and majesty. At the end, was Ling, holding onto the tip of the flicking tail, letting it toss and fling him into the air before he returned to grab it and hold on again.

"You have caught the dragon's tail, my friend." Jolie laughed. *"Now what will you do with it?"*

"I believe that I will take Refuge," Ling replied.

An announcement came over the mall's loudspeaker, "the judges ask you all to go to the side of the courtyard of the school you believe has won the challenge."

The parking lot to the West filled, then overfilled, a sea of students and supporters flooding the grounds, pressing the challengers back to the East until they were a line against the portable fence.

"The judges declare the winners of the challenge to be the Temple School of the Lohans!" Mister Yinchen shouted over the crowd. Cheers burst from the crowd like fireworks. Temple students old and new hugged and congratulated each other.

At the East fence, Rance shook hands with the challenging school's champion.

Yinchen caught Jolie's eye and winked.

Then Sifu sagged, stumbled, and began to collapse.

"Sifu, what's wrong?" Jolie caught him, quickly joined by other senior students.

"Let's get him somewhere quiet," an older student who was a doctor said. "Someone, find Rance." Jolie looked around. Everyone, except herself, was too old to run through the crowd. She looked up at Mister Yinchen. He had seen and was already on his way to the stairs. Jolie took off like a hare, toward the east fence and Rance.

CHAPTER TWENTY-NINE

It felt like the whole world was gathered in the hospital waiting room. Nearly every student Sifu had taught in decades had been at The Challenge. Some recognized there was nothing they could do now, and had gone home to await news. Others could not stay away.

It reminded Jolie of the first time Bodhi had overdosed; the time he had pulled through. Bodhi's Kung Fu family had all been there, waiting, determined to wait until they knew their friend would be all right or until it was over.

Jolie had seen then how Sifu and the school made a family--a family she was now part of, a family where she belonged. This family would always welcome her back, their hearts open to her. They would always wish the best for her.

True friends.

Iris had wanted to take Jolie to tea. Topi had wanted to take her to dinner, but all Jolie wanted to do was to be at the hospital with her friends. Iris and Topi would just have to understand.

Rose and Wrangler came, bringing sandwiches. Mickey and her girls brought healthy snacks and little packages of tissue. Jolie suspected Marty had helped a few of the over twenty-one crowd to some stress reduction in the parking lot, but Tru stayed right by Jolie, holding her hand, never leaving, never saying anything. She didn't need to.

Everyone's eyes were rimmed with red, their demo costumes wrinkled and smelling ripe. After the first twelve hours, students began taking breaks in rotating shifts so they could change and grab a shower.

Rance's girlfriend from California appeared from somewhere. She sat quietly in the corner, watching the group. She seemed to understand that she was not important right now--not even to Rance. Rance was a part of this family--a big part, and if she had been entertaining fantasies that he would move away with her, she was reconsidering how unlikely that was.

"He's going to be all right, isn't he, Jo?" Hugo's voice broke.

"I don't know, Hugo. I hope so."

"But you must know. You always know," Hugo reasoned. "You knew about Remy. You knew about Bodhi."

"Not enough." *I never know enough.*

"Anything is better than nothing," Hugo insisted.

"No. It's not," Jolie disagreed. "Knowing a little and not being able to do anything about it is the worst." She and Jiu caught each other's eyes. Death was not foreign to them, but after losing Bodhi, it would shatter Jiu to lose Sifu as well. Part of her wanted to share that when she touched Sifu, she saw him pass on later in life, an older man, if not a lot older. But she was afraid to say it. What if she gave her friends false hope and she was wrong?

"He knows so much--he works out and does all that longevity stuff. How could he be sick?" Brutus said, too loudly.

One of the older students squatted down in front of the bereft teen.

"You know, the doctors told Sifu's mom when he was nine that he was going to die. She refused to accept it and took him to the new Kung Fu school that had just opened near where they lived. Master Share Lew had just emigrated to the United States and had no intention of teaching kids who weren't Chinese, but he agreed to teach that little boy. Every year that Sifu lived--every year we had him teaching and guiding us, has been a gift and I am so grateful I got the chance to know him and learn from him. It has changed my life."

"Mine too." Brutus sniffled.

"Come on, let's take a little walk and get some fresh air." The man took the boy by the shoulders, and they walked outside where Brutus could grieve more privately.

Rance came over. "Is Brutus all right?"

"He's just feeling overwhelmed, like the rest of us," Jolie said. "Did you know Sifu was sick, Rance?"

"I knew the stories about him as a little kid, but no. Like the rest of them," he gestured to the students gathered in the hospital waiting room, "I thought he would be here forever--that I would move away and start my school, but Sifu would always be there to answer questions or remind me the right way to do a form. How do we go on without him?"

"We're not there yet," Jolie reminded him. "But when the time does come, we go on the way he would expect us to--the way he *taught* us to." She did not realize that she had gotten the attention of the whole room, but people were nodding. Some repeated her words; "the way he taught us to."

"*We* are his legacy," one of the old students added. They all knew it was true.

"It's some legacy," Jolie muttered. Hugo took her hand and squeezed it.

"I'm always going to love you, you know, Jolie," he said quietly.

"I know. Me too." And she did. She could see him, an older, happy man with kids. Love is love, whatever form it evolves into. The trust and affection she and her friends had for one another would bind their lives together.

The doctor student who had been nearest Jolie and Sifu when Sifu collapsed came out of the Emergency Room doors. Everyone looked up expectantly.

"He's going to be okay," the man announced, choking back tears. "He's weak, but it looks like he'll pull through."

Emotion bursts over the room like a dammed-up waterfall that's suddenly released. Students hugged each other, stupid-silly smiles of relief on their faces, their eyes wet, their spirits lighter.

"So, he's going to be okay. Will you go then?" Jolie asked Rance, glancing at the girlfriend. If Sifu had not made it, that would have been the end of any conversation about Rance moving to California, but now that question was in play again.

"He'll need me," Rance replied. "The school will need me. My life is here, with all of them." He indicated their chosen family hugging, crying, and smiling in relief. "What about you, Jo? What will you choose?"

"We know you must have realized why we wanted to have this meeting, Jolie," Iris said. She was dressed up, but conservatively for her for a night out. The restaurant was a good one, white tablecloth, low lights, and really good food. Iris and Topi had listened to Jolie's account of her adventures, marveled at her resilience, and apologized for not being there when she needed them.

Jolie knew this part was coming. She had been waiting for it.

"Sifu's illness required some time and sensitivity, Jo, but as much as it's been fun to show Topi around Las Vegas, he has a job and a family in New Orleans and he can't stay here forever," Iris opened the hard part of the conversation. "I understand that my being called away probably made it seem like I didn't care--that I didn't want you. That's bullshit. It's just not true. The timing was terrible, it was an incredibly unfortunate situation, but the delay was never about me not wanting you to be part of my life, Jo. I want us to be the family we talked about being when Faith was alive--even if you do come with a tagalong demon.

"I also realize, however, that I am not blood family, and legally, or perhaps even in your heart, that may be important to you. So, if you decide you want to live in New Orleans, I'll be disappointed, but I won't fall apart. We can visit. I will always be here for you, and I will always be your friend, and I will always be the executor of the education trust that Faith left you, so you had better start thinking about what university you're going to go to after you graduate high school. School starts here in a few weeks."

Topi was sitting next to Jolie, so it was easy for him to take her hands. She didn't mind. Even after twelve years apart, whatever she saw when she touched him, she knew it would be okay.

"I know you have probably thought more than once that because of what happened between your mom and me and Tessa, you would not be welcome in our family, especially now that we have children. But that is not the truth in our hearts, Jolie. You were never responsible for Jessie Lynn's choices. You were the victim of them as much as she was. There were complications, but they have all been ironed out now. You can come back with me to New Orleans if you want. It is your home. *We* are your home. We too were blessed to know Mem and because of her influence in our lives, we think we understand you. But if you want to stay here in Las Vegas, because of the school, your friends, and the life you have here, we, too, will understand. You will still have a place with us whenever you want it, to visit or to live. And I hope you will include us in the conversation about where you might choose to go to university."

Jolie studied their faces, remembering, weighing, and forecasting what life would be like under the different options.

"I love you, Topi," she said finally. "And for many years it was my dream to come home to you and the family in New Orleans, but I am not the same person I was last December. I've found people who've helped me understand myself and the world better. I found Red Rock, and Rose, and Sifu, and my friends, and Ling. And I'm not ready to leave them. I know I will learn a lot someday when I come back to New Orleans, but right now, there are still things I need to learn here that I can't learn somewhere else. So, I want to stay here, in Las Vegas. After all, it is the brightest spot on Earth."

"Buddhas and bodhisattvas who abide in all the directions, please think of me," Ling had once again taken the form he had relinquished at the end of his last human incarnation, looking like Older Brother Ling as he recited the words before Sifu, now named Dashi of his lineage, and the students attending the Refuge ceremony.

"For now, until the end of this life, I take refuge at the feet of the Buddha," Ling went on. "Shunning desire and all its illusions." Gathered in the temple school with all Jolie's friends present, the teenage girl stood proudly beside the demon. "I take refuge in the wisdom of the dharma and the welcome of the sangha. From now until the end of this life." A life built of his own choices, yet to be revealed.

Jolie thought about the words. She had one life as Jolie Figg-Boulet, and she wanted it to count for something. Maybe now it did. Though she had struggled to find her path, the one she had chosen brought her to this moment and that was not a bad thing.

"I hold this master, and this community to be my spiritual family of the heart and my dearest, most trusted friends," Ling finished.

"I hold this master, and this community to be my spiritual family of the heart and my dearest, most trusted friends," Jolie repeated in a whisper.

Ling turned to her, smiling. *"How could I ever have forgotten you?"*

"You were always an idiot, Jing Ling," she teased him affectionately.

"And you were always wise beyond your years, Little Sister." He bowed in respect.

High in the sky overhead, the golden dragon trumpeted, its voice vibrating the school's walls. Sifu raised his eyebrows and smiled, shaking his head.

"We have indeed caught the dragon's tail," Ling said.

"Yes, we have." Jolie smiled.

And the dragon had brought them home.

www.ingramcontent.com/pod-product-compliance
Lightning Source LLC
Chambersburg PA
CBHW051526200726
48295CB00029B/672